Diary of a *Single*
Wedding Planner

VIOLET HOWE

www.violethowe.com

Cover Design: Robin Ludwig Design, Inc.

www.gobookcoverdesign.com

Published by Charbar Productions, LLC

(p-v10)

ISBN: 0996496807
ISBN-13: 978-0-9964968-0-3

Dedication

For My Knight, who has given me the incredible gift of being able to pursue my dreams. Your love allows me to grow, evolve, and be the best me I can be. I thank you for that. I love you. I love us.

For My Son, who is my heart walking outside my body. Being your mom is the greatest blessing of my life. You inspire me every day and give me the courage to take on the world. I love you, Boo.

Books by Violet Howe

<u>Tales Behind the Veils</u>

Diary of a Single Wedding Planner

Diary of a Wedding Planner in Love

Diary of an Engaged Wedding Planner

Maggie

<u>The Cedar Creek Collection</u>

Cedar Creek Mysteries:

The Ghost in the Curve

The Glow in the Woods

Cedar Creek Families:

Building Fences

Crossing Paths

Visit www.violethowe.com to subscribe to Violet's monthly newsletter for news on upcoming releases, events, sales, and other tidbits.

Or join her Facebook reader group, the UltraViolets, to be the first to know all things Violet and get exclusive content and giveaways.

Acknowledgments

I don't have enough room to acknowledge everyone who has been a part of bringing this book to fruition, but I've tried to at least mention the key people. If I missed your name, it's not because I didn't appreciate your efforts. It's because I'm past forty and I don't sleep enough. Please know I appreciated it when you did whatever it was.

My sincerest thanks and heartfelt gratitude to:

Dad and Bev: Since the moment I decided to pursue this lifelong dream, your support and encouragement has been unfailing. You have been with me every step of the way, learned the industry with me, talked me off the ledge numerous times, and given me the bolstering I needed to press on. We wouldn't be here without you.

Aunt Zona: Thank you for being my rock, my constant, and my source of wisdom and Southern sayings. We should write a book of Zona-isms for life lessons. I appreciate your support and encouragement.

My parents, Bobby and Sherry: Thank you for instilling in me a love of writing and reading, especially the finer arts of escape literature! A special thanks to the Queen for her vast knowledge of grammar and all things literary. Thank you for your love and support.

Jan: My other mother and bestest good friend. I could write an entire book acknowledging all you've done for me and what your friendship means to me, but for now, I'll just say thanks and I love ya.

Heather: I can't see the keyboard because I am bowing down to you, ye goddess of knowledge and wisdom. Without your invaluable guidance, I would still be bumbling along. Your friendship is extra icing on the cake.

Bonnie (and Sandy too!): Beta-reader-extraordinaire and lifelong best friend. Your input and insight helped me shape this story and bring it to life. Thanks for going above and beyond when called upon. Every. Time.

Roberta and Angela: Your support has been unfaltering. Thank you for reading, for printing, for feedback, and for love & encouragement. You ladies are not only neighbors or friends, you're family!

Karin, Molly, Kim, and Kathy: You ladies rock! Thank you for taking the time to read and give me feedback. You each gave me influence that improved and shaped the final project.

Christine: Your feedback and your questions have pushed me to discover new things about my characters and delve deeper into my story. I love what you've brought out of me. Thanks for putting up with the craaaaaazy.

Lesley: You are my audience! Your love for Tyler was the final boost I needed to show this baby to the world.

Kalon: Thank you for representing the guy POV. You always give me insight in a completely different direction, and I hope you never stop.

Max: Girl, what have we not been through together? You had to be a part of this, and I can't thank you enough for bequeathing to me your title for my series. They might have gotten a limo, but we got a book series.

Beth: Thanks for your artistic insight with the cover design and for introducing me to Outlander. You restored my love of reading.

Jody Wenke: Who else would I have asked about photography and websites? Your friendship is one of my favorite wedding gifts. Thanks for your support. (I'm still determined to prove Andy Wenke wrong.)

Susan P: You gave me the courage to veer off the path and journey on new adventures. I am forever grateful for your friendship and your influence.

Kathy, Suzanne, Susan W, and Joann: You ladies introduced me to a whole new world that changed my life forever. To you and to Marion, Ken, Bill, Diane, Lisa, Michelle, and Joan: You were the best example of what it means to belong to a team, and my time with you remains one of the greatest experiences of my life.

Small Group—Suzann, Nick, Molly, Frank, Melissa, T: Thanks for being family, there for me through thick and thin and all that life has to offer. I appreciate you "thinking about me."

And finally to the loyal followers of the Goddess Howe blog: Thanks for sticking me with since the beginning of this journey. Your comments and your support encourage and inspire me.

October

Saturday, October 5th

I've always said I didn't want an ordinary life. Nothing average or mundane for me. But as I stared at the rather ample naked derriere wiggling two inches from my face today, I realized I should have been more specific with my goals. Definitely not ordinary, but not exactly what I had in mind.

The Texas-flag tattoo emblazoned across the left cheek waved at me as she shifted her weight from foot to foot. The flag was distorted and stretched, as was the large yellow rose on the right cheek, both tattoos dotted with dimples and pock marks. An uneven script scrawled out "The Yellow Rose of Texas" across the top of her rump.

Her entire bridal party—her closest friends and relatives, mind you— had left her high and dry. They'd stormed off the elevator as I tried to enter it, a flurry of daffodil-yellow silk, spouting and sputtering about their dear loved one, Tonya the bride.

"That's it! We're done!" They sounded off in a chorus of clucking hens.

"We ain't goin' back in there. She can get ready on her own!"

"Yeah, she can get ready on her own!"

"Known her since third grade and she's gonna talk to me like that?"

"Third grade? She's my first cousin. I've known her since the day she was born. She's always been that way. I don't know why y'all acting all surprised."

I felt more than a little uneasy about what all this meant for our schedule. The ceremony was supposed to start in fifteen minutes. The bride should have already been downstairs and loaded in the carriage to make her way to the hotel's beach.

My unease grew to panic when I knocked on Tonya's door and she opened it clad only in a skimpy little satin robe.

"Honey, you're supposed to be dressed and downstairs already."

1

I tried to say it as sweetly as possible, but I'm sure my panic came through. My Southern accent kicked in thick, which usually only happens when I'm panicked or frustrated. Or pissed. Or drunk.

"Do you think I don't know that?" she asked, arching a perfectly drawn-on eyebrow. "Do you think somehow when I booked this wedding and had invitations printed and planned the entire damned event, I somehow didn't realize what time the ceremony started? And just who the hell are you anyway?"

Well, alrighty then. Obviously this was going to be a fun day.

"Um, I'm Tyler Warren. I'm assisting Lillian with your wedding today."

"Fine. Those bitches left me with my nails wet." She held up both hands to show me the glossy, fresh manicure. "How the hell am I supposed to get dressed with wet nails?" she asked, arching both eyebrows now and glaring at me like I was somehow responsible for this.

"Oh." My mind spun with the limited time frame I had available, the amount of clothing she still needed to put on, and the amount of time it would take to get her in the carriage and to the ceremony.

"Give me just a second to let Lillian know we'll be down shortly." I smiled what I hoped was my sweetest smile and stepped backward into the hallway.

She slammed the door as I frantically dialed Lillian's cell.

"You'd better be calling to tell me she is in the carriage and on her way," Lillian said. "It is hotter than Hades out here. I have several people looking like they're about to faint, and I may possibly dunk a cranky, tuxedoed five-year-old headfirst in the lake. The bridesmaids say she is not even dressed. Tell me you are on top of this, and my ceremony will not run late."

Lillian Graham has been doing weddings since Moses's mother got married, and her weddings do *not* run late. Even after working for her for three years, I still get nervous as all hell assisting one of her events. No one else in the office has that effect on me. I don't even get nervous with my own clients. But with Lillian? Sheesh.

I felt like I might throw up a bit when I opened my mouth to answer her, but I swallowed hard and tried to sound calm.

"Yes, yes, I'm on top of it. Getting her dressed now and we'll be right down." I lied to my boss and hung up on her.

Tonya swung open the door on my first knock.

"Do you have more calls to make, or can you help me get dressed now? I don't want to be late for my own wedding." She stood there tapping her pudgy little foot with both hands on her hips.

I've often wondered why people freak out and become monsters on their wedding day. It seems to me if it's a happy occasion, if you're marrying someone you love, and if all your family and friends have come to see you be happy and get hitched, the least you could do is be nice about it.

"Okay, let's get you dressed and to your ceremony!" It was probably the most sickeningly false voice I have ever used.

Tonya led me into the room waving her fingers to dry her nails. I struggled to keep from staring, but I was fascinated by her. Never in all my days had I seen anyone so colorful!

Tonya was about five feet two and well over three hundred pounds. She wore a royal purple satin robe with huge yellow flowers all over it. Though it barely skimmed the bottom of her rump, she seemed perfectly at ease nearly naked in front of a total stranger.

Tonya's hair glowed a bright, shocking orange. Not red. Not auburn. Orange. A fiery, neon orange curling in cascades of flames around and below her shoulders.

An iridescent smudge of purple shadow covered her eyelids, and greasy black liner outlined the entire rim of her blue eyes. A thick, black fringe of false eyelashes fluttered and flapped with every wink.

The bright, bubble-gum pink smear on each cheek matched the slick gloss on her lips. I thought perhaps she would be more attractive without makeup. And without her present scowl.

"Here," she said, gingerly holding out a pair of pantyhose between her French-manicured fingers. "Put these on."

I swear for a minute I thought she meant for me to wear them. Then it dawned on me with sickened recognition that she wanted me to put the pantyhose on her. Ewww.

I stared at her a bit dumbfounded. I have been asked to do many things in this line of work. It's definitely not as glamorous as the star-crossed wannabes imagine it. But never in the multitude of weddings have I ever been expected to put on another human being's pantyhose. I thought surely she was joking. Surely, there was a bridesmaid left hiding in the room to do this. Surely, a meteor could come crashing into the hotel at that moment and create a hole to swallow me up.

As a girl with abundant thighs myself, it is my personal belief that support pantyhose are a relic left over from some medieval torture chamber. I have never been happier with the fashion world than when they decided pantyhose were out of style and we could all go bare-legged.

Putting on hose is an all-out swearing, sweating, pushing, pulling, aerobic activity that borders on assault. My granny used to say it's like shoving two pounds of lard in a one-pound sack. To go through this torture against your own thighs within the privacy of your own room with the shades pulled down tight is one thing. But with someone else's sweaty thighs? I was repulsed. It must have shown.

"It ain't like I got any other options," she said, placing one hand on her hip and waving the other in such a dramatic flourish I almost laughed at the absurdity of the situation. "Them bitches all left me."

I wondered briefly if this was the task that pushed them out the door.

"Those selfish no-good whores got themselves ready and didn't do a damned thing to help me. And now here I am, on *my* wedding day. *My* day. It's about *me*. It's not about *them*. They're lucky I even invited them. I didn't have to! They oughtta be thanking me! Kissing my ass! Doing all they can to show me some appreciation, don'tcha think?"

My phone vibrated on my hip, and I ignored it. I knew it was Lillian, but I had no idea what to tell her.

"Okay," I said with a deep breath. "Let's do this."

She propped her foot up on the ottoman in the room. I knelt on the carpet to begin the task at hand, taking another deep breath and thinking I truly do not get paid enough to do this.

I carefully slid one leg of the hose over her French-manicured toes and then over her calloused heel. So far so good. It wigged me out a little to touch someone's feet, but I kept telling myself to be a professional. To square my shoulders and get it done.

We made it over her ankle and started up her leg with no problem, but as I got to the largest part of her calf just below the knee, things got more difficult. And awkward.

When I put on my own hose, I have to start working my fingers all the way around the leg to make sure the hose come up evenly. Not so easy to do on someone else's leg. I twisted, scooted, and bent my arms like we were playing Twister. All to get the hose over one knee.

Her legs were slick with perfumed lotion, which didn't mix well with my own palms damp with nervousness and the sheen of her perspiration. The moisture caused my hands to slip and slide, but it did the opposite for the hose as they adhered to the stickiness and refused to budge.

To keep from thinking about how this would work above the knee, I went ahead and started on the other leg. Over the toes, up the calf, over the knee. Then we had reached the point of no return. I had to get the hose up her thighs and over her bum.

My phone vibrated again, and I shut it completely off. I wasn't sure I could hold my composure on the phone while facing the monumental task ahead of me. Better to deal with the consequences later and climb the mountain in front of me now.

It was one of the hardest and most uncomfortable workouts of my entire life. I tugged. I pulled. I did little circles around her on the floor until my knees were carpet burned. All the while praying my fingernails wouldn't pop through the strained nylon and spark a run.

Tonya stretched. She danced. She did squats. She wriggled, and jiggled, and wiggled to try and help put everything where it needed to be without the use of her hands.

"Maybe you could spread your legs a little farther?" I never thought I would ever have occasion to say that to another woman.

"Wait, no, that pulls the hose tighter," I said as her balance wobbled from trying to stand at a straddle with the hose around her thighs.

I strained to wedge my hands between her legs, but there was no space between the fleshy abundance of her upper thighs. We were both outright sweating now, and the scent of us mixed with her lotion nauseated me. It was a nightmare beyond what I could have dreamed up.

Bit by bit and inch by inch, the hose were slowly coming up, but that meant my hands were slowly getting closer to the nether regions, which I had no desire to reach. I silently prayed a bridesmaid or family member would come walking in. Or a housekeeper. Or an alien. I didn't care at that point. I did not want to have my hands all up in this girl's hoohah.

She grunted and squatted again as I tried to heave the nylon across her dimpled upper thighs. I sighed and sank back on my knees behind her, catching my breath for a moment as I summoned the courage to finish the job.

It was at this point that she hiked the robe up out of the way.

Commando.

No lacy big-girl panties in sight. Nothing. Nada.

Just The Yellow Rose of Texas fluttering in my face. My hands faltered, and I considered what other jobs I could do if I quit this one at that very moment.

As I contemplated the need for more specific life goals other than "not ordinary," Tonya shifted her weight and cleared her throat. I realized I'd been staring at her butt for an awkwardly long pause.

I took another deep breath and wrangled the nylon past Tonya's lady parts, determined to finish the deed and get out of that position. Let me tell you, if I never have to do that again, it will be too soon. The material strained as I hoisted it over the fleshiest part of her cheeks and settled it around her midsection. I thought the waistband might cut off my circulation if I didn't get my fingers out as quickly as possible.

"Okay, get my dress," she commanded with a sweep of her arm and a point of her finger, as though completely oblivious to our unfortunate bonding experience and the effect it had on me.

I walked to the closet in somewhat of a fog, feeling both violated and underappreciated. I slid open the mirrored door and gasped out loud before I could catch myself.

"Isn't it beautiful?" Tonya asked. "Custom made. The only one like it in the whole world."

"Wow! It's . . ." I struggled for composure and tried to find any leftover reserves of calm facade and polite bullshit not used up in the nylon project. "Amazing!" was what I finally came up with.

I could say it was purple, but that would be a tragic understatement. It was more like an optical assault of purple. Shocking brighter-than-you-can-imagine purple. The satin jacket had shoulder pads and huge puffy sleeves that would have done any 80s prom photo proud. The voluminous, floor-length, A-line skirt shimmered with layers of organza over royal purple.

"Purple's my favorite color," she said with a huge smile.

"Mine too," I responded, hoping my eyes matched the smile plastered on my face.

I like purple, I do, but this was a bit much purple. Over the top and then some. Some green to be exact.

A brilliant emerald-green satin bodice peeked out from underneath the jacket, coordinating with the humongous emerald-green bow and ribbons that trailed down the back of the skirt to the floor. A thin layer of green tulle was gathered around the hips in some sort of ode to a bustle. I had definitely never seen anything like it.

When the queen for a day was clothed in her royal garb, I handed her the exquisite bouquet from the floral box on the counter and headed for the door.

"Wait!" she said. "My veil!"

I felt a little apprehensive to even look in the direction she pointed. With good reason. Plumes of purple feathers waved at me from the Styrofoam head on the corner table. At the base of the feathers was an emerald-green satin hat, surrounded by a pouf of purple tulle barely long enough to cover her face.

The contrast of the purple veil and green hat against the neon orange of her hair was like Picasso on crack. The entire visage of purple satin, organza, feathers and eye shadow was practically enough to turn me against the hue forever.

I have always believed every bride should wear a gown reflective of her personality and tastes. I am also a proponent of women of any size being fashionable and stylish. But there is always an exception to every rule. Lines need to be drawn sometimes. It is possible that three hundred pounds of satin and organza in colors vivid enough to produce light may be the place to draw one.

I loaded Barney the Bride into her elegant carriage, and the driver nudged the horses into action. I considered turning the other way and running. It would take them several minutes to navigate around the pool area and down the long wooden boardwalk that ran along the lake to the beach. I could have been in my car and gone by the time they arrived at the ceremony site and Lillian looked for me. I would still have to see her eventually, though, so I turned my phone on and faced the inevitable.

She answered after the first ring and yelled into the phone, "Where are you?"

I had never heard her yell before. Lillian is a formidable lady, fully capable of ripping a person to shreds without a second thought, and she doesn't even have to raise her voice to do it.

I didn't get a chance to answer her.

"Are we calling the whole bloody thing off, Tylah?" Her British accent sounded even more intimidating when she yelled, dropping the *er* from my name as she always did.

"She's almost there. We, um, hit a little complication," I answered.

"What happened? Did you turn your phone off? I've been trying to call you and it kept going straight to voice mail. What complication?"

This wasn't something I was sure I ever wanted anyone to know about, and it definitely wasn't anything I was prepared to discuss right then.

"I'll explain later. She'll be there soon." I hung up on my boss for the second time in one day.

Tonya's sweaty wedding guests looked at her with more contempt than joy when she finally pulled up in the carriage, an hour past the time they were put out to fry in the blazing Florida sun. More than a few grumbled and complained loudly, although her groom did manage a smile.

As I watched at Barney the Bride and her groom, I wondered for the millionth time if there really was someone for everyone. Was this guy some poor, masochistic chump who mistakes abuse for charm? Or was he just as volatile as his bride, an even match in poor health and behavior?

Maybe they were blissfully happy together. Maybe they were both fortunate enough to have found "the one." But I've learned while doing weddings that just because people are getting married, it doesn't mean they're happy. Or that they'll stay married.

Sunday, October 6th

I woke up just before dawn, feeling all bright-eyed and bushy-tailed. I don't get it. If I have to be up early for work, it's all I can do to drag my butt out of bed and into the shower. But this morning, when I had a late wedding and could have slept in, I was wide awake and full of energy.

Granted, it's probably because I went to bed around seven last night. I was exhausted after my WrestleMania session with Tonya's pantyhose and my frosty encounter with Lillian. She had been none too pleased with me for bringing Barney the Bride down late and turning off my phone. (I don't think the heat and the fact she had no shade to stand in helped.) No sooner had Barney sashayed down the aisle to snag her groom than Lillian peered down her nose at me to say, "Tylah, your services are no longer needed today."

I normally stay through the ceremony to help her with the reception until cake-cutting time, but she dismissed me before the vows were even read. She said it all matter-of-fact, too, so I knew there was no room for discussion. I was just relieved she ended the sentence with the word *today*. It is never a good idea to be on Lillian's bad side.

It's not that I don't like Lillian. I do. I admire her. She is an incredibly smart and strong woman. Able to orchestrate the most complicated of events with ease and grace. I think I kind of view her through a set of glasses with one lens of fear, another of respect, and neither rose-colored. Maybe it's because I look up to her so much that I always seem to screw up in her presence. I guess I get nervous.

I was too keyed up to go back to sleep this morning with yesterday replaying in my head, so as soon as the sun rose, I got out of bed. I even put on a pair of shorts and some running shoes, feeling all ambitious about the day. But then I remembered how much I loathe running, so I ate a bowl of Cheerios instead.

By the time eight o'clock rolled around, I had already vacuumed the entire apartment, started a load of laundry, and tweezed my eyebrows. I still don't get how my brows can be perfectly clear of strays when I go to bed and morph into furry kiwi by the time I get up. Seems like that many spontaneous hairs sprouting out of my head in my sleep would wake me.

By nine, I had cleaned the bathroom and emptied a week of take-out containers from the fridge. I really should go to the grocery store more often and eat at home, but the whole process of shopping, then cooking, and then cleaning is not worth it for only me, especially on wedding nights. It's much easier to grab takeout. (Hence, my jeans getting tighter and my need to get over my hatred for running.)

I was still pumping adrenaline and amazed at how much energy I had. To the point that, for one insane moment, I actually considered getting up at sunrise every morning. Luckily, that moment passed before any damage was done.

With the whole apartment pretty well spic and span, I decided to venture into my closet and clean it out a bit. I didn't get far.

The first box I pulled down was filled with pictures of Cabe. My heart pinched in my chest, and I sank onto the floor in my bedroom holding the box. I probably should have just buried it under the bed, but I didn't.

I still can't believe it's been almost a year since my best friend galloped across the country to follow some chick and marry her. I also can't believe the jerk hasn't called me in nine months. Which is why I packed up all his pictures and anything that reminded me of him and shoved it in the top of my closet.

How do you just drop off the face of the earth and not talk to a friend? Your best friend even? To go from being inseparable for four years, talking every day, and hanging out pretty much all the time, to just not talking for nine months. All because of *her*. Thank you, Monica.

I reached in the box and pulled out a photo of the three of us at a downtown concert right after they met. We'd had a blast that night. I looked like a total dork in the picture, of course. The humidity had wreaked havoc on my unruly curls, making me look like I had strands of chocolate cotton candy swirling around my head.

Monica looked picture perfect. Monica *always* looked picture perfect. Her blond pixie cut was never out of place. Her nail polish was never chipped. She never had an oily forehead or smudges of eyeliner beneath her eyes. And her dancer's body was, well, a dancer's body. I bet she was a size zero. Which I never understood. How can anyone actually be a size zero? Zero means nothing. Nada. Zilch. So if you were really a size zero, you would be invisible.

Cabe towered above both of us at six feet four. It was a great picture of him standing between us and pulling us close, happiness lighting up his entire face. His clear, blue eyes danced for the camera as he laughed. I looked back and forth from his eyes to hers, almost the same exact shade of blue, and then to my own greenish-brown, quite muted in comparison.

I dropped the photo back in the box and pulled out another. Cabe and me. At the coffee shop where I worked when I first moved here. Where we met. I called him Plain Coffee because that's what he ordered every day.

Another picture—this one of Cabe and me in the Keys. Holy Cow, I looked skinny. I guess I was, back then. Still nursing the wounds of a painful breakup that drove me to leave home in Georgia and move all the way to Orlando. Cabe's friendship helped me heal. Plain Coffee ended up being one of the best friends I ever had.

God, I wished I could talk to him. He would have roared with laughter at my pantyhose encounter. I closed my eyes, still hearing his deep, rumbling laugh in my memories. Until my cell phone rang in the living room. I nearly broke my ankle trying to get to it, spilling the photos across the carpet in the process.

I think I may have actually hoped it was him. Like I had telepathically summoned him or something. But it was just Melanie. Well, that's rude, I guess. She's not "just Melanie." She plucked me from barista hell at the coffee shop and whisked me away to weddings world, talking her bosses, Laura and Lillian, into hiring me with no experience at all.

"What's up, Mel?"

"How'd the wedding go? I thought you were going to text me last night when you finished," Melanie said.

"Let's just say tonight might be our last wedding together, because I'm probably getting fired tomorrow."

"She can't fire you," Mel said. "Laura won't let her. Laura loves you. That's the beauty of having two bosses. What happened?"

I recounted the entire story to Mel, pausing quite frequently for her to recover from laughter and then repeating parts of the story on speaker for her husband, Paul.

"Did you take any pictures?" Mel asked when she finally caught her breath.

"Lord, no!" I said. "What was I going to do? Ask if I could take a selfie with her tattoo?"

"Not of her butt, Tyler! Her dress. Did you get a picture of that dress?"

"No, but I'm sure the photographer will be happy to give you a copy."

"I am so glad that wasn't my client. I don't think I could have kept a straight face," she said to me, and then to Paul with her face away from the phone, "I'm getting to it, honey. Hold your horses."

"What's he want?" I asked.

"Christopher called, and he's free Wednesday night," Mel answered.

I groaned.

Melanie and Paul have been trying to set me up with this guy Paul works with for over a month now. My love life must have reached pretty pathetic lows if my friend's husband is seeking out men from work for me to date. They both have been singing Christopher's praises every time I go over to their house for dinner or we meet up for a night out together.

"Come on, Tyler. This guy's a great catch. He's successful. Hard working."

Paul piped up in the background. "She means he's rich."

"Paul, stop. He's a really nice guy, Tyler. A real gentleman. So polite. Very interesting to talk to with all his travel stories. You'll have a great time."

"So you say," I replied, shaking my head in doubt. "But if he's that flippin' awesome, why is he single? I mean, seriously."

"You're single," Paul called out.

"Paul, stop it! Go away! Tyler, just go out with him. If you don't like him, you don't ever have to see him again, and Paul will leave us both alone about it."

"Alright, alright!" I caved. It wasn't like I had any better plans on a Wednesday night.

"Great. I'll give him your number. Now, can you be at the staircase at four? I need to drop off the toasting glasses before I come to photos. Should be a pretty easy wedding."

"Well, hey, if your bride's dressed and I didn't have to dress her, then it'll be easier than yesterday's wedding," I said.

Mel laughed. "I promise you will not have to dress anyone tonight. In fact, I'll work the ceremony and you can just head straight over to set up reception right after photos. How's that?"

"Wow! I feel honored. You must be convinced I'm getting fired. You never choose ceremony over reception."

"You know I loathe ceremonies. Standing around forever waiting for everyone to get there so it can start, then waiting for the ceremony to end, and then standing around again waiting for the photographer to finish. Aargh. Slit my wrists already. At least with the reception setup, I can be busy."

"Yeah, yeah. It's a tough job, but somebody's got to do it."

"Maybe not you, after tomorrow," Mel teased.

"Oh, not fair. I'm hanging up now."

For the record, everyone was dressed at tonight's wedding, and they were nice. Which made the time standing around much easier to bear.

Monday, October 7th

The office was quiet this morning except for Chaz's ever-present jazz music playing softly from his office. Mondays were typically an off day since we work the weekends, but in October, there's pretty much no such thing as a day off. The milder weather, plus less-crowded beaches and theme parks, makes October the busiest wedding month of the year for Central Florida. June and July are way too hot.

"Who's there?" Laura called out in a playful, dramatic voice from the other side of the building. "Who goes there?"

I knew she'd be in the office. Laura never took Mondays off, no matter what month it was. As co-owner of the salon, she not only had her own events to plan and execute, but all the aspects of running the business as well. Marketing, accounting, taxes, insurance. All the crap that comes with the glory.

"It's me!" I answered, walking across the open salon area toward her office. I was relieved to see Lillian's office dark. I dreaded the conversation I knew was coming as I had no desire to be stripped to the bone by her teeth and talons.

"What's shaking?" Laura tucked her reading glasses into her long, dark hair and gave me a smile. I plopped into one of her comfy overstuffed chairs, pulled one of the pillows out from behind my back, and put it over my face.

She laughed the sweet, deep, gravelly laugh I absolutely love. I swear I would be an entirely different human being if Laura could be my mom.

"Aw! What's the matter? Why are you hiding your face this morning? Did you have a late night?" She chuckled again as I pulled the pillow down and fought back tears. Somehow the warm security of Laura's voice made me want to cry.

"I screwed up again. I swear, Laura, every time I work one of her weddings I screw something up. Why is that?"

"What happened? I talked to her this morning and she didn't mention anything, so you can't have done anything too bad. Let's get you some coffee and talk about it." She took me by the hand and led me back to our tiny kitchen.

I gave her the briefest summary I could of what happened, pausing for her to gasp and cover her mouth when I got to the commando part.

"Come here, honey!" Laura put her arms around me in a big hug, and I wanted to melt. I'm such a big baby sometimes.

"The Yellow Rose of Texas, huh? Wow." She laughed again and let me go. "Well, it sounds to me you did everything you could to ensure our bride was taken care of. You helped her in her time of need, you stayed calm in the face of a difficult situation, and you got her to the wedding dressed and feeling pretty. So I think you did fine. I would definitely rather you keep your phone on so we can always reach you, but I understand you were in a situation. You made a decision that may not have been what you would do next time."

Laura has an amazing ability to say "don't ever do that again" and make it sound like a good thing. I've never met anyone so kind, patient, and compassionate. In the three years I've worked here, I've never heard her raise her voice or lose her temper, yet she is authoritative and in control. I wonder if her sons have ever heard her lose it. They're both in college now, but could you raise two teenage boys and never yell?

I shrugged as I took the coffee she offered. "I'm not sure Lillian will see it that way. She was furious."

"Well, you have to remember Lillian ran an entire hotel empire where multiple properties in multiple countries all depended on her leadership and organization skills. She was responsible for a lot of people. She made the company very successful because she ran a tight ship with little room for error. So she tends to get a little tense when things don't go as planned," Laura said.

"Didn't you tell me once she started out at the front desk of one of those hotels?" I asked. I don't know why, but I always found it comforting to picture Lillian as a front desk clerk. I'd love to be all noble and say it was because it inspired me to work hard and make my way to the top. But nah . . . I just liked picturing her in a silly front-desk uniform with someone telling her when she could take a fifteen-minute break.

"Yes, she did. Worked her way into upper management and ended up running the entire company. That's why she comes across so tough. She expects people to do as she commands. You and I both know brides aren't always in that mindset."

"Aren't you forgetting the part about her marrying the boss's son? I think that's an important little detail in her climb to the top," Chaz said, slinking in through the door frame and leaning against it with a Cheshire-cat grin.

I swear the man has sonar hearing when it comes to gossip. He loves dirt on anyone, and he has a plethora of Lillian's dirt since they worked together at the hotel long ago. She brought him on board here as a senior planner when he was laid off about six months ago. Senior planner, my ass. Granted, he knows more about weddings than I did when I started, but not by much. They're tight, though, him and Lillian. If I didn't know how incredibly fond he is of men, I would swear they have a cougar thing going on.

"Oh, Chaz. Stop it!" Laura waved him away. "Yes, she married the owner's son, but that's not why she took the company from two properties to a worldwide network of resorts and clubs. So let's not throw daggers and be petty. She was very good at what she did."

"So was he evidently!" Chaz laughed loudly at his own joke. "I heard he was quite talented in pleasing the ladies." He reached up and grabbed the top of the doorframe, stretching his long, skinny limbs and yawning loudly.

Laura arched an eyebrow at him and shook her head. "Well, I don't know if I would necessarily call them ladies, but it's neither here nor there. We're not discussing that. I was only trying to help Tyler keep Lillian's temper in perspective," she said before turning to me. "Don't brood over this, Tyler. Lillian's bark is much worse than her bite. She's got a heart of gold, and you know she adores you."

Adores was probably reaching a bit. Maybe *tolerates* would be more appropriate. I mean, Lillian must like me somewhat or I wouldn't still be working here. But I have never felt any warm fuzzies from her. Not even in the beginning, before I was screwing up her events.

I didn't have a clue about weddings when Melanie hired me. I honestly didn't even know event planning was a real job until we met. No one in my tiny little hometown was an event planner. If you had a baby shower or a wedding or something, your aunts and cousins helped plan it. Mostly planned it for you and told you what to do, but they called it helping. Maybe that was one good thing about getting jilted and leaving home never to return. When and if I get married now, I get to do my own planning.

Laura returned to her office, and I followed Chaz back to his, still thinking about Lillian. "Why did she leave the hotel business if she was so successful?"

He exhaled sharply and shook his head. "Everyone has a limit to how much they can take. She was the powerhouse building the company up. He was the wealthy playboy who gave her free rein as long as she turned a blind eye to his adventures. When he moved a buxom blonde into the penthouse suite of the downtown tower, Lillian called foul. She thought he'd come in line. Instead, he sued for divorce and tried to fire her from the company. But her attorneys took care of her. She's not hurting."

"Wow." I couldn't imagine Lillian in that situation. She's such a force to be reckoned with. Who would have the balls to cheat on her?

I bet she probably handled it much better than I did when it happened to me. Then again, I was much younger at the time, and I didn't have attorneys to fight for me. Which is another good thing, I suppose. At least my college sweetheart was kind enough to dump me and break my heart before we got married. No lawyers needed.

I was still deep in thought when I heard the salon door open. I knew it was Lillian even before I heard her ask Laura if I was in the office. I cringed and waited for the summons.

"Tylah, could you come here, please?" Lillian called out.

I scurried over to her office with the same sick feeling I used to get when my mother found out I'd skipped class.

"Yes, ma'am?" I said, standing at attention in her doorway. In stark contrast to Laura's warm and fluffy office, Lillian's is sleek and modern with a glass desk and two black, straight-back chairs. No pillows. Not a single picture on the walls. Only one lone mirror.

"Here," she said, handing me a purple bouquet in a clear vase. "Tonya wanted you to have her bouquet. I kept it in my fridge last night, so there may be a few broken stems. I think overall it fared well. I understand you had quite the mission to perform in helping her get ready. She was appreciative of your efforts."

I took the heavy bouquet from her and blurted out, "Sorry we were late."

"Me too," she said. "It was hot and uncomfortable, but from what I hear, you had cause to be uncomfortable as well."

Lillian glanced in the mirror and ran her hand through her short white hair. "Thank you for helping her. Trashy, selfish girl that she is. A mere peasant. This marriage will not last. She is four months pregnant now with what he thinks is his child. I have my doubts."

She rubbed her eyes and shook her head with a slight shudder. "They did things on the dance floor no one with any self-respect would ever do. Horrors. But it's behind us now. Enjoy the flowers." She waved her hand in dismissal to me and turned on her computer.

"Um, yes, ma'am," I nodded and backed out of her office, much like a servant leaving the presence of the queen.

I stumbled back to my desk in a daze.

"That's it? That's all she said?" Melanie asked as we ate lunch. "I figured she would at least ream you for turning your phone off. I mean, you couldn't really help the bride being late."

"She didn't even mention the phone. I think my intimate encounter with the bride's backside earned me some kind of brownie points."

"I guess. I can't believe the girl told Lillian about you putting on her pantyhose. I'm thinking I would have kept that to myself," Mel said, stuffing a huge bite of salad in her mouth.

"I just don't know why I got so worked up. I need to learn to chill," I said as I munched on my fries. "It's not like Lillian's mean. I just feel like I can't quite do my best around her. Like no matter how much I want to impress her and please her, something always goes wrong."

"I think you're reading too much into things, Tyler. If she thought you were screwing up, she would have told you. It sounds to me like she pretty much said you'd done a good job."

"Maybe. I know there is no way in hell Lillian would have been down on her knees risking a hernia to pull pantyhose up over some girl's butt. At the same time, there is no way I could've told her I wasn't going to do whatever I could to take care of the bride."

Melanie nodded in agreement. "You're right about that. But I guess in the end it's okay since the bride was happy and Lillian still loves you."

"I think *love* is too strong a word. Scratch that, and let's say she still *likes* me. At least enough that I get to keep my job for now."

Tuesday, October 8th

Nice eye candy in the hotel lobby today as we were doing photos. Tall, dark, Italian. Wearing his suit rather well, I must say! He came over to ask how long we would need the staircase and offered to block it off for us. Not a single soul had tried to use the stairs, so I think he was just saying hello. I didn't mind. He was quite a looker. We stood and talked for a few minutes while the photographer finished up. He offered me his card, "in case the bride and groom need something while they are staying at the hotel." I offered him mine, "in case the bride and groom can't reach me or the hotel has a question."

Isn't it funny the dances we go through in this ritual of meeting someone? Why can't we simply say, "I find you attractive and would like to have another conversation past this one. Call me." Wouldn't it make everything simpler? Why can't we just be straightforward?

You would think I would be used to the game by now. I should be much better at playing it. Lord knows I've gotten enough practice.

Maybe he'll call. Maybe he won't. We'll see.

The rest of the wedding went well enough, but I had a first today I sincerely hope is a last. We had finished pictures at the hotel and had everyone ready to go at the wedding chapel. The bride was tucked away in the dressing room while we waited for a few straggling guests to arrive and be seated.

Sondra, the mother of the groom, approached me outside to suggest we put plastic cups in the dressing rooms. I thought she wanted water, so I reminded her the dressing room held a small fridge with water bottles inside.

Yeah, she didn't want water.

"Oh, we saw those, thank you." Sondra nodded as she smiled. "I'm not sure how to put this delicately, but . . . " she hesitated and twisted her hands together as she glanced over her shoulder, "that bathroom stall in there is quite narrow. Especially for a bride in a dress with a large train and layers and layers of tulle."

She leaned in to whisper. "It is virtually impossible for a bride to hit the toilet without being able to see where she's going, and you can only get so many people in that tiny stall to hold up the dress. A plastic cup would have come in handy."

For a moment, I just stared at her in confusion. I wasn't sure what a plastic cup had to do with the bride and her dress and peeing. But she cleared it up for me right away.

"We ended up using the candy dish that was sitting on the dresser. She filled it right up, and then we rinsed it out in the sink afterward and set it upside down to dry. But a plastic cup would have been much easier to maneuver up under her dress, I think."

My mouth dropped open as she walked away.

They used a candy dish?!? For her to pee in???

It raised way more questions than I had answers for.

I mean, the circumference of the candy dish—or a plastic cup, for that matter—is much smaller than the opening of the toilet. Was it really that much easier to hit?

Someone obviously held it for her. Who got that job? I've never seen that on a list of maid of honor duties.

I hope to God it wasn't the mother of the groom. What a way to start off with your mother-in-law! Normally it's enough to worry about saying something offensive without being concerned you're going to splash her with pee.

How deep was the candy dish? What if there was overflow? Was someone up under the skirt helping her aim and judging capacity? I don't think I want to know the answers to these questions. And yet, my mind can't help but ask.

I recovered my composure enough to tell the poor housekeeper to please wear rubber gloves and dispose of the candy dish. As far as I'm concerned, no amount of "rinsing out" would make it suitable for candy again.

Wednesday, October 9th

So tonight was blind date night. Melanie was way more into it than I was. She must have texted me twenty times while I was getting ready, and then when I didn't text her back quickly enough, she called.

"Are you excited?" Mel asked.

"Umm, I'd say more nervous than excited."

"Why? This is a good thing." She sounded so disappointed I almost wanted to pretend to be excited just to make her happy.

"You know how I feel about blind dates, Mel," I said.

"I do, but Christopher's a nice guy. He's not going to show up barefooted, I promise."

I laughed at Mel and cringed at the memory she referred to. I was probably sixteen at the time, and my mother's best friend had insisted I go out with her nephew. Doris described Sammy as a "long, tall, good-lookin' drink of water." She would drawl out *long* and *tall* into pretty much two-syllable words and then rush through *good-lookin' drink of water* like she was running out of oxygen.

He was tall alright, but evidently Doris and I have vastly differing opinions on what constitutes good-lookin'. Of course, it didn't help that he showed up barefoot to take me out to dinner. I opened the door in my brand-new dress to greet a scrawny giant of a boy wearing a rebel-flag tank top, a pair of cut-off denim shorts, and no shoes.

He smiled down at me, revealing a large gap of two to three teeth missing on the bottom and a couple of top teeth ready to jump ship at any moment.

I decided right then and there I'd need to see someone up close and in person before I ever let anyone set me up on a date. Melanie had a lot of faith in Paul's opinion, though, and I had a lot of faith in Melanie. So much so that I even agreed to let Christopher pick me up at my house and drive me on the date.

It started out wonderful enough. He arrived on time with a gorgeous bouquet. I was relieved to see Paul actually did have good taste in men. Christopher was tall and muscular, with dark, wavy, tousled brown hair and eyes the color of dark honey. He flashed a gorgeous white smile and kissed me on the cheek as he handed me the flowers.

The shiny new Porsche in my driveway was another nice surprise. I've always been a sucker for a nice ride. This one was black, sleek, and plush. I don't consider myself a real material girl, but I think a handsome, rich guy in an expensive car is not a bad way to start a date.

The afternoon's heavy rains had subsided, but water still filled the potholes along the road. Christopher swerved to miss one and ended up splashing into the water running along the curb. All conversation stopped. His mood changed immediately. He stopped at the next parking lot entrance, got out of the car without a word, and grabbed a white towel from behind the driver's seat. After drying every single drop of water from the right front fender, he got back in and continued our drive.

After the third time, I asked if he'd recently washed his car.

"No," he replied. "I don't want street water ruining my finish."

Now I don't know a lot about cars, but I don't think they could charge as much as they do for a Porsche if splashing in a puddle would ruin it. My admiration for the car quickly soured as I sat and waited for him to dry it off every few minutes.

My annoyance lifted somewhat when we pulled into the most sought-after restaurant in Orlando. Reservations were usually booked up months in advance, but Christopher whipped right into valet like he owned the place. I felt a little like Cinderella at the ball when the valet opened the car door and my handsome prince-for-the-night extended his hand to escort me up the steep stairs at the entrance.

The hostess greeted Christopher by name and with a fond smile. She led us to a small table for two set against a curve in the back windows. I gazed out at the incredible view of the lake, wondering if this was his regular table and how often he brought dates here.

He smiled and thanked the hostess as she replaced my white linen napkin with a black one. I glanced around at the other diners and hoped my little black dress was up to par.

After a few questions about what I liked and disliked, Christopher asked if he could order for me. I was hesitant to say yes at first, especially since I hadn't even seen the menu, but I decided what the hell. I'll go with it.

I had no need to worry. He started with an amazing antipasto platter and a bottle of wine, followed by soup so good I wanted to sop my bread in it. I didn't, but I sure wanted to. (You can take the girl out of the country, but you can't take all the country out of the girl.)

Christopher behaved as a perfect gentleman throughout the entire meal. Asking me questions, actually listening to the answers, and being extremely attentive to my comfort and needs. I was thinking I could definitely get used to that kind of treatment.

The wine coaxed me into a warm and fuzzy haze as soft jazz played in the background and Christopher wooed me with tales of his exotic travel escapades. It seemed there was nowhere this man had not been. Frolicking with penguins in Antarctica, camping with the aborigine in Australia, backpacking across Europe, and sleeping under the stars on safari in Africa. I felt like I was in an episode on the Travel Channel. Definitely a far cry from that sixteen-year-old country girl and barefoot Sammy.

As we shared a decadent slice of chocolate-lava cake for dessert, I felt certain Paul and Melanie had stumbled upon the most wonderful man on the planet. I was mesmerized. I could certainly overlook an obsession with water droplets on fenders.

He casually reached his hand across the table with palm outstretched. I placed my hand in his with a giddy schoolgirl giggle. I couldn't tell if my stomach flipping was from butterflies or a result of too much rich food and a third glass of wine. It didn't matter. I was having a fantastic time. Truly enjoying his company. I didn't want the night to end.

Evidently, neither did he. As he stroked the back of my hand with his fingers and sent slight shivers down my spine, he leaned toward me above the low candle in the center of the table and whispered, "I want to bathe you."

Thinking the wine had messed up my hearing, I cocked my head to one side and said, "I'm sorry. What did you say?"

"I want to bathe you. I want to put you in a tub of warm, soapy suds, and bathe you from head to toe."

I shook my head slightly to clear the wine fuzz and try to understand what my gorgeous, perfect date was telling me. I pulled my hand from his and leaned closer.

"I'm sorry, it sounded like you said you wanted to *bathe* me?"

He nodded in what I am sure he meant as a seductive manner, licking his bottom lip ever so slowly.

I shuddered, but not in the giggly, shivers-down-my-spine way I'd felt a few minutes before.

He leaned toward me and spoke low, his voice husky with desire. "I want to take you back to your apartment, undress you, pick you up in my arms and put you in the tub to bathe every last inch of you."

He blew a kiss in the air as he purred out the last part. I cracked up laughing. Hard. Loud. Like other people around us staring at me loud.

Christopher looked both surprised and embarrassed. He sat back in his chair and took a sip of wine as he looked at the patrons around us then back to me.

I tried to stop laughing, but it was damned good wine. The harder I fought for composure, the more it eluded me.

I mean, never in my entire life has anyone told me they wanted to bathe me. Is this a thing? A fetish? To bathe people? I've never heard of it. Don't get me wrong. I love a good bubble bath as much as the next girl. But on the first date?

Had I somehow given him the impression I was up for a bath? I stopped laughing and dabbed my running mascara with the black napkin.

"Excuse me," I said, leaning toward him across the table "but what exactly did I do or say tonight to make you think I was the kind of girl you could take home and *bathe* on the first date?"

"What do you mean?" he answered. "I find you beautiful, and I want to bathe you. It's a sensual thing."

"I'm sure it is. But I don't want to be bathed by someone I barely know. If you'll excuse me, I'm going to the ladies room."

I gathered my shawl and my purse and tried to walk as dignified as possible, although the remnants of the wine fuzz gave me a slight sway I couldn't control.

I looked at myself in the bathroom mirror and wondered how the evening had plummeted so abruptly. Maybe I overreacted. Maybe it wasn't a big deal. I mean, I could overlook his other water obsession, so why not this?

Perhaps it was that he expected it so quickly. Sure, I wanted him to find me attractive. I had certainly hoped he would kiss me good night. I might have even invited him in for a few minutes when he dropped me off. But I wanted him to desire spending time with me. To desire getting to know me. To find out who I am and what makes me tick. Share who he is and what makes him tick. Then, perhaps if our ticks lined up and our interests matched, maybe just maybe after we'd held hands and swapped spit— cuddled and petted a bit, trusted and shared—I *might* consider letting him bathe me.

Bathing seems so, I don't know, personal? So intimate. Even more so than sex in some way. I would have to feel completely and totally comfortable with someone to lay there and be bathed. Definitely not a first date event for me.

When I returned to the table, Christopher had paid the check and stood waiting for me. We left the restaurant in silence, and after only two stops to dry the car, he pulled into my driveway and cut the engine.

He looked at me intently, resting his left arm across the steering wheel and reaching over to put his right hand on my knee. I didn't move it, but I didn't necessarily want it there either.

"I'm sorry if I offended you," he said. "I didn't mean to. I find you attractive, and I wanted to see more of you."

"Evidently so," I said, shifting my leg out from under his hand.

"I didn't mean it like that. I mean, yes, I did want to see more of you, but I meant it like I wanted to go out with you again."

I nodded and smiled, unsure how to respond. I looked out the window and away from him.

"So," he said, "can I come inside for a while? No bath, just talking?"

I turned back to him, wondering if I was an insane, unreasonable person making too much out of this. There were so many wonderful things about him, so much I liked. Here was a handsome, wealthy, interesting man being straightforward and upfront with me about what he wanted. Hadn't I asked for that? Hadn't I wished for a straight shooter? So why couldn't I get past him offering to bathe me?

I didn't know. But I couldn't. "I don't think that's a good idea," I answered.

"Okay. Well, can I see you again?" he asked.

"I don't think that's a good idea either," I answered. Part of me felt guilty for turning the dude down. He'd been a perfect gentleman right up until he became Mr. Bubble. Even after, really. Polite as ever. Not pushing the issue or getting offended.

"Okay," he said. "Well, I bought you a gift. I intended to give it to you after your bath, but since that won't be happening, I'd like to go ahead and give it to you now."

He reached into the tight space behind my seat and pulled out an unmistakable pink-striped Victoria's Secret bag.

My eyes widened in shock as I sank back against the window away from the bag.

He reached inside and pulled out a sheer, white mesh thong with a bright pink satin rose prominently placed right above the G-string in the back.

"I got this for you today. I've been picturing you in it all night long. Paul showed me a picture of you, so I got the large to make sure it would fit. I can't stop imagining how fine your deliciously round derriere would look in this. Especially after a nice, hot bath."

"Okay, good night. I would say thank you for a lovely evening, but I'm a bit creeped out right now. Take care, and please don't bother to call."

I hauled my deliciously round derriere out of the super-clean Porsche, mentally noting I probably wouldn't want to ride in a car so low to the ground all the time anyway.

As I came around the front of the car he yelled, "Here!"

I shouldn't have turned, but I did, instinctively reaching to catch the pink-striped bag before it hit me square in the face.

"The gift was for you," he said. "I want you to have it. If I don't get to see you again, at least I can picture you wearing it. If you change your mind, you have my number."

Mr. Bubble pulled away, carefully avoiding the water on the side of my street. Between the car and the bath, this guy has some serious issues with cleanliness.

So yeah. I don't do blind dates. Or baths. I think I'll be a shower-only girl from here on out.

Thursday, October 10th

I debated over how much to tell Melanie today. She and Paul both wanted so badly for last night to go well. It was downright awkward to tell her I didn't like their dream date because he wanted to bathe me and dress me in a thong he bought me before we ever met. A *large* thong, I might add. (Never mind it was the correct size. That's not the point.)

The details ended up spewing out as we stood by the coffee machine. After she got over her initial shock and we laughed a bit, she apologized profusely and said she might murder Paul.

"It's not his fault, Mel. I'm pretty sure Christopher didn't tell him about his fetish for bubble baths, and I don't think he called Paul to get a size before making the thong purchase."

"Are you kidding me?" Mel asked. "We've been married almost fifteen years. The man has no clue what size panties *I* wear. He doesn't have a clue what to get you, trust me!"

"Well, chalk it up to another dating adventure and a new pair of panties I doubt I'll ever wear," I said.

"Hell, I'd wear 'em," Mel said. "He's not gonna know either way. Why turn down Victoria's Secret?"

I laughed with Mel about it, but I couldn't shake feeling a little depressed about the whole thing. I tried to go into it without expecting much, but then it seemed so good. I think I got my hopes up. I thought for a little bit that I had finally found someone to be excited about again. It's been a long time since I felt that way.

Not that I haven't had dates here and there that went well, but I don't remember really feeling excited to be with someone since Dwayne. Well, in the beginning with Dwayne, that is. All I felt in the end was a stabbing pain in my chest.

We'd known each other our whole lives, but it wasn't until our senior year that Cupid struck. It was the first time I'd ever been in love, complete with all the giddy, giggly, silly-ass things we say and do at that age. I wore his class ring on my index finger with a Dr. Scholl's corn pad stuffed beneath it so it wouldn't fall off. I drew hearts with our initials inside them all over notebooks, book covers, and chalkboards.

I'm embarrassed to say how many times I wrote my name as Tyler Davis, practicing so many variations of a capital D that I could have been a calligrapher if I only needed to do that one letter. I even scribbled out *Mrs. Dwayne Howard Davis* a few times on scraps of paper when no one was looking.

I thought I was moving up in the alphabet. Warren gets called last for everything. Davis was near the top. I chuckled out loud at the memory of my young priorities. Once you get out of school, the world is no longer structured in alphabetical order. But at the time, I thought I was scoring a great coup in upward mobility.

We were together three years. My last year of high school and my first two—well, my *only* two—years of college. By the end of our first year, I had already built the white-picket fence in my head *and* named the babies I thought we'd raise together.

The ringing of the office phone sucked me back into present day, the nostalgia of puppy love still wafting through my brain.

It was Rob, one of our grooms for March. He seemed upset but polite as he explained he and his bride, Megan, would not be getting married after all. He wanted to cancel the wedding contract and any vendors already booked, including the photographer, venue, caterer and florist. I extended my sympathies and told him we'd take care of the cancellations.

Laura said she'd put the file aside to sit for a day or so. Sometimes couples make decisions in the heat of an argument or a moment of doubt that change after they make up. Better to hold off canceling until they're sure the wedding's not happening than to stress out trying to rebook vendors after releasing them.

So later this afternoon, Megan called. She was freaking out, asking Laura if everything had already been canceled. Laura assured her nothing had been done yet.

But then she asked if she could change the groom's name on the contract instead of cancelling. She wanted everything she had booked—the venue, photographer, florist, and caterer. All the details arranged for her and Rob—flowers, menu, cake, linens. She wanted the same wedding but with a different guy. Seems she went back home for a wedding shower and ran into her high school sweetheart. Old flames die hard, I guess.

The whole thing hit really close to home. Partly because I'd been thinking about my old flame, my first love, and partly because I thought I knew a teensy bit about what Rob was feeling.

"Poor guy, huh?" Laura said.

"Yep," I answered, still mulling over my own memories.

"Well, at least he knows now. Better than after he married her, right?"

"I guess," I said. "Doesn't make it any easier, though. My boyfriend dumped me and got married a month later. At the time, I wasn't thinking he had done me any favors."

"He got married a month later?" Laura lifted her eyebrows almost to her hairline as she sank back in her chair. "Whoa. Was he already seeing her while you two were together?"

"I think so. I certainly didn't know about it. In fact, I thought he was going to propose. He said we needed to talk, and I started practicing my acceptance speech in my head. I was even cursing myself for not having my nails painted to look pretty for the ring. That wasn't what he had in mind, though."

"What did he say? He just told you he was marrying someone else?" Laura had leaned forward, resting her chin in her hands as she propped her elbows on her desk.

"No! I got the 'I think we need time apart' speech. The 'it's not you, it's me,' and my personal favorite, the 'I feel like we have so much life ahead of us that we can't really be tied down and make a commitment to one person' speech." Funny how I could remember how I felt that night as though it happened yesterday.

The air had left my lungs when he spoke, and I felt like I'd been punched in the gut. Like the world spun an extra loop or tilted too far to one side or something. Nauseous and dizzy.

"One day he was my whole world. The next day he wasn't even on my planet." I could feel my throat tighten as Laura shook her head in commiseration. "I was a mess for weeks. Couldn't eat. Couldn't drink. Couldn't sleep. I lost fifteen pounds in two weeks. I probably could have fit into a size six for the first time in my life *if* I'd been able to drag myself to a store to shop."

"But wait, how did you find out he was getting married?" Laura asked.

"His grandmother told me," I said. "Mama sent me to the store to buy milk. Probably to get me out of the house more than anything. I ran into his grandma in the grocery store and was stupid enough to ask how he was doing. I mean, I thought he might have been taking it hard, too."

Mrs. Dolores had given me a huge hug, squeezing me tight and telling me how much she missed me, which ripped my heart anew. I had thought she would be my grandma, too. That his family would be my family.

"She'd always been real sweet to me," I told Laura. "I hate that she had to be the one to break the news. She looked so confused when I asked how he was doing, and then she said she thought somebody would have told me already."

I had no idea what she was going to say, but I remember wanting to put my hands over my ears because I was sure it was nothing I wanted to know.

I could still hear her voice in my head, sweet and apologetic as she'd leaned in close and patted my arm. "Honey, Dwayne got married. Last weekend. He's on his honeymoon in New Orleans right now."

I felt as though the blood had stopped rushing through my body for a moment. I couldn't speak. Couldn't breathe. I thought I might pass out right there in the potato chips aisle.

"It had only been one month, Laura. One month since he gave me his speech about being too young to commit and having our whole lives ahead of us. I thought he just had cold feet and needed time to figure things out. Three years together and one month after he broke up with me, he got married. I guess he figured it out, didn't he?"

I felt the anger wash over me again. You'd think after five years I'd be totally over it and it wouldn't be that big of a deal. But he was my first love. I gave him my heart, my dreams, my virginity. In return, I got betrayed. And it still hurts. I think maybe it always will.

Laura was staring at me with an intense expression.

"People in my hometown probably still talk about me running out of that store like I was on fire," I said. "I have no idea who I bumped into on the way out. I just knew I had to get out."

"So is that when you moved away from home?" she asked, her voice a quiet whisper.

"Yep. The very next day. I packed my clothes and kept running. I quit college, quit my job, left my mother standing on the porch crying, and I ran."

"Why Orlando? Did you know people here?" Laura asked.

"Nope. Didn't know a soul. We came to the Magic Kingdom the summer before I turned thirteen. The summer before my dad died. I had happy memories here. I couldn't think of any place I'd rather be."

"Wow," Laura said. "I had wondered what made you move away from your family and come down here on your own. I had no idea, honey. I'm sorry that happened to you."

"Me too." I smiled, trying to lighten the conversation. I suddenly felt self-conscious that I had just poured my life story out to my boss. "But I'm okay now, right? It's all good."

"I guess. It obviously still bothers you," Laura said. "Have you talked to him since then? Did you see him after that?"

"No, I haven't. He's still right there in that little town working at his dad's lumber yard. Right where he swore he never wanted to be. Two kids, I think. Maybe three by now. I don't really keep up with him."

"Is that why you don't go home much?" Laura asked.

"Yeah, I guess so. It's like I associate home with bad memories, so I don't want to go back, you know?" I stood up and cleared my throat, ready to end my impromptu therapy session. "I'm sorry I got into all that. I guess he's just been on my mind the last couple of days for some reason, and then with Megan doing what she did . . ."

"Oh, no. Don't apologize. I would like to think we could talk and share things together without needing apologies. I'm glad to have a little glimpse or a little insight. And I, for one, think he made a dreadful mistake. But his loss was my gain, and I'm so happy you're here with us."

I smiled and nodded back at her, feeling the tightening in my throat I always feel when Laura is sweet to me. She and Lillian both make me want to cry. Just for completely different reasons.

Friday, October 11th

A frantic text message summoning me to a bride's room fifteen minutes before photos start is never a good sign.

I knew something was off when I entered the room. No excitement. No laughter. No last-minute preparations or animated chatter. Just an eerie quiet.

Janet, the bride, stood gazing out the window. From the look of the yellowed tulle and the ruffled, tiered skirt of her wedding gown, it was an antique or a family heirloom. She didn't turn to acknowledge me when I entered. The silent bridesmaids returned my greeting with briefly fleeting pasted-on smiles, which faded as their eyes widened and flicked toward the bride. I got the distinct impression something was horribly wrong, and they expected me to fix it.

My mind raced through possibilities. I scanned my memories for details of their relationship and any signs of trouble. They were an older couple, both in their late forties. Her first marriage, his third. Maybe she was having cold feet?

"Janet? Honey? Is everything okay?"

She turned then, and I was struck again by what an attractive lady she was. Her soft, honey blond hair framed her face in beautiful waves straight from a hair product commercial. Her brilliant green eyes had sparkled and danced when we met, but today they seemed paralyzed in sadness. The lines in her pretty face were a little more prominent.

It confused me. Janet had been so happy to get married. Overjoyed to find love late in life. Excited about every little detail of the wedding. I couldn't figure out what had changed.

When she spoke, I had to lean in to hear her despite our close proximity. "I found this dress when I was twenty-three. I was helping my friend shop for her wedding dress and envious of her getting married. I saw this gown hanging there, and I wanted more than anything to try it on. I went back to the store the next weekend all by myself. I put it on and knew this was the dress I wanted to wear in my wedding. I wasn't even dating anyone at the time, but I bought it. I put it on layaway and never told anyone. I figured I could hold onto it until I got married. I didn't think it would be twenty-four years, you know?"

She smiled at me as a huge tear rolled down her cheek.

"I put it on again when Ray and I first got engaged a year ago. I was amazed it still fit. Ecstatic! I automatically had my something old!" She chuckled as she dabbed at her eyes with a lace handkerchief. "I didn't put it on again until today. It's old. Fragile. I didn't want anything to happen to it."

She took a deep breath and gazed back out the window.

"So I put it on today for my *wedding*," she said, stressing the word as she spread her hands in the air and motioned to the hubbub in the room around her, "and this happened!"

She raised her left arm, and I saw it. The seam of the dress had completely ripped free, from just under her arm all the way to the bottom of the bodice. I gasped out loud before I could stop myself.

"And this," she said, turning so I could see the huge hole in the middle of the seam on her right side. Tears rolled freely down her cheeks.

"Okay," I said, mustering up my best confidence-boosting voice, "we can fix this. We can." I nodded several times and flashed a huge smile, all the while trying to figure out how on earth I could fix it in time for pictures in ten minutes.

"You can?" she asked, her face lighting up as her eyes dared to dance ever so slightly. The other bridesmaids came to life, chiming in around us. One saying, "I told you she'd fix it." Another saying, "It's going to be fine!" And one bitchy one muttering, "How are you going to fix that?"

I had no clue, but I sure didn't intend to say that out loud.

"Let me make a call. I'll be right back." I smiled as I backed toward the door. "Hold on, okay? We'll get you fixed up and down the aisle!" I made the universal "atta girl!" symbol with my fist swinging triumphantly in the air. Then, realizing how stupid that must look, I smoothed my hair back and cleared my throat before stepping into the hallway to call our favorite seamstress, Eileen.

The universe smiled down on me today. Or on Janet. Or both. Eileen happened to be in the hotel already, finishing up with Melanie's bridesmaids.

I've never doubted her prowess and expertise, but she proved her brilliance all over again today. The amazing Eileen took material from the lining of the skirt and stitched it inside the bodice. Then she stitched over

31

the frayed seams to create a slight ruffled effect. It wouldn't hold through much sitting or dancing, but it would get Janet down the aisle.

We missed photos before the ceremony, but I assured Janet we would have plenty of time to get pictures afterward. Not to mention the pictures would look much better without her busting out of her dress.

Thankfully from the time I said we could fix it, her spirits lifted. Every detail is important to a bride, but not having skin bulging out of the dress is a pretty big detail. I hated seeing her so distraught and depressed when she thought the dress was ruined.

I kept thinking all day about that 23-year-old girl who went and picked out a gown and the dreams that went with it, paying forward with hope that someday she would wear the gown for her own fairy tale. I cannot even begin to imagine how much faith it took to keep that dress for twenty-four years. How often must she have felt like throwing the damned thing away and giving up. I probably would have thought the dress was bad luck and gotten rid of it to try and stop the curse.

I wonder how many times she may have moved to a new place, or how many times a relationship fell apart, or how many lonely nights she spent with that dress hanging in the closet, taunting her and daring her to keep on dreaming.

How excited she must have been to finally find love and somehow still fit into her 23-year-old dream. How devastated she must have been when they zipped the bodice and those seams gave way.

I guess sometimes my dreams feel like that. Fragile bits of fabric held together by memories of what I wanted to be. Ripped apart a bit, disintegrated somewhat, but still with me. I know there is someone out there for me. I know my dream of finding true love will happen. I just need to have faith. I can't give up. Maybe I should go dress shopping and buy myself a reminder to hang in the closet.

Saturday, October 12th

Before I started doing weddings, I never knew how exhausting it could be to watch drunk people party. I feel hungover from just watching them tonight, and I didn't even drink.

I knew it was gonna be bad when I walked in the dressing room before pictures and they had already finished off a bottle of champagne. I told Rebecca several times she needed to eat something and lay off the alcohol, but when I went back in to get her for the ceremony she was drunker than Cooter Brown's dog. (It occurs to me as I write that phrase that although I have heard it my entire life, I have no idea who Cooter Brown was or why on earth his dog was drunk. But anyway!)

I should have known when Rebecca chose "Save a Horse, Ride a Cowboy" for her bridal processional that it was going to be a rowdy night. We ended up closing the bar an hour early after two people passed out and one lady threw up in the bathroom sink. At least Rebecca managed to stay upright all night, which was quite the accomplishment since she walked down the aisle giggling and burping behind her bouquet before slurring her way through her vows.

She went to all that trouble, planning out the most minute details for her event, and how much of it will she remember? I guess it doesn't really matter. She and Tim gushed about how wonderful everything was as I put them in the limo at the end of the night, and her parents kept remarking about what a great job I did.

I just think that if it's one of the most important events of your life, you'd want to remember it.

Maybe I'm getting old. I can't remember the last time I went out partying. Working a wedding every Friday and Saturday night kind of puts a damper on the weekend. Nowadays, going out means catching a drink or two after a wedding with the people I worked with that night. The florist, the DJ, the photographer. I go out with Mel and Paul sometimes, but it's usually just dinner or a movie on a weeknight.

I used to go out all the time. Especially when I worked at the coffee shop. I still keep in touch with those friends, but it's hard to connect with everyone's diverse schedules. Cabe and I had a group we hung out with—mostly his friends from growing up and his sister Galen and her friends—all of whom I stopped seeing when he left.

I guess I kind of cocooned a little when he moved. I didn't want to be around anyone for a while. Didn't want to go out and be reminded he was gone. Then it became normal to just go to work and come home. I should look at the calendar to see when I have a weekend night off and call some of the old coffee shop gang to get together. Definitely would have to be after October, though. Or maybe Halloween. That would be a cool night to go out. I think I'll call a few people tomorrow and see what everyone's doing for Halloween.

But for now, I'm headed to bed. Sober and exhausted.

Sunday, October 13th

Mr. Hotel Man called today. Wanted to check and see how this weekend's wedding went. He said they'd be happy to book any future brides and grooms, and he'd love to work with me again. What's up with that? He calls my cell phone on a Sunday afternoon to tell me I can book future brides and grooms at his hotel? Is he running for salesman of the year for the resort, or is he leading up to asking me out? He kept it short and sweet, so maybe it was just a courtesy business call. But who does that? On a Sunday afternoon?

I think he likes me.

Monday, October 14th

Wow. Just wow. I left my desk to get a cup of coffee and missed a call from Cabe. I haven't heard a peep from the man for nine freakin' months, and then the one time he calls, I'm not by my phone. I would have been totally caught off guard, though, so it was probably a good thing I had a warning.

Of course, I immediately went to Melanie's desk and shoved my phone in her face. Never mind that she was in the middle of a cake design discussion with Chaz.

"He called?" Mel shrieked when she saw his name on the screen. She looked up at me with her mouth wide open.

I nodded.

"Who called?" Chaz asked.

"Did you call him back?" Mel asked, handing me back the phone.

"No! I came to show you first."

"Call who back?" Chaz asked.

"I don't know if I'm going to call right back. I think when you don't call me for nine months, it's perfectly acceptable to make you wait for a call back."

"Let who wait? Who called?" Chaz asked.

"Don't do that, Tyler. Call him," Mel said.

"Call who? Will somebody tell me who we're talking about?" Chaz shouted.

"Cabe!" Mel and I yelled in unison.

"Who the hell is Cabe?" Chaz asked.

"Nine months, Mel. Nine months and I've only heard from him twice. One call from a concert where I couldn't hear a word he said and a text to thank me for sending his mother a birthday card. Why should I call him

36

back at all?"

"Maybe he has a good reason," Mel offered.

"Who is Cabe?" Chaz tapped his hands on the desk in frustration.

"What would be a good reason for not calling your best friend for nine months?" I crossed my arms and arched my eyebrow, twisting my lips in anger.

"Okay, got it. Cabe's your best friend. Next clue?" Chaz seemed quite pleased with himself.

"*Was* my best friend," I corrected him.

"Oh, he still is," Mel said. She turned to explain to Chaz. "Tyler and Cabe were inseparable. They did everything together. The closest of friends. Should have gotten married, but neither of them had the guts to make a move."

"Ha!" I scoffed. "Marry him? Never. Not even a consideration." I looked at Chaz. "We were just friends."

"With benefits?" asked Chaz.

"No benefits!" I said.

Mel laughed and leaned across her desk toward Chaz. "Just friends, my patootie. Chaz, honey, do you frequently take out of town trips for the weekend with someone who is just a friend? Have sleepovers on a weekly basis? Call each other a bazillion times a day, text like crazy, and finish each other's sentences? These two were perfect for each other and too stupid to see it. You should have seen the way this guy looked at her. Like she hung the moon."

I shook my head as Chaz looked from Mel to me. "She's mistaken. She wanted there to be more than there was. We were friends."

Cabe was actually my first friend here. I met him the day I started at the coffee shop five years ago. He came in and stressed that he wanted "plain coffee." He was a systems programmer and came in a couple of days a week with his laptop to work for a few hours. His *coffice*, he called it. We started hanging out, and soon we were spending all our time together. It was comfortable. Easy. No stress. No pressure. We had this weird chemistry that worked. Sure, there was some physical tension between us, but neither of us ever acted on it. In fact, we discussed many times how we treasured the friendship too much to screw it up by trying anything further.

No matter who I went out with, and no matter who he went out with, we were always there for each other. Prospective partners knew upfront we were a package deal. If you dated me, you got Cabe. If you dated Cabe, you got me.

My mother never got it. Never understood.

"But why do you spend so much time with him if you're not dating? You're never going to find someone if you're always with Cabe. Boys aren't going to come up and talk to you if you're already with a guy. They'll assume you're together. Are you sure he's not gay? He must be gay. How can he spend so much time with you and not be gay? Are you sure he's not attracted to you and he's just not saying so? Maybe you should make the first move. Maybe you should simply ask him if he's interested."

Oh, good grief. It was never ending with her.

But we didn't care what other people thought. We were partners in adventure. Dance buddies. We were best friends. And we knew we could count on each other.

Until Monica.

"Okaaay, so what happened?" Chaz asked. "Why haven't you heard from him? Why haven't I heard about him? Do tell, girl." He sat on the edge of his seat, awaiting the new dirt.

"He left," I said. "He moved to Seattle."

"You told him to!" Mel slapped her folder against my leg.

"Why'd you do that?" Chaz asked.

"Because I wanted him to be happy. He met a girl who made him happy. They were perfect for each other. They fell in love hard and fast, and we thought he'd finally found the one. Until she decided to move back home to Seattle."

Cabe had showed up at my apartment around midnight that night, crying like I'd never seen before. I mean, he'd always been one to tear up over a good movie here and there. *The Notebook* got him every time. But nothing like that night. He was devastated.

We talked 'til four in the morning, and he asked what I thought he should do.

I told him he should follow her.

"If you love her, if she's the one you want to spend your life with, then you go where she goes. Your job doesn't matter. Your family doesn't matter. None of it does. If she's the one, and you can't imagine life without her, then you follow her."

It was what he wanted to hear and what I wanted to believe love should be. He arranged a transfer with his company, agreeing to give up his remote office status and show up at a desk in a cubicle every day. Within a month, my best friend was gone.

We had been spending less time together since they started dating, but I always knew he was right there if I needed him. Suddenly, he lived all the way across the country, and I felt his absence in the pit of my stomach.

"But I don't get this," Chaz said. "If you guys were so close, why haven't you heard from him since he left?"

"Because she's his chocolate chip cookie." Melanie purred the words, sitting back in her chair with her arms crossed, obviously satisfied with herself. Her words stung too much for me to even comment.

"What does that mean?" Chaz asked.

Melanie nodded for me to answer, but it wasn't something I wanted to talk about. Still too painful, even though it all happened months ago.

"Don't take it personally," Cabe had said about a month after he moved. "You didn't do anything wrong. Monica likes you, she really does. But she, well, *we*, feel like maybe I'm not fully committing to the whole relationship thing if you're still my closest friend. You know? Monica has to be my closest friend now. I don't know if I can be as close to her as I should be if you're still around. I mean, I'm closer to you than I've ever been with anyone. You get me. You and I kind of have our own language. Our own vibe. It makes it hard for Monica. For *us*, I mean. It's kind of like chocolate chip cookies when you're on a diet. You just can't stay away from them. If they're around, you're gonna want a cookie. Therefore, the best thing to do is not have chocolate chip cookies around, you know?"

Being across the country wasn't good enough. He severed our ties. I became a chocolate chip cookie and lost the best friend I'd ever had. It's not like cookies weren't already the enemy of my ample thighs. Now they had to gash open a hole in my heart as well.

"So the two of you didn't get along?" Chaz asked. "You and Monica?"

"I thought we did! I thought she and I were friends. We hung out together all the time when they were still here. If there was a problem, I didn't know about it."

"Okay, so she's a catty bitch who was nice to your face and then sunk her talons in him once she got him away from you," Chaz said, crossing his legs and clasping his hands on his knee. "Go on. What happened next?"

I swear the man should have his own talk show or something. He thrives on gossip like a baby on breast milk.

"He called again less than a month later. This time to tell me they'd driven to Big Sur and gotten married with nobody there except her sister and her mom. He said he was sorry I couldn't come." I could feel the hurt and anger unleashing within me all over again.

"Would you have gone?" Chaz the interviewer asked.

"I don't know. I think it would have been awkward to watch him marry someone who didn't want me around, you know? I mean, I would have been the chocolate chip cookie skulking in the background. Anyway, I wasn't invited."

"And she hasn't heard from him since the wedding day," Melanie added.

"Whoa, Nelly!" Chaz gasped, sitting back in his chair. "So he meant it, huh?"

"Well, technically, that's not true, Mel. There was the concert call and the text about his mom's birthday." I don't know why I felt like I needed to defend Cabe.

"No way, girl," Chaz said, shaking his head. "Don't you call that boy back!"

"Don't you listen to him! He doesn't know what he's talking about," Mel said.

"Honey, if there is one thing I do know, it is men." Chaz pointed his finger and pursed his lips. "This one does not deserve a callback. Let it go, girl."

"No, I'm gonna call him back," I said.

"I wouldn't." Chaz uncrossed his legs and crossed his arms simultaneously.

"She will," Mel said. "She wants to talk to him. No matter what." She nodded her head again, smug in her assessment.

I turned and went back to my desk, my stomach twisted in knots. She was right, of course. I knew I would call him back the minute I saw the missed call. I needed time to compose myself, though. To gather my thoughts. I decided I'd go for nonchalant. As though I hadn't even noticed how much time had passed.

My hand shook as I dialed his number. He answered on the first ring.

"What's up, Buttercup?"

His voice cut through me like a knife. So deep. So throaty. So Cabe.

I swallowed back tears and called forth sarcasm, the great camouflage for all emotion.

"Wow! Could it be? Could this actually be my very best friend? Who skipped town, got married, and then dropped off the face of the planet? Is he calling to talk to little ole me?"

"Very funny," he said.

"So how's married life? Are you able to enjoy a cookie now without the world ending?"

So much for the nonchalant approach. He went silent, and I worried he may have hung up on me.

"Hello? Dude, are you there? Cabe? Did you call and say hello and hang up?"

"I'm here. You off today?"

"No, why?"

"I want to see you."

I sat back in my chair and raised my eyebrows in surprise.

"Where are you?" I asked.

"Here. In town. Can I see you?"

Conflict coiled my insides. Excitement he was in town and wanted to see me. Hurt that he hadn't let me know he was coming.

"Sure. When?" I asked, my voice clipped as I tried to remind myself to be nice. After all, he was calling and asking to see me, right? It's not like I heard from someone else that he came and went without even telling me.

"Right now?" His voice sounded off. A little hoarse. Emotional, maybe?

"Um, I don't know. I'm working."

"On a Monday?" he asked.

"Yeah. October. Crazy busy. Can we meet up later?" I cringed, waiting for him to say they had plans later. I suddenly very much wanted to see him. I hoped I hadn't missed my only opportunity.

"Okay. What time?"

"Oh, I don't know. Wanna meet for dinner?" I selfishly hoped he wouldn't bring Monica.

"Can you maybe leave early this afternoon? Maybe we could meet at like four?"

"Um, sure. I can do that. Are you okay?" I could definitely detect emotion in his voice now. It didn't sound happy.

"Yeah, I just need to see you."

"Okay. Four o'clock then. Where are you staying?" I started to ask if Monica was coming with him but decided against it. I'd find out soon enough.

"I'll meet you by the lake. On the bench."

The lake. The bench. Our favorite spot. My heart tugged. We both loved this little lake tucked away at the back of one of the older neighborhoods in town. Mediterranean-style mansions lined the perimeter. They'd been built back in the 20s with stucco, tile roofs, and colorful porcelain accents. We used to sit on the bench for hours, feeding the ducks and making up stories about imaginary characters living in each house. In our stories, they lived incredibly dramatic lives. We created outrageous circumstances and dialogue for our make-believe residents, laughing our heads off at their antics. It was a game we thoroughly enjoyed. The kind of crazy stuff that no one else understood.

"Okay, see you at four."

"See you then." He hung up and my feelings swirled in a whirlpool of anticipation, giddiness, hurt, and resentment. One minute I couldn't wait for four o'clock to get here. The next I wanted to call him back, tell him I was busy, and I didn't have time to talk.

As the day progressed, my raging thoughts built to a tempest. How can you just drop someone's friendship and disappear? Especially your best friend? On some level, I understood his relationship needed to come first. If I married someone, I wouldn't want some other chick hanging around being his best friend and confidante. So I got that. Really, I did. I wanted what was best for Cabe. I wanted him to be happy even more than I wanted me to be happy. So if me being gone would make him happy, then I was willing to do that for him. I did do it. But it hurt like hell.

It still hurts now, more than I've cared to admit all this time. I don't like feeling like I didn't matter. Like our friendship didn't matter. I wanted to be as important to him as he was to me. I thought I was. But evidently, I was only a chocolate chip cookie.

I couldn't even focus on the files on my desk. The more I thought about it, the madder I got. I decided I didn't want to be at his beck and call. Who calls someone up after virtually no contact for months and expects them to drop everything and be available? What kind of idiot person says, "Okay, I'll be there"?

I snatched my phone and texted him to say something came up. We'd have to meet tomorrow instead. A stronger person probably would have canceled altogether, but I wanted to see him. As much as I needed to make a point, I also missed my friend.

Part of me hoped he would say tomorrow wouldn't work. Then I could feel justified somehow and stay mad at him forever. Another part of me wanted him to insist on seeing me today as though he couldn't wait any longer.

He did neither. He just texted me back.

"Tomorrow at the lake at four. Got it."

Pins and needles here.

Tuesday, October 15th

The clock moved as slow as molasses today. By the time I got to the office this morning, I'd worked myself into a frenzy over putting Cabe off last night, especially since he sounded upset. Maybe he didn't call to let me know he was coming home because something was terribly wrong. Like an emergency that required him to come home with no notice. What if he has cancer or something? What if his mom is sick? What if Monica is sick? What could have made him sound so sad?

I felt guilty for not going to him yesterday. Here I was, criticizing him for being a bad friend, yet I was being completely selfish and not thinking about him. It took considerable effort all day to resist the temptation to call and ask if he wanted to meet earlier. How funny that after so long without any contact, I felt like I had to analyze and pre-think something as simple as calling Cabe. It used to be so natural and normal. It didn't require thought or planning. But suddenly it felt like trying to figure out the dance steps with some guy I just met. Aargh.

By two-thirty, I couldn't stand it any longer. I left the office, figuring I'd rather be on the road and headed toward him than sitting at my desk watching the clock every five minutes. Time wasn't moving fast enough, and I wasn't getting anything done anyway.

I stopped by a deli to pick up a sandwich and check my hair and makeup in the ladies' room. How odd. I don't think I've ever checked my hair and makeup to see Cabe before. He's seen me first thing in the morning numerous times when we crashed on each other's couches. More often than not after a raucous evening out that didn't exactly make for the best appearance the morning after. He's brought me Gatorade and saltines when I was throwing up nonstop with the flu, held my hair back while I puked, and then wiped my face with a wet cloth while I lay motionless on the bathroom floor. I usually never bothered to put on makeup if we were hanging out, so it felt weird to suddenly be all self-conscious about how I looked.

"It's just Cabe," I kept telling myself. Not seeing him for so many months combined with a tad bit of insecurity about our friendship had me rattled. Stupid, I know. It's not like he would have sacrificed his relationship with Monica to save our friendship if I had looked prettier. Maybe it was a girl thing. You want someone to see you looking great and thinking you have fared well without them. Which I had. But it hadn't always been easy.

Even though I arrived twenty minutes early, he was already there. My heart lifted as soon as I saw him on the bench. I felt nothing but complete happiness. No hurt or resentment. No self-consciousness or awkwardness. Just Cabe. My best friend. I could relax and completely be myself. More so than I have ever been with anyone else.

I snuck up behind him and reached my hands around to cover his eyes.

"I'll give you three chances to guess who I am, and the first two don't count."

He grabbed my hands and tried to pull me over the back of the bench and into his lap as he laughed. I wrenched free and he stood up, turning to hug me. His face shocked me. He had a full, messy, thick, curly, Grizzly Adams beard going on.

"What the hell? Is this some kind of Seattle thing?" I asked, tugging on his beard. He laughed again, and I could see his perfect white teeth hidden in all that funky hair. He had such an incredible smile. Dazzling, the girls would say, which I teased him about without mercy.

His sandy blond hair had darkened since he left, and it hung shaggy around his face with thick curls almost grazing his shoulders. He looked thin, much thinner than I had ever seen him. His flannel shirt hung on his shoulders and the blue T-shirt underneath didn't touch his chest or ribs. He seemed to be swimming in his khaki pants.

"Does that girl never cook for you?" I asked. "Or does eating all that organic hipster food not keep the meat on your bones?"

His smile faded and tears welled in his eyes, the moisture intensifying the clear blue.

"What? Cabe, what? What is it?"

He reached out his arms and I fell into them, squeezing him as hard as I could. Trying to make up for months without his big bear hugs.

"What's going on?" I didn't want to let go of him, but I wanted to know what was wrong. Every horrible disease imaginable flashed in my brain as I tried to figure out what could cause such a drastic weight loss in this guy who had been so muscular and meaty.

"She left me, Ty. She doesn't love me. She doesn't want me anymore." His voice broke and sobs racked his body as he squeezed me so tight I couldn't breathe. I struggled to twist my head from one side to the other against his chest, trying to find air. He let me go and almost shoved me away from him as he turned toward the lake, wiping his eyes with closed fists like a little kid.

"What? When? Oh, Cabe, I am so sorry. What happened?"

He squatted by the lake, pulling strands of grass to toss in the water as he spoke.

"Three months ago. She'd been working a lot, gone all the time. I didn't see much of her. She spent most of her time with her friend Kristen. Going out after work every night. Coming in all hours. We were fighting a bunch. I mean, hell, I was lonely. I moved all the way across the frickin' country to be with someone who was never home. I finally asked if she would rather be married to Kristen. I meant it as a rhetorical question, but she said yes. She said they were in love, and she couldn't pretend with me anymore."

I sank on the bench and exhaled. I didn't even know I'd been holding my breath.

"Wow."

"Yeah," he said. "Wow."

He stood up and faced me, his hands in his back pockets. He looked so thin, so fragile. I had never seen this Cabe. This broken shell of the incredibly confident and outgoing boy I knew so well. My heart hurt to see him in such pain.

"She moved out that weekend. No talking it over. No counseling. Nothing. She moved in with Kristen, moved on with her life, and left me to pick up the pieces. She didn't even want anything from the apartment. Furniture, dishes. None of it. It was like she wanted nothing at all to do with our life. She just left and never looked back."

A selfish, immature part of me shouted somewhere deep inside, *"Hey, I know how that feels."* Luckily, I shoved it back to the depths from which it came. Now was not the time to be nursing my own wounds. His were much more threatening at the moment.

"Cabe, I'm so sorry. I don't know what to say. I can't even imagine what you must be feeling. I'm sorry. Are you okay? Well, obviously not. Stupid question. I'm sorry. And I'm sorry I keep saying I'm sorry. I just . . . I don't . . . I just . . ."

"Yeah. Me too," he said. He came and sat on the bench beside me. I leaned my head on his shoulder, resting my hand on his thigh.

We sat there for a few minutes in total silence before it dawned on me. I wish it hadn't. I wish I could have never thought it. Because I feel like I must be a self-absorbed, vile creature if that popped into my head at a time when my very best friend on Earth hurt so desperately. But it did pop into my head. No matter how hard I tried to swallow it back down, I couldn't. Then, I heard myself blurt it out, even though I was thinking the whole time that I shouldn't.

"This happened three months ago? Why didn't you call me? I mean, I would think you would have wanted to talk to me."

I know, I know. Could I be any more self-absorbed? Really? The dude's wife left him for another chick. He's lost like fifty pounds in grief. Here I am concerned because I wasn't the first person he called. I am truly a terrible person. A terrible friend. But my feelings were hurt.

Cabe didn't look at me when he answered. "I couldn't. I couldn't talk to anyone. I was a zombie. I went to work, came home, and slept. I slept any time I wasn't at work. I couldn't eat. I just wanted to sleep so I didn't feel the pain."

I knew that feeling. All too well. I remembered the utter hopelessness when Dwayne left. Not wanting to talk to anyone because somehow talking about it made it more real. Unavoidable. Hearing what other people had to say made it harder to bear. Despite their best intentions and their most carefully-worded clichés of comfort, nothing helped. Talking about only made it worse.

So I understood. Really, I did. But it still hurt. Like another nail in the coffin of our friendship. I felt even more unnecessary to him. Even more disconnected. How could I have been his best friend if this terrible, horrible thing happened to him, and he didn't even want to talk to me about it?

"My manager suggested maybe I take some time off. I hadn't showered in days. I looked and smelled like hell. I wasn't exactly a productive employee, ya know?"

No matter how bad I felt for him and for feeling the way I did, I couldn't stop. I had to ask the question burning the back of my throat.

"Cabe, how long have you been back in town?"

He sat up and leaned forward, resting his elbows on knees. He turned his head away from me and when he spoke, I had to strain to hear him.

"About two months. It took me a few days to clear out the apartment. I sold some stuff. Left some in storage. Packed up the rest and drove back across the country with way too much time and highway for so much on my brain. I gave up everything for her. Left my mom and my sister. Hell, I married her. Swore to spend the rest of my life with her. Gave her my name. Now's it's all gone. It's bullshit."

I battled within myself. I knew he was hurting. It honestly had nothing to do with me. It wasn't personal. He was processing. Taking one day at a time. But anger boiled inside of me. Anger at Monica for doing this to my friend. Anger at Cabe for diminishing my presence in his life to a chocolate-chip cookie. Anger for him not calling, e-mailing, or texting. For not in any way giving a shit what was happening in my life for the past nine months. Anger at Dwayne for being an epic fail and giving me all the experience I needed to know what Cabe was feeling. And more anger at Cabe for not even coming to me when the very reason we'd been separated tossed him aside.

"So how many of those houses have people getting a divorce?" He nodded toward the Mediterranean mansions lining the little lake. When we created lives for our imaginary residents, at least one family ended up on the rocks. We figured it was a statistical probability and needed to be acknowledged. Life wasn't all happy endings, so amid the parties and extravagant lifestyles we imagined them having, we also crafted all sorts of sordid and twisted things to happen behind the walls across the lake.

I didn't feel like playing the game right then, but I didn't trust myself to say what I should in my current emotional state. So I played.

"Two," I answered. "That one on the left, and the third house over. The husband is a movie producer. He's been in LA filming for a year. His wife is bored. She's been rebuffed by the pool boy and the gardener. So she set her sights on the neighbor three doors down, who was recently laid off from his job in a research laboratory. He's sitting home alone all day."

"No, you missed what's right in front of your eyes, Ty. In between that house and the guy three doors down is a sexy blond lady who has stolen the neighbor's heart and ravished her body. Now she'll leave her husband and kids behind and take off with the blonde in that red Ferrari."

My heart sank. I was at a loss for what to say to make him feel better.

"Dude, again, I'm sorry. I won't offer any stupid clichés like 'it's her loss' or 'time heals all wounds.' Those won't help. I'm just going to say it sucks. And I'm sorry. I'm here."

He took my hand and kissed the back of it. "I missed you, Ty. It's so good to see you. You being here already makes me feel better."

The late afternoon sun illuminated the pain in his eyes, but he managed a lopsided smile as he pulled my hand tight against his chest, hugging my arm close. My heart melted as we locked eyes, and I saw the desperate plea in his gaze. How could I have been upset with him?

We stayed an hour longer, not saying much at all.

"Are you hungry? You want something to eat?" I asked, my Southern heritage coming through. There is no tragedy or loss that cannot be made better by throwing food at it. Preferably something fried.

"Nah. I'm good. I don't eat much anymore. Not much of an appetite."

"Where you stayin'?" I asked.

"Mama's. She's been cooking these big meals every night trying to get me to eat, but I don't want anything. The fridge is packed with leftovers. She keeps having to throw stuff out to put more in."

I thought of Maggie, and how this must be killing her. Cabe had always been her big, strapping boy. A true mama's boy. She raised him and his sister Galen on her own after their dad left on Cabe's third birthday. She was a tough lady who would move heaven and earth for her kids. I couldn't imagine how she felt seeing him so distraught. She hated him moving to Seattle. I'm sure not being included in his wedding devastated her. So some part of her must be happy to have him home, no matter what the circumstances. I knew I was.

I patted the hand that held mine.

"Well, I was worried you were going to tell me you had cancer. Or Maggie was sick. So I guess all things considered, things could be worse."

He groaned a bit, shaking his head. "I guess so."

"You wanna watch a movie or something?" I wanted to bring him out of the funk.

"No, but thanks. I just wanted you. To hear your voice and see your sweet smile. To feel like someone loved me. Other than Mama, you know."

"I do love ya, sweetie. Always will. You know that." My heart clenched a bit at feeling like he needed me after all.

He kissed the back of my hand again and let it go, standing up to stretch his arms wide. It was a Cabe move I had seen a thousand times. It made me suddenly ache for the way things used to be between us. Then the selfish little bitch inside my head whispered that with Monica gone, it could be that way again. I'm so horrible.

Wednesday, October 16th

I slept in intermittent spurts last night. Kept thinking about Cabe and Monica. His situation and our situation. I couldn't stop my whirring brain from obsessing over everything. If I hadn't had a cake tasting today, I would have called in sick to sleep. But at least I got to eat cake.

Our entire wedding industry is focused around the bride. But there are two people getting married, and one of them generally gets lost in the shuffle. Part of this is because men don't typically care about flowers, dresses, and place cards. As long as the food is good and the bar is serving, most grooms are happy to let the bride figure out the rest of the details.

I always encourage the bride to ask for her groom's input, especially in areas like music or menus where he may actually care. I think it's a good idea to remind her as she goes into marriage that she needs to consider his opinion and what he wants. The groom should have at least a tiny stake in his own wedding. It doesn't always work, but I do make a point of trying.

Other than menu tastings, cake tastings are often one of the only planning meetings a groom enjoys. Most men like sampling food for free, especially yummy cakes.

My groom today, Jerry, was no exception. He particularly liked the chocolate cake with raspberry filling. But his bride, Joanna, wouldn't even consider it. She wanted a white cake. I suggested perhaps she could do the larger layer in white with the smaller second layer in chocolate for Jerry. Nope. She didn't want a dark cake. I could tell Jerry was a little peeved, but he said okay and she seemed determined, so I let it drop.

Jerry pretty much checked out from that point, a little irritated but overall bored. Until Joanna told the pastry chef she wanted Gerber daisies on the cake.

"No," he said. "No daisies. I want roses on the cake. Red roses."

Joanna turned and looked at him like he had two heads.

"Red? Nothing in this wedding is red," she said.

"I want red roses." He issued the challenge.

Joanna crossed her arms and slid one knee over the other, her left foot bopping up and down as it dangled. "First of all, you know I hate roses. There are no roses in this wedding. I am having Gerber daisies in purple, orange, pink, and yellow. No roses and no red!"

"The last time I checked, this was my wedding, too. And *she*"—he pointed to me as I shrank from him—"said you need to consider my opinions. My opinion is I want red roses on this damned cake. And I want it to be chocolate."

"A wedding cake is not chocolate." Joanna clenched her teeth and hissed the words. "That's not what people expect when they see a wedding cake. Nor will they expect to see red roses on the cake when there's no red anywhere else at all. And no roses!" I sensed perhaps there were other sources of tension that had nothing to do with cake.

"Well, I didn't expect to go into debt to marry you!" Jerry shouted. "I didn't expect to be told to ask my brother to be my best man instead of Chuck, my best friend since third grade. I also didn't expect half of my family to not be invited so your mother could invite anyone who's ever been related to her. Or that I would be guilted into wearing a white tuxedo, which I think is ridiculous. So if I have to deal with all that shit I didn't expect, then I think people will survive seeing red roses on a chocolate cake. If you want me to be standing there waiting for you at the altar, then this cake will be chocolate and have red roses."

Joanna's mouth dropped open and then closed. A couple of times. She looked like she couldn't decide whether to kill him or cry.

I tried to think of something to say but struggled.

"Um. Um. Maybe you could compromise and have red Gerbers. Then it would be the color Jerry wants and the flowers—"

"No. Red roses and chocolate cake." Jerry set his jaw as he spoke, glaring at Joanna with such venom that I seriously questioned if we would even make it to the wedding day. Much less how long they might make it afterward.

Joanna stared back at him for a moment. Then, in an almost imperceptible surrender, she blinked back whatever moisture might have gathered and nodded.

"Okay. Red roses. Chocolate cake." Joanna turned to her rather uncomfortable pastry chef, and the cake was ordered.

I doubt Jerry honestly gave two hoots what color the flowers were on the cake. But something obviously made him feel like he needed to take a stand and be heard.

We get such a small glimpse into people's relationships in my job. We see the big day. The plans that go into it. The emotions surrounding it. But we don't see the behind the scenes. How they treat each other when no one is looking. How their relationship really ticks.

I wonder what Cabe and Monica were like when it was just them. By themselves in Seattle. What was their behind-the-scenes like? What the hell happened to make her just take off? I mean, obviously she had some things going on with her sexual identity. I certainly didn't see that coming from the time I spent with her.

But why would she let him move to Seattle and marry him if she was wrestling with her own demons? It just doesn't make sense.

Cabe said in Seattle Monica was never home. When they were here, she couldn't get enough of him. She seemed completely enamored. Always touching him. Holding his hand, stroking his back, hand on his thigh. She watched him intently and reacted to his every movement. She talked about him as though he were Adonis himself. From the first night they met, she pursued him relentlessly. It was her who made the first move. And the second and the third. I know. I was there. I saw it with my own eyes. So I don't understand what happened once they moved.

As much as I would never want to see Monica again, part of me would love to hear her side of the story. Why did she do this to Cabe? What was their underlying issue that brought things to a head? Was it really as simple as her discovering she liked girls?

When I got home tonight, I sent Cabe a text.

"How you doing?"

He responded *"fine"* and nothing else. Not sure where we go from here. I guess I should sit back and see what he does. What he needs. Practice what I preach, I guess. Respect? Consideration? Putting someone else first? I guess it applies in friendship just like in marriage.

Thursday, October 17th

Laura hired a new assistant Monday. It hasn't even been a full week, and I already want to fire her. We've been short-handed ever since our assistant Carmen went into labor at Olive Garden last month. Her water broke between the salad and entrée. (The manager was kind enough to give her an entire order of breadsticks to take to the hospital with her.)

Since no one has time to do interviews in crazy-busy October, Laura brought in her sister-in-law's niece, Charlotte. I understand wanting to help out family—or in this case, family of family—but I don't think this girl has ever even attended a wedding. All I can say after her first week is I hope she marries well. I don't see running corporations or navigating upper management in her future.

I gave her a wedding file yesterday with a letter paper-clipped to the front of it. I stuck a yellow Post-it note on the letter saying, "Mail this to the client. Address in file." I thought it was pretty simple. Self-explanatory.

This afternoon, I needed the file and went to ask her for it. She looked at me like I was stupid and told me with the slightest bit of attitude that she mailed it to the client like I asked.

Yep. She mailed the entire freakin' wedding file to the client. Folder and all.

I explained I had only wanted the letter mailed to the client. That's why I clipped it to the front with the note on it.

She shrugged and continued to look at me as though I were daft as she calmly replied, "Your note said 'Mail this to the client.' It didn't say mail the letter."

Are you kidding me?!

Today, Melanie had her fold save-the-date letters and put them in envelopes. Charlotte threw away twelve envelopes and stamps because she addressed them and stamped them upside down. Now, I'm not a total hard-ass. I can understand it happening once or maybe twice. It's mindless work. Easy to get distracted. But twelve times? Wouldn't you start paying attention real close after two or three?

What we do is not brain surgery, but it does help to have a brain and know how to use it. I hope I wasn't this clueless on my first day.

No word from Cabe today. I texted *"Hey."* He didn't text back.

Friday, October 18th

Lillian's heart made a covert, undercover appearance today. It doesn't happen often, but it restores my faith in her every time.

She popped in my office this morning and asked for my car keys. I immediately dug into my purse for my keys and handed them over to her, even though I had no earthly idea what she was going to do with my car. Funny how when she asks for something, people do it without question.

After she'd been gone about ten minutes, curiosity got the best of me. I got to my car just as she closed the trunk.

"What did you put in there?" I asked.

Lillian looked startled, uncharacteristically nervous, and slightly out of breath.

"Oh. I need you to take something to Carmen today."

One would think she would've asked me *before* putting it in my car, but that's not Lillian's style. She pretty much expects we'll do whatever she needs. Granted, we usually do, even if we have to rearrange the heavens to do so.

"Sure," I answered.

"You mustn't look in the trunk until you get to her house, and you absolutely must not tell her who it is from. Do you understand?" She asked the question in the form of a statement. I knew my only option was yes.

She handed me back my keys before getting into her Cadillac and driving away. It took every bit of honor in my heart to keep from immediately whipping the trunk open to look. Okay, so it had nothing to do with honor. I was actually scared she was secretly watching me from some vantage point. Like it was a test.

I went back inside to keep from being tempted and called Carmen to see if she was available. I started to say I needed to drop off something for

Lillian but then remembered I wasn't allowed. What was it, and why on earth could I not tell Carmen who it came from? Why couldn't Lillian just drop it off herself?

The questions ate away at my productivity until I finally packed up my desk and told Laura I was heading out early. I was a bundle of nervous energy the whole way to Carmen's house. As excited as I was to see her and hold sweet baby Lila, I was also chomping at the bit to know what the back of my car held.

I brought Carmen out and opened the trunk with breathless anticipation. It was filled to the brim. Enough diapers and wipes to stock a daycare. A plethora of adorable dresses with all the matching accessories. Rattles, pacifiers, and teething rings. A playpen and a bouncy chair. It looked like Lillian bought out several aisles of a Babies "R" Us. Everything you could ever need for a baby crammed into the trunk of my car. I stood there with my mouth open in amazement as Carmen burst into hysterical tears and laughter.

She handed me Lila and started rummaging through all the stuff like it was Christmas morning and she couldn't decide what to open first. She turned to me with teary eyes and thanked me profusely.

"It wasn't me!" I said. I couldn't take credit for the bounty, but I couldn't reveal the source either. Luckily, Carmen has worked for Lillian for quite a while. She immediately guessed.

"Doña Lillian. She comes across all tough, like she don't wanna be bothered. But she gotta bigger heart than anyone I ever met." Carmen smiled through her tears. Then she raised her finger and wagged it at me. "Now don't you dare tell her I guessed. You let her have her secret."

We talked about the office and about her new life as a mommy. I told her about Cabe coming back, of course. I stayed until time for Lila's bath and then came home.

I kept thinking about Lillian tonight. What causes someone to hide behind such a strong facade? Is it fear? Is it not wanting to be hurt? Maybe it was what happened with her husband, but Chaz says she's been a tough old bird as long as he's known her. Long before the divorce. Maybe Laura's right and it was her position at the resorts. Always needing to be in charge. Not wanting people to question her authority.

I don't know. I know she grew up with modest means in England, but I've never heard how she came to be in the United States or what she was like when she was younger. I can't picture her as a carefree girl in pigtails or a frisky teenager in a short skirt.

How sad to work side by side with someone yet not really know them at all. Probably because I avoid her most of the time. She's been on my mind so much lately. I wish I could see this caring side of her more often. I think starting tomorrow I'm going to make an effort to get to know Lillian better.

On a more depressing note, I've texted Cabe the last two days with no response. None. Nada. I keep trying to remember how I felt when I didn't want to talk to anyone. He could at least acknowledge me with a text back, though. I hope he's okay. Maybe I should call. But then again, if he's not returning my texts, why would he want me to pick up the phone and call? After all, he's been here two months without any contact. It's not like he's dying to talk to me now. I guess I'll leave him alone and go by what he asks for. If he reaches out, I'm here. Otherwise, it's like he's still in Seattle. Except I know he's not.

Saturday, October 19th

We should offer a class on what it means to be a maid of honor. Some of these girls seem to think their sole purpose is to wear the dress and look pretty in the pictures. Tonight's bride, Amber, left her white sneakers in the dressing room. They had obviously only been worn a couple of times, if that. No dirt, no smudges, no funk at all. I asked Amber's maid of honor to take them to her at the reception.

She refused.

"No!" she shrieked. "I'm not carrying shoes that have been on someone's feet."

The other bridesmaids kept walking to the bus as though they hadn't heard the exchange. I knew they had.

I was flabbergasted. Were these not Amber's closest friends? The ladies chosen to stand beside her on this most important day? And her maid of honor? The one chosen above all the others as her closest?

I wasn't willing to drop it. "They're not someone's shoes. They're Amber's shoes. You're her maid of honor."

"So? That doesn't mean I have to carry her shoes. That's disgusting. You do it."

"You're already going to the reception. I'm not," I told her. "You'll see Amber and put your stuff wherever she has her stuff. It only makes sense for you to take her shoes."

She groaned as she spun back to face me. "Fine. I'll take the damned shoes if it means that much to you." She snatched the shoes from my hand and stomped onto the bus.

Maybe it's not even a bridesmaid etiquette class that's needed. Maybe it's a few guidelines for what it means to be a friend. To help carry a burden, make the load lighter. To have someone's back.

If a pair of shoes was too much for her, how on earth would she stand by Amber in the nastier and more painful aspects of life?

I didn't hear from Cabe today. I hope he knows I'm here. Willing to help in whatever way I can, although I'm not at all sure what I could possibly do. Too bad it's not as simple as carrying his sneakers.

Sunday, October 20th

Today's parents of the groom provided another example of the tried-and-true rule I've learned while doing weddings. When a man remarries, he chooses one of two things. Either the second wife is as far removed from the first wife as possible in looks and personality, or she is a younger, thinner, spitting image of wife number one.

In this case, young trophy wife Beth could have passed for a younger sister to the groom's mom, Ellen. Same frame, same build, same hair color and eye color. They even laughed in a similar way. I had to hand it to Ellen. She was as nice and gracious as can be. Such an attractive lady despite her years. Still, it must be hard as a woman to not only lose your marriage but then to see yourself replaced with what you used to look like.

I think I'd be resentful as all hell. Pissed for an awfully long time. Like pretty much anytime I saw my younger-me. Of course, I'd be mad the other way as well. My ex, Dwayne, married somebody that looked nothing at all like me and I still felt resentful.

Being replaced bites either way, I think.

I checked my phone after the wedding to see if Cabe had called or texted. He hadn't, but Mr. Hotel Man had left a message. He said he had a guest in the hotel who wanted to order flowers. He thought I might know a good florist. Okay, dude. I know the hotel front desk would easily be able to recommend a florist to a guest. Why's he calling? If he's going to ask me out, why doesn't he just do it already?

Monday, October 21st

Lillian's generosity rubbed off on me this morning. I stopped to buy bagels for everyone. I got Lillian's favorite chive cream cheese, and I even remembered to buy her Lay's chips. I crunched them up on the bagel with the cream cheese, just the way she does it, and then I poured her a cup of her special hot tea. I gallantly swept into her office, picturing a huge smile spreading across her face and her inviting me to sit and chat for a while. Instead, she peered over her red glasses like I had approached the queen without a summons.

My confidence plummeted. I wondered what the hell I was thinking, which made me stumble and splatter tea all over her desk. She didn't say a word. She continued typing on her keyboard while I got paper towels and wiped the desk and the damaged paperwork. I wanted to kick myself in my own ass. Once again, in my efforts to please Lillian, I had screwed up and made a mess of things. Happens every time.

As I finished cleaning and turned to leave her office with handfuls of wet paper towels, I heard a long sigh and a very quiet, virtually inaudible, "Thanks for the bagel."

I turned back to make sure I had actually heard it, but her eyes were fixed on the screen and her fingers were tapping away. If she'd said anything, she didn't plan on repeating it. Oh well.

Mr. Hotel Man finally got up the nerve to ask me out. He called to see if I'd go to the Food & Art Festival with him. I'm not so sure I want to go, though. At first, I felt interested and wanted him to ask. Now I don't know. I do this all the time. I meet someone I think I'd like to go out with, but then if they do ask me out, I change my mind. So fickle.

I said I'd go but told him I prefer to drive my own car and meet him there. One, it's safer. Two, I can go home when I get ready to.

Still no word from Cabe.

Tuesday, October 22nd

My wedding party had just arrived for their rehearsal when Cabe texted me.

"Dinner tonight?"

For a week, I've heard nothing from this man. No texts, no calls, nothing. Then he ever so casually asks if I want to have dinner. This is one of the many reasons why I never dated him. He is freakin' clueless.

However, since I am working hard on being a patient and understanding friend, I said yes. (Well, that and the fact that I had no dinner plans. Plus, I did want to see him.)

"Sure. At a rehearsal now. Shouldn't be too late."

"Let's cook. I'll bring it. Your place. What time?"

It's been over a year since we cooked at my place. It used to be a regular occurrence. At least a couple of times a week, every week. We were one helluva dynamic team in the kitchen. We loved finding a great recipe and then deviating from it as much as possible.

I haven't cooked much at all since he went to Seattle. Partly for nostalgia and missing my buddy, and partly because it makes no sense to buy all the ingredients and make an entire meal for one person. I felt more than a little thrilled at his suggestion for tonight.

"Should be home by eight," I answered.

"See ya then. Do you have red wine?"

"Nope."

"I'll get some."

My whole mood turned around. I knew my freezer held no good dinner prospects, so the thought of arriving home to a hot meal was enticing. Of course, I looked forward to seeing Cabe again without all the stress of his big announcement. I also hoped he would explain what his deal was with not calling and not texting me back.

He didn't. We made it through the entire meal—prep, cooking, eating, cleaning up—and not one word about not hearing from him. He seemed in a much better mood than when we met at the lake, and he ate heartily, which was good since he was still skin and bones. He pretty well acted like nothing had ever happened, and things were back to normal.

I know I probably should have let it go, but I couldn't.

"So, did you get my texts?" I asked. He lay sprawled out on my couch while I sat on the floor with my back against the overstuffed chair in the corner.

"Yeah."

We sat in silence for as long as I could possibly manage to stand it without speaking. About one minute.

"You just didn't bother to respond?"

He put his arm over his face and turned his head toward the back of the couch.

"Are you trying to hide?" I asked. "You realize I can see you, right?"

He shifted to sitting and took a deep swig from his wine glass, but he still didn't speak.

"Hello? What's up, dude?"

(I know. I need to work on my patience. I'll start on it tomorrow.)

(Maybe.)

(Probably not.)

"I dunno, Ty."

"You don't know what? That I can see you? Or why you completely ignored my texts and didn't bother calling me for a week? Or while we're discussing it, why you didn't call me for the first two months since you got back? Do you have any idea how that feels? What if I had run into you somewhere in town? What if I went out with some friends and bumped into you? That would've sucked. I thought we were friends. Like, I thought we were *best* friends. I understand you felt like you needed to dump me for your marriage, but I don't understand why you came back and didn't feel like you wanted to talk to me at all. Especially when you were obviously going through something where I would think you would want a friend to talk to. I feel like maybe I was delusional in thinking we were close. What the hell is your deal, dude?"

(Okay, I kind of vomited all that out before I realized what was happening. So much for putting his needs before my own. But I was pissed.)

"I don't have a deal, Tyler. I'm sorry. The last thing I wanted to do was hurt you again. You *are* my best friend, and I did want to talk to you. But it's embarrassing. Humiliating. I didn't want to face you. I know what I did hurt you. And I know you let it go because you were trying to make me happy and make Monica happy. So I feel like a complete ass, Ty. I gave up on what we had for something that wasn't even real. For someone who evidently didn't love me and definitely wasn't worth giving up a friendship for. I didn't feel right calling you up and leaning on you to get me through it after I walked away from you. But now you're pissed because I didn't call you, and I ended up hurting you anyway. I can't freakin' win."

He stood up and tossed back the rest of his wine before putting the empty glass in the sink.

His words stunned me. I felt like a jerk for bringing it up and waving the "what about me?" flag. My heart hurt to hear he felt like he couldn't call me. At the same time, the twisted part of me felt happy it wasn't because he didn't need me anymore. Not like happy he was unhappy or anything. Just happy I did matter after all.

I stood on the other side of the counter, facing him at the sink.

"You total dork," I said. "Did you like miss the whole point of being best friends? Friends stand by one another and try to help each other. Look out for each other. Yeah, you're right. It hurt when you broke ties with me for Monica. I ain't gonna lie about that. It sucked. But I don't think you did it maliciously. You were doing what you thought was best for your relationship. I got that. I not only got it, I agreed with it. I knew you couldn't have been fully in that relationship with us being so close. Monica would have gone nuts, more so than she already was, I mean, and you would have always felt torn. Plus, that was me encouraging you to leave everything behind, including me, and follow her to Seattle. Remember? I told you to go?"

It dawned on me then that maybe that had been bad advice. It seemed right at the time, but given how everything turned out, I wondered if he was upset with me for telling him to go.

"Oh wow. I guess that didn't really work out so well, huh? You're not mad at me, are you? For encouraging you to go? Because I thought . . ."

"No, Tyler. You didn't drug me and tie me up and send me on a one-way flight to Seattle. I made the decision to go. What you told me at the time was right. If I wanted to spend my life with Monica, then I needed to go. But evidently she didn't want to spend her life with me."

His face crumpled, and his eyes got glassy. No tears fell, but I could see my friend was still very much in pain. I needed to say something to make him feel better. Something profound.

"Rejection sucks."

Alright, so maybe it wasn't profound, but it was all I could come up with. We both stood silent for a minute as I tried to figure out how to lighten the mood.

"I think the first thing you need to do is shave off that god-awful growth all over your face. You look like some maniacal creature who's been wandering the Alaskan wilderness. Or I guess the Seattle wilderness. Don't they have a lot of woods there? I've never been, but they spent a lot of time in the woods in *Twilight*." I smiled at him and hoped he'd smile back.

"Oh, please. Tell me you did not just use *Twilight* as your geographical basis of knowledge."

Ah, there it was. A bit of a smile. A glimpse of the Cabe I knew and loved.

"You wanna shave it off?" he asked.

I walked around the bar into the kitchen and grabbed his beard with both hands.

"It's so scruffy and wild. Rough. Do you have anything hiding in there?" I pulled sections of the beard apart, mimicking a monkey grooming its mate.

"There may be. I don't know. I haven't spent a whole lot of time looking in a mirror lately. I guess my masculine pride is a bit wounded since my wife left me for lady bits."

It felt odd to hear him say "my wife." We hadn't really talked since their spur-of-the-moment wedding, so I'd never heard him say those words or refer to her like that. It bothered me, but I don't know why. I mean, I knew he was married. Maybe it was because she hurt him so badly, but I felt resentful that she got to be his wife. Not that I wanted to be. Lord, no! But Cabe was an awesome guy. One in a million. Whoever he called "my wife" should have been worthy of the title.

"Well, if you were trying to establish masculinity by morphing into a grizzly bear, you accomplished it. I think your strong cheekbones and prominent jawline are plenty masculine enough without the beard, though. Even if you do have your mother's dimples."

"Let's shave it. I'm assuming you have a razor," he said. He looked excited to get rid of it.

"Not for that! Good God, man, what the hell do you think I'm shaving here? My legs have never on their worst day been that far gone, and without getting too personal, we'll say nothing else has either. I think we need a machete or some pruning shears for this beard."

"Let's go buy razors. I want to shave this off. I want you to shave this off. Let's do it," he said.

"Right now? It's almost eleven o'clock. I have a wedding tomorrow," I whined, but I was already putting my shoes on and grabbing my purse. I wanted nothing more than to shave that hideous beard off his face. I think for me, and maybe even for him, it was symbolic of Monica and what she'd done to him. I wanted her gone.

So we went and bought razors, shaving cream, aftershave, some KitKat bars and a bottle of cheap drugstore wine. Then we ventured into my bathroom to rid Cabe's face of his wife's betrayal.

I looked up at him as I sat on my bathroom counter straddling the sink. "Okay. We already established I've never had to shave this much hair. What do we do? Do you just wet it and then put on shaving cream like I do with my legs? Should we cut it with scissors first? How will the razor get through all that?"

"You're asking me? I have no idea. I've never shaved this much hair before either. You do it. Then if it's all jacked up I can always blame you."

"I don't know what to do! I'm scared I'll cut you. Give you scars for life."

"I think I already have those," he said. I think he meant to try and be funny, but his face fell a bit when he said it. I didn't want him sliding back into darkness so soon, so I grabbed the scissors and started trimming.

"I still think I would do better with hedge clippers," I said. "I have no idea what I'm doing."

Once I had it cut down some, I lathered him up and took the razor to his face. I was so scared I would cut him that my hand shook. As I worked, the hair fell all over me, the sink, the floor, and the countertop. This man had a lot of facial hair happening. I tried to spread my legs further and lean backward so he could lean forward over the sink, but hair still went everywhere.

It's funny that I can be so close to him physically and not be weirded out. I mean, shaving a guy's face is kind of a personal thing. (Not as personal as *bathing* someone, but still personal.) Being crammed together in my tiny bathroom put us in really close proximity with my legs spread wide around his as he leaned into the sink. I could feel his breath as he exhaled and smell the sweet bitterness of wine on his tongue with our faces only inches apart.

If this was a date, I'd be freaking out. Worried my breath smelled, or my thighs looked fat in this position. I'd be nervous he was looking down my top and expecting this to lead somewhere. I'd be obsessing over whether or not I wanted it to and what would happen if it did. I'd be wondering if it meant anything that I was shaving him and if I should be worried about him taking it the wrong way.

Luckily, it was just Cabe. I didn't have to go through all that. It didn't matter because it wasn't a date. (Wouldn't that be a really weird date—to shave someone? I bet there's some kinky sexual fetish for that, too, but thankfully I am unaware.) There was no tension. No awkwardness. Just me and Cabe. As comfortable and easy as it's always been.

I hear people say they're married to their best friend. I think that must be the best relationship of all. If I could have what Cabe and I have in friendship and fun but also have the physical attraction and romantic feelings, then that would be the bomb-diggety to end all searching. Does it exist? Is it possible to be utterly uninhibited and not at all self-conscious, and yet be in love? Because it seems like once you introduce love—sex, passion, romance—then it all gets messed up and scary. You have something to lose. You can be rejected. Or betrayed. Your heart, your hopes, your dreams can all be annihilated.

And yes, Cabe did hurt me. He did leave me. But it wasn't rejection really. It wasn't because I wasn't good enough or pretty enough or thin enough. It wasn't because he didn't want me or like me, or even love me. Because we are friends, not lovers. It's different.

I think love screws it up. Maybe you get love or you get friendship. Only the very lucky get both.

Wednesday, October 23rd

Laura asked me today to train Charlotte on an event this weekend. She must be joking. In addition to sending my client the entire wedding file, Charlotte also told a bride her wedding was cancelled when it wasn't, told another bride the groom was ridiculously smoking hot and she would date him in a heartbeat, and ordered a cake covered in daisies for a bride who had very emphatically requested *no* daisies anywhere at her wedding.

Charlotte says she saw DAISIES in all caps in the file and figured they were important, so she asked the chef to add them to the cake. I asked if she bothered to read any of the comments regarding daisies. Nope. Saw the word in all caps and figured the bride must like them.

Good Lord, help us. Now I'm supposed to take her to an actual wedding? Where she could screw up someone's life? Well, maybe not their life, but a pretty darned important day in their life.

That's the flip side of doing weddings. Everyone thinks it must be so much fun, but it's a helluva lot of stress. This is the day a little girl has dreamed of her whole life. The day her mama has planned since the doctor said, "It's a girl." And the day her daddy has dreaded paying for since that same day, so he wants every single penny accounted for. He wants to know what he's getting for his money.

Something as simple as the wrong color napkins can send a bride or family member into a complete the-sky-is-falling-and-you-ruined-our-wedding-and-our-life kind of meltdown.

I remember all too well my first event. What a disaster! I really did ruin someone's wedding, and at the time, I thought I had ruined their lives.

The bride's parents had surprised her with a beautiful white carriage pulled by six white ponies. They intended for Nancy to make a grand entrance to her outdoor ceremony like Cinderella coming to the ball. A loving and extravagant gift from her parents intended to make a statement about their princess's worth.

Let's just say I wasn't exactly the fairy godmother in this scenario.

Laura told me to escort Nancy and her bridesmaids down a hallway and outside to the waiting carriage. Once Nancy departed in the carriage, I was to call Laura and then escort the bridesmaids back inside to another hallway where the groomsmen would be waiting to walk them down the aisle.

I was as much in awe of the carriage and ponies as Nancy was. As she petted the ponies, the sun's rays caught the shimmer of her dress and it sparkled like magic. I felt all warm and fuzzy inside. I knew without a doubt this had to be the best job anyone ever had. I wanted to hug myself with joy at my good fortune, and hers, of course.

When I called Laura and told her Nancy was in the carriage and ready to get married, she said to send her.

I smiled at Nancy as she straightened her veil and settled herself on the seat. "Good luck! You look beautiful! Like a princess!"

Her father sat tall and proud next to his beloved daughter as her bridesmaids sniffled and waved goodbye. I fought back tears. The carriage driver said to me, "So are we good to go, or is someone going to tell me when?"

I have replayed those words in my head a million times since that day. I am sure that is how he said it. But I would like to say again: IT WAS MY FIRST WEDDING.

It turns out the carriage ride is usually a two-part process. The bride and her father board the carriage, and they are sent to a staging area. A manager from the carriage company waits for them to arrive at the staging area and then goes to a vantage point where he can communicate with Laura at the ceremony site. When the ceremony is under way and it's time for the bride to arrive, Laura gives a signal to the manager and he motions the carriage driver to pull forward.

Well, on that particular day of all days, the carriage manager had an emergency situation and needed to leave. The carriage driver thought we knew. Unfortunately, Laura didn't get the message, and I was freakin' clueless. So when he asked me if he was good to go, what he actually meant was, "Am I driving the bride to the ceremony right now, or am I stopping at the staging area like normal and waiting for someone to tell me when to go?"

Since I had no knowledge of the protocol, I answered enthusiastically, "You are good to go! Take this beautiful bride to meet her groom!"

It all went to hell in a handbasket from there.

While guests were still standing around talking and waiting for seating to begin, Nancy made her appearance in the carriage. A quick-thinking guest grabbed Frank the groom and dragged him out of sight to prevent him seeing Nancy while her mother and sister screamed at the carriage driver to go away.

I didn't know then what had gone wrong, but I knew in that moment how much responsibility it was to be involved with someone's wedding. One moment Nancy was shining in the sun, a princess enjoying the glory of her day. Then with one sentence from me, she had become a crying, embarrassed, and confused mess. The incredible gift from her parents, meant to exalt their daughter, morphed into a disaster that humiliated her.

Now, I could go on all day long about how a carriage and horses don't do anything to show a person's worth, or that it was a simple mistake and it didn't ruin anything in the grand scheme of life.

But the truth is, it was her very special day. For her, it was ruined. If Nancy and Frank are married for fifty years, it will be the same disaster story every time they tell anyone about their wedding.

Oh, well. At least this weekend's event doesn't have a carriage for Charlotte to mess up. But it's still somebody's wedding.

Thursday, October 24th

Why do I even answer when my mother calls? I didn't have time to talk, but I always fear the one time I let it go to voice mail she'll be calling to tell me someone is dead or ill. Another false alarm today, though.

"I gotta go, Mama. I just stepped out of the shower, and I'm running late."

"Oh! Where you goin'? Anything fun?" Mama asked, oblivious to the "gotta go" part.

"Cabe and I are going to a movie."

"Who?"

"Cabe, Mama. He's back." Sort of shows how much we don't talk that she didn't know this already.

"I thought his name was Gabe."

"You always think that, and I tell you every time it is Cabe. Short for Cable."

"Cable. What kind of name is that? It's so weird. Who would name a child Cable?"

"You say that every time, too. I've told you a hundred times he was named after his father's brother, who died in Vietnam. His name was Cable."

"Still an odd name. He's not Southern, is he?"

"No, Mom. He's from Ohio." I cannot count the number of times we've had this exact same conversation since I met Cabe five years ago.

"Ohio? How'd he end up in Florida? Isn't he the gay one?"

"Mama, why do you keep saying that? No, he's not gay." She could not let go of her theory that any boy who spent so much time with a girl without wanting to date her or sleep with her must be gay.

"There's a gay boy here now. Lives up in the old Ramsey house. They

70

say he's got it decorated something incredible. Like out of a magazine. I haven't seen it, but some of them from the Rotary Club went up there for tea. Said it was beautiful. Very tastefully done."

"That's nice. Okay, Mama, I need to get ready."

"Doesn't he like to cook and go antique shopping with you? Are you sure he's not gay?" I have no idea why this topic is so important to her. We haven't discussed Cabe in months, and the first time I mention his name to her, I am right back to defending his sexuality. She hasn't even asked why he's back or what happened to him in Seattle. We're right back to the same conversation we had before he even left.

"Mama! He's not gay. He's married. To a woman. Well, he's getting divorced, but he married a woman."

"Well, that don't mean a thing. I hear a lot of gay men get married to try to fit into society. Sometimes they even have children. I bet that's why he got divorced. He's gay, sugar."

"No, Mama, he's not, but his wife is. Which is why he's getting divorced. Besides, what does it matter if Cabe is gay or not? He's my best friend. I don't care if he's gay, so why should you?"

"Because I don't want you pining away after him and getting disappointed! Tyler Lorraine, don't you go getting all huffy with me. Being all defensive. All I did was suggest maybe you don't know your friend as well as you think. I want you to be aware of your surroundings, that's all."

"Mama! I'm not pining away after Cabe. We are just friends. You know what? I'm not gonna do this today. I'm going to hang up. I'm hanging up the phone now, Mama. Bye. Love you. I'm hanging up. You hang up, too."

I hung up on her protests. She drives me nuts. I will never understand how I was born and raised in her influence and turned out so different. Although, come to think of it, none of my siblings are like her either. Tanya, Carrie, Brad. None of us are really like Mama. Thank the Lord. Although, the older Tanya gets, the more I'm worried she may succumb.

Cabe rang the doorbell before I finished my hair, so I yelled for him to come on in. When I walked into the living room for us to leave, I nearly burst out laughing. There he sat in a beautiful pale pink Oxford shirt. I could hear my mother saying "I told you so" in my head.

Friday, October 25th

I want to have a serious conversation with whoever saw fit to sell modern-day brides on the idea the entire world is in indentured servitude to them on their wedding day. Much of the blame lies on these stupid television shows glorifying the Bridezilla image. A spoiled brat of a bride stomping her feet and demanding she gets what she wants simply because she's a bride. They've done a disservice to the entire institution of marriage, I think. What union can start on a good foot if it's hijacked by the whims of a self-absorbed prima donna?

Today's darling diva experienced an all-out meltdown of epic proportions when her roses were not the same shade of white as her gown.

"Look at these flowers!" Brittany screamed, shaking the bouquet in my face. "What color does this look like to you?"

"Um . . . white?" I responded.

"They are not white!" she shouted. She tossed the bouquet back into the floral box and grabbed her wedding gown from the steamer rack. "This is white! I specifically ordered white roses because I'm wearing a white gown for a reason. It signifies purity and innocence on my wedding day. I did not maintain my purity for nineteen years for nothing. I want white roses. Those roses are not white!"

I stifled a scoffing laugh at Brittany's concern over being seen as pure and innocent, willing to bet she was neither.

I looked back in the box at the roses, which were clearly white, though not nearly as white as the gown she held.

"They are white roses, Brittany, but the white in a rose is not the same as a manufactured white satin fabric. The roses aren't going to be that white. They don't come that white."

"Aaarrgghh!" She growled as she grabbed the roses from the box and held them up to the dress. "They are supposed to match this dress. This is unacceptable, and I expect you to do something about it. I am not happy right now."

I felt so sorry for her groom in that moment. I also felt thankful for my professional censor. It shushes my internal voice, which would have said to her, "So what, bitch? I'm not happy right now either. Suck it up. Do you think I can just pull a new bouquet from my rump because you don't like the one you have?"

Instead, my professional censor made me say this:

"Brittany, I understand your concern. I agree with you the roses are not the same shade of white as the dress." (*Let them know they have been heard and you understand their concern.*) "Unfortunately, this is the white rose bouquet we ordered from the florist. We are unable to change the color of the roses." (*Give them the bad news—the facts—sandwiched in between two nice statements.*) "However, it is a stunning bouquet. You are going to look amazing in your dress walking down the aisle to marry the man of your dreams. No one is even going to think about the roses when they get blown away by how gorgeous you look." (*Finish off with a sticky sweet reassuring statement they can't disagree with. Laura Wedding Strategy # 427 for Problems on the Wedding Day.*)

Brittany wasn't feeling sticky sweet. "Cut the bullshit, Tyler. The roses aren't white. I ordered white. I intend to walk down the aisle in my white dress carrying white roses. So I suggest you get on the phone with someone and do something. Mother, would you please make her do something? Don't just stand there. Ugh."

Her mom, Caroline, lifted the roses gingerly from the box. "Honey, these are white roses," she said. "As white as they come."

"They're not white!" Brittany screamed. "Why does everyone keep saying that? Look, look!" She snatched the bouquet from her mother and held it up to the dress. "They are *ivory*! The dress is white. The bouquet is not."

I gritted my teeth and tried one more time. "Well, the roses aren't going to be the same shade of white as your dress, Brittany. The roses are made by nature. The dress is made by man. This is nature's white."

"It's ivory! Cream! It contrasts with my dress. I think you used the wrong roses. I want a new bouquet, and I want it to be white. Mother?" Brittany turned to Caroline with her chin held high in defiance.

One of the bridesmaids held up her phone for Brittany to see. "It says here ivory roses mean fidelity and commitment. Why don't you use the ivory roses, Brittany?"

"Shut up, Abby. If you want ivory roses on your wedding day, then if and when you have a wedding, you can have ivory roses. Today is *my* wedding. I want *white* roses, and I am not walking down the aisle until I get them." Brittany glared the bridesmaid back to the couch with the others.

I was about to go off on the bitch, so I decided it would be best if I left the room.

"Let me take the bouquet over to the dinner room and see what Renee, the florist, can do," I said. Brittany turned on her heel and flounced back into the bedroom, slamming the door behind her.

"Thank you, Tyler," Caroline graciously said. Her face flushed red with embarrassment, but I felt no pity for her. She had created this monster, after all.

I hope whenever I have kids, I have the courage to say no to them. I hope in my efforts to provide for them and give their hearts' desires, I never lose sight of the fact that handing them everything only makes them nasty and spoiled. It helps no one. A healthy dose of disappointment and struggle can go a long way in shaping a person. Not that roses failing to be white enough can even be considered a "struggle."

Freakin' Bridezillas!

Saturday, October 26th

So I guess in all fairness, I should say Charlotte didn't *ruin* the wedding today. I don't think she'll be making senior planner any time soon, but it could have been much worse.

First, she poked herself while pinning on the groomsmen's boutonnieres. Not like a little pin prick where you say ouch and keep working. She gouged her finger and bled on the groomsman's shirt. A big, bloody spot right up front and center just below his bow tie. How one does that while pinning a flower on a lapel, I don't even know, but she did.

Then she forgot to give the best man the rings. Which I know I should have double-checked, but I handed them to her and said, "Go give these to the best man." He was in the next room. I kind of thought she could handle that without follow up. My bad. So that was a first for me—walking down the aisle in the middle of the ceremony to hand my clients their rings. Not cool.

I sent her to the reception site with instructions to put the toasting glasses on the head table, the cake knife and server on the cake table, and the place cards in alphabetical order on the marble table outside the dinner room. I realize in hindsight it may have been a bit much to expect, but they were all pretty simple tasks. Or so I thought.

I arrived at the reception site mere minutes before the guests and found the place cards in random-ass lines on the marble table with no uniformity and no thought given to presentation. Okay, my bad. I should have given more specific directions and suggested she make it look nice. I thought the fact it was someone's wedding might make that an unstated goal, but evidently not.

Then I noticed they were not all in alphabetical order. Charlotte came be-bopping out of the dinner room as I was freaking out trying to fix the cards.

"Charlotte! The guests will be here any minute, and the place cards are not in order!"

"Yes, they are! They were wrapped in rubber bands by table, so I put them out that way. I know you said put them in alphabetical order, but I didn't know if you meant by last name or first name. Then some said "guest" so I did a whole row of G's over here. Whoever is a guest can get theirs from that row."

"Charlotte, the people don't know what table they are seated at, so they won't know which table to look for. And the guests of the guests won't have any idea whose card is whose to look for table numbers . . . oh, never mind. Scoop up all these cards, and we'll put them on a table inside the dinner room. They have to be in alphabetical order by last name so when people walk up, they look for their name *in order* to find out which table to go to."

I gritted my teeth before entering the dinner room, half expecting it to be a disaster from her presence alone. Oh, sweet relief to see all the tables set, the DJ in place, and the cake on its stand (without daisies). I exhaled and headed to the head table to check the toasting glasses.

It wasn't hard to find them. They were on the table between the bride and groom's chairs. Still in the box. Still wrapped in plastic bubble wrap. Price tags still on the bottom.

To be fair, all I told Charlotte was to put the toasting glasses on the head table. I never said, "Take them out of the freakin' box, unwrap them, rinse them out, take off the price tags, put the box away." Silly me. Who knew I was such an inept manager??? It's funny how you assume people will figure things out when they seem like simple concepts.

After frantically unwrapping and washing the toasting glasses, I made my way over to the cake table to find exactly what I expected at that point. The cake knife and server were still wrapped up in tissue paper inside their box on the table. Although, I must say she added a flower beside the box. I guess I should give her an A for creativity. But seriously?? Did she expect the bride and groom to unwrap their toasting glasses in order to toast each other and then unwrap their cake knife and server in order to slice the cake and feed each other?

I tried to remind myself about a giddy little planner who sent the carriage at the wrong time, but surely this was different. My mistake had been a lack of knowledge about the process. Which I guess is technically still ignorance, but this had to be a different level of ignorant.

Oh, well. The bride and groom were happy. That's all that matters, right?

Sunday, October 27th

Melanie and I had a ten o'clock ceremony this morning with a brunch afterward. No special dances, no cake cutting, no open bar. A laid-back, everybody-happy, small affair with an older bride and groom and thirty of their closest friends. We were done by noon, so we headed over to see Carmen and the baby. She asked us to bring her a cheeseburger and fries, and you would've thought we brought her gold bars as excited as she got over her quarter pounder with cheese. Mel went straight for Lila, as always. All babies love Mel. The woman is a baby whisperer. I hate that she and Paul were never able to have one of their own. It kills her.

"When are you going to bring Lila to the office?" I asked.

"I need to, I know. It's such a production to go anywhere. It takes me forever to load everything up and get out of the house. Lillian came by Thursday night. She brought Lila the cutest little outfit. She still insists I named this baby after her!" Carmen laughed. I wondered if she had mentioned the trunk full of goodies to Lillian, but I didn't want to ask in front of Melanie.

We talked for a while about Lila, then we caught her up on current events in wedding world, and of course, we told her all about Charlotte.

"I hope she quits before I get back," Carmen said. "I will not be able to put up with it. I will go off on that girl." Carmen shook her head and took Lila from Mel to nurse.

"Did Tyler tell you Cabe is back?" Melanie asked as Carmen got settled on the couch with Lila.

"Yes," she said. "I say karma is a bitch, my friend. He's getting what's coming to him for doing Tyler like he did."

"What?! No, Carmen don't even say that!" I said.

"I'm serious. It wasn't right how he did you. That girl was no good for him from the start. Forcing him to give up his friends and family. Moving him way out there. Then she goes and leaves him? She'll get what's coming to her, but right now he gets what's coming to him. Mark my words, chica. Karma is real."

"I feel sorry for him," Melanie said.

"I don't," Carmen said. "He didn't have no business moving out there. He needed to stay here. Look after his mama." Carmen nodded her head and looked to me for agreement, but I wasn't sure how I felt about it. I definitely didn't think Cabe did anything to deserve Monica hurting him. As glad as I was to have him back here, I would give up being able to see him all over again for him to be happy. Even if it meant him being in Seattle without any contact. I hated seeing him hurt.

I looked back and forth between Mel and Carmen, who were still discussing Cabe's return. They were my closest friends. They were here for me when he moved to Seattle and dropped off the planet. They kept me afloat when Cabe dumped me as a chocolate chip cookie. I didn't expect Carmen to welcome him back with open arms. She was protective of me like I was protective of him. I understood that.

Mel, on the other hand, seemed to have become Cabe's biggest champion. She refused to back down from her assertion that we were more than friends. I knew she had always harbored hopes that Cabe and I would end up together, but I guess I didn't realize how much hope she was holding on to.

"I don't know," Mel said. "I always thought Cabe really loved Tyler. I think she just kept shutting him down and not giving him a chance, so he took off to find love somewhere else. There's no way he would have even been with Monica if Tyler had ever given him the slightest hint there could be more between them. Now he's back, and hopefully she'll see what's right in front of her."

My head swung around to face Melanie like it was on a swivel. "Excuse me? I'm sorry, I think you've confused me with someone else. What are you talking about?"

"Humph!" Carmen grunted. "Tyler ain't wanting none of him, are you?" She turned to me but never stopped talking to Melanie. "My girl wants a man who knows what he wants and isn't afraid to reach out and take it, right, Tyler? They been friends too long to be getting all up in each other's business. If he wanted it, he woulda told her a long time ago. If you wanted him, you would've known it a long time ago, right, girl?"

I nodded slowly, somewhat dazed at how I had become the ball in their tennis match. Carmen nodded as well, rocking back and forth as Lila nursed.

"Yeah, that's right," she said, clearly on her soap box now. "Tyler, you don't settle for nobody. You wait until the right man comes and sweeps you off your feet. A man you can't live without. Makes you feel like a better woman just by being by your side. Don't settle for no bullshit man who don't know what he wants. And you damned sure don't want no man who's been divorced. Oh, no, girl. You wait and get one that is yours and yours alone. Don't be signing up for no baggage."

"Yes, ma'am." I saluted her dramatically and laughed.

Mel shook her head. "She can't keep waiting for some magical man to sweep her off her feet, Carmen. Real men have real issues, just like real women do. There's no such thing as Prince Charming. You can't overlook the great men that may already be there waiting for some perfect ideal that doesn't exist."

"Pshhtt. That's bull. There's a Prince Charming for everyone. I got mine. You got yours. Tyler will get hers." Carmen refused to be swayed.

I kept thinking about their playful disagreement long after Lila had been put to bed and Melanie and I had said our goodbyes and headed home.

All the movies, the books, the fairy tales—they all sell us Prince Charming. THE ONE. When he arrives, you will know immediately that he is The One. Stars will twinkle, birds will sing, and all will be well. The fairy tales don't get into financial problems, health problems, conflicts with the in-laws, or a mid-life crisis. They don't mention arguing over the housework, working second jobs to pay the bills, or not showering all day with a new baby. They never show you the Prince's faults or point out that the Princess has some stuff to work on herself.

In reality, I know Melanie is right. There's no one riding in on a white stallion to rescue me from life. It's not only unrealistic, it probably keeps a lot of great people from getting a fair chance at being in a relationship. It sets up men to fail since they can't possibly be that perfect or actually rescue someone. It sets women up to fail because they have set their sights so high they feel as though they've missed out on something or settled the moment it's not perfect.

From what I've seen in real life, no one actually lives happily ever after. Carmen said she and Melanie had their Prince Charmings. But I can name several things about Paul and Oscar that really irritate their wives. I am sure Oscar and Paul could point out some faults in their ladies as well. Melanie and Paul never thought their fairy tale wouldn't include children, and I know for a fact Carmen and Oscar didn't expect the emergency costs incurred when Carmen went into labor early at the Olive Garden.

But even though Mel is right, I don't care. I'm with Carmen. I want the fairy tale. He doesn't have to ride in on a horse, and after Mr. Bubble I don't particularly care for him pulling up in a Porsche, but I want Prince Charming.

I want someone to sweep me off my feet. To know without any doubt he is The One. Because if he's The One and it's meant to be, then I'm safe.

It can't go wrong, right? No more painful break-ups and devastating hurt.

I want a passionate, romantic, and legendary love. At the same time, I want solid, honest, and real. Someone who thinks I am the absolute greatest thing walking despite my faults and shortcomings. I know no one is perfect. I'm okay knowing my Prince Charming will have some faults of his own. But I refuse to give up on the Happily Ever After.

For now though, I'm still stuck trying to find the Once Upon A Time. You can't have the happy ending without a beginning, right?

Monday, October 28th

'Til death do us part can be a scary concept. I couldn't imagine going to a car lot and having the salesman tell me to pick one car I'd have to keep for the rest of my life without ever having another. But that's what we sell in the wedding business. Step right up and pick a bride. For life.

Melanie's groom today, Wardell, was feeling the weight of the decision in a big way. When I escorted the guys into the holding room after pre-ceremony photos, Wardell hung back, letting all the other guys go in without him.

"You okay, Wardell?" I asked.

"Have you seen her?"

A common question from grooms on their wedding day. Tradition torments them with the belief that it is bad luck for the groom to see his bride on the wedding day.

"I haven't," I said, "but Melanie says she looks gorgeous!"

He leaned forward and whispered, "I don't know if I can do this."

"What do you mean, Wardell?" At least that's what I think I said. My mind was saying "Oh crap! Oh crap! Oh crap!", so I hope my mouth said something better.

"I don't know. I love her. But we talking about the rest of my life, ya know? Like old man, gray-haired, crippled and shit. It's all over after today."

I didn't know what to tell him, so I used something I saw Laura write in a card to a bride and groom once.

"Wardell, out of all the world and all the people, the two of you have chosen each other to wake up to. It's a beautiful gift to give and receive. I'm sure you'll be just fine."

Actually, I added the "I'm sure you'll be just fine" part for reassurance.

"You don't get it." He put his hand on his chest and patted it, his voice filled with emotion. "I do choose her, and I do love her. And she loves me. I'm grateful for that. But this means I get one cereal every day for the rest of my life. Like every damned morning, I'm gonna know as soon as I open my eyes, that's the only cereal in the house. The only cereal I'm allowed to eat. That scares the hell out of me. How can anybody eat one cereal every day the rest of their life and not get sick and tired of it?"

I couldn't tell this man I had my own doubts and fears about this, so I decided to take his clever analogy and run with it.

"Wardell, what's your absolute, most favorite cereal?"

He thought about it a minute before answering.

"Frosted Flakes."

"That's awesome," I said. "Now, no one in their right mind would tell you to eat Frosted Flakes every day. It wouldn't be healthy. But what if you could eat Frosted Flakes every day and it be good for you? What if no one could tell you not to eat it? You'd get to have your very favorite thing every day. And think about this . . . you're the only one that gets the Frosted Flakes."

I was grasping at straws, but I've never professed to be a relationship counselor. Far from it.

He looked away for a moment as though considering this option and what it would look like for him. Then he grinned, just a little at first and then a wide, toothy gold grin. A visible swagger settled over him, and Wardell was back in action.

"You all right, girl. You alright!" He gave me a little fist bump and opened the door to join his groomsmen.

When the ceremony ended, Wardell came back down the aisle like he'd won the jackpot of all lotteries. He pretty much floated beside Marquisha as they made their way toward me amid the shouts of congratulations.

He made eye contact with me right as they passed, pausing for the briefest of moments to say, "Frosted Flakes, baby! Every day! You know that's right!"

I hope it is. I really hope it is.

Thursday, October 31st

Mom called today to ask if I had a date for Halloween. I didn't, and I wasn't nearly as upset about it as she was. I had made plans to go downtown with some of my old coffee shop friends. No date, no drama. Just dancing, one of my absolute favorite things to do. I invited Cabe, but he didn't feel up to being around people. He says that a lot. Some days I feel sorry for him and other days I want to tell him to snap out of it and start living.

"Are you wearing a costume?" Mom asked.

"Yeah, but nothing fancy. I got a cat-ear headband, and I'll paint on some whiskers. I'm wearing a black dress and black tights," I said.

"Well, that's original," she said with more than a hint of sarcasm. "Why don't you put some thought in it and come up with a good costume? You were always so creative."

"We're not going to a costume party or anything, Mom. We're going to stop by some bars and go dancing. I don't want to have some elaborate costume I can't dance in."

"I just think if you're going to dress up, you ought to put in the effort and do it right."

"Mom, I'm twenty-five years old. I'm not going trick-or-treating. It doesn't matter what costume I wear. We're going out. It's not a big deal," I said, rolling my eyes and wondering why I answered the phone.

"Your sister says Erin is going to be Raggedy Ann and Eric is Raggedy Andy. Do people still have Raggedy Ann dolls? I don't think anyone will know who they are. I wonder why on earth she would pick that. Undoubtedly, there was something else the kids wanted to be."

Sounds like Tanya had gotten quite the earful about my niece and nephew's costumes. Of course, Tanya wouldn't care. She doesn't let Mom get to her the way I do. She simply does what she wants to do. It doesn't bother her if Mom doesn't like it.

"Maybe it was an easy costume to do," I offered.

"No, she sewed them. Made them matching outfits with aprons and overalls. Stockings, too. There's no telling how long it took her. She's always complaining she has no time, but then she puts more on her plate. Now why couldn't she just go to Wal-Mart and buy them a costume already made? That would have made more sense."

"I don't know, Mom. I guess that's not what she wanted to do."

"So why don't you have a date tonight?"

I wondered how long it would take to bring her back around to that popular topic of conversation.

"I'm going out with friends, Mom. It's a big group of us. No one has dates."

"You need to get new friends. You need friends who will introduce you to someone. You need to go out with someone other than Gabe."

"Cabe, Mom," I interjected.

"You never meet anyone new. All the men you meet are either getting married already or coming in town for a wedding and leaving right after it. You need to meet local men."

She was right on that count. Every wedding serves up a handful of groomsmen and a bevy of guests, usually with at least a couple of single ones in the group. Sometimes the single ones are great-looking, fun guys. Occasionally, one seems either interested or interesting, or both. But I'm working, and they're partying. Then they go back home to their own lives, and I greet the next group.

"I did meet someone local, Mom. He works at a hotel. We're going out next month." What the hell? Why did I say that? Why did I even tell her about him? I have no idea what's going on with him and whether or not I even want to go out with him, and now I blabbed about it to my mother?

"Really? Well, why haven't you said something? Who is he? What does he do? Does he go to church? Is he divorced? I know at your age there's a high probability anyone you date might have been married before, and I don't think you should rule that out. Why aren't you going out with him tonight?"

Immediate regret for my big mouth. I wanted so badly to say, "This would be why I haven't said anything." Instead I said, "It's only been a few phone calls. We haven't gotten into a whole lot yet."

"Well, you need to ask these questions! Don't wait until your heart is involved before your head gets the facts. You need to be your own best advocate."

"I know, Mom, I know. I need to go get ready. I'll talk to you later."

"How long can it take to put on a cat-ear headband? Please put some effort in. I'll tell Tanya to send you pictures of Erin and Eric. She texted me some, but I still can't figure out how to open pictures on this new phone. Don't eat too much candy, okay? You know it goes straight to your hips, and it's not worth it. Love you! Happy Halloween!"

Amazing how a conversation with my mother can make me feel like I got the trick instead of the treat.

I had a great time tonight, though, cat-ears and all. There's nothing I love more than dancing, and we danced the night away. It's so fun to just hang on the dance floor with the girls without the pressure of worrying about a guy.

Some poor dude came up and tried desperately to have a conversation with me. He literally screamed over the music. "So, where ya from?"

"What?"

"Where ya from?"

"Here. I live here."

"Wow. That's cool. So what do you do?"

"What?"

"What is your job?"

"I kind of just want to dance."

"What?"

"I don't want to talk. I only want to dance."

"Oh. Right. Do you have any brothers or sisters?"

I turned and danced away from him. The poor guy has probably been told he needs to talk to women and ask them questions to get to know them better. I myself have complained that guys need to be more straightforward and let you know they're interested. The middle of dance floor surrounded by blaring music is not the place to put it in action, though. We're all trying to figure it out, buddy. Kudos to you for trying. Tonight, I just wanted to dance.

November

Saturday, November 2nd

When you hear the bride's name is Diamond Starr, you automatically think stripper or porn queen. Stripper, in this case. The groom, Billy, owns a chain of upscale gentlemen's clubs (strip joints) in Manhattan. Diamond is his main attraction. Personally and professionally, it seems.

Chaz said she was born Elizabeth Anne but changed her legal name to Diamond Starr after she dropped out of college to pursue her lucrative dancing career. Diamond Sparkl Starr according to the marriage license.

I'm not sure what I expected, but she wasn't it. She stood a little under five feet, and I think her thigh might have been as big around as my arm. I've been dying all day to ask if the long cascade of dark brown hair hanging well below her hips is a wig, but I couldn't figure out how to work it into conversation. I do know with absolute certainty her boobs are fake. I encountered them up close and personal when I went to her room.

Diamond looked like a tiny living doll. By which I mean a nude doll wearing nothing but white lace garters, thigh highs and heels—Stripper Barbie. Hard to look at and hard to look away from. As if I didn't have enough self-esteem issues when I look in a mirror. I awkwardly averted my gaze and tried to speak casually, but it's hard for me to be casual when people are naked.

Maybe it's my conservative upbringing or my mother's own obsession with being fully covered at all times. I don't know, but I definitely felt overdressed in this forced encounter with someone so comfortable with her body she's made a career out of sharing it.

Diamond rushed forward to shake my hand and tell me how much she appreciated me being there with Chaz for her big day. I think she said something about Chaz raving about me. I'm not sure. I can, however, report there are two light bulbs out in the chandelier in the Gardenia Suite.

She finally released my hand and introduced me to her bridesmaids, who thankfully were clothed. Albeit in the sheerest of sheer cotton candy pink, wearing nothing but white thongs underneath. And yes, it was sheer enough for me to know that.

I nodded as I shook hands with Vanity, Destiny, Vixen, and Carla. (Carla was Diamond's cousin. She didn't have a stage name.) If we've ever had a more beautiful group of bridesmaids, I don't remember them. None of them had spared any expense in their quest for cleavage, and they didn't share my inclination toward modesty. Laugher erupted all around when I offered to step outside so Diamond could finish dressing.

"Don't worry about me!" Diamond said. "I paid a fortune for these puppies. I fully intend to show them off to anyone who will look." She emphasized the puppies' size and prominence with a playful juggle.

I couldn't help but look. I have never in my life seen such humongous boobies up close and personal. I tried to look away, but they fascinated me. Maintaining eye contact proved damned near impossible. No wonder men have a terrible time with it.

I struggled to focus on her face as she stood there with her hands on her hips, making no effort to cover herself or get dressed. As if drawn by invisible magnets and without any conscious thought on my part, my eyes kept glancing at her massive breasts.

She laughed and said, "It's okay. Go ahead and look." She cupped her hands underneath and lifted them up like a pair of bowling balls. "Aren't they beautiful?" she asked. "You have to touch them. You just have to. You will not believe how natural they feel."

She leaned her chest toward me, and I took a couple of steps backward. "Nope, that's okay. I'll take your word for it!"

"No, seriously," said Vixen. "You have to touch those things. Mine are hard as glass." With no warning at all, Vixen grabbed my hand and mashed it against her breast. Yep. Hard as glass. I tried to jerk my hand away, but she quickly switched it over to Diamond's breast. Which I must admit by comparison felt soft and squishy.

"See?" Diamond said. "Aren't they amazing? Don't they feel natural?"

I pulled my hand back and blinked several times, nodding. I had no idea whether or not they felt "natural". In all honesty, mine are the only breasts I've ever touched. I pretty much have to squeeze my elbows together to get enough cleavage to even justify a monthly self-exam. But if I had to imagine what every teenage boy thinks a breast would feel like, it's probably exactly like what I had just felt.

"She got them in Brazil. Best on the market," said Carla, as though we were discussing a new set of tires Diamond bought for her car.

"I bet," I answered with a nervous sigh. Between this and the pantyhose incident with Barney the Bride, I've started thinking maybe I need to work somewhere in a cubicle away from people. I've never considered myself a prude or anything, but I don't think it's normal to keep ending up in situations where I'm touching other people's bodies against my will. It's just plain weird.

"Uh-oh, we got you all freaked out," Diamond said, seeming genuinely concerned at my discomfort. "I'm so sorry. We forget how shy people can be about their bodies."

I suddenly felt as though I'd done something wrong or outside the norm. Maybe I am a bit reserved, but am I supposed to be perfectly comfortable feeling up some woman's breasts I only just met? Or any woman? In the circles I travel in, breast groping is not a socially acceptable greeting. No one I know goes around grabbing each other's tatas for comparison.

I made my way to the door, willing my eyes not to look at Diamond's prized possessions. "No, no, you're fine. I need to go check on a few things. I'll be back. When you're dressed."

Later, when we were finished with the post-ceremony pictures, I watched Billy escort Diamond to the limo as I walked behind them carrying her train and her bouquet. His right hand caressed the small of her back as they walked. His left caressed a glass of champagne.

He was a good-looking guy, tall and broad-shouldered, with soft green eyes. Probably mid-forties, I would guess. His shaved head highlighted the large crescent-shaped scar above his left ear, the smaller jagged scar over his right eye, and the large hole in the center of the back of his head, like a bullet wound. I was torn between wanting to know bad enough to ask and wanting to be professional enough to remain silent. As my granny would say, he'd seen some scrapping in his day.

I wondered if Diamond would still be dancing in his clubs after the wedding and how all that would work. The boss's wife up on stage. I mean, how is that a "Honey, I'm headed to work" kind of job, especially when he is right there in the club watching it all? Does he walk people over to her pole and introduce his wife? And if he's already watched her make all her moves for every patron who comes in, then what constitutes a sexy night at home? Baking cookies and watching television? I don't get it.

Diamond stopped short as we reached the limo. "Oh, no! My dancing shoes. I left them at the hotel. Is there any way I can go get them?"

"Are you kidding me, Di? We're already missing the party," Billy said. "Just dance in what you're wearing."

"Honey, I can't dance in these things!"

She lifted the lace hem of her exquisite gown and revealed a stunning pair of gorgeous strappy stilettos with distinctive red soles. Clearly, I was quite distracted earlier in the dressing room if I did not notice Louboutins. Maybe I should have been looking at the floor instead of the ceiling.

They were from this year's wedding collection, at least three inches high with a sharply-pointed toe. I wouldn't have been able to walk in those things, much less dance in them. Heck, I probably couldn't have stood still in them.

Billy was clearly not as impressed as I was. "I paid fifteen-hundred dollars for a pair of shoes you can't dance in? You gotta be kidding me," he said.

"I have to get my dance shoes. I'm not going to my own wedding without being able to dance." Diamond stood her ground outside the limo. Billy shrugged and got in the car, already pouring more champagne. He didn't even bother to help his new bride get in.

"Can we go to the room? It won't take but a minute for me to change shoes," she asked.

"Um, sure," I answered.

I stepped to the back of the car to call Chaz as the limo driver helped Diamond get in.

"But we're already late!" Chaz whined. I rolled my eyes and sighed. I could only deal with one diva at a time.

I offered to go to the room with Diamond to keep it quick and prevent a huge delay, which appeased Chaz enough to get him off the phone.

Just when my feet thought we were done for the night.

Billy was chomping to bits to get to the party, so he stayed in the limo while I escorted Diamond up to the Gardenia Suite to get her dancing shoes.

"I can't believe he thought I could dance in these damned things," she said as we entered the suite. She kicked off the Louboutins and flung them across the foyer with her toes. I cringed to see them bounce across the floor.

"I know, right?" I felt like finally I could commiserate with Diamond on something. There was no way humanly possible to dance in those stilettos.

But then I saw what she was strapping on. Her "dancing shoes" were at least five inches high, much higher than the Louboutins. They were clear Lucite with a huge platform under the ball of her foot, and a thick, clear Lucite heel with sparkling crystals floating in some gel-like substance. She stood and stomped each foot lightly on the floor, activating lights in the heel that morphed from red to green then blue, purple and pink.

Ohhhhhhhhhhh. It slowly dawned on me. Her *DANCING SHOES*. Yeah. So much for commiseration and bonding with this bride. I had nothing.

I ended up staying for most of the reception just to watch this party happen. I saw things I've never seen before and probably will never see again.

Man, that girl sure knew how to use those shoes.

Sunday, November 3rd

My head is killing me. The throbbing and aching have not gotten better, but my vision is no longer blurry, so I guess that's a good sign.

After this morning's ceremony, the wedding party boarded a pontoon boat for a brief cruise before joining the rest of the guests at the cocktail brunch.

The boat driver wasn't too keen on pouring champagne and navigating a boat, so Laura suggested I stay with them. Floating around the lake with a light breeze in my hair and the sun shining on my shoulders? Sign me up! I mean, what could be so hard about serving champagne and strawberries to a group of happy, fun people?

For one, it would have helped if I knew how to open a champagne bottle. As the boat sailed away with the wedding party posing and waving for the photographer on the dock, I realized that even though I've attended plenty of New Year's Eves, weddings, parties, etc., I've never needed to open a bottle. Someone else always did it. I've been in the back hallway of hundreds of receptions as champagne popped and poured, but always in the capable hands of servers and banquet captains.

I knew, of course, that I had to place my thumb beneath the cork and push it off, but the wire contraption underneath the foil wrapper threw me. I twisted it, lifted it, pulled it, tugged it. Nothing worked.

It didn't take long for the wedding party to tire of making faces at the photographer and turn to watch me struggle with the bottle. Panic set in at the thought of looking like a complete idiot when my whole purpose on the boat was to open the champagne, and I couldn't do it. What kind of wedding planner doesn't know how to open champagne? Why didn't I pay attention to this as an important skill to learn for my career?

I peered closely at the bottle, as if it were the problem instead of me.

"Wow, this is a tough one," I said as I tilted it. I'm not sure why it never occurred to me that pointing the cork directly at my face could be a bad idea. I think maybe embarrassment at my lack of prowess had dulled my thinking, but I was also sure my thumb needed to push the cork for it pop.

Turns out I knew even less about champagne than I thought. The cork actually can come flying out without your thumb pushing it. Forcefully, in fact. If you're twisting the wire while turning the bottle in all different directions, the pressure build-up inside can pop a cork with a velocity that is quite impressive.

One minute I was twisting the wire in puzzlement. The next minute I was coming to as I lay flat on my back on the bottom of the boat with the entire wedding party and the boat driver bent over me in a circle looking concerned. I vaguely remember hearing the pop, and I sort of remember feeling the cork slamming into my face. They said I went right over backward like I'd been hit with a sledgehammer. Thank God I didn't fall off the boat. Or lose an eye.

It definitely cut the cruise short and killed the festivities. I went to first aid while Laura finished the wedding on her own. Luckily, it was a small event with virtually no set-up.

Deep black and blue circles formed pretty much immediately under my eyes, and now my forehead appears to be sprouting a small unicorn horn. All week, I've been so excited to have a Saturday night off so Cabe and I could go dancing. But with my head throbbing and my mythical creature appendage looking like it will break through my skin at any moment, we ended up sitting this one out on the couch with a big bowl of ice cream and a bunch of leftover strawberries. Cabe, of course, had a marvelous time with the whole situation. His jokes and comments were never-ending. I probably would have throttled him if my head hadn't hurt so badly.

Thursday, November 7th

Mr. Hotel Man called today to confirm for this weekend's Festival. I considered telling him something came up and I needed to cancel. I'm not sure I want to spend an evening with this guy. I don't know much about him at all. I wish we'd talked on the phone a little more. What if we don't even remotely have anything in common besides knowing each other from work?

What if he's boring? Or rude? What if he's a sex fiend? Or a serial killer? I should have asked if anyone in the office knows him. Outside of work, I mean.

Why did I agree to go? More importantly, why am I now freaking out?

I sort of hoped he was calling today to back out. Then I'd be off the hook. But no. He jumped right in with "Hey beautiful! Just calling to make sure we're on for Saturday. I can't wait to see you again."

I hope he's not a creeper or stalker. I hope he's a nice guy. An interesting guy. I hope I'm overreacting. He didn't say anything out of the ordinary. He just showed polite interest. I'm sure it'll be okay. He can't possibly be as bad as Mr. Bubble and his non-waterproof Porsche, right?

I guess I should try to be at least a little excited about this. I mean, I did start out interested in him. He looked pretty good in a suit, and he's been nothing but nice to me. But I feel like every time I get excited about a guy and look forward to going out with him, he ends up being a royal jerk or totally weird or something. Call me gun-shy. I'm wary, especially of the ones who seem too good to be true.

How sad it must be for the nice guys to put their best out there, trying to be polite and courteous as they navigate treacherous dating waters. Meanwhile, girls like me who have been burned by the jerks rarely give the nice guys a chance. We're looking for how they're going to disappoint us.

How they're not what they seem. Our vision becomes blurry and the good traits aren't clear. I do want to find a good guy amidst all the bad apples, but I guiltily admit I'm not very open-minded in giving people the benefit of the doubt. I need to work on that. I'm going to be receptive to Mr. Hotel Man. I'm going to focus on his positives!

Saturday, November 9th

I don't even know where to start. What to say. What to write.

Tonight was quite possibly the worst date I ever had.

Quite possibly the worst date *anyone* ever had. In the entire history of dating.

Oh. My. God.

Did this really happen?

It started with an issue with Mr. Hotel Man's car. He needed to get dropped off at the reception hall and ride with me. It was an omen for the evening to come. I should have canceled right then.

He came screeching up as the passenger in a dirty Honda Accord driven by a pretty blond woman in a pink suit. As he opened the door to get out, he leaned over and kissed her on the cheek. "I won't be home late. I'll try not to wake you."

"It's fine," she replied. "I'm going in late tomorrow, but you'll need to drive me so you have the car."

I probably should have said hello or acknowledged her in some way, but I was a little confused as to what was going on. I'm sure my face showed it.

Who the hell was she? A sister? Roommate? Friend? Who was this random, beautiful person he kisses on the cheek and tries not wake up late at night? I waved a hesitant goodbye in the general direction of the car, which had already pulled away.

"Hello, Beautiful!" he said, completely oblivious to my confusion. "You're even prettier than I remembered. I've been looking forward to seeing you again."

"Was that your sister?" I asked.

"Debbie? Um, no. She's my wife."

It is highly possible a weird noise somewhere between a gasp and a snort escaped me.

"Your wife?" I tried to ask, but although I mouthed the right words, all that came out was this weird gurgle.

"My ex-wife. Well, soon-to-be ex-wife. We're going to file the paperwork soon. Just a formality, really."

"Your wife." This time I found my voice and made the right noise. I even got my mouth to close after I said it. I think it had been open since he first spoke. "Your wife." I repeated it one more time, more of a statement to myself to confirm what was sinking in.

"Yeah. Oh man, you're weirded out, aren't you? I guess I should have said something, but I didn't want you to be, well, weirded out like you are now. It's all good. I mean, you saw her. You met her. She knows where I am, that we're going out tonight."

"Your . . . wife . . . knows we are going out tonight. Is this a date?"

"Yes. I mean, I hope so. I thought it was. Don't freak out. Really. She's been dating someone for the past couple of months. We're both moving on, I promise."

"So why *didn't* you tell me? And why did you kiss her goodbye and tell her you won't wake her up tonight?"

He shook his head and laughed, reaching for my hand, which I quickly pulled away.

"Come on. Seriously, it's not a big deal. I kissed her on the cheek because it's a habit. We've been married for ten years. She's my best friend. I'll always care about her, but we fell out of love a long time ago. We're okay with it. It's not like I kissed her on the mouth or anything."

He crossed his arms, like *he* was aggravated with *me* for this. He wasn't nearly as handsome as I remembered from the lobby. He'd been wearing a suit then. He looked different now. Less suave. More pig. A pig wearing a plaid shirt and a pair of jeans.

"Why are you still living together?" I asked.

"Money. It costs a lot to get a divorce, even when we both agree to it. We figured there's no reason for us to pay for separate places. Our lease isn't up until the end of the year. We're fine with living together. I mean, we're not sleeping together or anything!"

He said that last part with an eye roll and a laugh that gave me serious doubts about the truth and validity of the statement.

"I don't know if I feel comfortable with this." The little voice inside my head was screaming at me to walk away. To simply say no and walk away. Unfortunately, I've been raised to always be nice. Polite. It makes it hard to be honest when it may hurt or bother the other person.

"Oh, Tyler. Don't be that way. It's not a big deal," he cocked his head to the side and made a silly-looking pouty face. I bet Debbie has seen that look often in the last ten years.

"You keep saying that, but it's a big deal to me. You. Are. Married."

"Technically, yes, but . . . you know what? Why don't you talk to Debbie? Here, I'll call her and you can . . ." He took his phone out of his pocket.

"No!" I stepped back again. "I'm not going to ask your wife's permission to go out with you."

"Oh, good Lord. I was supposed to have the car. But then she got called into work and she needed it. If she hadn't needed the car, we'd already be at the festival having a good time." He shrugged and rolled his eyes as though the car was the problem.

"So if she hadn't needed the car—wait, you share a car? This keeps getting better and better—would you have even told me you were married?" I crossed my arms in irritation. I don't know if I would have gone out with him had I known he was still married and in the process of getting a divorce. That's some messy stuff I probably wouldn't have stepped in. But either way, it would have been nice to have the information from the get-go. I was pissed.

"I would've told you. It wouldn't have been the first thing I mentioned, though. Not because I'm trying to be dishonest or hide anything. If I wanted to hide it, I wouldn't have had Deb bring me and introduce the two of you. Look, I met you. I liked you. I haven't been out with anyone since we decided to divorce. Haven't even asked anyone out. It took me how many phone calls to get around to actually asking you? I didn't want to start the first date I've had in over a decade by announcing I'm technically still married. So I'm sorry. It's definitely not how I meant for this evening to go. To upset you or piss you off or whatever you're feeling. I just wanted to spend time with you. Talk to you and get to know you better."

His voice got softer as he talked, and almost against my will I started to feel sorry for him. He was in a rough spot. The voice in my head was loudly screaming, "AARGH! He wasn't upfront with you. He's married and going through a divorce. Go home. Don't waste your time. This is not your Prince Charming!"

He smiled what might have been a charming, handsome smile under other circumstances. "Look, if you want, I can call a cab and head back home. Or, and I would ask that you hear me out before you answer," he said, lifting his hand in protest when I started to speak, "hold on—we could go to the festival. Not as a date. Just two people going to a festival, enjoying good food and good art. Getting to know each other. No expectations. I'm an open book. I'll tell you anything you want to know. Nothing to hide."

I know I shouldn't have. I know I'm crazy for even considering it much less doing it. But I have that stupid-ass issue with not being able to tell people no. To tell them how I feel. Especially when he was being so nice and trying so hard. I didn't want to hurt his feelings, so I agreed to go to the festival. The voice inside my head threw her hands in the air and walked away.

Mr. Hotel Man, who had become Mr. Technically Married, tried to be all friendly as we walked to the car. At first, I tried to stay pissed off, but it made no sense to go with him and be mad the whole night, so I chose to have a good time. Well, I tried.

"By the way," Mr. Technically Married said as we pulled into the festival lot. "I have bad knees. I'm not able to walk far. Could you drop me off at the front gate and then park the car?"

The night took another step down the path of terrible dates, even though it was technically no longer a date. I looked at him with a mixture of disbelief and contempt.

"We're at a food and art festival. You have to walk the whole thing. It's, like, two miles all the way around. Did you realize this?" I asked.

"Oh, I know that!" He spoke with an easy smile. "I took some painkillers before I left the house, so I should be good to walk for a while. I didn't want to waste them on the parking lot."

Normally, I would never hold an injury or medical condition against someone. But when adding up this dude's points on the score card of possible second dates, everything counted. Against him. On top of not being upfront with me, not having his own car, obviously not having much in his bank account, still being *married* and still living with his *wife*, he had bad knees and couldn't walk. This guy was falling into the negative point range. Stellar. Oh lucky me.

"Okay." My voice was completely devoid of sympathy. "I'll drop you off and park the car."

My resolve to enjoy the festival was waning as I walked across the parking lot toward Mr. Technically-Married-with-Bad-Knees. I tried to self-encourage, but unfortunately, I asked the question you should never, ever, ever ask. What else could go wrong? Because there *was* more.

He stopped walking right before the entrance. "Um, it's a little tight this week. A few extra expenses this month. If you'd be willing to pay tonight, I can make it up to you with dinner after the first!" He said it unbelievably cheerful, like I had won the grand prize.

"Are you kidding me?" came flying out of my mouth before I could censor it. Although, I might have said it even if my censor kicked in.

He laughed and did the head cocked to the side, pouty face thing again.

"Maybe this is not a good idea," I said.

"Oh, come on! We're already here! It's a beautiful night. Not a cloud in the sky. We're at the winter festival. Food, art, music. I'll pay you back. I can even send you a check if you don't want to go to dinner."

Like I would take a check from Mr. Technically-Married-with-Bad-Knees-and-Bad-Finances.

"Please, Tyler? I really want to have a nice night out. I'll pay you back. Please?"

I swear he fluttered his eyelashes. What's so stupid is, had this guy been upfront with me, told me he's going through a divorce and wanted to get out of the house for a fun night, I might have been okay with going—as friends. But I felt like the whole thing was a bamboozle. Like I got set up. Hook, line, and sinker. But we were already at the festival, and I felt like an ass for just turning around and going home. So I paid for his frickin' ticket and in we went.

"Why don't we get one dish at each booth?" he asked. "Then it won't cost you so much, and we can try more things. We'll just split it," he said.

I didn't want to share anything with him at that point, but since I was paying for everything we ate, it did make sense to share. The first booth was a sausage pepper stew. It smelled delicious, and I stepped into line without even asking him.

"Oooh, sausage and peppers. Good thing I took my antacids!" He rubbed his hands together and took a big whiff of the aroma.

I turned to him, trying to decide whether or not I should even ask. I was sure I didn't want to know.

"Your antacids?" I was a glutton for punishment.

"Yeah, I have irritable bowel syndrome and a few other gastrointestinal issues. I'm not supposed to eat any spicy foods," he said.

"You have irritable bowel syndrome, and we came to an international food festival?" I thought surely I must be on Candid Camera or Punk'd. Someone was going to jump out at any moment and let me know this whole "date" had been a joke. Then we'd laugh, and Mr. Used-to-be-Hottie-Hotel-Man would say something like, "I can't believe you fell for all that."

But no cameras appeared, and the only thing he said was disgusting.

"It's fine! I love spicy food. I just take a lot of antacids and guzzle some Mylanta beforehand. Keeps the gas at bay. I'll probably be up all night with diarrhea." He cracked up laughing. "I might still have gas depending on what we eat and how long we walk, but we're outside and it's a pretty open space."

Few times in my life have I ever been rendered completely speechless, but my brain was not capable of generating a response to my married first date with no money and bad knees having noxious gas throughout the date and then going home to crap out everything we just ate. Maybe married people discuss that sort of thing, but I'm not the type to talk about pooping on a first date. Even when it's technically not a date. I don't want a mental image of a man camping out on the toilet with diarrhea, no matter how hot he is.

My appetite for sausage and peppers was gone. He scarfed it up, filling the tank for the unpleasant night to come. Unpleasant is actually an understatement. I'm getting nauseous just recalling it. The whole thing quickly went downhill like a mudslide. A noxious mudslide. With explosions and fumes and aromas not meant for the written word. From both ends, I might add, since the breath is not immune to gastrointestinal distress.

Part of me truly felt sorry for the guy. What a hot mess. His marriage ending, finances screwed up, no car of his own, knees blown, constant diarrhea, flatulence, and breath that smells like ass. This poor dude has to re-enter the dating world with all those attributes after a decade on the bench.

But the more selfish part of me could not believe what a miserable "date" this was. I hated to be rude or ugly, but the last straw had been broken. In several pieces. I could not wait to get away from him.

Mr. Bad-Breath-Bad-Knees-Bad-Date didn't say too much on the way back to the car. Like a pouty child being made to leave the park when he still wants to play. We rode to his house in silence. I didn't even pull into the driveway. I stopped the car in the street for him to get out. He had the audacity to lean in close with his ass-breath and whisper, "I had a good time tonight. I appreciate you giving me a chance after we got off to a rocky start. I can't wait to see you again."

I laughed. A shaky, nervous, I-may-just-go-off-on-you-asshole laugh.

He didn't seem to notice.

I pulled away without even saying goodnight.

Where the hell is Prince Charming??? He needs to hurry up and come. These dates are killing me.

Sunday, November 10th

Only one wedding today, just a ceremony. I enjoy those. Outside of confirming the florist, organist and photographer, I don't have a whole lot to do ahead of time, and I only need to be onsite an hour and a half before and about an hour after. I was finished and headed home a little after noon, which was great since I've been in a funk all day. Irritable and grumpy.

Melanie called this afternoon to invite me to Thanksgiving with her and Paul. She has three sisters, two brothers, and Lord only knows how many aunts, uncles, and cousins. It's an absolute madhouse when they all get together. Always a good time, though. They're all so cool about including me, but I can't help feeling like an outsider.

For the past few years (*before Monica*), I've spent Thanksgiving with Cabe at his mom's, which I love. Maggie is so laid-back and sweet. An incredible cook, too. We'd all eat ourselves beyond stuffed then crash on the couches and the floor to watch movies the rest of the day. Pausing every now and then to nosh on leftovers, of course.

It was usually just me and Cabe, his sister Galen, and his mom. Occasionally an extra if Galen was dating someone or a family member was visiting. No tension or drama, though. No fussing and fighting. Simply a relaxing, fun time.

Cabe hasn't mentioned me coming over this year, and I don't want to bring it up or assume. Too many unknowns and uncertainties since he's come back. I must say, if I can't be with my own family, I'd rather be with Cabe and his.

I miss my family most around the holidays. All it takes to make me a blubbering mess is one holiday movie where everyone is celebrating together in their funky sweaters, drinking egg nog, and singing Christmas carols. It makes me think about all of them and how far away I am.

It's funny how much I yearn for home sometimes when I so desperately wanted to get away from there growing up. I don't think it's the place I miss, though, but more the people and the feeling of belonging. Being part of something bigger than yourself. I have a very large extended family, so sometimes it feels a little strange to be only me living here by myself. Party of one.

I don't think I could ever move back home. My mother and I would probably drive each other nuts for one thing. I don't know. I definitely feel like I'm at a place in life where I want to belong. To something. To someone. People tell you not to look for a relationship. To be okay being on your own. Which I think I am in many ways. It doesn't mean I don't want someone though. Someone to come home to. Someone to laugh with, cry with, talk with. Just be with. I'm beginning to wonder if it exists for me, especially considering the prospects I've seen lately from the dating market.

I look at brides day in and day out and wonder what the crap is wrong with me. I mean, some of them are beautiful; some of them are not. Some are nice; some are total bitches. Some have health issues or children from past relationships. Some are just plain kooky or weird.

Yet, each of them comes to us because they've found someone who said, "You're the one. Out of all the world and all the girls, you're it. You're my Frosted Flakes."

I'm not stupid enough to think every bride we meet has a great relationship or that all these relationships last, but I do wonder why the hell I can't find anyone if all these other people did.

Both my sisters were married by the time they were my age. My mother already had four kids by the time she was my age. When is it my turn?

I swear I hear my poor mother saying to me now, "You'll find someone when you quit looking." Which may be the stupidest thing that woman has ever said to me. If I stopped looking, how would I find someone? And how the hay do you stop looking? Do you suddenly decide to become a monk and not notice anyone? Shun all social activity that makes it blatantly obvious you don't have a date? Maybe I should just quit my job so I'm not exposed to the endless cheese fest of people getting married and finding their soul mates.

It might be easier to try and follow my mother's advice then.

Okay, Universe. Here we go. I am officially announcing I have quit looking. My eyes are closed. Not peeking. Not a bit. (Did you send someone yet?)

Tuesday, November 12th

Out of nowhere, Lillian popped into my office and threw a file on my desk today.

"I need this budget revised. Type up a cover letter to go with it and send it to the bride. Make sure you put the revised total in the system. Also, double-check with the pastry chef for this weekend's event. I'm not sure she has the illustration for the cake request. I'll have my cell if you need to text me, but I'll be in a City Council meeting and I won't be able to talk."

I scribbled bullet points of her instructions on my notepad.

"Revise budget, cover letter, mail it, input it, and check on cake request. Got it."

At the exact moment I said "Got it", my brain asked "Why?" So I looked at Lillian and asked, "Why?"

Her eyes widened as her head tilted slightly to one side. I tried to backpedal.

"Um, I mean, um, no, it's okay, I can, I mean, will, get this done. I didn't mean . . . I guess I . . . I was just wondering why you're giving this to me," I smiled and gave a little shrug, wondering for the millionth time why I become a babbling idiot in front of this woman.

I wished I had just taken the file and gotten it done, but I didn't understand why she was handing it to me. Lillian had never given me any of her clerical work before. Carmen always did everything for Lillian, and I do mean *everything*. Since Carmen left for maternity leave, Lillian had been doing quite a bit more on her own, which I knew she didn't like. The whole office knew she didn't like it. She was quite vocal about it. I guess I assumed when Charlotte came on board Lillian would give her work to Charlotte. She was technically Lillian's assistant now.

"Whatever do you mean *why*?" Lillian asked. The British accent is so intimidating, I swear.

"Um, well, I don't mind doing it, of course, but I thought Charlotte was handling things for you."

"Humph," she snorted. "I wouldn't trust that twit to pour my coffee. She is completely daft. Not a brain cell in her head. I fear someday she will run out the front door, and the authorities will find her cavorting in a field of daisies singing *Fa La La*. I have been managing with much difficulty on my own thus far, but I have to be at this meeting and this cannot wait. I trust your abilities to handle it thoroughly and competently in a timely manner."

Out the door she went without waiting for any reply. I could have been momentarily pissed. After all, Lillian threw this on my desk to be completed right away with no thought or consideration to what I already had planned or any commitments I already made.

I wasn't pissed, though. I was over-the-moon beaming. Lillian felt I was thorough and competent. Yes, I realize it was in comparison to Charlotte, so the bar was not real high, but still. Lillian trusts me with her good-deed secrets, and she respects that I can complete my work efficiently.

She likes me. She likes me! Lillian likes me.

Friday, November 15th

One of my favorite things about my job is the moment right before the bride walks down the aisle. It's like I'm standing outside a window looking into someone else's life for a brief span of time. A very intimate, personal moment no one else should be allowed to witness. However, by nature of standing there waiting for music cues to open the door and send her down the aisle, I get to see it.

The majority of the time, it is a bride with her father. The last magical interchange between a little girl and her daddy before he transfers her heart to another and she becomes a woman and a wife. Everything this man has done to bring her to this point—all the sacrifices, the heartaches, the joys, the memories—it all comes together in this moment. She is entering the next phase in her life and leaving her old one behind. That touching, poignant exchange can melt the hardest of hearts, and I love it.

I am sure much of my affinity for it is because of my dad being gone and the fact that we will never have that moment. But I'm also just a sucker for sappy emotions.

I've heard some incredibly moving sentiments standing there holding the door, and they have filled me at times with envy and at times with hope. You can tell so much about the relationship between father and daughter through the words they share there.

Unfortunately, my glimpse is not always positive. Sometimes what it reveals is uncomfortable for all of us, and I wish I could shut the window.

Today, as I sent the maid of honor through the doors and pulled them closed, Sidney the bride stepped into the foyer and up to the mirror. She checked her lipstick and hair, which pretty much every bride does, and then she took the arm her dad offered. I cued the organist to change the music and turned to gaze through their "window" for my favorite moment.

I gave Sidney a big smile and said, "Ready?"

She smiled back and nodded, adjusting her bouquet and turning to smile at her dad. I felt a twinge of excitement knowing the magic was about to happen. The moment when she thanks him for everything he has done in her life, and he tells her how incredible she is and how he's never been prouder. I took a deep breath in hopes I wouldn't tear up and look like a total sap when they started.

As the organist fired up the traditional wedding march, Sidney's dad moved closer to her. I looked quickly at the ground so as not to seem too intrusive, but I did lean forward to make sure I could hear their declarations of love and tenderness.

Instead, I got this.

"This is the stupidest choice you've ever made, and I've never been more disappointed in you. If you'll turn around and walk out of here right now, we can leave and forget all about this. Your mother and I will never bring it up again. You won't hear another word about it. Don't worry about the money. It would be worth it to me to sacrifice the money to get you away from this sorry-ass son-of-a-bitch. So just say the word."

I couldn't help looking up and staring at them in shock. The wedding march built to its loudest point where I would normally swing open the doors and send them down the aisle to her waiting groom as I smiled with warm fuzzies inside. My hand hesitated on the door handle, though, not sure of her answer.

Sidney didn't react at all. She didn't even look at her father. She looked straight forward toward the doors, her groom, and her future. Then without any emotion at all, she said, "Dad, we've had this conversation. We're not having it again. I love you."

Then, she looked to me and gave a slight nod, her head held high.

So I swung it open. And away they went. Into the next phase of her life.

Wow. Just wow.

Saturday, November 16th

I don't get the universe's sense of humor sometimes. Especially when it seems directed at me. The photographer didn't like the lighting angles at our outdoor ceremony today, so he asked me to move the seated guests over to the right about four feet and turn them more north. I had barely begun my request at the end of the aisle when the universe decided to have a little fun at my expense.

A huge flock of birds flew over as I spoke, one of them depositing a wet, messy glop of bird poop in my face above my right eyebrow. A bird literally shat on my face! (Is that the correct past tense? I don't think I've ever written it before.) Based on the disgusted looks of shock and horror on the guests' faces, it was bad.

I attempted to finish my speech, but I could feel the bird droppings sliding ever so slowly down my forehead. I gave up the moment it dripped from my browbone onto my cheek. I stopped mid-sentence and ran to the bathroom.

It was in my hair, on my forehead, all up in my eyebrow, and still oozing down my cheek when I got to the mirror. I scrubbed nearly all the makeup off on one side of my face with those rough, cardboard-like paper towels in the hotel restroom. I used the liquid soap from the bathroom in my hair, vigorously combing through my bangs and the scalp beneath them with my fingers. It still didn't feel clean, but I knew I had to go back out in front of the guests. With a huge clump of wet hair right in the front.

At least no one complained about moving the chairs after my bird-feces shower. Sympathy for me, I'm sure.

My humiliation didn't end there, though.

Cabe had dropped me off at work this morning to take my car to get the oil changed. When he picked me up after the wedding, my makeup was still half gone, and my wet hair had dried into a limp, crunchy mess hanging across my eyebrow. As luck would have it, he'd purchased tickets for us to see a movie right after he picked me up. I had no time to go home and shower.

Thankfully, we were at the drive-in theater in Lakeland, so I just stayed in the car where I wouldn't be seen. But I swear every time I moved my head, I could smell bird poop.

Monday, November 18th

Cabe called and asked if I was free for dinner tonight. Two nights ago we did the double feature at the drive-in and didn't get home until after two. Last night, we listened to a jazz group at a bar downtown and rolled in a little after midnight. I needed to do laundry and run some errands tonight, not to mention get some sleep, but he is so damned persuasive when he wants something.

"Come on, Ty. It's dinner. You're going to eat anyway. It might as well be with me. I'll come over after we eat and help with your laundry. Okay, I'm not going to lie and say I'll help with your laundry, but I'll come hang out and watch you do your laundry," he said.

"It's not just laundry, dude. I need mouthwash and laundry detergent. I gotta return the lamp we got at Lowe's since it's too big for my end table. Then I need to check my mail at the post office. I have a lot of running around to do."

"So swing by and pick me up. We'll get it done. Then we'll eat dinner and go back to your place for laundry! Sounds like a blockbuster evening to me! What time shall I be ready?"

"You want to run errands with me? You so need to get a life!"

"Look who's talking. I'm offering to give up other exciting things I could be doing in order to hang out with you. But for you, this is actually your planned agenda for the evening. Who needs a life? Hmm?"

"Okay, okay. I'll pick you up around five. Wait, why don't you drive to my place and leave your car there? Then I can come home straight from work and I won't have to take you all the way back home after this exhausting evening," I said.

Errands ended up being fun. Of course. I swear Cabe and I can have a good time anywhere doing anything. We ended up staying in Target for over an hour. Cabe happened to wear a red V-neck T-shirt and a pair of khakis, which blended close enough with Target's employee uniform that customers keep stopping him to ask him questions.

He took his new "job" very seriously, walking people around the store trying to find what they were looking for. He even started going up and asking customers if he could help them with anything. All the while, he was making eye contact with me as I followed along like some weird Target stalker. Mouthing things and rolling his eyes, cracking me up in general. Cabe is simply hysterical. Naturally funny. He doesn't have to work at it or be conscious about it.

"I bet I get good comments," he said while on a break from helping people. "I bet I get nominated for employee of the month. Corporate will be all like—'What? Who? Wait, we have to find this man. We need him to be the face of the brand. We need him to train all our employees on how to treat the customers.' I'll be a Target movie star. I'll be in all their ads." He struck a pose near a rack of baby clothes, a creepy Vanna White smile plastered across his face.

I laughed and pulled him away from his dreams of stardom. "I bet someone has already reported you for being a creep and impersonating an employee. Any minute now security is going to bust out from behind the strollers and arrest you. I'll be too embarrassed to ever shop in Target again."

"But you'll come visit me in jail, right?" he asked.

"If I'm not in jail right beside you as an accomplice! I'll even bring you good coffee, because I'm thinking you won't be getting that expensive stuff you like in the slammer."

"Didn't think about that. We better get out of here before I get caught. I can't live without my organic fair-trade coffee," he said, pretending to look around for security as he tiptoed away from the racks.

We finished my errands, and Cabe suggested we eat at the Japanese steakhouse.

"It takes too long," I whined. "You have to sit through the whole show, and then it takes forever to get the check when they're done. Let's just grab a pizza."

"Oh, come on. I'm craving teriyaki shrimp. We can sit at a normal table where they bring the food to you without seeing the chef make butter fly and build an onion volcano."

"They have normal tables? Wait, are you sure?" I asked.

"Yeah. They always ask at the podium if you want a Hibachi chef or not," he answered.

"Then why in the hell do we always sit around that hot grill of a table and watch some dude throw shrimp tails in his paper chef hat?"

"Because I like it. It's like a double bang for your buck. Dinner and a show." He spread his arms and nodded like he had made an amazing announcement. "Eh? Eh? How 'bout it? Wanna see a dinner show, or sit at a regular table and be bored?"

I rolled my eyes, but he already knew I'd say yes. I've never been good at saying no to him. It's been worse since he's come back home. I think I've been so happy to have him back that I pretty much do whatever he wants. I should probably get that in check before he starts really taking advantage of it.

The seating hostess at the podium asked if we wanted the Hibachi grill or a booth. Cabe answered a booth, shooting me an eye roll as though he was being forced to do the lamest thing on Earth at my request.

She gathered two menus and said, "Follow me." She led us around the bar and into a long hallway with gold lanterns and paintings of dragons on bright red walls. The farther down the hallway we got, the less decorated it was. Eventually, the hallway was dark. We could barely see the hostess ahead of us. Luckily, I did see her turn to her left, and then the light at the end of the hallway outlined her silhouette and made it easier to see. This new hallway had no color or adornment at all. When we reached the end, the room was equally as dull and boring.

No bright red walls like the main restaurant, but more of a grayish-beige color that wasn't even a color at all. No festive lanterns or silk dragon kites hung from the ceiling. A lonely painting of a pagoda high upon a mountain adorned one wall. The others were bare. Plain brown booths lined both sides of the room with a couple of sets of dark brown tables and chairs in the center. Only one other couple and one family sat in this dining area. They all looked at us with a strange mixture of pity and camaraderie, as though we were new arrivals to some captive situation.

When we were seated, the hostess said, "Someone will be by shortly to take your order." Then she was gone.

"Wow," Cabe said. "I feel like we got banished." He drew his shoulders up tall and scrunched his face. "You no want Hibachi grill? Fine, we banish you to back room to eat table scraps," he said in a terrible attempt at a bad Asian accent.

The menu featured all Chinese entrees, not the Hibachi fare we normally get.

"Dude, it's not even the same menu. I thought it would be the same food only cooked in the back instead of right in front of you."

Cabe looked around the restaurant and turned completely around to see the exterior door leading out to the parking lot. "Do you know what this is?" He whirled back to me and then turned back around again. "Do you know where we are?"

"Um, at the Japanese steakhouse?" I answered, uncertain of what he was asking. Had we traveled through some time and space continuum I was unaware of?

"We're at the Chinese restaurant," he leaned low across the table toward me as he whispered.

"What?" I asked, looking at the front door to get my bearings. "What do you mean?"

He whispered again, holding his menu up to shield his face from the other patrons.

"They did banish us. When you pull into this shopping center, you can see the huge entrance to the steakhouse, but a couple of doors down is a little Chinese restaurant. It doesn't even have a name. The neon light just says 'Chinese' in red letters. We've been banished to China. You don't want Hibachi?" His terrible Asian accent came out again. "No steak for you. You go to China and eat lo mein."

"You're kidding. Why would they send us to a different restaurant?" I asked, but as I looked out the front door and into the parking lot beyond, I could tell he was right. We were no longer in the steakhouse. We were in a completely different restaurant.

Cabe started doing an impression of Seinfeld's Soup Nazi, saying "No steak for you!" over and over again.

I couldn't help but laugh at him. I swear no matter where we are and what we are doing, he makes me laugh. I guess maybe we have the same sense of humor or something. I mean, what he was doing in Target wasn't that hilarious when I explain it here, but when it was happening it was so funny I couldn't stop laughing. My laughter seems to be a catalyst for him, because the more I laugh, the funnier he gets. Every time. I've never had more fun with anyone than I do with Cabe.

When we got back to my apartment after our Chinese debacle of a meal, we sat in my car laughing about the night and how crazy it all was. Suddenly, Cabe got quiet. He shifted his weight in the seat and rubbed his long fingers down his thighs, sighing heavily.

"What?" I asked. "What happened? What did I miss?"

His entire demeanor had changed. He stared out the passenger window, his jaw clenched tight and his smile gone.

"Hello?" I placed my hand on his arm, but he flinched slightly so I pulled it away. "What's wrong?"

"I don't know," he said. "I felt . . . happy tonight. But then I thought about everything that's happened, and I remembered that my life is shit right now. I shouldn't be happy."

"Cabe, that's a total crock. Of course you're allowed to be happy. You've been unhappy. You've been miserable. It's okay to be happy. It's okay to laugh," I said.

"No, it's not. I'm living in my mother's pool house, Ty. I have pretty much screwed myself out of any kind of promotion at work since they now view me as unstable. I'm going through a divorce, which I never expected to do. I'm flat broke from moving cross-country twice. I feel like in the last year, I just picked up my life and scattered it to the winds. I have no idea how to put it back together. I don't know what my next step is. I'm not even sure who I am at this point. Or what's real anymore. But I do know I have nothing to be happy about right now."

He exhaled a quick rush of air as he opened the car door, and he was out before I could even process what happened. One minute he was fine, full of joy and being the old Cabe I remembered, and then a cloud rolled in over him and the broken Cabe was there in his place, vulnerable and exposed.

I got out and followed him. "Cabe, wait," I said, but he kept walking. "Dude, listen to me. You can still be happy. Cabe, wait. You're going to figure this out. Cabe, please wait."

He didn't. He got into his car and drove away without a word.

I still feel confused. I don't even understand what happened. It was so quick, so sudden. I absolutely adore the silly, goofy, fun, lovable man that he is. To see him wrestling with regret and self-doubt kills me. He's always been the strong, confident one in our pairing, and I've always been the hot mess. I'm not sure I know how to step up to the plate.

Maybe I should have stopped him from driving. Maybe I should call to see if he's okay. Or maybe I should just leave him alone and call tomorrow. Let him do the whole man-retreating-to-his-cave thing. I don't know.

In a weird way, I remember feeling the pain I saw in him tonight. I remember when I first moved here, and I had no idea who I was or where to find me. My idea of myself, my definition of who I was, had been defined by another person and what I thought I had with him. When that got stripped away, I felt exposed. I felt lost. God, I don't ever want to feel that way again. I don't ever want that haunted, dark emptiness in my brain and in my soul.

I wonder if that's why I haven't found anyone yet. If maybe that's why everyone I go out with has some glaring default I can't ignore or abide. Maybe as much as I say I want someone to spend my life with, I also don't want anyone to be able to hurt me. Maybe being alone is not such a bad thing. It's safe.

Tuesday, November 19th

Cabe called at six this morning.

"I hope I didn't wake you, but I haven't been able to sleep. I just wanted to say I'm sorry. I didn't mean to wig out and disappear."

"It's okay, Cabe. Are you alright?" I asked, yawning.

"Yes. No. I don't know. Sometimes I think I'm okay, and then something triggers a memory or a thought, and I'm right back where I was. I don't know how to accept where I am, Tyler. I didn't intend to be here. I thought when I picked up everything and moved, it was a commitment to something that was going to last. And it didn't. I feel like I got no say in it. Like, we went into this life together, made these promises—these vows— then she changed her mind and I had to come home with my tail between my legs. That's not how I thought it was going to turn out.

"I thought I loved her, you know? I thought I wanted to spend the rest of my life with her. But evidently, I didn't even really know her. That's messed up. How did I screw up that bad? How did I not see it? Shouldn't I have known my wife was gay? I don't even know what I feel at this point. Angry. Bitter. Stupid. Like I did the wrong thing. Made the wrong choice. Now I can't undo it. I can't go back, and I'm not sure how to go forward. It pisses me off."

His voice spewed with anger. I welcomed it, though. Anger he could use as fuel to get over this.

"You should be pissed off, Cabe. What Monica did was wrong! Unfair. If she wasn't sure she wanted to be with you, she shouldn't have married you. Screw her! She doesn't deserve you."

I thought encouraging the anger would help. It didn't make him angry, though.

"You're right," he said. "Why would you marry someone if you weren't sure? I mean, I thought I was sure, but now I don't know. So maybe she was sure, but then after she married me, I did something. Or didn't do something? Maybe she did love me, then something happened and she stopped."

"Cabe, it's not you. You can't think that. She was confused. Maybe she's been struggling with her sexuality for a long time. Who knows? I don't know why she did what she did, but you can't say it was you. You didn't do anything."

"How do you know, Ty? You don't know what I did or didn't do. A relationship doesn't fail because of just one person. It takes two to make it. It takes two to break it. Evidently, I didn't do something right. Emotionally or physically. Or both."

I understood the hurt and anguish of betrayal and what it does to your confidence and self-esteem. But I couldn't imagine the double whammy of not only being left for another but having no way at all to compete.

"Look, sweetie, what that chick had, God didn't give you. That wasn't something you could change. If Monica had feelings or needs she got fulfilled from another woman, it's not like you could have done something to supply that, you know? It was probably something she's been dealing with for a while. This girl happened to be the one who helped Monica be open about who she was. You can't beat yourself up."

"You don't understand, Ty. It still comes down to me not being enough. I couldn't keep her. I couldn't make her happy. We never should have gotten married."

His anger had gone, and he sounded empty again. I felt completely helpless. How come we can send documents, videos, and pictures instantaneously across the wires, but we can't figure out how to hug someone through the phone?

"You want me to come over?" I asked.

"No. I'm fine." He took a couple of deep breaths. When he spoke again, his voice was steady. "Sorry. I called to apologize and ended up going off on a rant. I'm a mess. Look, Ty. I had a great time with you last night. I'm sorry I screwed it up. I'll talk to you later."

"Wait, Cabe. Don't hang up. Let me come over. We'll get breakfast. I don't want you to be by yourself." I couldn't even hear him breathing. I thought maybe he had hung up. "Cabe?" Still no answer. I stayed on the line just in case. After an eternity of silence, I heard him sigh.

"No. I'm fine. I need to be by myself. I'll talk to you later." Then he was gone.

I wanted to drive over there despite what he'd said, but a quick check of my calendar reminded me I have a planning session this morning. So now when I finish my coffee, I get to go listen to a happy couple gush about how in love they are. How excited they are. How beautiful their wedding will be.

I can't even warn them it may not all work out the way they plan. Within a few years, maybe less, she may stop trying and he may stop caring. She may become a closet alcoholic, and he may fall for some pretty little thing at work. Her parents may interfere too much, and he may lose his job and their house.

It's all so stupid. These people come here and spend thousands of dollars on a wedding, and in the end, it's all a crap shoot. No one knows what the future brings or if the other person is going to hold up their end of the bargain. Hell, even if they do hold up their end, something like cancer or a car accident or Alzheimer's steps in and robs you blind.

No matter how pretty the dress is, no matter how gorgeous the flowers are, and no matter how many people show up to watch your vows, the whole thing can be ended with the stroke of a pen. It doesn't even have to be mutually agreed upon. The whole 'til death do we part is a joke. It's a hope to strive for. A hope that nothing else tears it apart before death. A hope death doesn't end it unexpectedly early.

Why do people do it? Why even try? Why are we willing to stand before our family and friends and pledge something that may mean nothing? Why are we willing to risk the pain, the suffering, the disappointment, the failure? And why do we get so gosh-darned excited about the prospect of it all? We march into it with music, flowers, ribbons, and bows. That's bullshit. We should go to all weddings wearing black and mourning the sacrifice of the heart.

Boy. I'm going to be a cheerful wedding planner today, huh?

Thursday, November 21st

And that's why I love this job! Just when I am about ready to completely give up on love and go live as a hermit in a cave somewhere, I get a wedding like today's and BOOM! My faith is restored. Somewhat, at least.

When you can feel the love in the room, when the happiness is contagious, and you can't help smiling just from being around the people attending, that's a great wedding! Boy, did I need it after the downers I've had this week.

Everyone was just so . . . *happy*. Happy to be there. Happy to be loved. Happy to be.

The bride and groom both kept thanking everyone for all the efforts being made on their behalf. Both sides of the family were gracious and delightful. Not a jerk or witch in the crowd! No complaints, all smiles. It was enough to make you want to puke, except they were all so nice it was hard to hate them or even feel nauseous.

I know they don't all work out. I know some marriages end in divorce and heartache like Cabe's or start off under bad circumstances like so many we see.

But every now and then—and it doesn't happen so often that I take it for granted—I get a glimpse of it and know it's real. Love, I mean. A couple comes along whose wedding isn't about the color of the linens, the fragrance of the roses, or whether or not the cake is tilting slightly to the right. None of those little details seem to matter. For them, it's a joyful occasion to share their love and excitement with closest family and friends.

Their guests aren't bitching about the hotel screwing up a wake-up call, or the dinner rolls being hard, or the place settings being too close together. Nope. They're just thrilled to know these two wonderful people who have met each other and made the world a better place by becoming partners.

I'm not a total sap, but I am definitely a hopeless romantic. I want to believe in love. I want to believe in happily-ever-after. I want to think it can exist, and we aren't all doomed to end up alone. Those weddings give me hope. Hope that love is real and being happy with another person is possible. It's not all heartache if love is attainable.

It sort of gives credibility to what I do for a living every single day. So on that note, I will drift off to sleep. At peace. Dreaming of love.

Friday, November 22nd

Laura and Lillian brought in lunch today to thank us for our hard work in the busy stretch of October and November. Laura said they could not be more proud of our team. Lillian nodded, dramatically lifting her iced tea in a toast. She was in a great mood today. More talkative than normal. Maybe she had the opportunity to thoroughly berate someone on her way in to work or something. I don't know, but she sure seemed quite jovial.

"So, Tyler, Laura tells me your friend Cabe has returned to nurse wounds from a sour marriage," Lillian said.

"Yeah, he has. It's really unfortunate," I answered. I glared at Melanie and Chaz. One of them must have told Laura. I certainly didn't.

"She asked," Melanie said defensively in response to my glare, holding her napkin up to hide her talking with her mouth full. She swallowed quickly before repeating herself. "Laura asked."

"I did," Laura said. "You've been quite busy lately. I asked Melanie about the lucky guy. When she said it was Cabe, I was confused since he'd moved away and gotten married."

"It didn't work out," I said.

"What does that mean?" Lillian asked.

"They're getting a divorce," I answered. I wondered how much of Cabe's personal details Melanie already shared.

"Divorce." Lillian spat the word out like it tasted bad. "Well, that's always dreadful. How's he doing?"

I thought about his meltdown Tuesday night and his tearful call Wednesday morning. "Um, okay, I guess. Not okay sometimes."

"You be careful with him, Tyler. Going through a divorce is very painful. It changes a person. During the metamorphosis, they are quite vulnerable and easily hurt," Lillian said, ever so casually dipping a steamed dumpling in the duck sauce with her chopsticks.

Her comment stabbed me a bit. I would never do anything to hurt Cabe. Did Lillian somehow think I would? Why would she tell me to be careful with him? I'm trying to help him.

"Careful with *him*?" Laura said. "She's the one who needs to be careful *she* doesn't get hurt. A man coming out of a divorce can be a dangerous time bomb. He's looking for someone to affirm his manhood and restore his confidence. He might be sending out messages he doesn't intend to deliver."

"Oh, Cabe wouldn't hurt Tyler," Melanie chimed in. "He adores her. You've seen the way he looks at her. The way he talks about her. That boy is crazy about Tyler. Always has been."

"All the more reason for her to be careful how involved she gets," Lillian said. "She can't be leading him to believe something that's not possible."

"She's not! Tyler cares a lot about Cabe. She was devastated when he left," Melanie said.

I whipped my head back and forth between them.

"Excuse me, guys, I'm sitting right here," I said, dramatically pointing to myself and making a large circle around me. "I can hear you!"

"All I am saying," said Lillian as though I had never spoken, "is that Tyler has daddy issues. She tends to attract men who think they can rescue her to feel masculine, but she rids of them quickly. This boy is in a fragile place. She needs to heed that."

"Daddy issues? I have daddy issues?" I put my box of noodles on the table and swung my entire upper body to face Lillian.

"You very well may, dear," Laura chimed in. "You lost your father at a very formative age. If so, no one faults you for it. It's a consequence of the hand you were dealt, but it's neither here nor there." She then turned to Lillian. "I just think it would be best if Tyler didn't spend all her time with him. You know, for both of their sakes."

I stood and stared at them all in amazement.

"I am right here. You are discussing me as though I can't hear you. I do not have daddy issues, and I'm not going to hurt Cabe. Cabe is not gonna hurt me. We are friends. Got it? I think I'll eat my lunch at my desk. I sincerely hope you can find another topic of conversation in my absence."

I walked to my office carrying my box of noodles and my indignation. How dare they sit there and discuss me—and not just me, but my mental and emotional health—like I wasn't even there.

My desk wasn't far enough away. I could still hear them.

"Why'd you have to go and say that?" Laura asked.

"Say what?" Lillian asked.

"That she has daddy issues," Laura answered. "You don't tell somebody they have daddy issues. You're not her therapist."

"As I recall, you agreed with me. Did you not?" Lillian said.

Laura's voice hushed to a whisper, but I could still hear her words. I could practically feel them prick me as she spoke.

"I said she may have. The poor thing lost her daddy at thirteen. How could she not? That would screw anyone up. You don't have to go pointing it out, though. I've told you before you don't necessarily have to share every piece of information you have, no matter its truth or value."

"Y'all mark my words," Melanie said, sounding like her mouth was full again. "They'll end up together. Tyler and Cabe love each other. They really do. She doesn't see it yet, but they truly love each other."

"I can still hear *you*!" I screamed.

I know I have issues, but I certainly don't want my issues to be office conversation. To be truthful, I've been told before, by a qualified therapist I might add, that I do indeed have some baggage stemming from losing my daddy. I suppose, in all honesty, I am aware that might factor into some of my relationship problems. My reluctance to commit battling with my desire to be loved. However, none of that has anything to do with me and Cabe. We're just friends. Why can't everyone get that?

Saturday, November 23rd

They say you marry the person and not their family, but the reality is you have to put up with the family, and the family has to put up with you. That lesson hurt my heart today, not for Ricky and Kim, the bride and groom, but for Ricky's poor sister, Amy.

I went to meet the girls at the elevator to take them to pre-ceremony photos, but Amy was missing.

"Where's Amy?" I asked.

"Upstairs," Kim answered sharply.

"Is she ready?" I asked.

"Who knows?" answered a bridesmaid.

"Well, she needs to be downstairs for photos. Is she coming soon?" I asked.

"Who knows?" answered another bridesmaid as they walked away from me toward the photographer.

"Um, ladies, wait, where is she?" I tagged along behind them like a puppy, but no one would answer me. When we reached Melanie, I told her I'd try to find the missing bridesmaid.

As I got off the elevator on Kim's floor, I saw Amy peeking out of a doorway a few rooms down.

"Can you help me?" she asked.

"Sure!" I said, relieved to have found her so easily. "What's up?"

As I got closer, I could see tears streaming down her face, her makeup an utter mess.

"What's wrong?"

"I must have gained weight since the last fitting. My dress won't zip." She turned for me to see the open back of her dress. The zipper was nowhere near touching.

"Oh, okay," I said casually, as though I saw this happen all the time and knew exactly how to fix it. Meanwhile, my mind raced trying to figure out how I was actually going to fix it and get her to pictures. I had no time.

Amy turned back to face me, and the faster she talked, the more she cried.

"They're all so skinny. They look so pretty in their dresses. Kim had to pick a different dress for me because I couldn't wear the strapless one with these boobs and these arms. I asked her if I could wear a jacket, but she got mad. Ricky told her she had to let me pick a different dress, which pissed her off even more. So they were fighting, and now all the bridesmaids hate me. I tried getting ready in there with them, but no one would talk to me. Plus, I didn't want to get undressed in front of them. So I came back here to our room to get dressed, but my husband had already taken the baby and gone downstairs. I couldn't get it zipped by myself, and now I'm late, and . . ."

"It's okay, it's okay. Calm down. It's okay!" I cut off her never-ending explanation and dabbed at her puffy eyes with a tissue from the bathroom.

"I had a baby six months ago," Amy said. "I've struggled to take off the baby weight. I mean, I wasn't skinny before, but I gained a lot with the pregnancy. I was working so hard to get it off before the wedding, but we've been eating out a lot and getting ready for the trip."

"It's okay. We'll get it zipped. You're gonna be fine. You'll be at your brother's wedding with your husband and your new baby, and you're going to have so much fun!"

I turned her around and tried to get the zipper closer together. The skin on her back was red and splotchy both from her crying and from fighting to get the zipper up. I pulled. I tugged. I yanked. The harder I tried and failed, the more upset Amy got. I texted Mel that we had a technical difficulty with the dress and would be there as soon as possible.

I wiped the sweat from her back with a towel and asked if she had any powder. I had to get the dress zipped, and I figured it was better to risk getting a bit of powder on the red dress than to have her entire back exposed.

By the time I dried and powdered her, she calmed down somewhat. I got the zipper above her lower back, but it wouldn't budge when I reached the area where her bra strap came across. It was my turn to sweat and panic. We were not even to the widest part of her back just below her shoulders.

I so wanted to get this poor girl zipped and to the wedding. Not only to keep Melanie on her time schedule but also to protect Amy from further humiliation by those skinny bridesmaids and her future bitch-in-law.

My fingers ached, and I had to put powder on my own hands they were sweating so much.

"Maybe I should just wear something else and tell Kim I can't be a bridesmaid. I don't want everyone waiting for me. She'll be furious if I make the wedding late. I'd rather drop out."

Amy's resignation made me even more determined to get the zipper up and get her to the wedding.

I tried to think of ways to get the dress to come together. If your jeans are too tight, you can lay down flat on the floor to redistribute the fat so they'll zip. I tried to think of any position I could put Amy in to redistribute her back fat. I couldn't lay her face down, because then the only thing shifting and redistributing would be her new mommy breasts coming around to the back. That wouldn't work.

Then I got a spark of genius and had her raise her arms a little so I could pull the dress up a bit. When I pulled it up, the excess material allowed me to zip a little more. So I pulled it up again, and I could zip a little more. We kept doing that until the whole dress zipped, but a good portion of it was now over her head. It took both of us working together to shimmy it back down ever so carefully over her body. I kept thinking about Janet and her seams splitting, and I prayed this dress could stand the pressure since it was newer and better made. We finally got it pulled over her, although it was beyond any definition of snug. I still don't know how that girl was managing to breathe.

"Let's do this," I said. "We'll get you to the ceremony. Then after it's over and you've taken family pictures, you can come up here and change into something more comfortable. Something you can breathe in. Just don't sit down at all between now and then, and try not to take any big, deep breaths, okay?"

Amy's gratitude was written all over face in her huge smile and happy eyes.

"Go fix your makeup, girl. We gotta get you downstairs!" I actually felt a little lump of emotion in my throat.

She hugged me as tightly as she could in her confined state, then she laughed and high-fived me. After a quick makeup touch-up, we headed to the wedding. Kim had done all the pre-ceremony photos without Amy, but at least she would be in the ceremony itself and all the post-ceremony photos with her brother and her family. I hope at some point Kim will realize what a big "B" she was today. And I secretly hope she gains a hundred pounds and isn't able to zip her dress someday.

I don't care what the photographer or the fashion magazines say. I think family relationships and people feeling comfortable are worth much more in the long run than the way the dresses look in the photos.

Monday, November 25th

It was so hard getting up and going in today. I just wanted to sleep. I actually considered just calling in sick and going back to bed, but I'm already losing an office day Thursday for Thanksgiving. Then I have a big wedding on Friday in addition to helping Lillian with hers on Saturday. Calling in was not an option.

I blame Cabe for my exhaustion. He came over last night after my wedding. We went to the store and spent way too much time debating what to cook and which wine to drink, so we got a late start with our meal. Then the DVD kept screwing up and skipping, so we ended up driving back to the store to return it and get a different one. We both fell asleep long before the credits rolled. I woke up when the music began looping for the DVD menu. Cabe was laid out on my couch, one arm hanging over the side and one leg thrown over the back. I didn't even bother waking him. I brushed my teeth and took a swipe at my makeup before climbing into bed. I pretty much forgot he was there until I flipped on the kitchen light this morning and heard him groan.

"Bright. Bright light." He put one of the couch pillows over his face and turned in toward the back of the couch.

"Oh, sorry, buddy. If you want, you can go climb into my bed." I opened the coffee jar and inhaled its intoxicating scent, hoping it would help awaken my brain.

"Oh, hell yeah, baby! I've been waiting for that invitation for years!" Cabe said sarcastically, giving a fist pump without even looking up from the couch.

"Yeah, right. Go curl up and sleep. Some of us have real jobs that require showing up to get paid. We don't all work in the computer world where everything is remote."

"Oh, please. You could do everything you're gonna do at the office from right here with a laptop and a phone. You don't have to go anywhere. But since you are, I'm going to take you up on that delicious offer and catch a few Z's. That stupid sofa bed at Mom's has been killing my back. This couch is definitely not an improvement."

He stood and stretched but then sat back down. "Coffee smells good," he said.

"You want some? Not too late to make you a cup," I offered.

"Nope. I'm going back to sleep. I intend to enjoy every single minute sleeping in a real bed." He stood again and headed to my room.

"When are you going to move out of your mom's pool house? Isn't there like some time frame where you officially become a slacker or a moocher?"

"Hey, I'm paying rent. It's not like I'm sleeping in her living room or something. It's a separate building," he said from my room.

"Well, we both know your mother loves having you there. She won't want you to leave no matter how long you stay. Maybe just buy a bed and put it in the pool house?"

"I thought you told me to go to sleep. How can I sleep if you keep talking to me and filling the air with the smell of coffee?" His voice was muffled in my pillows.

"Sorry, dude. I'll be out of here in a few. I gotta spread some peanut butter on a bagel and pour my coffee in a to-go cup. Sleep tight. Lock the bottom lock when you leave and set the alarm. We should probably get you another key." Cabe had held the extra key to my apartment until he left for Seattle and we decided a more local friend would be a better option.

I got no response, so I assumed he went back to sleep. I envied him and wished I could curl up beside him. I mean, not in a sexual way. Or a couples way. I mean just to sleep. Just to be able to sleep late. You know, not to have to go to work. I mean, in a friend way. Okay, now I am actually spending time explaining myself to myself in my journal. Whatever.

He was gone when I got home this afternoon, but he made the bed and left a note on my pillow.

"This bed is so freakin' heavenly. If I had a truck, I might steal it. I don't think it would fit in the pool house, though, so I'm thinking maybe you could move in there and I'll move in here. J/K. Hope you had a great day. C"

It really is a comfortable bed.

Wednesday, November 27th

My cell phone rang as I unlocked the door to my apartment tonight.

"Well, hello beautiful," said Mr. Bad-Knees-Bad-Breath-Technically-Married-Hotel-Man. "Where've you been all my life?"

Ugh. Just ugh.

"Somewhere else, I guess. What's up?" I asked, cursing myself for not recognizing his number. They invented voice mail to avoid calls like that one.

"Deb and I were wondering if you wanted to come over for Thanksgiving tomorrow."

"Um, no. I really do not want to come over and have Thanksgiving dinner with you and your *wife*."

"Well, she's bringing her boyfriend, and her dad will be there. I thought maybe it might be nice if you were there with me."

What delusional planet does this man live on? Did he think we were a couple?

"I don't think so," I said. I wondered if I was required by the conventions of politeness to thank him for inviting me when I wasn't at all thankful he asked.

"Alright. I know it's short notice. You probably have plans. But, hey! I'm getting paid this weekend, so you let me know when you're available. It's on me this time. Remember I couldn't pay the night of the festival?"

"Oh, I remember. You know what? Let's just call it even. Don't worry about it."

"No, no, no. I fully intend to take you out and pay for it this time. You let me know where you want to go. We'll make it happen."

Even if I did want to go out with him again, and I most certainly did not, I wouldn't know how to pick a restaurant that wouldn't require him to walk and wouldn't leave him with dire fits of gas and diarrhea. I thought it best to be as upfront and honest as possible.

"Look, I appreciate you offering, but I'm not interested."

"Well, I think you need to give it another chance," he said. "That was a bad pick, you know, with all the walking and the food and all. I don't think you really got to know me. We could pick a quiet place to sit and talk."

It's much easier to be honest about not liking people when they're complete jerks, but he wasn't a jerk. I really don't think he has any idea how disgusting he comes across. He's just doing his best to navigate his return to the dating world. Trying to put himself out there. I see that. I can appreciate it. It doesn't mean I want to go out with him again, though.

"Thank you, but no. I'm not interested. Sorry it didn't work out. Have a happy Thanksgiving."

I ended the call before he could say anything else. I have a bad habit of being polite to a fault and dragging things out far beyond where I want them to go. I need to change that, so I'm proud of myself for being honest. Even though I do feel sorry for him.

Cabe called tonight to ask what I was doing for Thanksgiving. He hasn't even mentioned it before now. I'd much rather be spending the day with him, but I already told Melanie and Paul I'd be there since he hadn't brought it up and I didn't want to invite myself.

Before we hung up he asked about this journal, though.

"What's up with the book on your nightstand?"

"What?" I asked, panicking a little when I remembered he was alone in my apartment Monday. In my room. With my journal. Just because he's my best friend doesn't mean I want him reading my thoughts. Especially ones about him.

"The diary or whatever it is on your nightstand."

"Did you read it?" I asked, horrified.

"No. What kind of dweeb picks up someone else's diary and reads it? Dang, Ty. Thanks for giving me some credit there."

I exhaled a sigh of relief. "No, it doesn't matter," I lied. "It's more of a work journal, actually. Laura gave us all one at the beginning of October. Everybody is always saying we should write a book because we encounter so many unique people with such interesting stories. So Laura told us to try and write a little about each wedding after it happened so we'd remember the details."

"Oh, so it's only about work stuff?" He sounded disappointed.

"Yeah, pretty much." I lied again. Well, not exactly a *lie*. It is about work stuff. Mostly. Partly. Some.

"Well, that's disappointing. I thought maybe you'd written about your hot, desirable best friend and how you're secretly crushing on him and wanting to take him down in the throes of passion."

"Yep. Busted. That's what I've been writing. In between you snoring and drooling on my couch and making my sheets smell like sweat. You caught me."

"I don't smell like sweat," he argued.

I wondered if he had read anything. If I was in his room and a journal was laying there, I would be reading that bad boy cover to cover. No way could I leave it uncracked. I wondered if he was really that much stronger or more honorable than me. I mean, it's not like there's anything incriminating in it. I haven't done anything to be incriminated for, but still. It's kind of private, and I hope he didn't read it.

"Alright, Buttercup," he said. "I gotta go roll out pie crusts. If you don't have anything to do after you leave Melanie and Paul's, swing by or give me a call. Tell Mel hey for me. And happy Thanksgiving, Ty."

"You too, Cabe."

There are many things in my life I am thankful for. He is definitely one of them.

Friday, November 29th

Oh boy. Oh Lord. Oh no. Oh dear. Oh God.

What do I do? What do I do? What do I do?

Cabe texted during my wedding to tell me he would be at my place with dinner and a movie when I got home.

He'd already finished a few drinks by the time I arrived, and he acted a little more buzzed than I'm used to seeing him. Especially since he was drinking alone.

"How was your wedding this evening, Ms. Wedding Planner?" he asked as he put a glass of wine in my hand.

"Good. Down the aisle, two 'I Dos', and they danced the night away. Another happy couple sent into wedded bliss," I said.

He toasted my glass and swigged deeply from his gin and tonic. I didn't even bother taking a sip from mine because I knew I needed to eat something first.

"Wow, chicken marsala," I said as I sat at the table. "You remembered my favorite. Aren't you sweet?" I was a bit surprised he made the dish since it's not something he likes.

"Hopefully it's as good as you remember." He poured himself another drink. The bottle of gin on the counter looked nearly empty.

"Dude, are you planning on being conscious for the movie? How many have you had?"

"We are celebrating, my dear. I haven't counted how many, and I'm not finished." He put his plate on the table and took a long swallow from his glass before sitting.

"Oh? Okay. What are we celebrating?" I felt more than a little concerned. We've celebrated many things over the years, but this was not his usual celebratory mood.

131

"As of today, I am no longer a married man. I signed the papers and Fed Ex'd them to the attorney. Everything is now finalized. They've been waiting for me. I've been waiting . . . on God only knows what. So a toast—" he raised his glass and motioned for me to raise mine—"to the end of my ill-fated marriage."

"Cabe, I'm sorry. I didn't know." I wasn't sure whether I was supposed to toast or not. This didn't seem like a good celebration.

"How could you, Ty? I didn't tell you. I didn't tell anyone. When you get engaged, you let the whole world know. But when she leaves you for another woman and your divorce gets finalized, you're not quite so keen on getting the word out." He drained his glass and shuddered.

I didn't know what to say or do. I could only imagine how horrible he must feel. I didn't know how to make it better. Saying "I'm sorry" is so inadequate sometimes.

"Well, maybe now you can move on," I said, and immediately ruled that inadequate as well.

He laughed, a sinister sort of chuckle that held no humor at all. "Right. Now I can move on! Now I am free to find the next woman who will trample my heart into a million pieces. I can start the whole dating nightmare again. I'm back on the market for all the bullshit that entails. Only now, I'm a marked man. I have a title. I am now Cabe Shaw comma divorced. And that 'comma, divorced' title automatically screams that I'm a failure at relationships." He got up and poured more gin than tonic in his glass.

"Cabe, divorce is so common these days. It doesn't brand you as a failure. It just means something didn't work out, that's all. You were open to love. You tried to make it work, and it didn't. Monica couldn't be completely vested in it. She had other stuff going on. That's not on you."

I stood and walked over to him, suddenly no longer hungry at all.

"Tyler, you've been out on dates. Be honest. If you find out a man is divorced, what is the first thing you think? Hmm? I waited until I was twenty-eight years old to get married. I didn't want to be divorced. I wanted to know when I said those vows, it was for keeps. Now I feel like I have this strike against me. Like I'm tainted." He essentially spit the words as he waved his glass in the air.

"I think anyone worth going out with will be willing to find out the truth. To get to know you and understand you. If not, they're not someone you should be dating. You're an incredible guy, Cabe. You truly are. I'm sorry this didn't work out. You put your heart out there, and it got broken. But it doesn't change who you are. It's not your label. Your title. It's just something that happened in your life."

"Easy for you to say, my dear. You're still single. You still get to check off the single box. I have to check off divorced from here on out," he said.

He walked back to the table, stumbling as he went.

There was nothing I could say. The best I could do was try to get his mind off this. I hoped getting some food in his stomach would at least help prevent a further drunken stupor. I thought maybe if I could get him safely to sleep for the night, he'd be better in the morning. Hungover, yes, but better. Things always look better in the morning, right?

We ate in silence. I'm sure it was delicious, but I didn't taste it. I kept watching Cabe.

I loaded the dishes in the dishwasher as he poured another drink, emptying the bottle. I wondered if he started with a full bottle when he got here. Cabe had never been a heavy drinker. If he drank a whole bottle of gin, it did not forebode well for the night ahead or the morning after.

"What movie did you get?" I asked.

"The Notebook."

"What? Are you freakin' insane? We're not watching The Notebook," I said.

He laughed, genuinely this time, though a bit more raucous than normal.

"I didn't get The Notebook. It's some Bruce Willis action thing. Blood and guts and shoot 'em up," he said.

"Good. I think you need some blood and guts right about now. I'm hoping you don't throw up your guts all over my sofa." I came and sat beside him, curling my legs underneath me. He rested his arm across my knee.

"No ma'am," he said. "I may not be able to hold onto my woman, but I'm still man enough to hold my liquor."

"Being a man has absolutely nothing to do with holding liquor, Cable Tucker Shaw. And your divorce has nothing to do with your manhood. You know that."

"Do I?" he asked. "Hmmph." He swirled the last of his drink around the ice cubes, staring into the liquid whirlpool.

I started the movie, knowing we probably wouldn't finish it. Not like either one of us really cared anyway. I'd never seen Cabe so messed up. I didn't know how to react. I felt sorry for him, angry that life dealt him these cards.

He slumped against my shoulder snoring not even halfway through the movie. My bottom leg fell asleep from being tucked under me so long, but I couldn't move without waking him because his arm was wrapped around my top knee. My leg slipped past numbness and into serious, aching pain. Plus, the glass of wine had gone right through me, and I seriously needed the restroom.

I tried to slide my leg out from under his arm, but pins and needles shot through me, and I jerked from the pain.

Cabe sat up and ran his hand through his hair, looking dazed and confused. He leaned back against the couch and closed his eyes again as I tried to stand without feeling my right leg. I hobbled down the hallway to the bathroom, limping on needles as the blood flow crept back through the muscles.

When I came back, he was lying on his side on the couch with his arm curled under his head. He opened his eyes, so I sat on the floor beside the couch and smiled at him.

"How you doin'?" I asked in my best impersonation of Joey from Friends.

"Great." He patted the couch beside him. "Come lay beside me."

"There's not room," I said. "These hips don't fit in that amount of space, dude."

"Come 'ere," he said.

He scooted as far as he could into the back of the couch as I sat beside him. "Lay down, Ty."

We've laid on the couch a million times, sprawled all over each other with feet, arms, and legs propped wherever was most comfortable. Something seemed different about this time, though. I hesitated and stayed put.

"Just hold me, Ty. I just want to be held." He lifted his left arm, and I shifted to lay facing him. He wrapped both arms around me and buried his face in my hair. He smelled of alcohol, cologne, and Cabe—a strangely intoxicating scent.

I tilted my head up to look at him, and before I even knew what was happening, we were kissing. His mouth closed over mine, his tongue sliding between my lips as though it was the most natural thing ever. I didn't resist. I don't know why. I know I should have. I should have been shocked. Indignant. Appalled. But a tiny little part of me had always wondered what it would be like to kiss Cabe. To be kissed by Cabe. I mean, we're just friends, and I'm perfectly fine with that. But can you ever really be friends with someone for so long, be around them so much, be so close, and not at least wonder what it would be like? I'm not saying I've been crushing on him or anything, but I'd be lying if I said I'd never thought about kissing him.

Can I just say, it was heavenly? For that brief moment before I came to my senses and ended it, it was this incredibly tender, passionate, seeking-needing-wanting-getting, kind of kiss. Nothing sloppy or all over my face. I've been kissed by a drunk guy or two in my day. There was nothing impaired going on here. He was playful and tentative as he explored with his tongue. I rolled mine against his, pushing my chest against him. Leaning into him. His hands stroked up and down my back, then into my hair to cup my head, pulling me closer still. His tongue retreated as his lips left mine to plant small kisses on my cheeks, my eyes, my forehead, and the tip of my nose. His mouth covered mine again, hungrier this time, more urgent.

It's been a long time since I've really been kissed. Really wanted to be kissed. Or even enjoyed kissing. But somewhere deep within my brain, an alarm sounded. This was Cabe. My best friend. We were crossing a line that couldn't be crossed. I pulled back from his mouth and placed my hand against his chest. He moved to kiss me again, but I pulled way back, scared if his lips touched mine again, I'd lose my resolve.

"Whoa, buddy. I think someone's had a bit too much to drink." I focused on mentally recited all the reasons I couldn't let him kiss me.

He was drunk, for one, which was enough reason on its own. He wasn't thinking clearly. Plus, I knew he'd been through an emotional wringer today. He needed to feel confident and desired. He was probably reaching out to get that without considering the consequences. This wasn't what he wanted. I mean, I'm sure in that moment it was what he wanted, but I knew in the grand scheme of life, it wasn't. I wasn't what he wanted. He needed affection and affirmation. He leaned forward and kissed the top of my head softly, still stroking my hair with his hand. I tried desperately to think of other reasons to say no.

We'd been friends through thick and thin, and we'd never gone anywhere near here. We couldn't go here now. It would change everything. Make everything awkward. It would introduce a whole other element into our relationship, but for all the wrong reasons. For Cabe, he was drunk and needed to feel like a man. For me, I hadn't had a decent date in over a year, and Cabe happened to be a damned good kisser.

So I pushed myself into a seated position and looked down at my best friend in the whole, wide world. He stared up at me with those intensely blue eyes, sad and bleary, searching my face as I searched his. His lips were swollen, and he looked so incredibly handsome I wavered a bit, almost willing to throw my sanity and reason to the wind for one night. Consequences be damned.

But it didn't feel right. Hell, I'd be basically be taking advantage of him since he wasn't in his right mind. I had to be the one to keep us on track. I tried to stand to walk away, but he caught my shoulder and pulled me down to meet him as he sat up. He kissed me again, not at all tentative this time. I tried hard to remember my own name, much less why I should not be allowing this man to continue doing something that felt so damned good. He shifted on the couch to pull me closer. Somehow, I resisted. From somewhere deep within my conscience, or perhaps from deep within my fears, I'm not sure which.

He opened his eyes and stared into mine, our faces still pressed close together. Close enough to feel his breath on my lips when he said, "Will you sleep with me?" His face clouded. His eyes grew dark. I saw desire there, but I also saw fear, rejection, and pain. "Ty? Will you sleep with me? Please?"

This was definitely not right. I turned away from him, but my legs felt shaky and I couldn't make myself stand. Waves of heat radiated from him, heat generated by our bodies so close together, and I scooted to the edge of the couch to try and get some distance between us. He reached to tuck a stray curl back behind my ear, and the caress of his fingers across my cheek sent a chill up my spine where the heat had been scorching me seconds before. I felt goosebumps explode across my skin, and I swallowed deeply before I turned to look at him, the words heavy in my throat.

"No, Cabe, I won't. Not because you're not man enough, or because you're not handsome enough, or desirable enough, or whatever else your screwed-up little brain is thinking right now. You are all those things and then some. It's not even because I don't want to. Because unfortunately, I would very much like to right now. But when we wake up in the morning, we'd look at each with regret. I don't want any regrets between us."

He slumped back down to the couch, but his eyes never left mine. His hand lingered lightly on my arm, his fingers tracing a circle across my skin as I struggled to continue, my voice cracking slightly when I spoke. "It'd be a line we couldn't uncross. It'd change everything, Cabe. Change us. I'm not willing to lose what we have just because you're drunk and I haven't had sex in a really long time. We mean so much more than that to me. And to you, too. Only you can't see that right now in your current state." I shot an exaggerated glance at his crotch and raised my eyebrows. "Mental and otherwise." I smiled as I looked up, hoping my joke made it more lighthearted.

He stared at me for a moment before his fingers left my arm, leaving a cold space where his warmth had been. He turned his head into the couch and crossed his arm over his face. I felt embarrassed suddenly, sitting there watching him as he dealt with rejection, mine and hers. I got up and went to brush my teeth and take my makeup off, leaving him in his pain since I couldn't take it away.

When I walked back in to say good night, he was asleep, his breathing steady and deep. I pulled a blanket from the closet and spread it over him. Then I leaned down and kissed the top of his head. Now he is out there, on my couch, sleeping away the night, while I am in here, in my bed, writing this and unable to sleep. I am so scared tomorrow we'll be different. I feel like I just got him back. It was so hard when he pulled away from me for her. Even harder still when he left, and I knew he was gone. I could feel his absence like a physical pain. Now he's here. He's back. Wounded, to be sure, but back. I can't risk letting anything else come between us. Not even us.

I wonder what he'll say in the morning. Will he be embarrassed? Will he be mad? Will he even remember? Ugh. I dread it. Cabe is the best relationship I've ever had. I so hope it's not all screwed up. I feel all Harry and Sally right now. Why can't men and women just be friends? Why does desire, sex, and wanting ever have to creep in? I mean, it's not like it's all his fault. I definitely didn't push him away right off the bat. But we've been up close and personal so many times before, and nothing has happened. We've never gone there. Maybe the curiosity built up, and now that we've dangled off the ledge, we'll be fine.

Man, that boy sure knows how to kiss.

Will I ever look at those lips again without remembering them on mine? Without tasting him in my mind?

He's touched me a million times before. Will he be able to touch me again without my skin feeling like it's on fire even as it ripples with chills and goosebumps?

Oh God, what have I done?

I hope he doesn't remember.

I hope I can forget.

Saturday, November 30th

When I woke this morning, he was gone. The blanket lay folded on the couch, the gin bottle had disappeared, and the kitchen was spotless. He left no note at all. My stomach twisted and clenched not knowing what he might be thinking. I waffled back and forth all morning about whether or not to call him. I got so distracted by it I put shaving cream in my hair instead of conditioner and forgot to turn on the coffee pot. So I headed out the door at least twenty minutes late with no coffee, already dreading calling Lillian to tell her I wouldn't be on time.

Luckily, her voice mail picked up, so I left a message. I don't know how Cabe fared this morning, but I felt run over by a Mack truck even though I only drank one glass of wine. I knew my condition had nothing to do with the wine, though. More likely lack of sleep. When I did finally doze off, I spent the night in and out of weird dreams that left me exhausted and worn out when I woke.

I started to text him when I got in the car, but I didn't want to be the first to make contact without knowing where he was with everything. Oh God. It was awkward already.

I jumped when the phone rang and answered it without even looking at the screen. I really need to stop doing that.

"You're not going to believe what I found out last night," Mama said. Bless her heart, she was about the last person I wanted to talk to right then. I figured whatever grapevine news she had to spread couldn't possibly hold my interest this morning. But boy, life sure has a way of catching you off guard, doesn't it?

"Guess who is officially divorced?" she asked.

At the time, I thought I honestly couldn't care less.

"I don't know, Mama. I'm on my way to work. Can I call you later?"

138

"Oh, you're gonna want to hear this. Are you sitting down?"

For a moment, I thought it may be one of my sisters, but not even my mother would be excited over one of her own daughters losing her marriage. I mean, the woman loves a good piece of gossip, but still. It wasn't one of my sisters, though.

"Dwayne Davis. Ellain left him for some truck driver over in Walton. Took both kids with her. I guess they've been keeping it all hush-hush since his mama is so sick with the cancer, but I stopped by the post office and Dwayne came in and told me all about it. She's been gone a couple of months. The divorce is already final. They just ain't told nobody."

My mind reeled. I screeched to a halt as I nearly ran a red light, whipping my head from side to side to watch for someone ready to slam into me or give me a ticket. Thankfully, the intersection was empty.

I don't fully understand why this news affected me, but so many emotions flooded through me all at once. Way too much for my tired brain to process.

"I didn't know his mama had cancer," I managed to say, trying to stop my hands from shaking on the wheel. I really should not have been driving.

So Dwayne was divorced. The woman he left me for, the marriage he left me for, had ended. (Is it just me, or is there a recurring theme happening in my life?)

"Oh yeah," Mama said. "She's been getting the chemo for about six months. I thought I told you. Don't you remember she got sick at the music festival and passed out? They thought she just got dehydrated? I know I told you. Well, maybe I told your sister Tanya. I was sure I told you, though."

I did feel bad for Dwayne's mama, but my brain kept screaming "Dwayne got divorced!"

I know this shouldn't have mattered to me in the least. We broke up so long ago, and my life is in a totally different place.

Some part of it, I am sure, was just pure evil joy that the relationship he replaced me with had failed. I admit that isn't a very nice way for me to feel, but oh well. His marriage hurt me on so many levels, and finding out it wasn't a happily-ever-after gave me some small measure of justice.

And as long as I'm being honest, I think part of my reaction to the news was because Dwayne was my first love. The first guy I gave my heart to, among other things. I think the girl I was back then will always hold a spot for him. I'm not saying I'm still carrying a torch for the guy, but I think first love is a powerful thing. So maybe in place of the torch, there is still a miniscule little flicker in my heart when it comes to Dwayne. A remnant of a flame perhaps. A burnt spot that's still tender.

I pulled into the parking lot at the convention center and pinned on my name tag, sticking myself in the process.

"Ouch!" I yelped, putting my finger in my mouth. "Mama, I gotta go. I'm late for work. I'll call you later." I locked the car door and started to walk as fast as possible toward the main lobby doors.

"Okay. I'll be at bingo tonight, but I should be home by eight if you want to call me then."

"Alright, Mama. I gotta go. Love you. Bye."

"Bye. Oh, and he asked for your number, so he's probably gonna call. Love you, bye."

"What!" I stopped in my tracks. "What? Mama? Mama? What?"

She had gone. My phone rang, and I answered, hoping Mama had called back but got Lillian instead.

"Where are you?"

"I'm walking in now. Be right there," I answered.

Pre-ceremony photos took forever. I felt certain I would throw up before they ended. I can't even describe my relief when Lillian asked me to cover the reception side. She normally doesn't like being among all the guests on the ceremony side, but this wedding brought a crapload of set-up for their reception. She wanted nothing to do with that. I welcomed it, though. Being busy would keep my mind off Dwayne and Cabe. Plus, doing set-up in the dinner room gave me a chance to be a bit more isolated. I was in no mood to fake a smile for a bunch of happy people while sending a bride down the aisle to almost certain doom.

I had just finished the place cards and started unwrapping the guest book when the phone rang. I saw the area code and knew immediately. I shouldn't have answered it. I know that. I knew that when it rang. But sometimes I don't always do what I should, and Dwayne Davis finally called me after telling me he needed time all those years ago. Nothing this side of hell could have kept me from answering that call.

"Hello?" I tried to sound confident. Or maybe sexy. Or maybe clueless as to who it was. Or to make an audible sound that didn't sound completely unintelligent.

"Well, hello darlin'."

It's been over five years. His voice rasped exactly the same as I remembered it. And I remembered it well. I wasn't going to tell him that, though. This was the complete and total A-hole who dumped me to marry someone else only a month later. The man who pummeled my heart and shattered the dreams of my youth.

"Who's this?" I asked, hoping it sounded nonchalant.

"You don't know who this is? I woulda thought you'd remember me. Has it been that long, darlin'?"

I hated him for his cocky self-assurance. I despised him calling me *darlin'* and acting like I should be happy to hear from him. Yet, in the deep recesses of my heart, a poor, broken-hearted, little lovesick girl jumped up and down at the sound of his voice. I think she must have been trapped in cobwebs all these years waiting for the call to come. I mentally told her to sit down and shut the hell up.

"I'm sorry, who is this?" I asked, determined to play this cool at all costs.

"Guurrl, you know who this is. How you been?"

Maybe his thick, Southern drawl did sound slower and more syrupy than I remembered. I wondered if time away from him had changed my memory or if he laid it on thicker for my benefit.

"I'm doing great, Dwayne. And you?"

"I'm doing good, darlin'. Surviving. Which is all any of us can do, ain't it? You heard about Mama?"

"Yes, I did. I was real sorry to hear. How's she holding up?"

"Oh, you know. She's tough as nails. Ain't nothin' can keep that woman down. She's driving Daddy nuts 'cause she won't stay off her feet and rest. She'll be fine. Too stubborn for cancer to take her out."

"Yeah," I said, smiling at the thought of his mama and her steely reserve.

"Granny's doing good, too," he said. "Gonna outlive us all, I swear."

He knew I'd been close with Mrs. Dolores. I thought again of that day in the grocery store, and my anger flared anew.

"How's your wife?" I asked, forcing him to admit the truth for the evil little part of me who was happy his marriage had ended.

"Ex-wife. I thought your mama would've told you. We didn't make it. Gave it our best try. I got two beautiful baby girls, though. They're my focus now. Making sure them babies are okay. What about you? Your mama said you ain't got married yet?"

I knew he was a daddy, but to hear him talk about his girls tugged at my heartstrings. I thought for so long I'd have his babies. Pain, anger, and loss washed over me as memories came flooding back.

I wish I'd been strong enough to hang up the phone. To not even talk to him or listen to him. Not give him any more space in my head. But this was the love of my life. Or so I had thought at one time. The boy I built all my dreams around. The one who nearly destroyed me. I could no more hang up on him in that moment than I could stop breathing.

In some twisted train of thought, I wanted to hear his voice just as much as I wanted to never hear it again. I felt happy he reached out to me. That he hadn't forgotten me. And stupidly enough, I felt some small measure of victory that the woman he left me for didn't get him in the end.

"Hello? You still there, girl?" he asked.

"Um, yeah. I mean, I'm still here, but no, I'm not married. I'm at work, though. I can't really talk right now."

"Alright. Well, I only wanted to say hey and see how you're doin'. Your mama said you wouldn't mind if I called."

"Oh, really?" I silently cursed my mother.

"Can I call you later?" he asked.

Tell him no, tell him no, tell him no, my brain screamed. "Sure," my mouth said.

When we hung up, I realized I had missed three calls from Lillian. She was going to kill me. I deleted the missed call notification from my phone and decided to play stupid.

I rushed into the dinner room to get everything set up, but my mind felt too fried to think. Between Cabe and the kissing and Dwayne and the darlin' talk, I didn't know if I was coming or going. Of course, a Lillian wedding automatically guaranteed I would screw up something even without the lack of sleep and the boy drama.

Boy, did I ever screw up. Big time. Really big.

One of the responsibilities for the reception side of the event is checking the table numbers against the table diagram to ensure each table is in the right place in the room. We usually have the hotel's table stands with numbers on them, but this couple had gotten really crafty and created centerpieces that incorporated names of locations they had visited. An Eiffel Tower and beret for Paris, a Statue of Liberty for New York, a miniature street car for San Francisco. The florist had taken the empty containers to fill with flowers and place in the room. We kept the little name signs so we could place them with the correct box and on the right table in the room according to the bride's diagram.

What a crazy day. Little details hiccupped everywhere. I felt pulled in a million directions trying to get every fire put out. I'd met with Stephanie and Tanner, the bride and groom, many times during their planning visits with Lillian, so I felt a personal connection with them. I wanted their day to go well, but I wasn't on my best game and things out of my control kept happening.

The van bringing the cake got rear-ended, which messed up the back of the bottom layer. One of the engraved toasting glasses came out of the box with the stem broken. We could get a replacement set but couldn't get them engraved. Three table linens were a different shade of ivory than the rest. Not too noticeable when the lights dimmed, but decisions had to be made on where to place them in the room for the least impact.

When the florist arrived with the centerpiece bases, I gave them the name signs and told them I'd be right back to help place them against the diagram. Unfortunately, I got busy greeting the guests as they arrived at the cocktail reception, sorting out a place card snafu, and gathering up the clothes and belongings the limo brought from the church dressing room. At some point in the chaos, one of the floral assistants told me she set the stands for me and double-checked each one. I thanked her profusely, but being the control freak I am, I fully intended to double-check for myself to see that it had been done right. Especially with the way things were going today.

But it didn't happen. Somehow one thing led to another and before I knew it, the time had slipped away. Stephanie decided she wanted her wedding party to wait and make their grand entrance at the dinner reception, so I scrambled to find an available banquet room for them, get a table and chairs set up, and have servers come and pass the hors d'oeuvres. I got their drink orders and had the bartender make up a tray of drinks and got a server to bring them. I got all the bridesmaids' bouquets and purses and deposited them at the head table. Then I helped Lillian bring in the other ceremony items from her car.

Lillian moved the guests into the dinner room while I bustled Stephanie's gown. Our DJ and emcee lined up the wedding party and verified the pronunciation of their names, and soon we were all standing outside the dinner room waiting for the announcements to begin. At least the chaos drove the men in my life from my mind momentarily.

As the DJ walked back to his microphone to start announcements, I asked the parents of the groom and parents of the bride if they knew where to find their tables. As I always do in case they haven't seen the dinner room. I never want them walking into a dark room as everyone cheers and claps only to find they have no idea where to go. I whipped out my room diagram and verified the groom's parents were seated at the London Table, and the bride's parents were seated at Cancun.

As I looked into the darkness to point out their tables, I realized something was terribly wrong. London and Cancun should have both been immediately adjacent to the head table. Front and center of the room between the wedding party and the dance floor. Prominently placed as the hosts of the party and the parents of the event's honored couple.

But the table that should have been London was already filled and clearly marked Boston. Where Cancun should have been was the New Orleans table, filled with those business associates who were so angry about the place cards.

Panic rose in my throat as the DJ greeted the guests and asked any lingerers to be seated for the announcement of the wedding party, my mouth going dry and nausea sweeping over me as I looked at the diagram in my hand and then back at the room in front of me. Not one single table in the right place.

The bride's parents had been relocated to the back corner of the room, near the bar. The groom's parents were a bit closer to the head table, but in the middle of the room and off to the side. The extended families were scattered throughout the room with no rhyme or reason.

As the groom's parents were announced, his mother grabbed my arm and said, "Where? Where do we go? You didn't tell us."

My mind frantically searched for a solution but found none. My job depends on me being able to think on my feet, to come up with solutions where none seem possible, and at all costs, to figure out how to keep the guests, the parents, and the bride and groom from ever realizing there is a problem. I had failed on so many levels. There was no way to fix this.

My shaking hand pointed to the London Table on the left side of the room as the guests stood to their feet and welcomed the groom's parents with thunderous applause. The groom's mother had never seen the diagram, so she had no idea her table was incorrect.

But when I turned back to face the bride's mother, we locked eyes and I had no doubt she knew. She pored over those lists of seating arrangement for months with her daughter. She knew where the groom's parents should be, and she could clearly see her table—the one right in front of her daughter and new son-in-law—already filled. I pointed to the Cancun Table all the way across the back of the room as the DJ announced them as the hosts of the evening.

She glared at me with a shocked expression as her husband pulled her arm and escorted her across the room to the back corner. Tears sprang to my eyes, and I fought the urge to throw up. Lillian's eyes followed the parents' path across the room and looked at me in confusion.

"Where are they going? Why is their table there?"

We had no time to talk as the DJ announced the first wedding party couple into the room dancing and shouting. I couldn't hear Lillian's questions over the roar of the crowd, but I clearly heard the bride's voice in my ear as she grabbed my arm.

"Tyler! It's wrong! The tables are wrong! My parents are in the back, and Tanner's parents are in the wrong place, too. It's all wrong. What happened?"

She looked bewildered. She put so much time into carefully placing each guest in a specific location, laboring to put family members in close proximity and acquaintances from work or college near each other to encourage mingling. The hard work and creativity they put into the centerpieces had gone awry, and it was all my fault. When the DJ introduced Mr. & Mrs. Tanner Jordan, Stephanie's face clouded over with tears, confusion, hurt and anger. Not the face of a beautiful bride ready to celebrate.

As soon as the doors closed behind them, I slid down the wall to the floor. My tears poured. This was a huge mistake. The entire room full of people already drank the water, ordered the wine, used the napkins, and settled in at their tables. No way to ask them to move to different seats at different tables. No way to drag the parents back to their rightful place in front of the head table or insult the guests at those prime tables by telling them they had displaced the parents and were meant to be put in the corner. It was done.

I had ruined their wedding.

People don't get it. They say it's "just a wedding." They diminish the details as trivial. But to a bride, each little detail is a component of a larger picture. A larger experience. A dream she holds in her heart of a magical day and how it will look. How it will sound. How it will be remembered.

All the planning. All the dreaming. All the details now overshadowed by the room configuration and everyone's emotions about it. Her parents were pissed. Understandably so. This was their only child. Their only wedding to host. And they were banished to the back corner of the room.

"What happened?" Lillian asked. My head snapped up as I remembered I still had to explain this to Lillian.

"I didn't check the diagram. I am so sorry, Lillian." I burst into tears again.

Lillian grabbed my arm by the elbow and lifted me gently to my feet. She leaned in close to my ear and whispered, "Take yourself to the restroom, splash your face, and dry your eyes. Meet me in the back hallway. Now go."

I nodded and headed to the restroom, trying not to make eye contact with the various employees and random people staring at me. I splashed water on my face and dried it with a paper towel, picking off the little random spots of paper that stuck to the dark circles under my eyes and the puffiness of my cheeks. When I came out of the bathroom to face the music, Renee the florist stood just outside the bathroom door with two crying members of her floral team.

"I'm sorry, Tyler," Renee said. "Evidently, we double-checked each sign against the box to make sure it matched the city name on the bottom of the box, but Addie failed to use the room diagram when she put them on the tables.

This made Addie cry harder, so I reached over and gave her a big hug.

"It's not your fault," I said. "I should have checked it. It's my responsibility."

"Well, we should have known," Renee said. "It's not like all the centerpieces were the same and it didn't matter which table they were on. Any time there are custom centerpieces, they need to be set according to the diagram."

She seemed to say that more to her team than to me, but I knew it was ultimately my fault.

I took a deep breath and squared my shoulders to go wait for Lillian in the back hallway. Before I could get there, she came out of the dinner room toward me, motioning and gesturing for me to come to her. Quickly.

I sped up my stride, apologizing again before I even reached her. She brushed away my words with a sweep of her hand and a shake of her head. She took me by the hand and led me into the dinner room.

"Stephanie has requested to speak with you," she said.

I almost turned and ran. I didn't want to face Stephanie. She'd been so nice throughout the entire planning process. Now I had let her down and ruined her day. So imagine my surprise when instead of anger or venom, Stephanie and Tanner greeted me with smiles and enveloped me in a huge hug.

"Tyler! You poor thing!" Stephanie said. "Lillian told us you've been running around trying to fix the cake, the toasting glasses, and everything else. No wonder you didn't have time to check the centerpieces. I'm so sorry you've had such a stressful day. Ours has been great, and that's because of you and Lillian. I haven't been stressed. I haven't been worried. I've had a wonderful day. If these tables are the worst of it, then I'm happy. My dad's boss moved everyone from their table, and Tanner's mom asked their neighbors to move. It's all good. We're married. We're all in the same room. Nothing else matters. Please don't be upset." Stephanie squeezed my hands in her own.

Tanner lifted his glass in the air. "Hey, I just got married! As long as the DJ's playing music, the bar's serving Heineken, and she's by my side, everything's okay!"

I didn't know what to say. We work with some of the nastiest, rudest, most ungrateful people on the planet. I get yelled at and cursed at for things beyond my control all the time. Yet on this day, when I got distracted and just plain screwed up, they offered me forgiveness and kindness. I'm used to standing up straight and staying calm through the cursing. The graciousness totally threw me.

As I drove home thinking back on the night, I felt grateful I'd been offered forgiveness, but I wasn't sure I wanted to forgive Dwayne. I wondered when and if he would call again. As if I haven't wasted enough time wondering when that man would call. At the same time, I was very painfully aware Cabe had been a no-show all day. No text. No call.

December

Sunday, December 1st

The doorbell this morning interrupted what might have been my deepest, most serene state of sleep ever. I heard the chime coming from the end of a long, dark tunnel, but I had no desire to go and find out what caused it. I'm not sure how many times it rang before I finally came out of the fog enough to realize someone was at my door. I squinted at the clock. 9:07 am. The doorbell chimed again.

I stumbled to the door yawning and wondering who in the hell would be ringing my doorbell on a Sunday morning. I looked through the peephole and stepped back in shock. I would not have been more surprised if Abraham Lincoln had been standing there, hat in hand.

Lillian stood on the other side, looking at her watch in a most irritated fashion. My brain panicked thinking I'd missed a wedding or a meeting. I replayed our conversations of last night, but after the dinner got underway, she didn't say much to me and sent me home early. I admit I was definitely not all there last night, but I think I would have remembered agreeing to meet her this morning. At my house no less. She had never even been here.

Realizing I had kept her waiting for quite a while, I flung open the door, hoping there were no dirty dishes in sight.

She had turned away, and I swear she almost looked disappointed when I opened it, as though she had been relieved to find me not home.

"Lillian?"

"Good morning, Tyler. I'm sorry I woke you. I forget the rest of the world does not awaken with the sunrise. I wanted to take you to breakfast," she said.

Shocked again. This had never happened.

"Oh, okay. I need to get dressed," I said. How funny that I never even stopped to question whether or not I wanted to go to breakfast or why she was asking. Lillian stood in my doorway telling me we were going to breakfast. All I needed to know.

"Would you like to come in while I get dressed?" I took a step back so she could enter. She hesitated for a moment and then cautiously stepped inside. I wondered with a mental smirk if she would turn up her nose at entering a "peasant's domicile."

"I'll only be a minute. Have a seat."

I stripped off my PJs and pulled a dress over my head in record time. In less than five minutes, I had my hair combed, teeth brushed, and a fresh coat of mascara on my eyes. They were swollen and puffy from crying last night and my abrupt wake-up this morning.

Lillian still stood just inside the door where I had left her. She seemed out of place.

"Ready?" she asked, turning to open the door as though she could not wait to leave.

"Where are we going?" I was still somewhat in a sleepy haze and a curious daze as to why I was leaving my house with Lillian.

"I don't care. Wherever you'd like," she answered.

We ended up at a small cafe a few blocks over, where we sat in awkward silence as we sipped our coffee and stared out the windows. Finally, she spoke.

"I'm worried about you," she said. "You seem very distracted lately. Making mistakes that are quite uncharacteristic. What's going on?"

I groaned inside—not audibly, of course—and wished I could crawl under the table.

"I am really sorry about last night," I started to say, but she interrupted me before I could finish.

"I didn't drive over to your apartment and bring you out of bed to chastise you for last night's errors. I am worried about you. What's going on?"

Lillian was definitely the last person on earth I would ever think of unloading all my troubles on, but before I knew what was happening, I had poured them out to her over blueberry pancakes. Dwayne and our marriage that didn't happen, his that did happen but didn't last. Cabe and our friendship, his marriage and divorce, and the kiss. My mother and my dead daddy. The life I thought I was gonna have and the life I am scared I may never have. All of it. Through it all, she ate her omelet and drank her coffee, occasionally nodding and sometimes slightly raising one eyebrow.

When I had given her every last detail of every last thing going on, she sat back and calmly folded her napkin.

"Tyler, what do you want to do with your life?"

Not what I expected her to say. "What?"

"Your life. Not Dwayne's life, or Cabe's life or your mother's life. Your life. What do *you* want to do with *your* life?"

I realized I didn't have an answer for her. I didn't know. I think for most of high school and college, I had wanted to be whatever it took to be with Dwayne. Then after that ended, I wanted to be whatever it took to be far away from him and everything associated with him. I kind of floated along in recovery mode until Cabe left, and then all my focus and energy had shifted to getting over that. Since he got back, I've spent most of my time trying to help him be okay.

I didn't really have a clear direction in mind for me. I enjoyed my job, but I hadn't set any job goals and didn't know what I wanted to do beyond this. I hadn't finished college, and my original choice of degree—nursing—no longer interested me. I only chose that because Mama said I'd be able to get a job wherever Dwayne did and work around his hours.

"I don't know," I answered. I felt ashamed.

"Well, then you need to figure it out. This is your life, Tyler. No one else's. The other people in your life are going to make decisions based on what they want in their life. Always. Even when it seems like they are interested in you, even when they genuinely do care about you, they are still going to make their decisions based on what works best for them. So you have to figure out what works for you. What will get you where you want to be. Then make sure any decision you make, no matter how small, will take you toward it."

My eyes welled up with tears from the lack of sleep, the overwhelming emotions of the last two days, and the fact that the one person who intimidated me most in the world was sitting across my pancakes from me asking deep life questions I had no answers for.

"Figure out who you are, Tyler. Allow these young men to figure out who they are. You are not defined by them. You are defined by you and the decisions you make." She paused as the server cleared her plate and refilled her coffee.

"I made the mistake once of choosing my life path based on what I thought a man wanted and what I thought I would have with him if I chose it. I learned the hard way the lesson I am trying to give you now. People will do what is best for them, even when it is not what is best for you. This Dwayne you thought you were to marry. Did he not make his choice without thought to you and your feelings?"

I nodded.

"And Cabe? He chose his path in life, to go to Seattle and marry this woman? Did he base that on what worked best for you?"

I absentmindedly nodded, then realized it was the incorrect response and quickly shook my head.

"They won't. Because they are making their decisions based on what is best for them. Now, if you have a firm idea of where you are headed, what you want to achieve, and where you want to be, and then you find a man who fits in that plan and supports you in reaching it—well, then by all means, have at him. But make it a conscious choice, Tyler. Be sure he is what you want. He needs to fit in your future. Don't just latch on to whoever is there, compromising your goals and yourself because you fancy accommodating him will be what is best. I did that. I can tell you it doesn't work."

"How did you meet your husband?" I asked.

"Remy?" She looked shocked, then raised both eyebrows and scrunched her face like she had to think about it in order to remember.

"We worked together. His father owned the hotel where I worked as an executive. I had the utmost respect for Remy's father, and he for me. I think he feared what would happen when he died and Remy took over the business. In some ways, I provided an insurance policy to ensure his legacy would survive. And it has. Without me, it seems."

She sipped her coffee and looked out the window. How odd that her answer seemed more about her father-in-law and less about her husband.

"Did you love him?" I asked.

"My dear, we are not here because I slid down walls in my business suit last night. Any love life of mine is ancient history and best not discussed lest the cobwebs overtake us both. Now, I have an assignment for you. I want you to come up with goals for your life. What do you want to achieve? Where do you want to be? In regards to travel, status, job, location, life? Write down some goals. Where you want to find yourself in three years, five years, ten. Where you want to be in a year. Then figure out the steps necessary to get you there. I will be more than happy to help you with that part if you wish, but you simply must have a destination before you can map out the trip."

Lillian gathered her purse and left a generous tip under her saucer. I took one last bite of the pancakes and drained the rest of my coffee before following her out.

We drove back to my apartment in silence.

"How did you know where I live?" I asked as she pulled into the parking lot.

"I am your employer, dear. I do have your address, and technology-challenged though I may be, I can use my GPS."

"Right. Got it."

"Now, you have the afternoon off, I believe. So you have plenty of time to figure out who Tyler wants to be. Until you know that, leave these silly men to their own devices. When you have yourself all figured out, there'll be plenty of time for them. You may be surprised what caliber of men you can attract when you know what you want."

I thanked her for breakfast and got out of the car feeling drained. The whole situation with Cabe, the past dredged up in Dwayne's call, and the disastrous wedding last night gave me a lot to process. Now to have Lillian show up on my doorstep with pep talks and life lessons proved too much. I considered taking her advice and writing out some goals, mostly out of fear she would ask for them tomorrow. But then I fell asleep.

I woke up around six, starving and needing a shower. My phone showed four missed calls. One from an unknown number, one from my mother and two from Cabe.

Guess who I called back?

"What's up, Buttercup?" he said.

I worried he might launch into an apology or an awkward conversation about the drunken events Friday night. He didn't. He rattled on about the football game he was watching for a few minutes before I blurted out, "Dwayne called."

"What? Like, Dweeb Dwayne?"

"Yes, Dweeb Dwayne. He got divorced and thought he'd call to say hi."

"Wow. No shit. When?"

"When did he get divorced or when did he call?" I asked.

"Both."

"He got divorced like a month ago, I guess, and he called yesterday."

"Okay. How'd that go?"

"Weird as all hell. He kept calling me darlin' and he asked if I was married."

"Really. How'd he get your number?"

"My mother gave it to him."

Cabe snorted on the other end of the line and said, "Nice!"

"I know, right? Strange hearing his voice after all this time. Surreal. Suddenly talking to him and hearing him. Took me back."

Cabe was silent.

"So yeah. That was my fun weekend highlight." I winced a bit as I said it, hoping the comment didn't lead into a conversation about our encounter on Friday night.

I certainly enjoyed kissing Cabe more than listening to Dwayne, but I didn't think it quite appropriate to mention that. Nor did I think I should tell him about completely destroying someone's wedding thanks to him and Dwayne screwing with my head. Or my boss showing up unannounced on a Sunday morning to tell me to drop all the men in my life and get a life of my own.

"Stellar," Cabe said. "Sounds like good times. You okay?"

"Yeah. I am. Just shaken up, I guess. He asked if he could call again."

"I hope you told him hell-to-the-no! What is he thinking?" Cabe said.

I rolled my eyes and bit my bottom lip, embarrassed to admit I'd said yes. Cabe read the answer in my silence.

"Oh no. Ty, you didn't say he could call you again? Why? Why would you do that? You've finally gotten over the guy and stopped moping around about him. You don't need him in your life. The dude dumped you. He left you for another woman. He doesn't get to just show up when he's done with her and pick back up where he left off."

"Nobody said he's picking back up where he left off, okay? I am well aware he dumped me, thank you very much. He caught me off guard. I didn't know what to say," I said.

"You just say screw you. It's pretty simple."

"Really? So if Monica called tonight and asked if she could call again sometime, you'd say screw you?"

More silence.

"I don't know what I'd say," Cabe finally said. "But I really hope I'd say no. I hope I'd tell her to kiss my ass and not give her the satisfaction of thinking I've been sitting here waiting for her to call."

"I don't think I gave him that impression, Cabe. I told him I was at work. He asked if he could call again. He probably just wants to catch up. He's bummed about his divorce and wants to talk someone."

Cabe laughed a sinister chuckle. "Yeah, okay. You just happen to be who he wants to talk to five years after walking out on you to marry someone he cheated with? Come on, Ty. Don't let this guy sucker you in. You're smarter than that."

As much as I hear what Lillian and Cabe are both saying, and as much as I know they're right, I can't *not* talk to Dwayne Davis. Call me a moth, call him a flame. But if that boy calls, I'll answer.

Monday, December 2nd

I didn't have to wait long this time. Cabe and I went bowling after work. Cabe had just left to head back to his mom's when my phone rang, so I figured he forgot something. I picked up the phone and said, "Hey! What's up?"

"Nothing much, darlin'. What's up with you?"

That familiar drawl immediately put a smile on my face. Am I crazy for that? I know it's been a long time, and I know he did me wrong. But back in the day, this was my guy. My first love. The one who made my heart beat faster. Old habits die hard.

"Just got home," I answered. "I went bowling."

I don't why I felt the need to add that. I think I wanted to let him know I had stuff happening. Out and about on the town. Not sitting home waiting for his call. Although now that I think about it, bowling doesn't exactly scream life of the party with a kicking social calendar.

"Bowling, huh? I haven't been bowling in years. Do you still throw the ball under-handed and use the bumper guards?"

I laughed, remembering how foolish I must have looked as a college student using bumper guards. "No, I've graduated to holding the ball with my fingers and throwing the proper way. You'd be proud of me. I even have a nice little dip thing going with my ankle crossing behind me. I look hot bowling."

Okay, as if it's not bad enough that I tossed out bowling as my social event to identify with, I professed that I look hot doing it.

"You always looked hot bowling, darlin'. Hell, you looked hot no matter what you was doin'. You tore the hell outta some bumper guards, that's all." He laughed, and I laughed with him.

Crazy or not, I felt young again. Beautiful. Wanted. Adored. All the

155

things he used to make me feel when life was fresh and opportunities lay endlessly out in front of us. Before I knew what love could do to you.

"At least I never bowled in cowboy boots," I said, full-on flirting and teasing.

"I wouldn't be caught dead in them sissified bowling shoes. They was like fourteen different colors. What if lightning struck me dead and I had to be buried in them shoes?"

"Yes, because they have so many lightning strikes inside bowling alleys. Besides, just because you got struck in those shoes doesn't mean they would bury you in them." I said.

"Well, I sure as hell hope not. I wanna be buried in my boots."

"I am sure you will be, Dwayne Davis." I laughed.

"I love the way you say my name. You know, the first and last name together like that. Nobody says my name the way you do," he said softly.

If I was crazy, then so be it. My heart soared on cloud nine. It seemed like no time had passed, no hurts had been done, and no life-shattering betrayal had ever happened. I realize it did happen, and this was probably an unhealthy phone call to indulge in, but God, it felt so good. I was taken back to a different time in life on that call, and it was freakin' awesome.

"How's your mama doin'?" I felt my drawl creeping in, as it often does when I talk to someone with a thick Southern accent. I had all but lost mine since moving here, but I slipped back into it easy as pie when I heard it.

"She's hangin'. Tough as ever. I told her I talked to you. She said hey."

I wondered what Martha Jean thought of him talking to me, if she had liked his wife and if she was okay with how he ended things with me. I always thought she and I had a pretty good relationship, but when I never heard one word from her after he broke things off, it added to the confusion and betrayal I felt.

"Tell her I said hello. I hope she's feeling better soon."

"I see your brother every now and then," Dwayne said. "Hard to believe he's in college. Makes me feel old. I remember him riding around with us all the time. Never shut up!"

I laughed as memories warmed my heart. So many good times. I had been deliriously happy once. I'd kept those happy memories stuffed deep inside me, scared to allow them to surface. Remembering good times with Dwayne always intertwined with the pain of him leaving, so I made a conscious effort to never think about them. Now they came rushing back, a sappy movie montage playing soft-focused in my mind.

My brother Brad had just turned eleven when Dwayne and I started dating. He idolized Dwayne. He started listening to country music because Dwayne did. He asked for cowboy boots for Christmas because Dwayne wore them. He wanted to dip tobacco because Dwayne did, but my mother threatened to kill him if he did.

"He adored you," I said.

"What's not to adore?" Dwayne asked.

I chuckled. "You really want to ask me that?"

My mind quickly switched from soft focus montage to replaying every fantasy conversation I'd ever had in which I got to tell him exactly what I thought of him and what he had done. I opened my mouth to vent, but my heart shut it, enjoying this time with him too much to ruin it by reminding us of the pain. He brought it up for me, though.

"Nah, I probably know what you'd say. I owe you an apology, girl. I did you wrong. I know that, and I know me saying I'm sorry ain't gonna do a whole helluva lot, but I'm sorry. Young and stupid. Scared. Didn't know what I wanted. What can I say other than I was a total ass and you didn't deserve it?"

Bam! I got the apology I'd waited five years for. The apology I thought I'd never get. Yet there it was, freely offered without me asking for it. Whether it held any merit in it or not, hearing him say he was sorry actually healed me a little bit. I felt vindicated. Restored in some small way. I'm sure he only reached out to me to make himself feel better because his wife left. I'm not stupid. I know apologizing had more to do with him than me, but it still felt good. Really good. So good that I wanted him to apologize more.

"You're right," I said. "There's not a whole lot else you can say. But why don't you try?"

I held my breath and waited to see what he would come up with. I wanted him to say he was never happy with her. That leaving me had been his biggest mistake. I wanted him to make up for the last five years and the tears I'd cried over him.

Instead, I got, "There ain't nothing I could say that you don't already know, girl."

I did know, but I still needed him to say it. I wanted him to make me feel better.

"Dwayne . . ." I stopped. I wasn't going to ask for it. It had to come from him. He left us in silence for a minute or two, maybe unsure of what I expected. More likely, unsure of what he wanted to give.

"So what are you up to now, darlin'? Your mama said you do weddings? Like what, you marry people—like a preacher?"

He had changed the subject. He had given me all I would get. I exhaled loudly, letting go of my anticipation and my hope.

"No, not like a preacher. I plan everything out for them. Help them book everything. Then I'm with them on the wedding day to make sure everything goes smoothly."

"Oh, like the movie? *The Wedding Planner*?" he asked.

"No," I said. "Same basic concept, but there was nothing realistic about that movie."

My mood had changed, and I no longer felt like riding the high of a stroll down memory lane. His attempt at an apology and his refusal to fulfill my unspoken request for adoration and groveling had made me irritable. I was ready for the conversation to end.

"So no groom for you, huh? I mean, your own. I would've figured you'd been married a long time ago. How'd you stay single this long?" he asked.

My anger flared, and I lashed out at him. "Everyone doesn't just up and marry the first piece of ass that comes along, Dwayne. Some of us want to take our time and find someone worth the wait. Something that will last."

"Ouch. I guess I deserve that. You always could put me in my place like nobody else, darlin'. I loved that about you. You never were afraid to stand up to me and give me what-for."

"You want a what-for, Dwayne? I'll give you one. You don't tell someone you need *time* and aren't ready to make a commitment, and then up and marry somebody else a month later. What were you thinkin'?"

"I don't know. We'd been together so long. Hell, everybody thought we was getting married. You wanted me to move off somewhere and live in some city or something. I didn't know if that was what I wanted."

"That makes no sense, Dwayne. You don't just dump one person and marry another because you don't know what you want. Did it ever cross your mind you could have talked to me? You could have told me you were having second thoughts? That you didn't want to move away?"

"Aw, hell, girl. You would have freaked out. Your world was a whole lot bigger than mine. You were dead set on leaving here. You wouldn't have been happy staying. I knew that. You knew that, too. Look where you are now. Far away from here, and you don't ever come home."

"I don't ever come home because—" I stopped. No way was I going to tell him I avoided coming home because of him. "You know what? Never mind. None of this matters. You did what you did, and I did what I did. It's all water under a bridge that washed out long ago. I gotta go, Dwayne."

"Aw, now. I didn't call to upset you. That wasn't my intent. I know I screwed up. With you, with my marriage, with my life. I just wanted to hear your voice. I'm sorry, darlin'."

I didn't speak. I couldn't speak. I hated him. I hated what he had done to me, and how he made me feel. I hated him calling me and being all sugary-sweet with me.

At the same time, I knew the young girl inside me would always love Dwayne Davis. My first serious relationship. My first real heartbreak. He was a part of me. Part of my history and my life. I didn't want to hang up angry. As much as I never wanted to hear from him again, I also wanted to think I would.

"I gotta go, Dwayne." I said, softer this time.

"Okay." We were both silent for what felt like an eternity, neither of us wanting to be the one to actually end the connection. Finally, he said, "Can I call you again?"

I leaned my head back against the sofa and closed my eyes. How was I supposed to answer that? I knew what Cabe would say. What Lillian would say. What I should say. I even opened my mouth to say it. But that young Tyler inside me told him yeah before I had the chance to talk her out of it.

"Whew!" Dwayne said. "You had me sweating bullets there, girl. I ain't never held my breath so long waiting for a girl to say I could call her."

His attempt to lighten the mood and be flirtatious made me irritated. With him and with my younger self for hi-jacking my voice.

"Good night, Dwayne."

"Good night, darlin'."

I wanted to call Cabe when I got off the phone, but the clock had long ago struck midnight. I already knew what he'd say, anyway. I could hear his voice over all the others in my head, expressing his warnings and disappointment.

If only I could sleep. If only they would all shut up in my head and just let me sleep.

Wednesday, December 4th

Cabe and I met up after work to do the Food Truck Festival downtown. We couldn't have asked for a more beautiful night, just crisp enough to wear a sweater without being cold. We sampled the lobster truck, the burrito truck, and one billed as the "World's Best Cuban Sandwich."

Cabe had a heyday with that one.

"How did they determine this?" he asked me. "Was there a statewide competition? Did they take the truck cross-country and earn a nationwide title before taking on the world? Can you imagine them loading the truck up on a cargo ship and unloading in . . . say, Madagascar? 'Excuse me, sir. Would you say this is the best damned Cuban sandwich you've ever had?' 'What's a Cuban sandwich?' 'That is. Now is it the best one you've ever had?' 'Why, yes. Yes, it is.' They could take Africa by storm. I can see this truck driving across the desert to all the malnourished children who don't even have clean water to brush their freakin' teeth. This guy's feeding them a sandwich with all this meat and butter and asking them, 'Is this the best sandwich you've ever had?' I mean, what goes into winning this title? Who declared this? Were there regulations?"

I laughed at him as I tasted the sandwich and found I wasn't impressed.

"I think since moving to Florida, I've become quite the Cuban Sandwich Connoisseur," I said. "Like, I should be deemed a judge or at least be consulted on such important decisions and declarations. No one asked me, though. I proclaim this to be quite an ordinary Cuban sandwich."

"I know, right? Can we protest?" Cabe asked. "We need to start a campaign for a re-vote." He finished off his sandwich with a flourish and motioned toward the funnel cake and fried Oreos.

"No, no, no," I said. "There are Oreos, and there are fried foods. To combine the two is like an oxymoron or something. They can't be in the same sentence. No grease on my Oreos."

"My dear, Oreos are pretty much made of lard. You realize that, right?" Cabe asked.

"So then there's no need to add grease, is there? An Oreo in itself is fat enough. I will go for a funnel cake, though."

We had just stepped in line for a funnel cake when my phone rang. I recognized the area code and knew it was him.

"Excuse me a minute. Go ahead and get a funnel cake and we'll split it," I told Cabe as I stepped out of line and away from the crowd.

"Well, hello darlin'," he said. I smiled in spite of myself. Ridiculous, I know. I didn't care, though. I wanted to talk to Dwayne.

"Hey you," I responded.

"What you up to?"

"I'm at a Food Truck Festival."

"A what? Food truck? What the hell is a food truck?" Dwayne asked.

I noticed Cabe staring at me from his place in the funnel cake line. I turned so I didn't have to see him.

"It's what it says it is. A truck that serves food," I said with a chuckle.

"Why would you order food cooked in a truck? Don't they have restaurants down there?"

I laughed, the nervous energy within me releasing louder than I intended. "They are restaurants. They drive around and cook inside the truck."

"That sounds disgusting. What do you eat?"

"I had a lobster roll and . . ."

"Lobster? From a truck? Girl, ain't you got better sense than that? You can't eat lobster off a truck. You're gonna get sick."

"No, no. It's good, I swear," I said.

Cabe startled me with a tap on the shoulder and a funnel cake tantalizingly waved under my nose.

"Oh! I gotta go. There's a funnel cake here with my name on it!" I laughed again, not because anything was funny but because I felt very nervous. Nervous about talking to Dwayne when I probably shouldn't be. Nervous that Cabe would ask who was on the phone, and I knew I had to tell him. He wouldn't be pleased.

"Well, alright. I just thought I'd say hey. You enjoy your lobster from a truck," Dwayne said.

"I already had the lobster. I'm eating a funnel cake now."

Cabe cocked his head to the side, his eyebrow lifted. I looked away.

"You take care, darlin'. Don't get sick," Dwayne said.

"I won't. Talk to you later!" I winced slightly as I hung up, thinking maybe I shouldn't have said that.

"Well, I sure don't need to ask who you were talking to." Cabe rolled his eyes and snapped the napkin out from under the plate.

"What do you mean?" I asked, knowing I was busted.

"Your Southern accent is dripping more sugar than this funnel cake, and you look like a sixteen-year-old who just met her favorite boy band singer. You're all giggly and drooling and shit."

"I am not drooling," I said. Although I could feel myself blushing, self-conscious under his scrutiny.

"Whatever," Cabe said. "I don't know what the hell you're doing, Ty. He's bad news."

"You don't even know him!" I protested.

"No, you're right, I don't." He lifted his hands and shrugged. "I only know I met a girl in a coffee shop who always looked like she'd just been kicked. I held her hair out of her face I don't know how many nights while she cried and puked from drinking her way past what he had done to her. I know I watched her turn down pretty much every single guy who *ever* looked her way because of this jerk. That's what I know. That, and there's no way he deserves the chance to hurt you again. He shouldn't even get the chance to talk to you, much less make your face light up like it's Christmas. I just don't know why you would even give him the time of day. Why would you even talk to him? Much less be happy about it."

Cabe turned and walked away from me as I stood there stunned by his outburst.

Embarrassment and outrage battled within me. What he said rang true, after all. Cabe was essentially defending me, his opinion of Dwayne based on what I had told him.

But Dwayne had a lot of good qualities, too. He wasn't a bad guy. He wasn't even a bad boyfriend. He just made a really bad choice. (Wait, am I to a point now where I'm defending Dwayne? That's messed up.)

Whether he spoke truth or not, though, his efforts to police my actions made me defiantly indignant. He wasn't my dad, after all. He couldn't tell me who I could or couldn't talk to. My decisions were mine to make, whether they were good decisions or not. I stormed after Cabe, anger being easier to channel than shame.

I was angry at him for calling me out. Probably angry at him for being right as well.

And despite enjoying the phone call, I was still pissed at Dwayne. Just because, well, just because of all the obvious reasons to be pissed at Dwayne. Although none of those seemed to keep me from wanting him to call and feeling good when he did.

Which, of course, made me mad at myself. I knew Cabe was right. I had no business engaging with Dwayne. Pride alone should have kept me from it. I just wanted to feel the way I used to. To go back in time, if even for a brief moment.

Cabe stopped at the end of the food truck row and turned back to wait for me. He put up his hand to stop me before I could say anything.

"I'm sorry, Ty. You're a grown woman. You can talk to whomever you want. It just seriously burns me up for this guy to think he can . . . you know what, never mind. It's your life. I just don't want to see you get hurt." He turned and walked away again, and I followed him in silence. I didn't want to see me hurt either. I wanted to be happy. I couldn't help that Dwayne's voice made me happy right now.

I tried to watch television when I got home. I tried checking e-mail. Then I tried to read a magazine. I even took a shower and thought about going to bed early. Get some sleep for a change. But I couldn't. I can only imagine how hard it is for an addict to stay away from their addiction, because try as I might, I could not keep myself from picking up the phone and dialing Dwayne Davis.

We talked for over two hours, covering everything from coaching his daughter's tee-ball team to the time the cops pulled up behind us as we were "parking" out behind his uncle's barn.

I dreaded looking at the clock, but he and I both had to be at work early. So I finally said, "Well, I guess we better get off here."

"Yeah, I guess so. I sure don't want to, though. I feel better talking to you than I've felt in years. I feel alive again," Dwayne said. Unfortunately, I knew exactly what he meant. We were silent again for a while, trying to prolong the inevitable, but eventually we said good night. What the hell am I doing?

Friday, December 6th

Dwayne called a little before noon.

"Hey," I said, smiling.

"I want to see you," he said.

"What?"

"Come see me. I'll start driving and meet you halfway."

I inhaled and held it. My stomach rolled, but I can't say if it was excitement or nausea. Or both. It was one thing to talk to Dwayne on the phone, hours away and safely not in my life. Seeing him in person seemed totally different. I wondered what he looked like after all this time. I wondered if I would still find him attractive. I was all at once certain I didn't want to see him and yet intrigued by what it would be like.

"I can't do that, Silly. I have stuff to do," I said while mentally going through my calendar to figure out if I could.

"Sure you can. We can meet in the middle, eat dinner, visit a while, and you can head back home and do your stuff."

"Dwayne, halfway is like three and a half hours. It's seven hours round trip."

"I know, but you only live once, right? Come on, girl. Come see me."

"I can't. I gotta work," I said, even as my brain plotted. Laura needed my help with a wedding Saturday, but I had no wedding of my own this weekend and no rehearsal tonight. Cabe and I had talked about seeing a movie, but we hadn't made any firm plans yet. This was actually a rare Friday night when I could take a road trip if I wanted to. I sort of wanted to.

"So let's meet later tonight. After you're done with work," he said.

I wavered. Seven hours of driving. Blech. Especially on a Friday night off coming out of busy October and November. Chilling with Cabe at a movie sounded much more relaxing. Curiosity was killing me, though. I hadn't seen Dwayne Davis in five years. I'd been going back and forth in my head for days between being excited to talk to him and never wanting to talk to him again. What would I feel if I actually saw him? The thought occurred to me that maybe then I would know. Maybe if I saw Dwayne, I would know once and for all if I wanted to pursue this, whatever it was, or if I wanted to tell him goodbye forever.

My heart clinched a little bit at the thought. Could I do that? Could I tell Dwayne goodbye again?

"Hello? You still there?" he asked.

"Yeah, I'm here. Okay, I'll meet you. Where and what time?"

I went to Melanie's office as soon as we hung up.

"Mel, I need to leave early, and I don't really want to get into a lot of explanation about what I'm doing or where I'm going. Could you tell Laura I had something come up and I'll be at her wedding tomorrow with no problem?"

"Sure, but what's up? What are you doing? Where are you going?" Mel asked.

"Didn't I just say I didn't want to get into it?" I stuck my tongue out at her playfully.

"Well, yeah, but I didn't think that meant me. If you want me to cover for you, don't I at least get to know what you're doing?" Then she got all excited and clapped her hands together, "Is it something with Cabe? Are you doing something to surprise him? Are you guys going away together?"

I felt a pang of guilt that it definitely didn't involve Cabe. I knew I'd have to call and tell him about my road trip, and he wouldn't be happy.

"No, it's not with Cabe, and I really can't get into it right now. I'll explain later, okay?" I didn't want anyone to know what my plan was because I didn't want anyone to talk me out of it.

"Alright. Everything okay, though? Should I be worried?" Mel asked.

"No, no. Everything's fine. I'll tell you all about it later."

I made it out of the building without seeing Laura, and I waited until I was an hour down the interstate before I called Cabe.

"What's up, Buttercup? What movie are we seeing?" he asked.

"Yeah, about that. I'm not going to be able to make the movie tonight. Something came up." I briefly toyed with the idea of lying and not telling him, but I knew I couldn't lie to Cabe.

"You okay?" he asked. Guilt and anxiety threatened to empty my stomach all over my car.

"Um . . . yeah. I'm fine. I'm driving to meet Dwayne." I paused and waited in the silence. In fact, I welcomed the silence because I didn't want to hear what he had to say.

"Really. Okay. How'd that come about?"

"He asked me to drive halfway and meet him."

"I thought you have a wedding tomorrow," Cabe said.

"I do. I'm coming back tonight. I'm driving to meet him, having dinner, and coming back."

"Why?" Cabe asked.

"I don't know, Cabe. Because he asked me to? Because I want to?"

"Why?" he asked.

"I dunno. Because at one time he was the love of my life. My first love. He was my everything. Talking to him again has reminded me of who I used to be. I see now how much I changed when he left me. I lost who I was. I guess I can't explain it. I just want to see him, Cabe. And he wants to see me."

"You do realize if his wife hadn't left him, you wouldn't be hearing from him at all? So it's not like he just missed you so terribly that he simply had to get in touch with you and see you. Don't be dumb about this, Ty."

His words stung, even though I expected them.

"I'm not being dumb, Cabe. But I have to know what it will be like to see him. I think in some ways, I never really let go of him. I need to know why. I know what you're saying is true, and I appreciate it. I thank you for worrying about me. This is something I need to do, though. To know what I feel when I see him. I think it will tell me a lot one way or another."

He paused for a minute and then said, "Okay, then let me go with you."

"What?"

"Let me go with you. There's no sense in you riding all that way by yourself, nervous and keyed up. If it doesn't go well, you're gonna be riding three hours back in a car alone. Let me go with you. I'll sit at another table so I'm not right up under you, but I wanna meet this dude. I want him to know someone is looking out for you."

My heart tugged in a strong gravitational pull back toward Cabe and home. What was I doing? Why on earth was I even giving Dwayne Davis the time of day? Much less seven plus hours out of my day? Why wasn't I heading out to a movie with Cabe? Safe. Not in danger of being hurt. This was a bad idea. Unfortunately, I was already in it and committed to it.

"Cabe, I'm an hour and a half out of town, about halfway to where we're meeting. Thank you, though. It means a lot that you would do that for me."

"Wow, so you just decided this and went for it. You weren't even going to tell me? You didn't want to discuss it first?" he asked.

I bit my tongue to keep from pointing out that he came back home for months before he bothered to contact me to discuss anything.

"It happened so quick, Cabe. He called today at work, and I made a decision. There wasn't anything to discuss."

"Wasn't there? What are you doing, Tyler? Do you want to get back together with him? To move back home and live with your mother? You going to play the part of wife number two and raise number one's kids with him? Where do you see this going?"

I had no answers. I hadn't thought ahead that far.

"I don't know, okay? I'm going to see him. I'm not marrying him or moving home with him. I'm just meeting him for dinner."

"Are you going to sleep with him?" he asked.

"Oh my God. I cannot even believe you asked me that," I said.

"Why not? Do you think it hasn't crossed his mind? Hasn't seen you in how many years? He's been separated from his wife so he probably hasn't been getting any action. I can speak personally for how frustrating that can be. You're rushing off to meet him at a moment's notice. Driving over three hours, I might add. You don't think he's got something on his mind?"

"Cabe, I don't want to argue with you. I'm going to have dinner with Dwayne, and that's all. I'll call you on my way back if you want."

"Whatever, Ty. You don't have to answer to me. I think you're making a mistake, but it's your mistake to make. Call me if you need me, not because you feel like you have to."

He hung up, and I almost turned the car around. I really wanted to see Dwayne Davis, though. I had to do it. I had to.

I spotted Dwayne's large red truck as soon as I pulled into the parking lot. He stood at the back of the truck, one knee bent with his foot behind him propped on the bumper. He had on cowboy boots, of course, and Wrangler jeans. His plaid shirt had pearl button snaps, and he wore a tall cowboy hat slung low on his head, shading his eyes in the setting sun. It was so far removed from what I see every day that I stifled a giggle.

He looked much skinnier than I remembered, by quite a bit. When we were in high school and college, his solid frame stayed muscular and lean, but he was a strapping guy. He seemed frail now, and I wondered if he had been ill.

His face seemed pretty much the same, but older. More haggard than I remembered.

I got out of the car and smoothed my skirt. I had gone home and changed into a cute little dress with a purple and orange paisley print. It was one of my favorites, cut generously in the hips with straps that crossed underneath my collarbone and went over my shoulders. Cabe always called it my hippie-chick dress. It was his favorite, too. Probably too bright for Dwayne's tastes, but I wanted to be bright, cheerful, and confident. I finished it off with my favorite boots and my trusty denim jacket.

I walked toward Dwayne, enjoying the slow, appreciative grin spreading across his face. Dwayne Davis. The love of my life. Right there in front of me, smiling and obviously happy to see me. I had a million flashes of that smile replaying in my head. Standing by his high school locker. Coming off the football field. Holding the hose as we washed his car. Looking up at me sitting in his lap. Lit up by the dashboard as he lay back in the driver's seat. Sneaking in the window of my dorm room.

He wrapped me in a big bear hug, which increased my amazement at how bony he felt. Definitely much thinner than before, no doubt about it. I had to strain to reach my arms all the way around him back then, but not now. Somehow I remembered him being taller, but he only stood an inch or two above me. Maybe being with Cabe's towering height all the time had messed with my memory.

"Well, hello darlin'. If you ain't a sight for sore eyes, I don't know what is. You smell downright edible. Let me look at you." He held me at arm's length, looking me up and down like a prized mule. He whistled low and motioned for me to turn around. I did a little twirl in my dress like a schoolgirl playing dress-up, completely reveling in having his attention once more.

"Damn, girl. I think you are even more beautiful than I remembered. I didn't think that was possible. How come you ain't just beating the boys off you with a stick?" he asked.

I thought about Cabe and how much he'd like to beat Dwayne with a stick.

"I don't know." There wasn't much else to say.

Dwayne took my hand, and it felt like the most natural thing in the world. Like we'd been holding hands only yesterday. There I was, strolling into a restaurant on Dwayne Davis's arm and feeling like a million bucks.

I noticed he favored his left leg with a slight limp.

"You okay?" I asked.

"Huh? Oh, that. I got into a bar fight over in Louisiana a few years ago. I went over there with my cousin to look at some horses. Don't remember much about the fight. Just playing pool and having a good time, and next thing I know I'm in a hospital with this here leg in traction. Had a ruptured kidney, four broke ribs, black eye, broke nose." He pointed to a spot on his nose. "See that little bump that right there? Kind of ridge-like? Yep. That's where it broke."

"Damn, boy. Did you even get a swing in?"

I hadn't thought about bar fights in years. Not since we broke up, most likely. The people I'm around on a daily basis don't really do the bar fight thing. I got a mental flash of Lillian in a bar fight and nearly burst out laughing.

"Probably. Hell, you know me. Always the first one swinging. But I don't remember a damned thing. Don't even know who hit me. Rayford—you remember him? Uncle Ray's oldest boy? He was in the bathroom when it happened, so he didn't see nothing. I laid in the hospital in Louisiana for damned near a month. Out of work a long time. Lost a bunch of weight.

Still got the limp."

"Yeah, I noticed you look a little thin."

"Well, I put some weight back on after all that, but this whole divorce thing tore me up. I couldn't eat nothing until I started talking to you, darlin'. I'm starving right now."

We made small talk throughout the meal, catching up on relatives and news from home. No awkward pauses or long silences. It felt oddly natural, like we'd never been apart. We slipped back into phrases and sayings we once used, bits and pieces of the intimate language each couple creates together.

I couldn't help comparing him with Cabe, though. I don't know why. I guess because that's who I eat with most of the time. I noticed little things right off. Dwayne ordered first. Cabe always makes a point of asking me what I want and telling the waitress before he orders. Dwayne talked with his mouth full, which I forgot about. He also doused his steak in ketchup, which I used to do until Cabe berated me about it being an insult to the chef.

I mean, it's not like Dwayne acted barbaric or anything, but it was certainly different than eating with Cabe. Which is okay. Nothing wrong with that. I just noticed, that's all.

While Dwayne complimented me on how nice I looked and how I hadn't changed, I kept thinking of all the ways he had changed. His eyes were still the color of melted milk chocolate, and they still twinkled with his mischievous allure. Deep lines crinkled in the corners, though. Telltale signs of aging and too many days in the sun. His hair was much shorter than I'd ever seen it, although I liked it better than the shaggy bangs that used to fall across his face. He was still a handsome man, no doubt about it. Every bit the charmer he had been. His stories kept me laughing, and his attention bolstered my confidence and made me lightheaded.

As I listened to him talk, though, I realized I remembered him being worldlier. More in charge. When we started dating, he had traveled quite a bit with his family, who had much more money than mine. Back then, I was in awe of his knowledge of the world and of life, which surpassed my meager understanding. Now I was the one who had left the small town environment and had my own tales to offer. The role reversal felt odd, but I liked it.

I noticed a large scar along his jawline and asked if that came from the Louisiana fight, too.

"Nah, that was a tractor accident. I tried to unhitch a bushhog. It jammed, so I got a crowbar. When that thing broke loose, it came right up and sliced me open. Broke my jaw. Had to have the damned thing wired shut for months. That's another reason I lost weight right there."

I thought about his wife and what it must have been like to be married to Dwayne all this time. After all, the life Ellain had was the one I had planned. Well, sort of. I envisioned us moving away and living in some big city somewhere. Now as I looked at him and listened to him talk about his life, I realized he never would have been happy anywhere else. Dwayne lived where he needed to be.

I pondered what Ellain thought about his bar fights and hospital stays in another state and nursing him through tractor accidents. Was it all she thought it would be when she said 'I do'? Obviously not, because she left, but was she happy with him for a time? They did have two kids together. Not that having kids means you're happy, but still.

For so long, I'd thought Ellain got something I was supposed to have. Like she took something from me. Now, sitting across from him and listening to highlights of his life since I last saw him, I didn't feel so sure about that. Would I have been happy? Would I have been okay with him lying in a hospital bed out of work because he got in a drunken bar fight while I had two kids to feed and support? Would I have been okay with him working at his daddy's lumber yard and farming his daddy's land? Would that have been enough for me?

When our meal had ended and the conversation had slowed, Dwayne walked me to my car.

"I don't want the night to end," he said. "I feel like I'm with a ghost, or an angel, or both. Like life has given me a second chance to see what I missed. What a complete idiot I was. You wanna go somewhere?"

I could see raw desire burning in his eyes, and Cabe's warning lights flashed in my head.

"Whaddya mean?" I asked, scared I knew the answer. I didn't want this to be about that.

"You know, find someplace private? We could keep talking. A little more reminiscing? Maybe a stroll down memory lane? I have some sweet memories of you and me."

Why did Cabe have to be right? Why couldn't Dwayne simply want dinner and conversation?

"I need to get back, Dwayne. I have to work in the morning."

"Alright, alright. I understand. Look, I just wanted to see you. You've made this ole boy the happiest I've been in a long time laying eyes on your pretty face. I ain't asking you for nothing else, and I ain't wanting you to feel like I'm trying to get you in the sack or something."

The alarm and panic must have shown on my face for him to say that.

"Not that I'd refuse if you offered," he laughed.

I shook off my unease and smiled. It was Dwayne, after all. I knew him. Even after all the time that had passed and all the changes in us both. It was still Dwayne.

"I ain't offering."

"I wouldn't expect you to," he said. "I woulda been shocked if you did, but you can't blame a boy for trying. Just like you can't blame me for leaning in just a little bit," he said as he leaned in, "and pulling you a little closer," he said as he pulled me in against him, "and trying for one little ole kiss."

Dwayne kissed me, and I let him. I wanted him to. I wanted to see what it would be like. I wanted to know what I would feel.

He seemed nervous. I definitely don't remember him ever being nervous before. But as he kissed me, I discovered I didn't remember a whole bunch about how it went back then. I know we did an awful lot of it, but for the life of me, I couldn't remember what it felt like to kiss Dwayne. Even more maddening, the most recent kiss I received was Cabe's, so that was what I kept thinking about and comparing it to.

It seemed like we couldn't get our heads at the right angle or something. No matter how our lips met, it felt awkward. Like it didn't work somehow. Our teeth bumped together once, and his tongue ended up swiping my chin a couple of times. Just messy, sloppy, uncoordinated. Like we didn't fit together anymore.

It was so weird to be kissing someone and expect to like kissing them, but instead feel confusion and uncertainty. When Cabe and I kissed, I wanted it with everything in me, even though I knew I shouldn't be kissing him. My body had surged with passion and desire, and that didn't happen in this kiss with Dwayne. I'm sure it came from so much time passing and all that happened between us. Maybe also because we had been flung together in this bumbling dinner meeting of the memories. Somehow, I just couldn't get into it. I thought I wanted Dwayne Davis to want me, be interested in me, and kiss me, but I couldn't drum up a truly passionate effort to kiss him back.

Evidently, he was oblivious to this.

"Damn, girl. You know how to rev up a boy's motor and get him on the start line. I had forgotten what a minx you were. I was such a fool, Tyler. Such a fool."

The words felt good to hear, which added more to my confusion over what I felt. Why did I want so badly for him to want me and yet not really know if I actually wanted him? I thought I would know right off the bat. Like I would see him and know immediately if this was a good thing or a bad thing. It didn't work that way. At times, it felt like I was where I was supposed to be, transported back to old times, happier ones, where I was completely comfortable to be by his side. Other times, I felt wildly out of place. Like Dwayne was a character in a play I used to star in, but I'd left the stage and that costume behind.

The whole night—the conversations, the laughter, the kissing, the hugging—it all felt like some surreal version of something I once knew.

He didn't seem to be experiencing any doubts, though.

"When can I see you again?" Dwayne asked. "You comin' home for Christmas?"

I shuddered a bit. Not in a good way.

"I don't know, Dwayne." His embrace suddenly felt claustrophobic, almost suffocating. I pulled away roughly and drew a deep breath.

It was one thing to meet him here in neutral territory when no one but Cabe even knew what I was doing.

But to go back home where our pasts were intertwined presented a completely different stress factor.

I hadn't been home for Christmas since the first year after I moved here.

Dwayne cocked his head to one side and grinned at me. "Undoubtedly no one in their right mind would get married on Christmas!"

"No, we don't do weddings on Christmas, but I don't know if this is a good idea."

"If what's a good idea? C'mon darlin'. I just wanna see ya again. Hell, I ain't seen you in years, and us talking again makes me remember how much fun we had. I know your mama would be thrilled to have you home for the holidays. You come home to see her, and then let this ole boy take you out to dinner again. It doesn't have to be any big deal."

"I don't know, Dwayne," I said again.

There was a time when Dwayne Davis standing in front of me begging me to come see him would have made my life complete. I could still feel small twinges of that overpowering attraction, the tattered remnants of first love still lingering in the recesses of my mind—despite the betrayal, the time that had passed, and the changes in my life. But while the girl I used to be was getting something she'd always wanted, the girl I'd become wasn't sure she wanted any part of it.

I felt dizzy and too warm. I needed air and space. I couldn't process all I was feeling, and I didn't want to be pushed either way. For reasons I still don't fully understand, I wasn't ready to completely sever ties with Dwayne, but I certainly wasn't about to commit to going back home to see him.

Definitely not the first time in my life I've seriously wished I had a therapist on call.

Dwayne took my hand in his and lightly stroked my palm with his thumb as he raised my chin with his other hand. His chocolate eyes were almost black in the dark parking lot, and I was struck by how handsome he still was, scars and all.

"I'll tell you what," he said. "Just tell me you'll think about it. That you'll consider comin' home for Christmas. Okay? Just think about it," he pleaded.

I probably should have said no right off the bat, but my head was so jumbled that I just gave some kind of noncommittal shrug which he immediately took as an affirmative gesture.

"Yes! Alright! You have made this country boy real happy, darlin'. You done gave me something to look forward to when I thought it would be the worst Christmas ever."

"Whoa, whoa, whoa. I didn't say I was coming," I protested, coming back to life a few seconds too late.

"You didn't say no, so I'll take it," Dwayne said. He drew me into his arms and laid another sloppy kiss on me before letting go. "You drive safe now, darlin'. Call me from the road if you need anything."

He turned and walked away, his cowboy boot heels clicking on the asphalt as he crossed to his truck.

I drove back in silence, replaying the entire encounter as I analyzed every moment and created alternate scenarios in my head. The phone rang about a half hour from home. I knew it was Cabe.

"Hey."

"Hey."

We both said nothing for a moment. Then I exhaled loudly, and he said, "You still with Dweeb?"

"His name is Dwayne."

"Oh, I know his name," Cabe said, his tone dripping with sarcasm. If I didn't know better, I'd have thought the boy was jealous. "Are you still with him?"

"Nope."

"Are you okay?" he asked.

"Yep."

More silence. I knew Cabe wanted answers. He even deserved them as a concerned friend, but I had none to give. I wasn't sure what had transpired and how I felt about it. All I had was more questions.

"Ty?" he said.

"Yes?" I answered.

"Don't be mad at me. I only wanted to—"

I interrupted him. "I'm not mad at you, Cabe. I'm just bewildered."

"Bewildered? Really? Who says that? Who says they're bewildered? I have never in my life heard another person say, 'Hey, I'm bewildered.' That's weird."

"Okay, Mr. Vocabulary, what word would you like me to say?"

"Well, I want you to say 'Cabe, you were right,' but that could mean a whole lot of things happened that I don't want to hear about, so for once in my life, I hope I was wrong."

"I didn't sleep with him."

"I didn't ask."

"Neither did he," I said, which technically was true, even though the offer was certainly insinuated.

"Really? Wow. Can't believe he passed up that opportunity. He's dumber than I thought."

"Oh, you! I can't believe you!" I acted shocked, but I smiled.

"How close to home are you?" he asked.

"About twenty minutes."

"Want me to come over? Do you need to talk?" he asked.

"No, thanks. I appreciate you offering, but I'm beat. I have Laura's wedding tomorrow. I'm kind of processing everything right now. We can talk later. I'm okay, though. I promise."

"Alright. Wanna go to the beach on Sunday? Hang out? Picnic, sit in the sand, talk about your ex-boyfriend?"

"Well, when you put it that way, who could refuse? Yeah. Let's go to the beach. Do you know if it's supposed to be cold?"

"Who cares?" Cabe said. "I'm a Floridian. I go to the beach year-round. We'll take blankets and dress warm."

"Okay." I paused, but when he didn't say anything else, I spoke. "Hey, Cabe?"

"Yeah?"

"Thanks for calling. For checking on me. Thanks for caring."

"No problem, Buttercup."

Saturday, December 7th

I probably should have just talked it out with Cabe. I should have known I'd never make it through an entire workday without everything pouring out of me, and since Laura was the person next to me all day, I ended up sharing the most recent episode of *The Life and Times of Tyler* with one of my bosses. Again. It's starting to be a bad habit, and I can only hope it doesn't doom my career.

I had yawned quite a few times when she asked what I did last night, and before I knew what was happening, I had recapped the whole dinner escapade.

"And how do you feel about it today?" Laura asked as we tied bows on favor boxes.

"Honestly? I'm not sure. I mean, I think I'm supposed to be mad at him. Cabe thinks I'm supposed to be mad at him, and I guess he's right."

"You can't base your feelings on what Cabe thinks you should do, Tyler. They're *your* feelings."

"I know, I just feel guilty. Like I'm doing something wrong. I know Dwayne hurt me, and I understand why Cabe thinks the way he does. I probably should be mad. But for some reason, I still want to talk to Dwayne."

Laura stacked the boxes carefully on the tray, her slender hands steadying the second tier as she spoke.

"I don't think you should feel guilty for wanting to talk to him. I mean, he was someone very important in your life. You spent quite a bit of time with him, invested a substantial amount of your emotions. It didn't end with a clean break. So I think you probably have unfinished business between you. The chapter is still open."

I dropped the stack of the boxes I was carrying in my haste to protest.

"Oh, no, I'm not saying I want to get back together with Dwayne. I can't see that happening. I just . . . I don't know."

Laura smiled as she bent to help me pick up the favors. "Tyler, just because the chapter is still open doesn't mean you're going to turn back the pages in the book. Sometimes in life, we transition out of one phase without the closure we need to fully move into the next phase. Maybe there are things left unsaid between you. Maybe there's healing to be done. I don't know. But I think you both are obviously still connected in some way, and I think you need to cut yourself some slack in figuring out what it means."

"I just feel like no matter what I do, it's the wrong thing. I feel bad *not* talking to him, but I feel bad talking to him, too."

"Look, we never have to feel bad about our feelings. They are simply that—feelings. It is how we choose to act upon them that gets us in trouble. Don't make any rash decisions or do anything drastic. Just feel what you're feeling and allow yourself to work through this without all the pressure of whether you should or shouldn't. There's a reason Dwayne is back in your life, and who knows what that means for either of you. Just ride it out. It will be revealed in its own time."

She patted my arm and walked away to check the song selections with the DJ, leaving me more confused and yet more at peace. Is that even possible?

Sunday, December 8th

Well, I can now cross "freeze to death on beach" off my bucket list. We took blankets and wore sweatshirts with gloves, but the wind whipping off the water proved too much for us. Poor Cabe. His first trip to the beach since moving back from Seattle, and the weather screwed him over.

We ended up in a little dive called Jack's Shack instead. We had a great view of the Atlantic with windows to block out the wind. I told him the highlights of my trip to see Dwayne, and he seemed mildly disinterested. This is one area where it is a disadvantage to have a dude as a best friend. If you're talking to a girl, you can give her every detail of the entire evening with every line of the conversation, and she'll be cool with it. She'll even ask questions to get a more complete picture.

Guys are different. Cabe wanted to know if Dwayne came on to me, if he paid for my dinner, if he asked to see me again, and if I wanted to see him again. That's it. He didn't care that Dwayne had lost a ton of weight, and he wasn't interested in my whole wishy-washy feelings over the whole thing. (I kind of glossed over the kiss part. I certainly didn't mention comparing Cabe's kiss to Dwayne's.) I summarized Laura's viewpoint that it was okay that I wanted to talk to Dwayne.

"Look, Ty," Cabe said in between bites of crab legs, "I think it's perfectly natural for you to be curious. I don't blame you for wanting to go see the guy and figuring out what's what. I think that's all it was, though. I mean, this guy's your past. He's not your future. You don't want to go back there and live, and he's damned sure not coming here. I think you guys might have had a lot in common then, but now you don't. So don't lead him on."

"Lead him on? How am I leading him on? I had dinner with him, that's all," I said.

177

"I realize that, but hell, he takes one look at you and he can clearly see how hot you are and that you have it together. Much more than he does right now. His wife just took off. He sees you as a way to make himself feel better. I'm just saying if you know it's not going anywhere and you can tell he thinks it might, you need to be aware of how you come across. Don't lead him on. Don't take him somewhere you have no intention of staying."

"So you're saying I shouldn't even talk to him?" I asked.

"I can't say you should or you shouldn't, but you need to seriously think about what you're doing. Especially when you're driving over three hours for dinner, ya know?"

The waitress came and refilled my Coke and Cabe's beer, and he switched the subject to a new blues band performing downtown. I couldn't help thinking about Dwayne, though, and wondering if I had screwed up by going to see him when I didn't know what I wanted.

"Brown Eyed Girl" came on the jukebox, and I started bouncing in my seat a little bit.

Cabe smiled, shaking his head as he wiped his mouth with his napkin. "Still love this song, huh? You never get tired of it, do you?"

I shook my head no as I swayed my shoulders and snapped my fingers, singing along with Van Morrison.

"When are we going out dancing?" I asked. "We used to go dancing all the time."

He put his napkin on the table and stretched his hand across to me.

"Let's go," he said.

"What? Leave? We're still eating."

"No, not leave. Let's dance. Get up." He stood up and grabbed my hand to pull me up with him.

"Cabe, no, oh my God, no. This is not a dancing place. No one is dancing." He continued pulling my arm. "Cabe, we can't dance here. I meant later, another time. We can't dance here."

"Why not?" he asked. "There's plenty of room, and this is your favorite song to dance to. Get up and let's dance."

"Cabe, no. I can't. We can't. They'll tell us to leave. Everybody will stare at us," I protested, but he had already pulled me to my feet.

"They're not going to ask us to leave because the place is damned near empty, and they need the business. Anyone staring at us will just be envying us because they wish they had the guts to get up and dance."

He wrapped his arm around my waist and lifted my other arm high, and we were dancing.

In the middle of the aisle at Jack's Shack, right beside our booth.

Once I got over my initial shock and embarrassment, I had a blast. I hadn't danced with Cabe in so long. I had forgotten how much fun it is with him leading. He twirled me, spun me, dipped me, and caught me in a whirlwind dance that left me breathless and laughing so hard I got a little dizzy from it all. When the song ended, the other five patrons in the restaurant applauded, and the waitress brought us another round of drinks on the house.

"It's so refreshing to see a young couple madly in love," she said as she set our drinks on the table. "You don't see the real deal every day."

"Oh, no ma'am, we aren't—" I started to protest but Cabe stopped me.

"Now, honey, don't be shy," he said to me before turning to the adoring waitress. "Ten years we've been together, and I still love this little lass just as much as the first day I saw her. She was only fifteen then. We had to sneak around so her parents didn't know we were dating. It was all worth it, though, as happy as we are today!"

I wanted to slink under the table and die of embarrassment. She beamed at us like she'd just heard the most romantic story ever.

"Aw, that's so sweet," she crooned. "I hope y'all never stop dancing."

"Oh, we won't," Cabe said, taking my hand across the table. "Me and my little brown-eyed girl will be dancing 'til our legs can't dance no more."

She smiled and walked away, at which point I yanked my hand out of Cabe's. He burst out laughing.

"You're terrible," I said.

"Me? What about you, traipsing about when you were only fifteen? Lying to your parents and sneaking around? You're one to talk about someone being terrible."

"I don't think I could have snuck anywhere at fifteen. My mother had us all on lockdown in her paranoia that one of us would get pregnant and not be able to finish school like she did. Besides, boys weren't even on my radar at that age. Not until senior year."

"Then you went on the warpath, breaking hearts and taking names," Cabe said, laughing.

"Um, no. Not exactly. What about you? Were you a heartbreaker at fifteen?" I asked.

"At fifteen? I wouldn't say heartbreaker, but I was aware of the ladies. Working my way through charm school by then."

"I bet you were," I said.

I'd seen high-school pictures of Cabe at his mom's house. Sandy blond hair, clear blue-gray, perfect white teeth, and eyelashes any girl would have killed for. I look back on my high-school photos and cringe. My mother felt convinced my thick, wavy brown hair worked best kept chin length so it didn't get unruly. Every picture of me before college looked like I wore a hedgehog on my head. Finally after I got out on my own and around other follically-challenged girls, I learned to just wash and wear with minimal product and let the waves fall as they may. I'd worn it long ever since. It was still thick and unruly, but the more I left it alone, the more it cooperated with me.

We sang Van Morrison songs at the top of our lungs all the way back from the beach. Cabe's passion for music is contagious. I swear that boy can listen to any kind of music and find value in it. He has certainly broadened my spectrum when it comes to that.

He headed home after dropping me off, and I didn't even notice the two missed calls from Dwayne until I plugged in the phone to charge before I went to bed. I didn't call him back. I preferred to go to sleep with Van Morrison in my head and dream of dancing the night away.

Monday, December 9th

Mama called at 9:45am. I should have already been at work, but it was a slow-moving Monday morning.

"So when were you going to tell me you're coming home for Christmas?" She sounded both pissed and excited.

"What? I'm not coming home for Christmas!"

"Well, that's not what I hear. I don't like being put on the spot, Tyler Lorraine. I would appreciate it if you would tell me what you're doing before I hear about it from someone else."

"Mama, I don't know what you heard, but I'm not—"

"Well, I walked in the bank first thing this morning and Gilda Robinson says I must be real excited about having you home for Christmas. Then she went on to say how sweet it is of you to help Dwayne through this rough time he's having. She says you're spending Christmas with him and his young'uns. Now I'd like to know when you were going to tell me you're coming home, and I would love to know when you were going to mention you're getting back together with Dwayne Davis."

Oh, the joys of dealing with small town grapevines. "Whoa, slow down a minute. First of all, I am not getting back together with Dwayne Davis."

"*Then* I went to the drug store to pick up my prescription, and Diane Smith tells me she heard I'm having a visitor for Christmas. Now, how do you think that made me feel? My own daughter isn't telling me what's going on. I'm the last to know. I raised you better than to do me that way."

"Mama, I didn't tell anybody I'm coming home. I'm not even—" She wouldn't let me finish.

"You didn't even tell me y'all were talking, much less getting back together. When did this happen? You didn't even wait for the ink to dry on them papers, did you? Does his whole family know? Did you tell your sisters? Am I the only one you're not talking to?"

"Mama! Please take a breath and let me talk! I am not getting back together with Dwayne Davis," I started.

"Then why on earth would you spend Christmas with him and his kids? Am I supposed to invite all of them over here when I didn't know anything about this? Do I need to buy presents for some young'uns I don't even know?"

"Good grief! Would you please just listen to me? I am not getting back together with Dwayne or spending Christmas with him and his kids. I'm not coming home for Christmas. Everything you're telling me is news to me, too. You didn't get left out of anything."

"Well, why on earth would everybody in town be telling me that if it's not true? Did they make it up?"

I groaned and slapped my palm against my forehead. "Maybe Dwayne is telling people that. I don't know."

"Why would Dwayne be telling people that, Tyler?"

"He asked me to come home for Christmas," I said, vowing silently to ream Dwayne out for his big mouth.

"So you have been talking to him! Are y'all getting back together?"

"No. We've talked a couple of times. It's not a big deal, so I didn't mention it."

"Not a big deal? You're coming here to spend Christmas with Dwayne Davis and his kids, and you don't think that's a big deal? You ain't been home to spend Christmas with your own mother in years, and you don't think it's a big deal that you're coming home for him?"

"I'm not coming home!" I started to say that if I had been planning on it, this phone call would have changed my mind. Luckily, I stopped before that flew out of my mouth.

"Why would he say you were?" she asked.

"I don't know! I will be happy to ask him the next time I talk to him. Like I told you, we've only talked a couple of times, and I've seen him once." I decided to go ahead and get it all out in the open while she was already pissed.

"You saw him? When? How? You saw Dwayne and you didn't tell me? Did you come home and *not tell me*?" she yelled, and I swear I thought she might cry.

Maybe full disclosure wasn't the best move, but it was too late to back up now.

"We met for dinner Friday night," I said, digging myself deeper.

"For dinner? Where?" she asked, still yelling.

"We both drove halfway," I said. "Look, Mama, it's not a big deal. If it was, I would have told you about it, I promise. You gave him my number. He called and asked me to meet him for dinner, and I did. That's it."

"He just called you up out of the blue, and you traipsed off to meet him for dinner? Ain't you got no self-pride? Good Lord in heaven, child, play a little bit hard to get." She did start to cry then.

"Mama, for Christ's sake," I started, but her loud shriek interrupted me.

"Don't you dare take the good Lord's name in vain on top of everything else you've done!"

"I'm not, I mean, I didn't mean to. Look, I have to go to work. If I decide to get back together with Dwayne, you'll be the first to know. Maybe the second, since I'm thinking Dwayne would need to know as well. But don't start getting your hopes up."

"He's got babies, Tyler. He ain't leaving them babies. He's got his daddy's business to run. Don't think you're gonna talk him into moving off down there. He already broke up with you one time for trying to make him leave here."

"That's great, Mama. Just great. I've had a couple of conversations with the boy and one dinner, and you've not only got us back together, but you've already got us breaking up. Has it ever occurred to you this is why I don't tell you stuff?"

"Don't you be hateful to me," she said, but I didn't let her finish.

"I'm hanging up, Mama. I have to go to work, and I'd rather do it without mascara pouring down my face. I've said all I'm going to say. I'm hanging up."

"Don't you dare hang up on me, Tyler Lorraine."

I pushed END CALL and looked around the room in shock. A few minutes ago, I had a peaceful, lazy Monday morning. Although my apartment still looked exactly the same, my mind felt like I had been ambushed in a war zone. My coffee wasn't even cold and my emotions were scattered all over the place.

I texted Cabe, *"I need to talk to you."*

He called me back immediately. "What's up, Buttercup? You okay?"

I told him the whole conversation, and by the end of it, he had me laughing at the absurdity of it all. Mama having a fit from seven hours away didn't have to affect my life. I hung up much calmer and more relaxed.

Until I got to work, that is, where the stress in the office was almost tangible.

One of Laura's March brides had called in hysterics. The father of the groom had stopped responding to treatment after battling cancer for several months. The doctors told them he likely had only weeks to live, so the bride and groom wanted to move the wedding up to happen as soon as possible. We scrambled all hands on deck in the office, with each of us calling vendors and venues to pull the entire wedding into the month of December.

The venue proved to be the biggest challenge. With so many holiday parties already on the books, no weekend nights were available, and the family needed a weekend to make travel easier for everyone's work schedules. The hotel they originally booked graciously offered to cancel the event without any penalty if we could find another venue. Which we couldn't.

So Lillian called a friend with a large yacht. He agreed to host the reception onboard if Laura could get one of the lakeside resorts to cater the event and arrange docking space for the yacht, which she did. The hotel offered lobby space in the convention center for the ceremony and agreed to duplicate the menu from the original venue as much as possible. We confirmed the new date of December 28th, roughly three weeks away. We even found a photographer, videographer, and DJ to be onboard. Literally.

The bride and groom were thankful beyond words. If the groom's dad could hold in there for three weeks, he would be able to be at his son's wedding.

It felt good to know so many people were willing to pull together in the face of tragedy, but I still felt sad. The happiest day of their life had a huge, dark cloud hanging over it. Even if his dad made the ceremony, he wouldn't be here long afterward. The whole thing tasted bittersweet.

It all, of course, made me think of my own sweet daddy not being able to walk either of my sisters down the aisle. If I ever do find my Prince Charming, my daddy won't be there to give me away. I settled into quite a gray funk thinking about Daddy and how alone Mama must have felt when he died. I still feel guilty for leaving her, even though she has two other daughters and a son who are equally responsible for her.

All that thinking led me to call Mama and apologize for this morning.

Somehow I ended up saying I'd come home for Christmas. She's overjoyed. I feel like I'm going to throw up.

Tuesday, December 10th

Dwayne finally returned my call and said he only told his mama about seeing me and trying to talk me into coming home for Christmas. I guess she translated that to his sister, who translated it around town, and that's how it got back to my mama. I asked him to please be a little more discreet in the future since I don't want my business to be the town topic of conversation.

"In the future? So are you saying we have one?" he asked.

Panic replaced annoyance. I couldn't answer that. I knew I didn't want to hang up the phone and never talk to him again, but I wasn't sure I wanted anything else beyond that either.

He laughed at my silence and said, "I'm kidding you, girl. Don't freak out. I ain't asking you for nothing. I'm just happy to be talking to you again. Although, my Christmas would be merrier if you were here."

I bit my lip. If I told him my plans to come home, he'd probably think it was for him and about him. Which wasn't the truth. The reason I decided to go home was Mama.

If I didn't tell him, there's no way he wouldn't find out. In fact, I'm sure me telling mama last night meant half the town already knew this morning.

"You still there?" he asked.

"Yeah, I'm here," I said with a sigh.

"You okay? I didn't upset you or anything, did I? I'm just talking. I don't want you thinking I'm getting all serious or something."

"No, Dwayne, you're fine. I'm fine. Just a little distracted this morning," I answered. Distracted was an understatement.

I'm about to go home for Christmas for the first time in years. I'm going to be with my mother twenty-four hours a day for several days. And then there's the little matter of telling my former flame, the man I thought was

185

the love of my life, that I'm coming home without making it seem like it has anything to do with him. Yeah, a little distracted.

"I'm coming home for Christmas," I said, the words rushing out of my mouth like making a confession to a priest.

"You are? Awesome! That's incredible! You've made me the happiest man on earth, I tell you what. You turned my whole Christmas around, for sure. That's great, Tyler. Thank you so much. Yeah! Best news I've had in a while. I can't wait to see you, darlin'. I'm gonna take you out for the best dinner you've ever had."

I wanted to stop him. To interrupt him and tell him I only planned to come home because I felt guilty about Mama. But he sounded so happy, so excited. I couldn't bring myself to knock him down. It makes me nervous as all hell that he was so elated. I know I'm not going to go home *to* see him, but I honestly can't say I'm going to go home and *not* see him either. I wasn't sure this was what Laura meant by just riding it out, but I guess one way or another I was going to find out what it all meant.

Tonight at dinner, I felt guilty even bringing it up to Cabe. I knew he'd think I was going home for Dwayne, too.

"By the way," I said as I casually twirled the pasta against the spoon, "I decided to go home for Christmas."

He stopped chewing and looked at me without saying anything. I stopped twirling and looked back.

"What?" I said. "Did you hear me?" I knew full well he had heard me.

He started chewing again, slowly and deliberately, and then washed it down with a drink of wine. He dabbed at his mouth with his napkin and sat back in his chair, still staring at me.

"What? Would you please say something?" I asked.

He just stared at me.

"Cabe, what? Say something. Why are you looking at me like that?" I put my silverware down and clasped my hands together in my lap. I wanted to know what he thought, but I dreaded him telling me.

He took another drink of wine and looked away from me, still silent. We sat for what seemed like an eternity. I finally picked up my fork and took another bite just to have something to do. Otherwise, I may have exploded from nervous energy and emotion.

Cabe put his napkin down and pushed his unfinished plate away. Then he got up and left the table without a word.

His reaction caught me off guard. Was he mad? Sad? Was he, I don't even know what? He'd been very vocal all along about whether I should be talking to Dwayne or entertaining anything at all with him, and I had no doubt he assumed my trip home was because of Dwayne. So why wasn't he saying anything? He'd never just walked away from me before. A few minutes went by, and I began to wonder if he was going to return at all. But then there he was, back in his seat and still looking at me with those incredibly blue eyes.

"Are you going to talk to me?" I asked.

He didn't answer right away. My heart beat so loudly in my ears I thought I might not be able to hear him when he did speak. But I could hear him fine, despite him speaking low and hushed, as though fighting to control his voice.

"I can't stop you from making your own decisions and living your own life. I can only tell you I think this is a mistake. I think this guy is focused on his own pain, and he's willing to do whatever it takes to numb that pain. I don't think he genuinely cares about you and what's best for you."

"Cabe, it's not about Dwayne," I said. "I'm going home to see Mama. You should have heard her when I called and told her. It's been three years since I've seen my family, and I want to go home to spend Christmas with them. It has nothing to do with Dwayne."

"Really? He starts calling, and out of the blue, you're suddenly all nostalgic and want to go home for the first time in three years. I'm not stupid, Tyler."

"What's that supposed to mean? I never said you were. Cabe, I'm not going home to see Dwayne."

"But you are going to see him, aren't you?" His tone bristled with accusation, accompanied by a brow arched so high it seemed to be pointing at me above his intense glare.

I felt uncomfortable answering, like I was guilty of something without knowing what.

"What do you want me to say, Cabe? Yes, I'm sure I'll see Dwayne while I'm there. Is that really such a bad thing? Is it terrible that I want to see him? To talk to him? I know it's probably because he's lonely, okay? I'm not stupid either. But maybe it feels good that he wants to see me and needs me. I feel like the tables have turned a little in my favor. With what the guy put me through, is it wrong to want to be on this side of the coin for a little bit? And maybe I'm just happy that after all these years, I can finally go home without being scared I might accidentally run into him. That I can see him without feeling my guts wrench. Is that wrong of me?"

Cabe sneered and took out his wallet to pay the check, his plate unfinished.

"I should have known," he said. "Ready to go?"

"Should have known what?" I asked, confused as to why he seemed so angry with me. He clearly thought I was doing something wrong. Either to me or to Dwayne, or both. Or to him somehow. He seemed to be taking it so personally. I just didn't understand why.

We rode back to my place in silence. I felt like I was in trouble. Like I had gotten caught skipping school or something and would get grounded when we got home.

He walked me upstairs to my door, but he hung back when I unlocked the door instead of standing with me like usual.

"You coming in?" I asked.

He shook his head no. I walked over and looked up at him. My heart hurt at the sadness I saw in his eyes.

"C'mon, Cabe, don't do this. I'm fine. I'm just going home for a visit. It's not about Dwayne. I'm not going home for him."

Suddenly, Cabe wrapped his arms around me and pulled me to him for an unexpectedly passionate kiss. It caught me off guard, and I don't even remember whether I kissed him back or stood there like a limp rag. He kissed me like it was the last time we would ever see each other. One hand twisted in my hair to pull me hard against his lips while the other planted firmly across my lower back holding me against his body. He held me so tightly, I could barely breathe. I felt like I might pass out, but I didn't know if it was from lack of air or the way he was completely blowing my mind by plundering my mouth.

Then, just as suddenly, he pulled away from me, and his eyes locked mine with an insane intensity before he abruptly let me go and walked down the stairs.

I stood there staring after him, my lips tingling from the contact and my heart stinging from his sudden absence. I felt unsteady as I walked to the stair railing to see him get into his car. I knew without a doubt he would turn and look up at me. I lifted my hand to wave goodbye when he did.

"When are you leaving?" he asked.

My head spun in a dizzy haze as I tried to figure out what just happened. I swallowed hard and forced my voice to sound nonchalant as I answered him.

"Uh, I don't know. I haven't figured that out yet. I have a wedding with Laura the Saturday before, so not until after that."

"Okay. I'd planned to tell you tonight that I have a surprise planned for you that Friday night. So please don't leave until after Friday, okay?"

I nodded. "Yeah, no problem. I have that wedding, so I'll be here Friday no matter what."

He got into his car and drove away.

What the hell?

Wednesday, December 11th

I had the weirdest dreams last night with people's faces and voices all mixed up. I would be talking to Cabe and suddenly realize it was Dwayne. Then I'd be talking to Dwayne and it would morph into Mr. Bad-Breath Bad-Knees, but his voice would be Cabe's. I think all this confusion speaks greatly to the benefits of strict monogamy. Not that I'm dating all these people. Actually, I'm not dating *any* of them. But they're all floating around in my head making me crazy. Er. Crazi-Er.

At least, I thought I was crazy, until I went into work and got reminded there are people *way* crazier than me walking around.

It goes without saying that people take wedding vows too lightly nowadays. The "sanctity" of marriage rarely exists. People trade spouses with the same consideration and thought they give to trading cars. (Sometimes even less so.)

Melanie got a call today from Greg, a groom she had two years ago. I remember the wedding. In fact, I think everyone in town remembers the wedding. Greg owned several race cars on the stock-car circuit, and he married one of the models hired to present trophies at the track. They had an Arabian Nights theme where Greg dressed as some sort of sheik and his buxom bride Belinda played princess. He spared no expense in creating his fantasy wedding, which included a camel and an elephant inside the reception. (Oh, good Lord, the number of permits and permissions Mel had to get to bring exotic animals into a food service location!)

The servers and bartenders all wore harem pants. Belly dancers and sword eaters entertained while guests smoked hookah pipes on the patio. They flew in traditional musicians from Saudi Arabia. Quite the magnificent, extravagant affair. Mel drew a firm line against having cobras in baskets, but other than that, they pretty much had no limits.

189

At any rate, Greg called today. The marriage lasted less than a year—shocker—and now Greg is engaged to Tabitha, a model and aspiring actress he met at a race. He wants the same exact event all over again. Same menu, same colors, same linens, same band. Bring back the camel and the elephant. Call up the belly dancers and get the same photographer booked. He wants it all the exact same way. The only catch (besides a different bride) is Greg doesn't want Tabitha to know he's already done this. Like not just already been married before, but already did this exact wedding.

How romantic.

It's wonderful he had such a great time the first go-round. It's awesome we did such a great job he wants us to do it all over again. But he doesn't want his bride to know.

What a nice way to start out a "lifelong" commitment to each other. With honesty, openness, and full disclosure. Total involvement and investment of both parties.

Partners are not interchangeable. You can't substitute one for another.

Ew. I wish sometimes we could just say no. We don't want to do your wedding. We don't want your money. We don't want to help you contribute to the divorce rate and the brokenness of society.

This job makes a mockery of love sometimes.

I didn't hear from Cabe or Dwayne today. Or Mama. The radio silence was somewhat peaceful.

Friday, December 13th

Tomorrow's bride and groom are the scariest people I've ever met.

Drago is an MMA fighter with massive biceps and a ripped body that looks chiseled out of stone, like a statue you'd see in a museum. Well, if that museum was in the hood. With the exception of his face, tattoos cover all visible skin on his body. Fully-inked sleeves encircle both arms and all the way around his neck right up to his jaw line. He even has a large skull tattooed on the back of his bald head and a small sword tattooed on his cheek. His tattoos don't scare me, though. I'm fine with tatts. I'm even fine with the multiple piercings in his eyebrow, and the bolt through his tongue. It's his eyes that freak me out.

Drago looks like he wants to kill somebody. Like, at all times. I've never seen him angry, nor do I ever want to see him angry. But I've never seen him happy either. In the few brief encounters I've had with Drago, he hasn't shown any emotion at all. Just a cold, impersonal stare that seemed to be sizing up what method would be most effective for killing me.

If Felicia is aware of the murderous-demon side of her fiancé, she doesn't let it show. She's a stunner. Long, lean, and muscular. She's tall, at least 5'10", but she still has to look up at Drago.

Felicia carries herself with the air of a woman who knows what she wants, knows what she's worth, and is in control. I don't get the impression Drago is her puppy dog, but I think he knows what he's got and appreciates it. After all, not that many grooms show up for an initial contract meeting for day-of coordination, and even less show up for final contract meetings. Especially big, huge, scary, tough-guy grooms.

While Drago scares me in a he-might-kill-me way, Felicia scares me for totally different reasons. If anything screws up at her wedding, she may eat me alive. She has a firm grasp on what she expects to happen, and she's done her research. She told me she only hired me because she knew she couldn't be everywhere on the wedding day. If she trusted a friend or relative to help out, then they might do something the way they wanted and not follow her instructions to a T. That would cause conflict. She figured if she hired someone—me—then I would have to do whatever she asked, the way she wanted it, or there'd be hell to pay.

Some people consider "day-of" coordination to be a piece of cake, but for me, not so much. I prefer being involved from the beginning so I can have some say-so in what vendors they hire and how it's all arranged. When I come in for day-of only, everything is already set. If it's been planned poorly or less than desirable vendors have been contracted, it's too late. But I'm still responsible for making sure everything goes smoothly. No matter how good of a coordinator I am, if the couple hired crappy people and didn't plan well, there is only so much I can pull out of my hat on the actual day. So to be responsible for how it all turns out when I had no input on the front end scares me.

Especially with a bride like Felicia who might claw me to death if anything goes wrong, and a groom like Drago who may actually kill me.

When I arrived for the rehearsal, everyone was already there. *Early*. That has *never* happened before. Rehearsals are notoriously, annoyingly late. I commented on how prompt they all were, and one of the bridesmaids informed me Felicia told them if they were late, they would no longer be part of the wedding party and would not be allowed to attend the wedding.

She means business. And they know it.

I got everyone lined up and showed them where to stand on the altar area, and then I took them to the back of the church to get them in processional order. I asked for the parents to step forward to lead the processional line.

I recognized Felicia's mom right away, but I couldn't find Drago's mom. I asked loudly if his mom could please step forward.

"She's not here," Felicia called out from the back of the church. "She got shot."

I thought I misunderstood. Undoubtedly, the bride did not just tell me the groom's mother got shot in the same calm, matter-of-fact voice she would use to say something like, she's stuck in traffic. Or her manicure ran late. Or her flight got delayed.

"I'm sorry, what?" I asked again just to be sure.

"Drago's mom got shot last night, so she's not here. She may make it tomorrow. I'll let you know in the morning."

Not a single person acted the least bit alarmed when Felicia said it. I mean, everyone but me obviously already knew, but why was no one reacting? Was this a common occurrence? Such uneventful news no one thought to mention it earlier? And this happened *last night???*

"Oh, okay," I said, trying to go along with the blasé crowd.

Drago didn't look upset. Neither did Felicia. No one seemed to be remotely bothered by the groom's mother getting shot. I wondered what the circumstances were, and I struggled not to ask the questions replaying over and over in my mind. What happened? Who shot her? Was it an accident? Where'd she get shot? Is this normal?

Instead, I turned back to the processional to see everyone looking impatiently at me. Throughout the rehearsal, the bridesmaids and groomsmen laughed or talked lightheartedly at various times, but I never saw a smile or any display of emotion from Drago. He stayed by Felicia's side without fail, and he did whatever I asked him to do politely. Always with that murderous glare, though. I wondered if perhaps he shot his mother, but then I admonished myself for even thinking it.

At the end of the proceedings, Felicia stepped forward and stood beside me to address her audience.

"Listen up, people. You need to be at your designated areas at your designated times tomorrow. Read your itineraries very carefully. Tardiness and lack of preparation will not be tolerated. You show up late to my wedding, and you will go home. You will not be a part of the day if you cannot honor my time schedule. I will not be stressed out, and I will not have Dra stressed out due to your lack of consideration. Got it?"

The wedding party and family members all nodded in unison.

"You've all met Tyler," she said, sweeping a long, manicured hand toward me. "Tomorrow she is acting on my behalf and with my authority. If she tells you to do something, I expect it to be done as though I had spoken to you myself. I do not want to hear any reports that anyone showed this lady anything but the utmost respect. Got it?"

Again, nods in unison.

"We are all following each other to the rehearsal dinner so none of you can get lost. Any questions?"

No one dared have any questions, including me.

She amazed me. While I could not imagine living day to day with a man who could and looked like he would kill me, I knew without any doubt he got nothing over on this woman. Truth be told, he might be scared of her, too.

Cabe's been a fan of Drago's for years, following his MMA career since the early days. He practically salivated when I told him we booked this wedding, and he completely freaked out when he found out I met his idol. He texted tonight that he was thinking about crashing the wedding tomorrow. Not a good idea in a group where the groom's mom has already been shot.

We haven't seen each other since the gloom and doom night that ended with the crazy-ass kiss. We've texted, of course, like always, but neither of us have mentioned the kiss or me going home. Classic avoidance.

I would love to know what's up with him just laying one on me like that, but I don't want to rock the boat with so much else going on. I'll wait for him to explain. I also want to avoid another lecture about Dwayne, who has called every day this week, by the way. I did try to call him back once, but it's been a crazy week, so we haven't connected. And that's fine with me. I think I need a little space from both of them.

Saturday, December 14th

Well, I never did find out why Drago's mama got shot, but I did eventually find out how. When I got to the dressing room Felicia told me Drago's mom would just rest at home, and then she moved right into giving me more set-up items and explicit instructions about the favors. One of the photographers said the groomsmen told him it was a drive-by in the neighborhood. His mom just happened to be sitting out on the porch in the crossfire. I didn't understand everyone's calmness, though. Pretty much no one even mentioned her all day. But then one of the servers overheard someone say Felicia went berserk on everyone at the hospital. She told them the shooting would not overshadow her wedding and everyone better be focused on the happy occasion. I couldn't help but imagine the poor groom's mom lying home alone while her son got married without her.

Unfortunately, I didn't have much time for contemplation because all my apprehensions about being a "day-of" coordinator rang true. The caterer, a friend Felicia assured me was a consummate professional, did not realize she had to bring skirted linen for the DJ table, gift table, place card table and head table. She only brought round linens for the guest tables. So I had to scramble to call around and get someone to loan us skirting for the night.

I so wanted to be like, *"Okay, Felicia, this is who you hired, and this is what she brought. So now you get bare-ass wood tables with banged-up metal edges and bent metal legs."* But I couldn't do it. I had to do whatever I could to make the event as flawless as possible. Not just because it's what Lillian and Laura expect of me, but because I don't know how to do anything else. It's someone's wedding. It has to be perfect. Or pretty freakin' close.

That would be how I found myself at Target at nine o'clock at night buying every fork they had since the caterer forgot to bring dessert forks for the cake.

I called Cabe on my way there to say, "You ain't gonna believe what happened now."

He went all teenage groupie on me. "You gotta take a picture with him for me."

"Um, no. I'm not walking up to Mr. Scary Dude whose mama just got shot and ask him to pose for a picture like some stalker girl."

"Come on, Ty. I would kill to meet this guy. He's freakin' tough. Can't you say you get pictures with all your brides and grooms or something?"

"I'll see what I can do, Cabe, but don't count on it. They're not warm and fuzzy. Oh great, they don't have one hundred dessert forks by themselves. I'm not buying full silverware sets just to get dessert forks. This is insane. Let me go so I can call this stupid caterer and see what we can come up with."

"Okay, but get a picture. Or an autograph. Tell him you need him to sign some paperwork or something. Get me an autograph at least!"

With the chaos of getting forks and handling all the other crap that popped up at this event, I never gave Cabe's request a second thought. Until I looked up and saw him standing by the railing along the dance floor, dressed up in slacks, a dress shirt, and a tie. I've seen him in a tie before, but not often. I was so dazzled by how handsome he looked that it took me a couple of seconds to wonder why he was standing there. I zigzagged along the outside of the dance floor making my way to him and trying not to get knocked out by the overzealous dancers.

"What are you doing here?" I asked.

"Well, hey, Buttercup! Glad to see you too!"

"Yeah. Glad to see you. Now what are you doing here?"

He laughed and smiled his most charming, forgive-me smile.

"I couldn't pass up the chance to meet Drago, so I thought I'd come help you with the wedding. There must be something I could do."

"You can't show up at somebody's wedding, freak. Felicia's going to go ballistic. She'll probably have you arrested or something." I looked around to see if her hawk eyes were already zoned in on him, but she stood with her back to us talking with guests.

"I'll work. I'll do whatever you tell me to. Just give me a job, and you'll never even know I'm here. Then maybe introduce me to Drago before the end of the night."

"Cabe, you can't be here. Dude, not cool."

With any other bride, it might have been okay, but not Felicia. I've bored him to tears with wedding details for years, so it would be nice for him to see first-hand. Not a wedding bordering on disaster like this one, though. I couldn't risk him doing something to upset Felicia.

"Give me twenty minutes. Give me a job to do, and let me be here for twenty minutes. I just want to see him, and then I'll go home. You don't even have to do the autograph or a picture or anything. Come on, Ty. I'd do it for you."

"Yes, except no one wanders into your office I would have any desire to meet." I knew he was right, though. If the tables were turned, he would do whatever he could to get me in and help me meet someone. I bit my lip and plunged into the realm of unprofessional bad decisions.

"Okay, you want a job? Go check the bathrooms. Make sure they have plenty of toilet paper, paper towels, soap. Make sure the trash cans aren't overflowing and that there's no mess." I crossed my arms and smiled at him, sure he would balk at doing it.

"Don't they have employees to do that?" he asked.

"Aha, so you're begging for a job and the first one I give you, I get attitude. Okay, time for you to go."

He rolled his eyes. "I'll do it;. I don't care. I'm just surprised they don't have employees to do that."

"They do, but I have to make sure everything is taken care of. Which includes keeping an eye on the bathrooms."

Cabe saluted me and headed toward the back of the building and the restrooms.

I scanned the crowd, relieved to find Felicia still smiling and in conversation. I went to check with the limo driver about the upcoming exit, and then to double-check the catering kitchen to make sure they were getting everything cleaned up in there.

Cabe came bouncing up to me with the hugest, goofiest grin I've ever seen him wear. Which is saying a lot because he has a lot of goofy grins.

"You're the best! You're awesome! I just met Drago in the bathroom! Did you know he was in there? Is that why you sent me? 'Cause I thought you were sending me to be a smartass, like to see if I would do it. Then I go busting up in there, and Drago is washing his hands in the sink. Do you have any idea what those hands are capable of? What they've done? What they can do? But there he was, lathering up with some pineapple scented soap. I tore off a couple of towels and handed them to him. I think he thought I was a bathroom attendant. But he said thank you. I wanted to like, shake his hand or something, but I figured that might be bad form. You know, in a bathroom, dude to dude. I mean, he had just washed and all, but still. You don't offer a shake in a bathroom. His biceps are huge, Ty. Way more massive than I thought from TV. I thought television added weight, but I swear he looks bigger in real life."

I noticed several servers standing around us by the kitchen entrance, all thoroughly engaged in Cabe's bathroom story. I grabbed his elbow and led him away from the kitchen, trying not to laugh at his exuberance.

"Okay, so now that you met your crush, can you please get outta here before you get caught?"

I saw Felicia walking toward me in my peripheral and spun to face her with a huge smile.

"Felicia, how can I help you?"

"There's no white wine at the bar. Why are they not offering white wine?" she asked without even a hint of the laughing bride I had seen minutes before.

"I will check on that right now," I said.

"Who's this?" she asked, looking at Cabe.

"This is my . . . um, associate, Cabe. He dropped off . . . some paperwork I needed to sign." I looked from her to Cabe, hoping he didn't say something stupid.

"Congratulations, you look stunning," he said, taking Felicia's hand lightly in his and bowing low to kiss the back of her hand. "We trust your evening has been all you had hoped."

I nearly died. I could not believe he just opened the door for Felicia to list everything she found wrong with the wedding. But she smiled and coyly pulled her hand away.

"And then some," she said, and I swear for a moment I thought she might even be flirting with Cabe. Apparently, no one can resist his baby blues.

"Cabe," I said, putting myself between the two of them, "I need to go and check on the wine. Would you please retrieve those papers I signed? They're in the kitchen."

"I'm all over it," he said before turning back to Felicia. "I wish you all the best in your new life together. Please don't hesitate to let us know if there is anything else we can do to make this evening special."

I glared at him, admiring him and wanting to kill him at the same time. Cabe excused himself and walked toward the kitchen as some guests came to tell Felicia they were leaving early, and I booked it over to the bartender to tell him to turn water into wine if he had to.

Felicia thanked me at the end of the night, telling me it couldn't have gone better if she had handled it herself—a huge compliment coming from her. Of course, she had no idea how much the caterer had screwed up, or that the DJ had lost the first dance CD, or that a snake had been found in the bathrooms when the set-up guys arrived. And that's why you hire a day-of coordinator, I guess. So you don't have to deal with any of the crap that happens at the event. Or any of the sub-par vendors you hired.

Cabe stayed until the bitter end. I must admit, having him with me to pack everything up helped my stress level. Drago and Felicia thanked me again as I escorted them to the limo, and I think Drago might have attempted a smile. Cabe walked along beside us carrying Felicia's bouquet and her overnight bag, beaming even more than the bride or the groom.

Silly boy.

Monday, December 16th

I spent the entire day yesterday Christmas shopping. If I'm going home this year, I need to be the best aunt ever and bring home stellar presents. Unfortunately, the most stellar presents must have all been purchased already. Probably by those insane people willing to give up sleep to shop on Black Friday. I traipsed all over town just to end up with some crappy mediocre toys and collapse in exhaustion as soon as I got home. Who knew shopping could be such a workout?

I had almost finished wrapping the gifts at my desk today when Charlotte said I needed to take a call because she didn't know what to say. It did not surprise me in the least that she didn't know what to say, but it still annoyed me. However, since I wasn't doing anything other than wrapping Christmas presents, I couldn't exactly refuse to take the call.

"This is Tyler, how can I help you?" I asked.

"You have a wedding scheduled this weekend for Travis Bradley. I thought you might like to know the groom is already married to someone else, and his divorce ain't final yet. You can call the Tampa courthouse and ask for case number DRT7V-21Y697."

"I'm sorry. Did you just say the groom is already married?" I asked in case I misunderstood.

"Yes ma'am. He's fighting about the child support and alimony, and he refuses to pay for half the house. So he ain't signed the papers and his divorce ain't final. That wench he's marrying don't know it. You can call the courthouse. It's public record."

I wrote down the number and asked for her name.

"I'd rather not say. I'm trying to make sure he does the right thing by his ex-wife and his kids." She hung up.

I took the memo to Laura, who called the groom, who quickly admitted the truth. He was none too happy we'd been alerted. He told Laura he didn't see why it mattered since he paid his event in full and we were contracted to put on his wedding.

Laura explained we had to have a marriage license to have a legal ceremony, which he would not be able to get if already married. He could still have the party he had contracted, but there'd be no pronouncement of husband and wife.

He was furious. I'm thinking he's going to be pretty willing to sign those papers now. Especially once his fiancée finds out he's still hitched and can't marry her this weekend.

Tuesday, December 17th

Dwayne called to firm up plans for when I'm home. He brought up Christmas again, which freaked me out a little. I mean, going to dinner with him where everyone and their brother would know about it was hard enough to contemplate. But to spend Christmas with him? Oh, good Lord, no! Way more than I want to bite off.

Spending the holiday together felt too fast and too forward. I wanted to be sure I was in control of what I was doing and not just going along with his plans. I opened my mouth to refuse, but he kept right on talking.

"This is our first Christmas since the divorce," Dwayne said. "They're gonna wake up here, then their mama will come get them around noon. It's gonna kill me. I'll tell ya the truth. I don't know how I can let 'em go on Christmas."

It still felt weird for me to think of Dwayne as a dad. We hadn't talked a whole lot about his kids, but I could tell when he did mention the girls he was crazy about them. I got the feeling he's a pretty good dad. I could hear the pain crackling in his voice when he talked about them leaving, and I felt sorry for him.

"Well, look at the bright side," I offered. "At least you get to see them waking up with Santa Claus. That's the best part, right?"

He didn't answer right away, and when he did, it was heavy with emotion.

"Yeah, I guess. I can't tell you how happy I am that you'll be here. That's going to keep me going, darlin'. Knowing even though they're leaving, I'll get to see you is at least a bright spot. Thank you," Dwayne said.

I felt trapped. I don't necessarily want to be Dwayne's pacifier for Christmas, but I also can't stand for anyone to be in pain. Especially not someone I care about, and the truth is whether I like it or not, I do still care about Dwayne.

"How's your mama? I'd like to see her while I'm home," I said to change the subject.

"Well, yeah, yeah. Of course. She wants to see you, too. We'll take a ride over there. Hell, we'll take a ride everywhere. You ain't been home in so long you won't even recognize a lot of things around here. I'll have to give you a tour!"

We talked for a while about stores that had closed and businesses that had opened, people who had married and divorced. A new highway had been built through town last year, and it cut right across his daddy's property. His grandmother had moved in with her youngest daughter.

It's funny how things stay frozen in my mind the same way they were when I left. Yet life goes on there. Things change and evolve. Just because I'm not there doesn't stop it from happening. I felt a twinge of anxiety about going back. Seeing what's changed and what has stayed the same. I know I've changed. A lot. I don't know if I'll still fit in there, or if I ever did. I guess it's only right that Dwayne be part of me figuring it all out. He's part of home for me. So completely ingrained in that world of my past that I can't separate the two completely. Not yet, anyway. It doesn't mean I won't ever be able to.

Thursday, December 19th

I called Cabe last night after yoga to find out what I should wear for my surprise tomorrow night. He's been stubbornly tight-lipped about it, which I suppose is the whole purpose of a surprise. But I hate not knowing. I make my living every day by being as prepared as possible. I plan out every single aspect to make sure there is no room for error or oversight. Surprises are not a good thing in my line of work. It means I didn't plan well enough and the unexpected happened. So it stresses me out to no end to be unprepared and unaware.

Cabe finds this amusing. He once took me to a zoo and made me go the entire day without looking at the map or brochure. I was a nervous wreck, certain we were missing exhibits and losing out on something spectacular by not studying the map. He prefers the whole, "let's see what happens and take it as it comes" approach. That so doesn't fly in the world of event planning.

"Can you at least tell me if I should dress warmly? Are we going to be outside?" I asked.

"It's December. In Florida. There's no way for me to know what the weather will be. Meteorologists don't even know, and they have advanced degrees. Why don't you wear something comfortable and bring a jacket?"

"A jacket? You say it so casually, like I'm a dude or something. I can't just bring a jacket. It has to match what I'm wearing. Am I going dressy with a long pea coat, or should I be casual with denim?"

"My mom always says it's better to be the best dressed in the room than the worst dressed. If you're overdressed, people will assume you're sophisticated. If you're underdressed, they'll think you have no class."

"Ah, a clue. So we're going someplace I need to dress up. Wow, fancy stuff."

"Just pearls of wisdom from my mama, not a clue for you to figure out," he said.

"Okay, Forrest Gump. Did you want to share anything else your mama says?" I teased him, like I always do, but he got really quiet.

"Hello? Are you still there?" I asked.

"Do you think she ever thinks of me? Like, do you think she sees things that remind her of me and she wonders where I am and what I'm doing?"

"Your mom?" I asked, a little slow on catching the transition.

"Yes, Tyler, my mom. I'm sitting here wondering if my mom ever thinks of me," he sneered. "Monica!" He sounded angry, but I realized it had nothing to do with me.

"I'm sure she does, Cabe," I said softly. "How could she not? You were an important part of her life. That doesn't just get wiped out of your brain."

"Humph," he snorted.

"What's up?" I asked. He had mentioned her much less lately, and I wondered what had triggered this.

"I got a package today," he said. "The landlady from Seattle cleaned out the storage shed where she put all the stuff I left there. She said she tried to find an address for Monica and couldn't, so she sent everything to me. Monica's baby pictures, some stuff from college, and what we had together. Pictures, cards, letters. Our wedding album. Things that say we had a life together, but now we don't. How is it that a year ago this girl filled my life every single day? Waking up next to her and going to bed next to her every night. My wife. And now? Nothing. I don't even know where she is. I used to talk to her multiple times a day, and now I haven't talked to her in months. How is that? How does someone go from being your everything to being nothing?"

I knew silence wasn't the best option, but I felt anything I said would be inadequate.

"I don't know, Ty. Does she think of me? Do I cross her mind? Does she even remember she had a husband?"

"You can't do this, Cabe. You can't go there. You gotta put that stuff away. Don't even go through it. Pack it up and put it away somewhere. Hell, just throw it all out."

"I've been looking at it all night. It's like a train wreck. I don't want to see it, but I can't help pulling the next thing out of the box."

"Oh boy. You can't do that. You gotta put it away."

He didn't say anything, and I suddenly wanted very much to be there with him. To take all those painful shards of memory and throw them far away so they couldn't hurt him anymore.

"I'm coming over," I said.

"Okay."

I knew he was in bad shape if he didn't even protest.

"I'll be right there." I grabbed a coat from the hall closet and put on my sneakers.

Pictures, letters, and mementos surrounded him, spread out all over his bed, end tables, coffee table and floor. I could tell he'd been crying. And drinking. His voice didn't belie it on the phone, but when I saw him I knew he was half in the bag.

I started picking up the remnants of his life with Monica, hating her more with every smiling photo of her I saw. I wanted to rip them all in two. I wanted to burn them and throw them in the pool. I wanted to tear her betrayal out of his heart and his mind. Pull her talons from his skin so he could heal and move on without her boring a hole into his brain every time he started to laugh.

Instead, I packed everything back into the box from Seattle, taking care to keep them from bending out of respect for Cabe's emotions.

When I had it all sealed away, I crawled up on the sofa bed and lay down beside my best friend, putting my arms around him. He lay his head on my shoulder, and I heard a strangled groan escape his throat.

"I don't want to be like this, Ty. I don't want to be broken. I don't want to feel like a failure. I wanna be okay."

"You are okay, baby. You're okay." I held him tightly against me, and he allowed me to hold. I gingerly kissed the top of his head and tried to think of some inspirational, healing words to say. None came. Not like he needed it. He seemed at peace in the silence. He shifted onto his side and threw his arm across my stomach. I turned to wrap him up tighter. His head lay against my chest now, tucked under my chin.

At some point, I dozed, waking to the familiar pins and needles in my arm and leg under Cabe. I pushed gently, and he rolled onto his other side without even waking up. I slid down further and massaged my arm to get the blood flowing, trying not to yelp in pain. Then I slipped back into a peaceful slumber, curled up next to my best friend and prepared to protect him from the world.

I awoke to the sound of the door opening and someone entering the pool house.

"Time to wake up, handsome! I made you fresh blueberry muffins!"

I sat up and locked eyes with Cabe's shocked mother.

"Hi, Maggie," I said, figuring casual and nonchalant was the way to go.

"Oh, hi. I'm so sorry, Tyler. I didn't . . . well, I mean, I didn't . . . I should have knocked."

"No, you're fine. I need to get up and get going."

I purposely pulled the covers back all the way so she could see Cabe and I both fully clothed. Even if we were adults, I didn't care to have Cabe's mother think I'd romp between the sheets with her son right under her own roof. Well, technically under her pool-house roof, but still.

"Don't go on my account," she said. She set the tray of muffins and coffee on the small dinette table and wiped her hands together. "I'm going to, um. Yeah. I'm going back to the house. Please make sure he gets up. He has a meeting this morning. Help yourself to a muffin. I didn't bring you coffee. I mean, I didn't know you were here. I should have checked the driveway, I suppose."

I felt embarrassed, although I hadn't done anything wrong. I had stayed there to support a friend. A friend whose mother wakes him up in the morning evidently, which is slightly creepy, I think.

He stirred and rolled over on the sofa bed, rubbing his eyes and yawning.

"Are you two going to talk all morning?" he asked.

"I brought you muffins and coffee," she told him.

"I'm just leaving," I said, smiling at Maggie and letting myself out the door. The morning walk of shame isn't the same when you didn't do anything naughty prior to the walk.

Friday, December 20th

Cabe called at six this morning and yelled, "Surprise!"

"What?" My mouth mumbled as my brain fought to slip back into deep sleep.

"Surprise!" he yelled again, and I resisted the urge to hang up on the man. Somehow pushing END CALL just doesn't have the same theatrical effect as slamming down the receiver. What's the point?

I yawned loudly to make sure he knew I had been asleep. "I don't get it. What's my surprise? That you're waking me up?"

"No, but today is your surprise day, so I am calling to say surprise."

"You are way too excited about this," I said.

"And you are way too *not* excited about this," he said. "Come on. Be at least a little bit curious."

"Curious? Are you kidding me? It's about to kill me not knowing what you're plotting. I'm beyond curious. You won't even tell me what to wear." I rolled out of bed and shuffled to the kitchen, balancing the phone on my shoulder as I started the coffee pot.

"You will look beautiful no matter what you wear. Be ready at four-thirty sharp. You can't be late!"

"Where are we going at four-thirty in the afternoon? Now I really don't know what to wear!"

"Dress for the evening, not the drive," he said.

"Oooh, so we're driving somewhere far away if we have to leave early, but we're dressing for dinner." I smiled, rather pleased with myself for deciphering his covert language.

"You are impossible," he said. "It's supposed to be a *surprise*. You aren't supposed to try to figure it out."

I didn't figure it out. I don't think I could have figured it out in a million years.

A couple of years ago, Cabe and I were having a conversation about life, something we discussed quite often before he starting dating Monica and moved away. Back when he seemed to be the calm, cool, collected one and I was the one randomly crying and getting emotional about the travesties of life. I babbled on that night about growing up in a small town and how I always dreamed about moving away to the big city. I thought people who lived in cities always went to art galleries and museums, attended the ballet, and ate big brunches every Sunday. At the time we talked, I realized even though I'd been living in the city for quite some time, I had yet to do any of those things. I swore then to make a point of visiting a museum or an art gallery once a month and to see at least one ballet before the end of the year. I kept my commitment to the museum and art galleries for the grand total of one month, but I did buy a ticket to see *The Nutcracker* with friends.

I never made it. The night of the ballet, Cabe called me from his bathroom floor, certain of his imminent death from food poisoning. He had tried a couple of friends since his mother and sister were out of town visiting relatives for the holidays, but got no answer.

He felt horrible about calling me, but given the seriousness of the situation, I surrendered my ticket without hesitation. We spent the entire night in the ER trying to get him hydrated and able to keep something down. So I missed *The Nutcracker*. He promised he'd make it up to me, but life got in the way. Or rather, Monica got in the way.

Tonight, Cabe, the best friend a girl could ever have, made good on his promise, and I finally got to see a real ballet. Wow. Beyond anything I thought it would be. Mesmerizing. Breathtaking. Beautiful. The sound of their feet on their stage. The strength of their legs. Their grace. The emotions they conveyed. And the costumes! Spectacular.

Cabe had seen *The Nutcracker* before. He's pretty much seen everything because his mom was a professional dancer before she had him and his sister Galen. Maggie made sure she exposed them to the arts from a very young age. Plays, Broadway shows, concerts, operas, ballets—you name it, Cabe has seen it.

Even he agreed tonight was special, though. A stellar cast and a thoroughly moving performance. It's funny, because I haven't thought much about it being Christmas, what with the trip home, the mama drama, the whole situation with Dwayne, Cabe being back home, and of course, the constant state of crazy that is my job. But tonight, watching Clara fight alongside the Nutcracker and then the Sugar Plum Fairy dancing—I felt a little bit nostalgic and misty-eyed about the holidays. I have only good memories of the holidays growing up. The first one without my dad sucked for sure, but I loved Christmas with my extended family. Lots of cousins, aunts and uncles. Everybody eating too much, playing card games, and opening presents. Singing Christmas carols on hayrides, decorating the tree, waking up early to see what Santa brought, my grandmother's egg custard pie. Warm thoughts flooded through me.

I've avoided home for so long. Scared of slipping back into the dark place I escaped when I crawled out of there and left. But that has caused me to miss so many good things. My family, my home. My baby brother is grown, a man now. My niece and nephew only know me from my pictures and occasional Skype calls over the internet. My grandmother passed away while I hid out down here.

Tonight's warm and fuzzy holiday mood made me see things from a different angle. I think I may actually be getting excited about going home for Christmas. Cabe's gift did more than just repay me for taking care of him or introduce me to the art of ballet. He restored my holiday spirit. I mean, I don't think I'll be humming Christmas carols all day tomorrow or anything, but I think I can push aside the tension about Mama, Dwayne, Cabe—all of it—and have some peace. 'Tis the season for peace, right?

Saturday, December 21st

What a whirlwind of a bizarre event! Travis didn't get his divorce. Because they had opted not to do a rehearsal last night, Diane didn't find out about her fiancé's marital status until two hours before she planned to marry him herself. Harry, the minister, went with Travis to tell her. As could be expected, it didn't go well. Diane's moods swung from fury to heartbreak and back to anger before she settled into embarrassment when the reality set in. All dressed up in a beautiful gown with fifty people here to celebrate a wedding that couldn't happen.

Harry suggested they do a "love ceremony", in which they pledge their love and commitment to each other, but without the pronouncement of husband and wife. No announcements by Harry or the DJ, and no wedding marquees in the convention center. It could not in any way be portrayed as a legal ceremony, but they could stand in front of their guests and promise to love each other, then celebrate with a reception. So many couples nowadays opt not to use the traditional vows that most of their guests probably wouldn't even realize the marriage didn't take place, unless, of course, the couple chose to share the news.

Diane disappointed me a little by going through with it. I expected a different reaction. She's either a pretty good actress, or she wasn't too concerned that the man she loves is a liar who doesn't want to support his children or be responsible for his obligations.

Funny what people are willing to overlook in order to get what they think they want.

Dwayne called just as I finished laundry and packing around nine.

"Hello, darlin'!"

"Hey, Dwayne." I smiled at the excitement in his voice sounding like a little kid knowing Santa is coming soon.

"What time are you leaving tomorrow?" he asked.

"I want to get on the road around seven, which should put me there early afternoon."

"My girls both have parts in the Christmas cantata tomorrow night at church, so you'll get to see them."

My peaceful feeling wavered like a hologram and then vanished completely. I hadn't even considered I would need to see Dwayne and his family at church. I mean, if his kids would be in the cantata, his ex-wife would be there, too. That old, familiar tension solidified in my belly like I had eaten bad chicken salad. Dang it. I didn't want to dread going home again when I just started to be excited about it. "Oh, wow. Ellain's going to be there, huh?"

I briefly considered illnesses that could befall me in the next twenty-four hours, but I knew my Mama was gonna make me go to church no matter what. I could have symptoms of the German measles and ebola while simultaneously bleeding from a missing limb, and that woman would still insist that if the church doors were open, that's where I needed to be.

"Well, yeah," Dwayne said, "but she'll be sitting with her family, so don't worry about her. If mama feels up to it, she wants to come, and I know a whole bunch of people who will be thrilled to see you."

I felt the panic rising up inside me, and I struggled to fight it. I had been so happy just a few moments before.

"I don't know, Dwayne. I don't want to be on display for everybody. I'd rather sit quietly in the back and hope no one notices me."

"Girl, yo mama has done told everybody who would listen that you're coming home. Ain't no way you're gonna sit in the back and nobody notice you. You'll probably get more attention than Calvin Thompson's three-month-old who is playing the Baby Jesus."

"Great," I said. "Upstaging the Baby Jesus the week of Christmas. Sure to win me brownie points in hell."

"Aw, they'll end up having to use a doll anyway. Ain't no way a three-month-old will lay up there in a bunch of hay for a whole cantata."

"Awesome, that's way more comforting. If it's not a real Baby Jesus, then it's not so bad." I rolled my eyes and shook my head even though he couldn't see me.

Dwayne made me promise I'd call if I needed anything on the road tomorrow. I hung up feeling slightly nauseous with my shoulders about two inches closer to my ears than they had been.

I texted Cabe, and he called right back.

"You rang?" he asked.

"Not technically," I answered.

"Yes, but 'you texted' just doesn't have the same ring to it. Get it? Ring to it?"

"Yeah, I get it. Look, I know me going home is a sensitive issue for us right now, but I'm freaking out and I really need to talk to you. Dwayne's kids are going to be in the cantata and his ex-wife will be there."

"What's a cantata?" he asked.

"Is that all you got out of that?" I sighed. "It's a concert of music and Christmas songs at the church. Did you hear the part about Dwayne's wife? Ex-wife?"

"Yeah, I just don't know why you care. You're not dating him, right? And you said you're not going home to see him. What does it matter if she's at the same church as you? God's big enough to love both of you, I'm thinking."

"No, I'm not dating him, but it's awkward. She knows who I am. I know who she is. And it's just . . . I don't know. It's weird."

"Why? It shouldn't be. You guys knew each other, like, five years ago. She doesn't know you now, and you don't know her. Y'all happened to be involved with the same man once upon a time. But neither one of you is involved with him now, so I don't see the problem."

He said it so cut-and-dry, like I was being unreasonable or something. I wished I hadn't even texted him.

"You don't get it," I said.

"No, you're right. I don't. Why do you care if she's going to be at church? She's not coming to your mom's for dinner, and it's not like you have to speak to her or anything. So unless there's a whole lot you're not telling me, it's not like you're going to have to deal with her or even see her again after this."

Logic wasn't what I wanted. I wanted to be distraught, overly dramatic, and indignant. Cabe wasn't cooperating.

"Alright, never mind. Sorry I bothered you." Okay, maybe I was being a little childish, but oh well.

"Well, alrighty then. Aren't we in a great mood this evening? Sorry if I didn't say what you wanted to hear," he said.

Oh, how I hated when he was right and sarcastic at the same time.

"I gotta go. Talk to you later." I hung up. Without saying goodbye. Without giving him a chance to say goodbye. Like a thirteen-year-old pouty girl.

My phone rang immediately.

"What?" I said.

"Did you really just hang up on me over something as stupid as Dweeb Davis's ex-wife going to church? Are you freakin' kidding me right now? Do you want me to come over there and bend you over my knee?" he asked.

"As much as you would probably derive intense pleasure from that, no, I don't think that's what I want at all. I want you to be a dutiful friend and be upset about what I'm upset about."

"I am a very dutiful friend, which is why I am telling you that you have absolutely no reason to be upset. Now tell me goodbye properly. I won't see you for days. You're leaving me here all alone for Christmas, and I refuse to be hung up on."

"I'm not leaving you here all alone. You have your mother and your sister. I'm sure some cousins or other relatives will stop by."

"Whatever eases your guilt."

"Aargh. You're such a pain in my butt."

He laughed, and I smiled. I swear I will never get tired of hearing his laughter.

"I'll miss you, buddy," I said.

"Yeah, yeah. I know you will. Call me when you get there. If you have any trouble on the road, I can be right there. Well, it may take me a couple of hours depending on how far you get, but you call and I'll come running."

"Wouldn't it be better to bring your car?"

"Yah, yah, yah," he said, mocking me in a nasal tone.

"Goodnight, Cabe," I said, still smiling.

"Night."

I felt 100% better. How does he always do that?

Sunday, December 22nd

Great weather today for driving! Although the slight chill in the air when I left morphed into a frigid blast by the time I got halfway to Mama's. I refused to close the convertible roof, though. The gorgeous blue sky and fluffy white clouds were worth wearing a couple extra layers. Besides, I just turned the heater on high and kept the windows up.

I hate to say it, but Cabe was right. I worried for nothing. The cantata went fine. The packed church held so many people I hadn't seen in forever. People I forgot I even knew. They knew me, though. Coming up all night to hug me and tell Mama how pretty I looked, which made her beam. So nice to make her happy for a change!

Dwayne stood just inside the doors as we entered, probably waiting on me to get there. He wrapped me in a huge hug and grabbed my hand to lead me to his mama, but I pulled it away and pretended to adjust something with my hair clip. It felt like too much to be holding hands in church like we were seventeen again.

Martha Jean's frail appearance shocked me. The strong, hefty woman in my memory worked alongside her boys on the farm and at the lumber mill, tough as an ox. My mind refused to accept the pale, scary-thin waif in the wheelchair before me as the woman I remembered. She smiled when Dwayne spoke, and I could tell she recognized me. She didn't say anything beyond hello and nice to see you, though, and I had to look away from the pain and misery in her eyes.

Dwayne sat with his mama, and I sat with mine, which alleviated any awkwardness and gossip from us sitting together. As it turns out, Ellain stayed in the back helping with the kids and their costumes. Which was fine by me.

As I write this from my old bed in my old bedroom, I feel like I'm having a flashback in some weird dream sequence. Mama hasn't changed a thing in here. My tie-dye rainbow comforter. The big peace sign poster from my hippie throwback phase in high school. So many memories in this room. A lifetime. Every ceiling tile, every plank of pink paneling, the curtains, the closet doors. So familiar to me. Like I never left in some ways, but at the same time, like I've been gone forever.

The bulletin board on the wall still has photos pinned to it, yellowed and curled from the sun coming through the window day after day. I barely recognize the girl in those pictures. So young and carefree. She had no idea what life had in store for her. I can't help but wonder as I look at those pep rallies, parties, and trips to the river if I would have done things differently if I'd known what would happen. Would I have left here on my own if I hadn't been running from Dwayne? If I had known how that relationship would end, would I have stayed in college and finished my degree? Would I still have gone to Orlando? What career would I have now?

Back then, I made choices for my life based on Dwayne's. If he'd been out of the picture, what would I have picked? What would I have done? I can't imagine I would have ever ended up doing weddings. Or meeting Lillian and Laura. Or Cabe. Hard to imagine my life without them all in it. And yet, it could have very easily been so. Different choices. Different turns.

I guess that all things considered, my life is pretty cool now. I don't intend to thank Dwayne or give him any kudos for breaking my heart, but all in all, it turned out okay. For me, at least. Him, not so much.

I'm going to sink under these covers and enjoy being home. It feels safe. It feels good.

Monday, December 23rd

Mama and I spent most of the morning at the grocery store and in the kitchen. She got the brilliant idea of hosting Christmas for the entire extended family at our house since I'm home this year. While I appreciate the sentiment, I don't think Mama's in a financial position to be supplying food for the whole bunch, and I certainly could have done without all the prep work. Believe you me, working alongside my mama in the kitchen is nothing at all like cooking with Cabe. And I'm not even allowed to drink some wine to help the process along. Aargh. She gave all my aunts and cousins a list of what each of them should bring, but she still felt she needed to make enough food for an army since she's hosting.

I made my escape when Dwayne called to say he left work early and wanted to meet up sooner than we had planned. I think if I'd been going anywhere else with anyone else, Mama would have told my butt to stay in the kitchen with her. She's all misty-eyed thinking we're getting back together, though, so she seemed all too willing to excuse me from my duties.

We stopped by Martha Jean's, which was hard. I didn't know what to say. It's hard enough to make small talk with someone I haven't seen in years, but to see his mama so uncomfortable and in pain made it even more awkward. We left there and visited his grandma, who greeted me like the prodigal child returning from war. My own mama showed less enthusiasm to see me than Mrs. Dolores.

When we left there, Dwayne turned and twisted along familiar roads, familiar routes. The miles we'd ridden hundreds of times before were peppered with subtle changes here and there. We listened to our music, laughed at old jokes and recounted stories of days gone by. The surreal déjà vu feeling persisted as I felt myself slipping back into the shell of the girl I

216

used to be, at once unsettling and yet familiar. She emerged within me almost like an alternate personality, someone I'd kept hidden but could now appreciate and experience once more.

He turned down a little dirt road, and I started laughing.

"What do you think you're doing?" I asked.

This little dirt road led to a whole other set of memories probably best forgotten. I wasn't nervous at all, though. I felt totally at ease, more-so than I had in years. I knew he wouldn't take me anywhere I didn't want to go.

He pulled off in the little clearing I knew so well, but the overgrowth and unkempt state amazed me.

"I guess no one comes out here anymore, huh?" I stepped high over tall grass and fallen logs, thankful like never before that Mama had saved my boots for me.

"Nah. There's a new swim hole up river a bit, and everybody pretty much goes there. Every now and then one of the old-timers still come here to fish, but the last flood washed it out so much you can't swim here no more. Too dangerous."

Everybody spent the entire summer here back in high school. In fact, any sunny day was an excuse to be on the river bank with a blanket and a cooler. Sunning, swimming, and perhaps sneaking an adult beverage or two.

Dwayne stopped walking near the bank, and it took me a minute to get my bearings. The flood had changed the course of the river. Moved it a little closer to the road. The long, wide, sandy bank of our youth was nowhere to be seen. Deep under water from the look of it.

He reached back and took my hand as he started walking again, and I let him. It felt good. It felt natural in our old stomping grounds. I had gone back in time and the world spun right again. He carefully navigated the bank, stepping over tree roots and then turning to help me over, one time even lifting me off the ground and over a twisted, gnarly piece.

I had no doubts where he was taking me, and I silently hoped the river and the ravages of time hadn't marred it. I didn't realize I was holding my breath until I crossed the last oak and let go of Dwayne's hand to duck under the leaning tree and enter our secret spot. We found it years ago while exploring along the river bank looking for a fishing place. We weren't the first ones to find it, or the last to visit it from the occasional beer bottles and food wrappers we'd find from time to time, but it had been our secret place. A special place we called our own.

The old tree leaned far to the left, away from the bank, undoubtedly the victim of a previous flood. Its roots twisted and buckled up out of the dirt, rising high enough on one side to meet the low-hanging branches that had turned downward seeking the water and the sun as the tree leaned. The two had eventually intertwined to form a small shelter at the base of the tree, a fortress of sorts with roots for walls and a dense canopy above that blocked out all the sun.

The large, flat, river boulder we called the floor was covered in soft, green moss—the only thing that could survive in the damp, shaded darkness. Dwayne plopped down on the ground and patted the moss beside him. I noticed as I sat that the shelter looked almost exactly as it had before. Granted, the lack of sunlight probably kept the overgrowth at bay, but someone had tended it well.

"I still come out here," he answered my unspoken question. "Always have. It's like the only place I can clear my head. Forget everything and just be. I love the sound of the water flowing. The wind in the trees. Birds, crickets. The world as God intended it to be. No traffic and nobody raising hell at me."

I turned and looked at him, wondering what his marriage had been like. Had he been happy? Had he regretted it? Had he really wanted her badly enough to throw me away? And had it been worth it? I still think no one walks down the aisle thinking they'll break up in the end. So what was the turning point? When did it become a mistake instead of a miracle? When did he know it wasn't what he thought it would be?

"Do you think you'd ever get married again?" I asked him.

If I thought about how it would sound, like maybe I was asking for myself, then I probably wouldn't have said it. But it was already out before I thought it through.

He lay on his back gazing up at the tiny patches of sky through the leaves. He looked younger somehow. Less haggard, less tired. Still skinnier than he should be, but the old Dwayne materialized from somewhere within the tormented man on the ground beside me.

"I guess so. I still believe in it. I think it's a good thing, marriage. Mine just didn't work out, that's all," he said without ever looking over at me.

"How you can say that? I mean, how can you still think it's good, after what happened?"

I thought about my own fears and the walls I'd put up. Not wanting to be vulnerable or be hurt. How could he even think of getting married again after what Ellain did to him? How could Cabe? How could anyone? I couldn't imagine throwing myself into such a heavy commitment again after someone betrayed me like that.

He turned his head toward me. His face looked funny from my angle, like it was upside-down and out of proportion.

"Because there has to be good, Tyler. Look at all the people that are married. Marriage isn't bad just because some of them don't work out. The people in the marriage screw up. That don't make marriage itself bad."

"I don't know," I said, looking away from him at the flowing water. "Seems like a lot of people are divorced. I would say I know more divorced people than married."

"Well, then you need to meet new people. Love makes the world go 'round, darlin'. Loving somebody and giving them your heart is about the scariest thing you can ever do, but it's the best damned feeling in the world. Ain't no way I'd give up on loving just because somebody screwed up. I ain't gonna let them screw me up because they are."

I looked at him and wondered how on earth he could say that to me. I'm sure he spoke based on his own recent experiences, but I couldn't help but feel like he had called me out. Like somehow he knew I shut myself off to other people because of what he did to me, and rather than apologize, again, for what he had done, he placed the blame on me for harboring it. Now, maybe he didn't mean that at all, but that's what I got out of it. It really made me think.

I slowly took in the gorgeous scenery around me. The dark, brown, muddy water swirling and churning past us. The gentle sway of the oaks and pines in the cold December breeze. The perfect blue sky peeking through here and there, without a cloud in sight. I sighed and inhaled the peace around me.

I never in a million years thought I'd ever be sitting here again. Let alone with Dwayne Davis. Just to think of this place would pretty much put me in a fetal position with intense pain and heartache. But here I sat. In no pain at all. It was simply a place. They were just memories. Moments in our past, mine and his. I watched the river carry a branch past me, dried leaves struggling to hold on and stay afloat as the water dipped and turned them about. Like my memories. Moving past me suddenly and carried away to a place they'd never been. I could see this place separate from the man now. I felt a new appreciation for its beauty and serenity.

I looked over at Dwayne, lying on his back with his eyes closed, and I saw him for what he was. A man. An overgrown boy I used to love. Someone who had loved me and made sweet memories with me, but then made a choice to love another. Maybe that choice didn't end like he thought it would, but he was still willing to love again, and he had two daughters he adored.

I couldn't hold the past against him any longer. I couldn't use his mistake to keep holding myself back either. So in a conscious and deliberate act of thinking, I forgave Dwayne Davis. I let him go. I allowed him to be human and make mistakes and let me down. I allowed him to move past what he had done and still be someone I enjoyed talking to. I allowed him to just be him, separate from me and my life.

About the time I had finished mentally separating us, Dwayne sat up and put us together. He leaned over ever so gently and put a light kiss on my cheek and then my lips. Softly. Tenderly. Like we were back in high school with him unsure if I'd say no.

He cupped my cheek in his hand and pulled himself up to get closer to me. His tongue rolled against mine, and I focused on being present in the moment. Not trying to go back. Not trying to remember what had been or recapture what was gone. Dwayne was there, I was there, and we were kissing. And that was okay. I didn't need to question it, analyze it, or have it be anything other than a man and a woman who shared an attraction for each other. It was like I'd stumbled into some out-of-body counseling experience where I could see everything so clearly and be able to look at it in a completely different way than before.

Evidently, we weren't both in that place of Zen. Dwayne leaned back an inch or so and looked at me, smiling his crooked little grin that used to drive me wild.

"Let's pick up where we left off, darlin'. Let's love each other. Hold each other. See where this thing can take us," he said, his voice husky with desire.

I felt no anger, no pressure, no confusion. I felt nothing but peace.

"Dwayne, we can't pick up where we left off. We left off with you marrying somebody else, and my heart shattered in a million pieces on the floor. You can't pick that up, honey. It's impossible." He started to speak but I lifted my fingers to his lips. "We're two entirely different people now. You've had a wife. And kids. And bar fights. I've had," I tried desperately to come up with something in my head to equate to wives and kids and bar fights, but I came up empty. It occurred to me that although there'd been many wonderful experiences in my life since I left, in many ways when Dwayne moved on with his life, I shut mine down. I realized how wrong I'd been to do that. How much I had cheated myself.

"I've had my own experiences," I finally finished. "All the things we've been through have changed us and shaped us, Dwayne. We don't even know each other anymore. Everything since we started talking again—every time we've seen each other—it's all about the past. About what we used to do, who we used to be. We aren't those people anymore."

I felt like I was channeling Oprah or something. Like these brilliant, insightful words were flowing from my mouth while the real me jumped up and down in the background saying, "Yeah, yeah, that's good, that's real good."

He pulled way back to look at me, his forehead scrunched up as he processed what I said.

"So then let's see if the people we are now hit it off," he said.

I laughed softly. "We live in different worlds, honey. We have different goals, different lives. You're not moving down there, and I definitely ain't moving back here!"

He turned his gaze to the water. He looked so crushed.

"Hey," I said, grabbing his hand. "We will always have what we had. A piece of my heart has always and will always belong to Dwayne Davis. You are part of me, part of my past, part of why I am who I am. Both good and bad!" I winked at him when his eyes darted toward me at that comment.

Dwayne shook his head and pulled his hand from mine. "I was such a fool, darlin'. I never should have let you go."

"Yep, you were," I said. I slapped him lightly on his back. "But you did. That's that. This is where we are now. Who knows how else it could have turned out? There's a million scenarios. We might have stayed together and proved your marriage theory solid. Or we might have made each other insanely miserable and ended up tearing each other apart any way. There's no way to know."

"When'd you get all wise and scholarly?" he asked.

I shrugged. "Must be all the nature, helping to clear my mind."

"City living is bad for your health, ya know."

"Maybe so, but for now, it's home." I thought about my cozy little apartment, all my friends from work, and Cabe. I missed my home. Which made me think about Mama probably going crazy wondering where we were and what was happening.

"I'm surprised Mama hasn't called," I said, reaching into my back pocket to pull out my phone.

"I'd be surprised if you get a signal out here," he laughed.

He was right. No signal at all.

"Wow. I haven't been anywhere completely off the grid in a very long time." I thought about how enticing it sounded to be somewhere no bride could reach. That would backfire though, because then they'd be even more frantic by the time you got back to them.

Dwayne stood and extended his hand to pull me up. I grabbed hold and stood, brushing off the back of my jeans with my phone hand. On the second swipe of my jeans, it went flying. The phone arced up high and then fell ever so slowly and gracefully right into the rushing water. It was like watching a disaster movie in slow motion.

"No!" I screamed, nearly diving in after it instinctively. Dwayne ran along the edge of the bank, looking like he'd jump in any minute. "It's no use," I said. "Forget it. I can't believe I just did that. Oh my God. My phone. Holy crap! My phone is gone."

I suddenly felt disconnected from the world, which I know is a bit dramatic, but I practically live on my phone. Between calls, texts, and e-mail, it is my line of constant communication with everyone around me. I felt punched in the gut as I searched the water for any miraculous floating, bobbing electronic. None appeared.

We both walked to the truck in a somber mood. Me for the loss of my phone; Dwayne for the loss of his safety net, I suppose. I guess it would have been kinder to give that speech after Christmas, but it happened so spur of the moment. The river moved me. I didn't plan to say it. Or feel it.

"You still want me to come over on Christmas?" I asked as he turned us around on the dirt road. He looked at me like a seven-year-old who's been offered a puppy.

"Would you? Please?"

I nodded, no longer feeling any conflict or tension about it. No uncertainty. All that Oprah channeling had mellowed me out for the moment.

"Sure," I said. "I don't want us to not be friends, Dwayne. I want us to stay in touch. We can hang out while I'm here."

He dropped me off without coming inside. Mama was fit to be tied and so stressed out in the kitchen she didn't even ask what had happened with Dwayne. My brother Brad had called to say he was staying at his girlfriend Kelly's for dinner, and my sister Carrie ended up working a double-shift at the restaurant. Mama had no help all afternoon. I felt bad about bailing on her, so I spent the rest of the night busting my butt to try and make up for it. A little after nine o'clock she finally turned and said, "Soo? How did your day with Dwayne go?"

"Good," I said.

She stopped stirring and peered at me over the top of her glasses.

"That's it? Good? Humph." She started stirring again, and I opened my mouth to elaborate, but decided not to. I didn't know for sure what all had transpired in me this afternoon, and I certainly wasn't ready for Mama to analyze it and pick it apart. Surprisingly, she didn't push it. I think she had too much else on her mind. Maybe it's a good thing we're hosting after all.

Tuesday, December 24th
Christmas Eve

At the risk of sounding like a soft-focus Hallmark commercial, today illustrated what a holiday's supposed to be. I've never felt so warm and fuzzy about my family before. Maybe being away for so long made me appreciate how cool it is to belong to the group. I've had great friends who have graciously invited me to be a part of their holidays since I left here, and I appreciated their inclusion. It's hard to be a part of someone else's holiday, though. You're always aware you aren't family. You don't really belong.

Today, I belonged. It was *my* family. *My* people. *My* aunts and uncles. *My* cousins. Some of whom look so much like me we could be siblings. And of course, my siblings were here today. It has been three years since me, Tanya, Carrie, and Brad have all been in the same place at the same time. I never thought too much about it before, but today I looked at my brother and sisters around me, and it felt cool. To be part of something. To have history. A connection no one can break or decide to walk away from. Which is kind of ironic considering I walked away, but distance can't make us not be siblings.

Several relatives from my dad's side were here, which was awesome. My life in Florida is so far removed from my dad. I loved hearing people talk about him today, telling stories and sharing funny memories of him. We laughed and laughed. What a great feeling to allow myself to remember him with laughter and joy. Free to share without fear of the emotion behind it. They all loved him like I did. They miss him like I do. No one in my daily circle had ever met my dad, so it's like he doesn't exist sometimes. Here, at home, in his house, surrounded by his family, I felt him with me today like I haven't in a really long time.

I guess maybe I moved on from Oprah to channel Shirley MacLaine or some psychic medium or something, but I literally felt my dad's presence laughing with us and reminding us of him.

There were entire blocks of time when I forgot to miss my phone. Normally, I check it every few minutes, but today a couple of hours would go by without me even reaching for it. Bizarre.

I didn't hear from Dwayne, but that didn't surprise me. I knew he had his kids for Christmas Eve, so I expected him to be preoccupied. Plus, I didn't know how he reacted to everything Oprah Me laid on him yesterday.

I called Cabe from our home phone this morning and told him mine was lost.

"I accidentally threw it in a river," I said.

"What the hell were you doing in a river?"

"I wasn't *in* the river. I was on the river bank. I was brushing grass off my butt and my phone went flying."

"Okay, then. Dare I ask why you were on a river bank with grass on your ass?"

"So, what is Santa Claus bringing you?" I didn't care to explain the whole Dwayne in the woods scenario, so I hoped Cabe wouldn't protest the subject change.

"A bottle of Bombay Sapphire if he doesn't check the list, and a bottle of Tanqueray or Gordon's if he does," he answered.

"He always checks the list. Twice, remember? He knows who's been naughty and nice! He should bring you an alarm clock so your mommy wouldn't have to come and wake your grown ass up in the morning to go to work."

"Very funny," he said in his snarky, nasal tone. "She only comes in if she can't sleep. She gets up and bakes. I had an alarm set on my phone to get my grown ass up, thank you very much. It went off about fifteen minutes after you left."

"What did your mom say about me being there?" I asked, curious if they talked about it at all. I hoped she didn't think less of me.

"Nothing, why?"

"Oh, just wondering." My nephew came running in to tell me they were looking for me, so I told Cabe I had to go.

"Well, Buttercup, keep the grass off your ass. I guess you're not going to explain that one. I probably don't want to know. I hope Santa brings you everything you wished for."

"Not likely! I don't think he's gonna cram Prince Charming down my mama's chimney."

"Prince Charming is a putz. He's overrated," Cabe snorted.

He may be right. A whole lot of things are turning out different than I thought on this trip, so it would be just my luck to have Prince Charming delivered and then find out he was some boring sop who drove me nuts. I mean, in all these stupid fairy tales, they pretty much meet one time before declaring love. What if the princess marries him and discovers he doesn't eat with a fork or he refuses to bathe? What if Charming is just his last name and not his one-word profile?

Wednesday, December 25th
Christmas Day

So much for the whole fa-la-la-la-la, peace on Earth malarkey.

The drama kicked off early this morning right after breakfast when my little brother announced his plans to go to his girlfriend's for the day. He simply finished his eggs, thanked Mama for his presents, kissed the top of her head, and said, "See ya later, I'm headed over to Kelly's."

I saw the look of shock on her face and braced myself for the inevitable storm.

"So early? I thought you were going over there for dinner tonight," she said.

"Nah. I told her I'd come on over right after breakfast," he said, putting on his coat and heading out the door.

"Well, when will you be home?" she asked.

"I don't know. I'll call ya. Bye, Ty. Merry Christmas!"

Just like that. Gone. No lengthy, drawn-out arguments or drama scenes. Well, not for him anyway.

I got to spend the next hour and a half listening to her cry and complain about how Brad spends too much time with Kelly and bends over backward for her. Mama feels like Kelly doesn't like her or show her the proper respect. She even complained this would be the first Christmas without Brad in the house. She didn't know if it could be Christmas at all without him there. Never mind that I haven't been home in three years before today. No sirree. My brother ruined Christmas by going to his girlfriend's house.

Mama complained all over again when my sisters arrived, and through the entire hubbub of presents, cooking, cleaning, and chasing around

226

Tanya's kids, Mama still did not let go of Brad's absence. She weaved it into every conversation.

"Mama, give it a rest," said Carrie, usually the one willing to tell her to cut her crap. "What did you think, that he'd just sit around here all day again? He's nineteen, Mama. He has a girlfriend. He hung out all day yesterday with the fam, so of course he wants to be with her today."

"Well, why couldn't they come over here?" Mama pouted.

"Did you invite her?" Carrie asked.

"What? Why would I need to invite her? She's over here all the time as it is. Never gives him a moment's peace. And if she ain't here, she's calling or texting."

"I'm sure her family is having something today," Tanya said. "He spent yesterday with us. Let him be with her today."

"I thought I'd finally have all my kids here together for Christmas," she cried.

"And you did, Ma. Yesterday!" Carrie showed her annoyance with a loud sigh and got up from the table, right in the middle of our card game.

"Where are you going?" Mama asked. "Aren't you gonna play?"

"I'm going to the bathroom, Mother!" Carrie yelled. It seemed to be a cue for everyone to get up and fix a drink or get a snack, so I took the opportunity to go in the kitchen and call Dwayne. I hadn't heard from him yet, and with the whole Brad situation, Mama wouldn't be too keen on me leaving. I figured I'd see if he wanted to come over here after his kids left. How awkward could it be?

The clock in the kitchen said a little after two, and he planned for Ellain to pick the girls up right around noon, so I figured it was safe to call. It rang four or five times and went to voice mail, so I left a message saying Merry Christmas and hung up.

Almost immediately, the phone rang.

"Hey! Merry Christmas!" I said.

A pissed-off female voice screamed into my ear. "Just who the hell is this, and why are you calling my husband?"

It was so unexpected I thought perhaps I had screwed up big time and called some random wrong number with my message, so I checked the caller ID. Sure enough, it said Dwayne Davis.

"Who is this?" she demanded.

"Who is this?" I asked back, still confused but pretty sure I knew who she was.

"This is the wife of the man you're calling, and I want to know who is calling my husband."

I heard Dwayne in the background, telling her to give him the phone and pleading with her to hang up.

They cursed and screamed at each other for a couple of minutes before

I went ahead and hung up on my end.

What the hell??? Were they still married? Had he played me somehow? They couldn't be, though. Mama had talked to other people in town who said he was divorced. If he was still married, why would he lie about it and insist I come to his house for Christmas? It's not like she wouldn't notice if I showed up on Christmas Day. So if he was telling the truth, and he was divorced, then why was his ex-wife calling me back all pissed off and laying claim to her husband? Didn't she leave him?

The phone rang again, and I picked it up and put it back down with no acknowledgment. I had no desire to be cursed at or yelled at. This is where it would be good to have my cell phone instead. The home phone is great for the dramatic receiver slam-down, but the cell phone is awesome for hitting *ignore* and making them go away. The phone rang again. I picked up and hung up again and switched the ringer off on the side of the phone.

"Who keeps calling?" Mama yelled from the dining room.

"Wrong number," I lied, not even wanting to go into it with everyone. I sat down and asked whose turn it was just as the phone rang again from the bedroom. Another advantage to a cell phone. There's only one of them to turn off.

"Well, who on earth?" Mama said, pushing back her chair to get up. "Why isn't the kitchen phone ringing? Did you do something to the phone?"

I stood back up and rushed to get to the kitchen before her. "I got it, Mama. I'll get it."

She beat me to it.

"Merry Christmas!" Mama crooned into the phone, not even bothering to say hello first. She stayed silent for a minute, and I cringed at the thought of her getting cursed at on my account. But then her voice changed and I knew it was Dwayne. "Well, hello there," she said, dripping sugar. "Did Santa Claus come to your house?"

I tried to motion to her that I didn't want to talk, but she paid no attention to me. She was all ears for Dwayne. "Now will we get to see you today? I sure hope so!" Mama giggled in response to whatever he said and ignored me. Then, he must have finally asked for me because she turned and said, "Here she is, honey."

She handed the phone to me, and I tried again to motion that I didn't want to take it. Her nose wrinkled up in a frown. "Tyler, take the phone. It's Dwayne."

Like I didn't know that.

I groaned and took the phone from her, hoping she'd go back to the dining room so I could have a private conversation.

"Hey, Ty! Merry Christmas!"

"Really, Dwayne? That's how you're going to start this?"

"I know, girl. You must be wondering what's going on over here."

"Um, yeah. That question had crossed my mind."

I could hear Ellain in the background on the other end, raising hell and telling Dwayne to "get that bitch off the phone."

"You seem to be having a lovely Christmas, Dwayne," I said. "I'm going to let you go now, so you can deal with the raving lunatic screaming at you. Goodbye."

I heard what sounded like "Tyler, wait!" but I hung up anyway. I turned around to see my mother, both of my sisters, one of my brother-in-laws, and my niece all standing in the kitchen staring at me.

"Don't ask," I said, throwing my hand up in their direction. They all scattered back to the dining room table as I passed them. Mama dared ask first, of course.

"What happened?"

"Mama, I don't want to talk about it. Can we just finish the card game?" I sat back down and picked up my cards, determined not to let Dwayne's issues ruin my day.

About an hour later, he rang our doorbell. I stepped out on the porch and pulled the door shut, careful not to let it slam this time.

"Tyler, darlin', I'm so sorry. I can't apologize enough," Dwayne said. "Ellain came over last night, crying and saying she missed the kids and missed our life. She didn't want to be without 'em on Christmas Eve, which I totally get, 'cause I didn't want to be away from 'em today, ya know? So anyway, she ended up spending the night."

I put my hand up and motioned for him to stop.

"I don't need to hear this," I said. "You don't have to tell me this."

"No, wait, I want you to know," he started, but I didn't let him finish.

"Dwayne, seriously, you don't have to tell me. You don't owe me any explanation this time. We aren't together, remember? You don't have to explain anything to me."

"It's just that she wants to get back together, and I don't know if I should. I mean, it's Christmas. The kids were so happy when they woke up and we were both there. I don't know what to do, Tyler."

"Wait a minute. Are you apologizing that your ex-wife cussed me out, or are you asking me for relationship advice?" I knew on some intellectual level none of this should matter to me in the least, but it struck a little too close. I sensed my inner Oprah channel starting to get a little fuzzy.

"No, I mean, yes. I mean, of course I'm apologizing, and I'm real sorry she did that. She thought you and I had gotten back together, and she's always been a little sensitive where you're concerned."

Okay, the inner channel completely switched from Oprah to Jerry Springer. Too much old baggage bubbling up in this scenario. I took a step back and waved one finger in the air. "*She* is sensitive about *me*? She stole my boyfriend right out from underneath me and married him before I even knew what happened, and *she* is sensitive? Oh, that's classic, Dwayne. That's just freakin' classic."

(I might add it is very possible I didn't say freakin' at all here, but I can't bring myself to write that word. It's bad enough I said it, on Christmas no less, and on my mama's front porch in full earshot of my entire eavesdropping family. But to write it feels extra sinful.)

"I know, darlin'," he tried to say.

"Do not even call me darlin'. I ain't your darlin' and I ain't been your darlin' since you left me for her. Let me tell you something, Dwayne Davis. I thought we had reached some kind of peaceful agreement yesterday, and I felt real good about that. Now I don't know what you have going on with the psycho bitch you married, but if you feel like this is the right thing for your kids, then your ass has no business on my porch. It needs to be back over there with her trying to work this out. If you don't think it's good for you and your kids, then you might want to get a restraining order because she seems a little cray-cray. Either way, I'm out of this dog fight. I don't have anything in it. No kids, no wives, no boyfriends, nothing. This time around, I'm sitting this one out. I wish you both all the best, but please get the hell off my porch and tell your crazy ex-wife, or wife, or whatever she is not to call here again."

My Southern accent is always thick when I'm angry, and after days of being influenced by those around me it blossomed to full-on drawl. I finished my speech and turned on my heel so fast a soap-opera casting agent would have hired me on the spot. I yanked at the handle of the screen door to pull it open dramatically, but my hand slipped off and my nail broke. I screamed out in pain, which only fueled my anger and frustration.

My sister Carrie opened the door and stepped out on the porch. When she determined he'd done nothing to make me scream, Carrie said, "Dwayne, I think she asked you to leave."

"Tyler, I'm sorry," he said.

"I know that, Dwayne. Really, I do. But I gotta be done, dude. Just let it go." I nudged Carrie to open the door. We walked back inside and left him to straighten out his own mess.

"You did good, baby," Carrie said.

"You don't think I overreacted?" I asked.

"No. I don't even know what happened, and I don't care. With Dwayne Davis involved, you needed to be chewing his ass."

So much for calm and peaceful Zen. Just when I thought I'd mastered the whole Oprah thing, too. Oh well.

Thursday, December 26th

The drive home seemed to take much longer than the drive up, mostly because it rained the whole way back. Overall, it had been a good visit, but I was anxious to be home. My home. In my own place, in my own life, in my own bed.

I hated being so disconnected without my phone. I wanted to call Cabe and talk about everything that had transpired. I also needed to make sure nothing significant had happened at work in my absence, so I decided to make a quick stop by the office before going to my apartment.

It was a little after six when I pulled in the parking lot, but I wasn't at all surprised to see Laura's car in the parking lot.

"Merry Christmas, sweetie!" She welcomed me with a huge hug and a hearty laugh. "How was your trip?"

"It was . . . good," I said as I hugged her back. "Interesting."

"Come sit and tell me about it. I'm been on the phone all day back and forth with my New Year's Eve bride and the hotel catering manager and I'm about to pull my hair out. I would welcome the distraction!"

"Chanel still isn't budging with the alcohol, huh?"

"No! She insists there be no alcohol served at all, but she wants the hotel to have punch bowls out so the room looks festive. She's asking for them to put colored water in the bowls. Aaron at the hotel is flat-out refusing, and of course, I don't blame him. I told her they could do different punch flavors to get colors, but she's being quite the stubborn minx."

"I still don't understand why on earth Chanel booked her wedding on New Year's Eve if she's so adamant about no drinking. I mean, I can understand her not wanting people to get trashed at her wedding, but New Year's Eve is kind of known for being a drinking and partying holiday. So why pick that date if you don't want anyone to party?"

Laura shook her head and rubbed the bridge of her nose as though fighting off a headache. "I don't know. And she extended the reception until two, so they are in the dinner room for seven hours with no bar, no wine, nothing. Aaron and his team are fit to be tied. He thinks the guests are going to be upset with the hotel. And he's probably right."

"I bet. Why can't she just do a champagne toast at midnight? No one is going to get drunk off one glass of champagne."

Laura shook her head again. "Won't do it. We even offered sparkling cider so there'd be no alcohol involved. She doesn't want it."

"Did you ever find out why? Is she in recovery? Someone in the family in recovery? Is it a religious thing?"

"I don't know. But like you said earlier, why have your wedding on the one night of the year most deeply associated with drinking if you're that adamant about not drinking? But enough about her. Tell me about your trip. I know you were very nervous about it."

"I was." I nodded, replaying the trip in my head and remembering my anxiety beforehand. "I don't know. It went much better than I expected, I guess. I enjoyed my time with my niece and nephew, my siblings. Even Mama. She and I had a pretty good visit this time. Long enough to enjoy, but short enough not to make us both crazy. I guess I was all worked up for nothing. They welcomed me with open arms."

"And what about the gentleman? Dwayne, I think? Did you see him?"

"Yep. I did. We hung out for a bit. We visited his mom and his grandma."

"How was that? How'd you feel about it?" She sat back in her chair and put her hands together. I felt like I was on a therapist's couch.

"You know what? You were right. I got closure. I was able to see him and spend time with him, but I know I don't have a future with him. I know my future's here."

She smiled so quickly that I almost sensed relief coming from her.

"Good! I am so glad. I know you dreaded going home, and that you've avoided it for a long time. I also know this young man factored heavily into that stress, and I am happy to see you at peace. You look lighter. Like the weight has been lifted."

She was right. I did feel lighter, like I dropped a ton of weight that's been holding me down. I got closure in a huge way on the trip, and not just with Dwayne. I mended my self-imposed separation from my family, and I no longer carried the trepidation and anxiety whenever I thought about home. Definitely not the same wounded girl who made that frantic drive to Florida years ago.

I nodded. "I think I'm ready to move forward. I'm done looking back." I held my head high as I said it, realizing perhaps for the first time how true it was.

She reached for my hands and clasped them tightly in hers. "I am so proud of you. You are such a strong, intelligent, young woman, and I look forward to seeing you sail forth into a bright future. On a personal note, I'll mention how relieved I am that you didn't come in and tell us you were resigning to move back home."

I shuddered at the thought. "Oh, no ma'am. Not a chance."

Laura laughed and released my hands. "Good. Now let me get back to figuring out how to appease Aaron and Chanel into meeting in the middle somehow. The two of them are definitely going to drive me to drink."

I called Cabe, hoping he'd be up for grabbing dinner or coming over. I got no answer, so I left him a message. I checked my voice mail and my e-mail, waiting around in hopes he'd call back. He didn't, though. I felt a bit deflated as I drove home, knowing he had no way of calling me once I left the office. I wanted so badly to talk to him. I have missed him so much.

Friday, December 27th

The week after Christmas and the week after New Year's are crazy-busy in our office. It seems like everyone who has any inclination at all to get engaged picks Christmas Eve or New Year's Eve to propose. Then they call us right away, ready to hire a planner.

I don't know which is worse—the clueless ones who have no idea what they want or what they're doing, or the people who have already decided every tiny little detail and refuse to budge in the face of reason.

One thing is for sure in this barrage of phone calls, though. If a groom is calling to plan the entire event, he's pretty much an anal, type A, control freak. Today, I got a phone call from the Mack Daddy of all organization.

Ricky and his fiancée got engaged on Christmas Day. In the forty-eight hours since she said yes, Ricky has already chosen their venues, completed a guest list, picked out a menu, and decided on cake flavors. He knows he wants a string trio for the ceremony and a DJ for the reception, and he has a music list and itinerary typed up for both. He asked how soon I could get him a contract to hire us as his planner, and I almost asked, "Why bother?"

This dude has put in way too many hours scouring the internet and planning this event. What would he have done if she had said no?

I congratulated him on the engagement and asked for the wedding date. When he answered me, I nearly hung up on him.

Their wedding is *three and a half years* away!

They are both freshmen in college and want to wait until after graduation to get married. Puh-leeze. Like you will even still be together after the next three years. Like any of these vendors would be willing to book an event three years out. Like these vendors will even still be here in three years. Well, okay, so they probably will, but will I?

I guess I need to seriously consider what I want from my career. During

234

my time away this week, I missed my job. I didn't dread coming back to work at all.

Come to think of it, I very rarely ever have a day where I am counting the hours until the end of my shift. I very much enjoy what I do. I think it's a great fit for me.

I mean, there are definitely downsides to the job. Working pretty much every weekend for one. And then there's the fact that we deal with stressed-out crazy people who think the world revolves simply for their own pleasure.

Then the other end of the spectrum is dealing with people who have blissfully found their mate and are oh-so-happy to no longer be alone. It sounds like it would be a good thing to be surrounded by, but it's like a bright beacon shining on my single status. It's kind of impossible for me not to obsess over finding Mr. Right if I'm constantly bombarded by people finding their match and committing to each other with public declarations of love.

I hate to sound bitter and cynical, but enough already. Sometimes I get sick of hearing how they met and how much they love each other. How she had given up and suddenly he came along, or he knew from the first time he saw her she was the one. Blah blah blah.

I've met some weird, screwed-up people in this line of work, and they still found somebody. So it makes me wonder what it says about me that I haven't.

I do realize all the fairy tales I see don't end up in happily ever after mode. In fact, quite a few of those screwed-up people I've met are in dysfunctional, unhealthy relationships. It still makes me feel hopeless, though. To see all these people who are somehow able to find each other amidst all the chaos and drama of life. Here they are. Walking down the aisle. And here I am. Not walking.

I'm willing to admit I've probably been my own worst roadblock. I've been more than a little apprehensive about committing to a relationship with someone because of my past heartbreak. But it ain't like Prince Charming came knocking and I just refused to give him the time of day. I ain't seen hide nor hair of him!

I'm okay if there's not going to be harp music and a soft focus light beam from heaven. I'm totally okay if he doesn't gallop in on a horse to sweep me away. My klutzy ass would probably fall off the back of the horse anyway.

But where is he? What's taking him so long?

It's enough to make a girl want to give up.

But that's where the flip side of this job comes in. Just when I think I'd be better off living life as a hermit, true love comes along and refills me with hope. I meet a couple or a family who clearly have something special, something real. In those moments, I know for certain that love does exist.

If I ever walk away from this job, I may lose that. That certainty. I might give up entirely and turn my back on love's very existence. I think about Dwayne that day in the woods. How willing he is to have faith in love and marriage. He chooses to still believe it can work despite everything he has seen to the contrary. I don't have that innate hope instilled in me.

So in some weird wacked-out way, the very job that makes me feel so shitty about love also fills me with hope and keeps me believing. It keeps me looking forward to the day those doors will swing open and it will be me walking down the aisle toward the one who will share my days and my nights.

So I guess I know the answer to my question. Yes, I'll still be here in three years. I'll keep planning events for the rest of the schmucks while I'm waiting around for a schmuck of my own.

Any day now. Hurry up, dude.

Saturday, December 28th

I did not know the state of Florida could be so cold. I seriously do not own clothes for freezing weather. Especially not clothes I could wear to work a wedding. Of course, I stayed warmer in my suit and my coat than many of the ladies attending the wedding tonight in their strappy little evening gowns. Check the weather channel before you pack, people. Florida isn't blazing hot year-round. I mean, granted, this wedding did get moved up from March, but still.

The ceremony was beautiful but so sad. I mean no disrespect at all by saying this, but the groom's father literally looked like death. I think sheer will and love for his son kept the poor man alive long enough to witness this marriage. He didn't even weigh one hundred pounds, and his skin seemed virtually transparent in his gray-blue state. Cancer totally sucks.

Everyone involved worked extra hard to try and make everything perfect for this family. Unfortunately, none of us could control the weather and the freak record-cold temperatures that moved in.

The guests seemed reluctant to leave the warm ceremony site inside the convention center to go board the yacht, and rightfully so. Even though we'd installed space heaters on the deck, the wind still whipped across it with a cold that cut to the bone. The yacht's owner and his captain had rearranged as much as possible to make room indoors, but capacity being what it was, some people had to be out on the deck.

The groom's dad spent most of post-ceremony pictures sitting in a large chair in the lobby, and when they needed him for a photo, the photographer posed everyone around him in the chair so he wouldn't have to move. He looked exhausted. His shallow breathing grew more labored as the night wore on, and his hands trembled terribly.

Even with his wheelchair, I knew he would get too cold going from the convention center to the hotel dock, so I borrowed a cart from housekeeping to drive him straight to the yacht. I even thought I'd go the extra mile and pull the cart all the way under the covered sidewalk to the door of the convention center to limit his exertion as much as possible. I was quite proud of myself for maneuvering such a tight fit with the cart. In fact, I might have even said out loud, "I am Tyler, here to save the day!" when no one was around to hear me. What a dork.

The rest of the wedding party walked to the dock with our entertainment manager Eric, while the groom's mom and brother helped me get his dad situated on the cart. The whole time, the groom's mom complained about the weather and how she couldn't believe it got this cold in Florida.

Once I had the three of them seated, I hopped back on and put it in gear, but when I started to back up, I found I was too close to the railing on the right side. I pulled forward a bit to try and change my angle, then reversed again, but I still couldn't clear the railing. I pulled forward and tried cutting the wheel harder to the left, but now the railing behind me was too close, and I couldn't back up as far. I turned the wheel back the other direction going forward, then put it in reverse again. This time I nearly hit the bench sitting against the railing. We were stuck. My clever maneuvering wasn't working on the way back out. I had somehow become Austin Powers and wedged the cart between the two railings.

"Is there a problem?" the mother asked. "It's freezing out here, and we'd like to get going."

"Oh yes, ma'am," I said. "I understand. I'm trying to back up without hitting anything."

My palms started to sweat despite the icy chill of the wind. I had no clue how to get us out, and I couldn't even change the plan and get him off the cart because he was penned in. He would have to slide across the seat and then crawl over the bench and inch between the cart and the railing. Which wasn't happening.

"Maybe if I move the bench?" the groom's brother asked.

"Oh. Yeah. I got it. I'll do it." It seemed wrong to have a member of the family pushing around a bench in his tux, so I jumped off to move it. It didn't budge.

"Let me help you," he said, handing his jacket to his mother. "Here, Mom. Put this on."

"Give it to your father, Adam. He's going to catch his death from cold. He's survived cancer this long only to freeze to death on a golf cart in Florida."

Guilt and embarrassment overwhelmed me. Adam and I moved the bench a few inches before I got back on the cart to try again.

"Maybe you should pull forward instead, a little more to the left, and then try to back up?" Adam suggested.

I turned the wheel like he said, but forgot to take it out of reverse, so when I let my foot off the break, the cart lurched backward and smacked the bench.

"That's reverse!" the mother yelled. "He said forward. You're going backward. Oh my God, we're all going to die. Have you ever even driven one of these before?"

In truth, only once or twice, which I didn't want to reveal at that point. I pulled forward again, trying to turn the wheel as Adam had suggested. My hands were shaking now, although whether from the cold or the state of my nerves, I don't know.

"Okay, now back up and cut the wheel to see if you can get it straightened out," Adam said.

I did as he said and cleared the railing to get the cart straight under the entranceway. Adam got back on as his mother loudly whispered, "Thank you, sweetheart. I don't think she knows what she's doing."

I couldn't even get mad at her, because clearly I didn't.

I backed the rest of the way down the covered sidewalk, cutting the wheel hard to make the turn between the two columns. I didn't make it. I smacked the column on the left hard. Hard enough to bust out the taillight. The groom's father groaned upon impact, and the mother screamed an obscenity I won't write.

"What are you doing?" she asked. "Are you trying to kill this poor man?"

Hot tears stung my eyes and I blinked them back furiously, embarrassed and frustrated. My good intentions had failed.

I pulled forward and grimaced at the huge black smear and splintered chunk of wood across the white column. I cut the wheel more and reversed again, but now the side of the cart veered dangerously close to hitting the other column so I stopped.

"Oh Lord in Heaven!" she shouted. "What are you doing? Is this some sort of joke? Can you please get someone else to drive us out of here?"

Her face quivered with emotion, scrunched up in rage and braced against the cold. I knew the entire event must be highly emotional for her, with her son getting married and her husband barely clinging to life. What might have been a minor incident with the cart at any other time only pushed her closer to the brink of what she could bear politely. I felt horrible, but it wasn't like I was screwing up on purpose.

"Ma'am, I'm sorry. I'm doing the best I can. I'm having a hard time, and I already feel incompetent. Your comments and your criticism are not helping."

"My husband is dying a slow, painful death. Your incompetence is going to speed up the process if you don't get him out of this cold."

I shifted back in my seat and eased forward to straighten out, then slowly backed up. The side of the cart scraped ever so slightly along the column as we passed it, but I kept going. Until the back tire slipped off the sidewalk and into the flower bed, throwing the groom's father off balance and against his wife's shoulder.

"Stop the damned cart!" she yelled. "You have no business driving this thing."

"Mom," Adam said, "just hush. You aren't helping. She's trying, okay?"

"Trying to kill your father," she said.

When I finally cleared the sidewalk railings and columns, I floored it and went as fast as the little banged-up cart could go. I figured the cold air wasn't nearly as damaging to him as more time in the cart with me. Best to get it over with quickly.

Laura stood ready to greet us at the dock, bundled in her coat, scarf, hat and gloves.

"Congratulations! How are you feeling?" she asked.

"We've all nearly died," the mother said, glaring at me with daggers surely meant to be deadly.

Adam gave me a brief smile as he struggled to get his father from the cart. "Thanks for trying. I know you meant well. We're all under a lot of stress, that's all."

Laura's gaze slowly changed to something along the lines of horrified confusion. Her eyes looked at me, shocked and questioning, but we had no time to talk. She needed to get them on the yacht to sail away into the frigid wind, and I needed to get the cart parked back under its shed before someone noticed the busted light and long scrapes along the side.

Guess I'll have some explaining to do tomorrow.

Monday, December 30th

I got my phone replaced today, and I am officially reconnected to the world! Of course, I called Cabe right away. I've been going through serious withdrawal without being able to talk to him whenever I wanted. I've called him from work a few times, but nothing like our normal constant flow of texts and calls. I felt like he moved to the other side of the world again.

He came over for dinner tonight, the first time I've seen him in over a week with my trip home and the weddings this past weekend. When I opened the door for him to come in, he looked like a giant compared to hanging around Dwayne last week. Cabe towers over me by about a foot at least. I think I like tall, though. Maybe I'll add tall to my list of characteristics for Mr. Perfect. I mean, if he's imaginary, I can request whatever qualities I want, right?

We rehashed all the details of my trip, and his sarcastic insight had me rolling. He even found a way to make my Austin Powers cart disaster funny somehow. I swear that boy can make me laugh in any situation.

We had eaten and talked and laughed for a couple of hours when he stood and stretched his arms wide.

"I gots to go," he said, yawning. "I have to get up early in the morning. We have a new program rollout launching on January 2nd. Lots to do still."

"Oh, is your mommy going to wake you up so you don't miss your meeting?" I asked in a singsong child's voice.

"No, my mommy isn't going to wake me up," he replied back mimicking my voice. "Smart-ass!"

I laughed and stood to hug him goodbye. He wrapped his arms around me and squeezed me tight in one of his signature bear hugs. I nestled my head against his chest and sighed contentedly.

"I'm glad you're home, Ty." He kissed the top of my head.

I laughed and leaned back to look up at him. "Aw. Did you miss me?" He locked his hands tight in the small of my back, holding me as I swayed back and forth laughing at him.

His eyes turned serious for a moment, and I thought he might lay another one of those random kisses on me that take my breath away and leave me dizzy. We definitely need to discuss those at some point and figure out what's up. Not tonight, though. I didn't want anything to ruin how happy I was just being with him.

Then without any warning, Cabe abruptly released his hold and let me go. "Night," he said as he let himself out the door.

"Good night," I replied, but he was already gone without ever looking back.

I wish I knew what goes on in his head. One minute he's here with me, smiling and happy. Then all of a sudden, he's somewhere else, not as happy. What is it that clouds that handsome smile?

Tuesday, December 31st
New Year's Eve

I felt so thankful to be working with Lillian's festive wedding tonight rather than Laura's alcohol-phobic bride. I've accepted that I have to work on New Year's Eve every year, but it helps if the event is at least fun. Tonight's was not only a good time but also one of those weddings that makes me feel lucky to do this job. A beautiful, happy wedding with beautiful, happy people from two sets of wealthy parents. They had spared no expense on decor, food, entertainment—you name it. An all-around fabulous event.

And to top it all off with whipped cream and a cherry, Lillian walked up while the crowd danced and mingled after dinner and said, "You did a great job tonight, Tyler. Thank you for your help."

She even gave me her signature nod at the end of it, a little habit I've noticed she has when paying a rare compliment. It's like the nod seals it. Like a queen making a decree.

I nearly fainted, but luckily I held my composure and just beamed at her, happy to have made her proud.

"Why don't you take off?" she said.

"What do you mean?"

"Take off. Get out of here. It's New Year's Eve. Surely, there's a party you can go to somewhere. You don't need to ring in the New Year working."

I was floored. Lillian is not the go-party-and-have-fun kind of boss. I thought I misunderstood.

"You mean, *leave?*" I asked.

"Well, yes, unless you consider it a party for all of us to crowd around a telly in the back hallway to watch some stupid ball of lights be dropped out of the sky." She arched an eyebrow at me and gave me a sly smile.

"But what about you? I don't want to leave you here alone," I said. "I mean, not that you're not capable of handling the wedding alone, but for New Year's, I meant."

"Ha!" She laughed. "The New Year has already begun, my dear. I am British, remember? The clock already struck midnight for me."

"Oh, right. Okay. I guess if you're sure." I hesitated in leaving, not only because I didn't want to shirk my duties but also because I didn't have a place to go. I didn't pay attention to anyone's party plans since I knew I was working. I went outside and dialed Cabe.

"Hey!" he shouted over loud music and laughter. "What's up, Buttercup?"

"Lillian says I can leave."

"What?" he shouted.

"I can leave. I can get off work now if I want."

"Cool! Come over. Galen is throwing a kick-ass party!"

His sister Galen lives in a high-rise downtown where she regularly throws great parties with all her artsy friends. Funky people, and sometimes a bit scary, but they definitely make lively partygoers. Cabe sounded like he'd thrown back a few and was feeling no pain.

"I don't know. I'm not really dressed for it. I don't think I have time to go home and change, then make it all the way downtown."

"Don't worry about it!" he screamed over someone shouting in the background. "No one cares how you're dressed. Just get your ass over here and let's sing Auld Lang Syne."

"Do you even know the words to Auld Lang Syne?" I asked, but he didn't answer. I could hear him talking to someone else in the room. I thought for a moment he'd forgotten me as his other conversation got more muffled and I heard loud laughter. But then he came back, "Hey! Are you coming?"

I didn't want to go to one of Galen's artsy parties wearing a navy suit. I also didn't want to show up completely sober and fresh out of a work shift when everyone else had been partying for hours. One of the things I've learned working weddings is it's no fun to be the sober, sane person in a room full of partying, celebrating, sloppy drunk people having a great time. As pathetic as it may be, my own comfy bed sounded more intriguing than the people yelling in the background behind Cabe.

"I don't think so. I'm not dressed for it, and everyone else is already in party mode. I think I'll go home and watch the ball drop on TV."

"By yourself?" he yelled. "Are you crazy? It's New Year's Eve. You have to be with people or it won't be a good year."

"I have never heard that wise parable. Did you get that from a fortune cookie?"

"Come on, Ty. Get your butt over here," he said, but then someone grabbed his phone and said, "Hello? Who's this?" Cabe took the phone back and said, "Don't mind him. He's a jerk when he's sober and worse when he's drunk." I heard the other voice protest in the background, and my bed kept sounding better and better.

"I'm going home, Cabe. I'll call you at midnight, okay?"

"You sure?" he asked.

"Yep. I'm sure. But I'll call you at midnight."

We hung up, and I went inside to say goodbye to the bride and groom. They were dancing alone with all the guests surrounding them, so I walked to the edge of the dance floor and watched.

"Thank you for everything," the woman next to me said, and I noticed it was the groom's mother, Nidia. A tall, beautiful lady who carried class and elegance in a way I had rarely seen.

"Oh, you're welcome. Lillian did it, though."

She smiled and turned back to the couple, gazing at them with love and admiration.

"They're such a beautiful couple," I said. "Today starts their happily ever after." I often borrowed the phrase from something one of our DJs uses at the end of the night. Sappy and sentimental for sure, but wedding guests loved it.

Nidia twisted the upper half of her body toward me, arms crossed at her waist.

"Oh, please tell me you don't buy into that," she said.

"Um, well," I started but didn't finish. I didn't know what to say.

Our business thrives on the whole fairy tale concept. It comes with the territory. If I were to reply honestly, I would admit I had my doubts. But then wouldn't that be a betrayal of sorts against my field?

"I've been married for forty-three years," she said, "and not a single one of those has been happily ever after. That is not to say I am not happily married or I have not been happy. I am and have been happy, most certainly. But love and marriage are work. This whole fairy tale concept does an incredible disservice to the commitment and selflessness required for love and marriage. People are quite imperfect. Loving them does not protect you from that. I look at my son and his beautiful bride, and I know there will be days they are not happy. She is not perfect. She has flaws, pains, emotions. She will have bad days. Sometimes bad months. Hopefully, not bad years. My son is not perfect."

She chuckled. "I know his flaws and imperfections all too well. The fairy tale suggests you will find the perfect one. It does not exist. What does exist is love. Support, patience, kindness, forgiveness, compassion, understanding. These exist. They are choices that must be made every day to maintain a marriage. I don't wish my son and his bride a happily ever after. I wish for them that they will make each other laugh. That they will support and encourage each other. Hold each other accountable. Uplift. Forgive. I wish for them the stamina it takes to choose love each and every day. For love is a verb. An action we choose. To love is to risk. To work through both the mundane and the unexpected. To love is to be completely vulnerable with no guarantee of safety. Because there is no happily ever after. There is only the choice to love."

"So why would anyone do it?" I asked, not caring if it ruined the facade of my field. I knew her words were true, but I was also angry this was the reality when I so desperately wanted the fantasy. "Why would people willingly open themselves when the chance of being hurt is so great? Why can't it be the way it is in fairy tales?"

She laughed softly and began to clap as their song ended. Then she leaned in toward me to be heard over the crowd's applause.

"You've missed the whole point, my dear." Her smile broadened, her eyes sparkling as though she was sharing some mysterious secret. "The whole beauty of love, of marriage, is that people do it in spite of the uncertainty. In spite of the work. The fact that we allow ourselves to love and be loved is the ultimate symbol of hope. It is the choosing that makes it so."

She moved forward onto the dance floor to hug her son and new daughter-in-law. I felt like I'd been visited by a fairy godmother or an ancient mystic. Like a New Year's Eve Love Fairy or something.

I bid them all my best wishes for a Happy New Year and a happy life. I found Lillian and told her good night and Happy New Year. Then I headed home to climb in my bed and watch the ball drop to start a new year with a new me. I had let go of a lot this year, and I looked forward to the new one with hope for what it would bring.

I couldn't stop thinking about what Nidia said on the way home. It made sense to me, but the idea of Mr. Perfect sounded much more appealing than some flawed, imperfect dude requiring work from me. The idea of love being a choice was a harder angle to market, for sure, making the fairy tale a much easier sell, I think.

I turned the key in the lock, thinking my neighbor's television sounded uncharacteristically loud. It wasn't until I swung the door open that I realized the noise came from inside my apartment, which completely freaked me out.

Until I saw Cabe. He stood in my kitchen, wearing a ridiculous paper hat with streamers coming out of the top. When he saw me, he blew one of those obnoxious paper horn things that unwind when you blow them and make a noise similar to a duck with laryngitis.

"Surprise!" he yelled. "Happy New Year!"

"Oh my God! How'd you get here? What are you doing here?" I asked him through a grin that spread across my face and throughout my being.

"I couldn't have you ring in the New Year alone! I told you, it's bad luck. Then you'd have a bad year, and I'd feel terrible about it. So I took a taxi 'cause Lord knows I don't need to be driving, and I came over here to do the countdown with my best good friend, Buttercup."

He grinned and raised his glass like a toast to me, and suddenly, there he was. The guy I'd been looking for all this time.

The one who laughs with me, cries with me, and dances with me at random restaurants. The one who cooks with me and watches movies with me. Who always calls right back when I text and always tells me what I need to hear, whether I want to or not. The one who always calls me on my shit when I'm being crazy. This handsome, charming guy with the most intense blue eyes and the most incredible smile. Who kisses with a passion I can't even describe and has a ton of flaws and imperfections. Loads of insecurities and fears.

He'd been right here in front of me the whole time, but I couldn't see him. I felt joy and relief wash over me. I'd found what I'd been searching for.

I walked straight over to him and wrapped both arms around his neck, laying the biggest, wettest, sloppiest kiss I could muster on those soft lips. If I surprised him, he didn't show it. He kissed me right back, both hands stroking up and down my back and pulling me closer.

"You have no idea how long I've been waiting for you to do that," Cabe said, covering my mouth with his as I arched my back against him and allowed myself to feel.

No hesitation, no holding back, no wondering.

I was kissing Cabe, the man I loved, and it was pretty freakin' awesome.

I heard the countdown begin on the television and pulled my mouth away on the 3, 2, 1. "Happy New Year, Cabe."

"Happy New Year, Ty."

"Oh, I think it will be. It may be my best year yet," I said, smiling as he pressed his lips to mine once again.

And that's all I'm gonna write for now.

Wanna Know What Happens Next?

Get a sneak peek now into
Diary of a Wedding Planner in Love,
Volume 2 in the Tales Behind the Veils series!

Wednesday, January 1st

You'd think a deputy sheriff could catch a fifty-two-year-old woman running in three-inch-heels. Now granted, he was wearing full gear and a bulletproof vest while she wore only a thin, slinky evening gown, but still. She was pretty far ahead of him before she ever kicked off her heels and ran barefoot. In all, twenty-six people ran. The cops caught two of them. I'm not sure if that says more about the sheriff's deputies or the bride's family.

Beth and Toby told us about their family feud in the initial planning session for the wedding. It had started decades before they were born, so long ago no one on either side seems to remember exactly how it began. Toby wanted to elope, but Beth felt certain they could prevent their wedding becoming a full-blown Montagues and Capulets showdown. Hmmph.

She counted on New Year's Eve hangovers working in her favor when she booked a midday brunch with a limited bar on January 1st. Unfortunately, I think her family subscribed more to the "hair of the dog" methodology.

Tonight's fiasco started on the dance floor when a heated exchange between two guests quickly escalated into a full-on eruption of flying fists, bodies slammed to the floor, kicks to the gut, and bloody noses. Family members from both sides rushed to join the melee, and it took seven security guards to break it up.

Beth got on the microphone, pleading with both sides to allow her and Toby to enjoy their day in peace. A grumbling truce settled uncomfortably over the room, but we pulled the bars as a precaution. No need to add more alcohol as fuel to simmering fires. Beth's father flipped out when he saw the bartenders rolling out, getting right up in Laura's face to express his displeasure.

True to Laura's reputation as the calm one of my two bosses, she never lost her cool. She did, however, seem a bit relieved when security stepped between them and asked him to leave. Beth's mother and two sisters went with him, along with several extended family members.

With most of Beth's family gone, the rest were too outnumbered to wreak much havoc, and Toby's family surprised me by settling down without taunting or gloating. Everyone grumbled about the lack of alcohol, but Beth and Toby were fine with it being pulled. They only had eyes for each other as they danced to song after song together.

Things seemed almost peaceful for the next half hour or so. The calm before the storm, I suppose, looking back on it all.

Laura and I stood talking near the patio doors when a flash of pink whirled past outside. I nearly broke my neck with the double-take when I saw Beth's sister, the maid of honor, riding the shoulders of one of Toby's cousins. She pulled his hair and scratched at his eyes as he spun in circles trying to buck her off. The seams of her tight pink satin dress had given way at some point, leaving her right butt cheek completely exposed.

I opened my mouth to yell for security, but the sound of glass shattering on the patio behind me drowned out my call for help. I grabbed Laura's arm and ducked instinctively. Beth's mother was standing over Toby's uncle, waving the stolen vodka bottle she'd broken over his head. Her pearls swung from left to right, and her hair flew loose from its once elegant chignon as she wheeled around looking for her next victim.

The entire room stampeded past us and out onto the patio as we stood in a state of disbelief and watched the whole disaster unfold. Father of the groom pitted against father of the bride as they scuffled on the ground. Beth's grandmother tripping people with her cane. Random cousins wielding stiletto heels like prison shanks.

Only Beth and Toby stayed on the dance floor, locked in a swaying embrace, seemingly oblivious to the apocalypse outside.

Laura and I pressed our faces to the glass as security fought their way onto the patio. I wasn't about to step outside. I harbored no grand delusions about breaking up any fights or putting myself anywhere in the vicinity of harm's way. Call me a coward, but these people had hidden in the bushes of a five-star resort in evening gowns and tuxedos to spring forth and attack smokers on the patio. Definitely out of my league and far outside the parameters of my job description. Besides, I've never been a fan of pain or blood. Especially when it's my own.

Eventually, the overwhelmed hotel security force called the cops. Deserters on both sides of the battle scattered at the first sound of sirens, jumping over shrubbery or bolting back through the convention center to exit from the other side. I think the scrappers in the center of the pile were too enthralled to hear the cops coming.

They sure heard them when the sirens came under the hotel entrance, though. They took off like rabbits in a greyhound race. Beth's dad swung by near the patio to let her sister jump in the back of the truck, but I never saw her mother again after she shucked her heels and left the deputy in her dust. They probably picked her up somewhere out on the highway.

Luckily, only three people needed medical attention. Well, I say that, but I should say only three people *who stayed to be examined* needed medical attention. I can't speak for the idiots who ran.

Beth and Toby just danced. Never left the ballroom the rest of the afternoon. If they noticed over half their guests had disappeared or been arrested, they didn't let on. After the final dance, they thanked Laura for a perfect event and told her to send them a bill for any destroyed property. Nice couple. I hope their love can survive without anyone getting killed.

There was a note from Cabe on my pillow when I got home.

Woke up in your bed. Don't remember much, so I hope I don't owe you any apologies. Let me take you to dinner tomorrow night either way. C.

Crazy boy. He fell asleep soon after the ball dropped last night. I slept curled up in his arms, finally happy and at peace. I can't believe I didn't realize that Prince Charming, The One I'd been searching for, had been right here the whole time. My best friend. My confidante. My dance partner. My love.

Visit your favorite online retailer to order Diary of a Wedding Planner in Love, Volume 2 in the Tales Behind the Veils series to keep reading Tyler's diary!

And the journey continues!

Volumes 3 & 4 are also available!
Diary of an Engaged Wedding Planner is Volume 3 in the
Tales Behind the Veils series and continues Tyler's story.

Maggie can be read as Volume 4 or as a standalone. This
seasoned romance features a beloved character from the
Tales Behind the Veils series with parallel stories telling of
Maggie's disastrous first love and her second chance at a
happily ever after.

Want more from Violet Howe?

Welcome to the small town of Cedar Creek! This quaint community is home to a collection of recurring characters who interact from book to book. While both Cedar Creek Mysteries and Cedar Creek Families feature stories of love, laughter, family, and friendships, Cedar Creek Mysteries have the added elements of suspense, mystery, and a ghost or two. We invite you to get to know the people of Cedar Creek!

Cedar Creek Families

Cedar Creek Mysteries

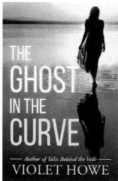
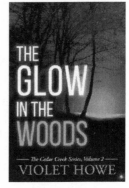

To purchase, visit your favorite online book retailer, or www.violethowe.com.

Photo Credit: Theresa Murphy

About the Author

Violet Howe enjoys writing romance and mystery with humor. She lives in Florida with her husband—her knight in shining armor—and their two handsome sons. They share their home with three adorable but spoiled dogs. When she's not writing, Violet is usually watching movies, reading, or planning her next travel adventure.

www.violethowe.com
Facebook.com/VioletHoweAuthor
Twitter: @Violet_Howe
Instagram.com/VioletHowe

Newsletter

Sign up at www.violethowe.com to be the first to know about Violet's new releases, giveaways, sales, and appearances. You can also find out about joining Violet's Facebook Reader Group, the Ultra Violets. And don't worry. She won't fill your email with a ton of messages or sell your address to anyone. Because nobody has time for that.

Thank You

Putting together a full-length novel is quite the undertaking. So is reading one with today's hectic schedules. Thank you so much for taking the time to read this book. It makes the effort all worthwhile.

If you liked it, then please tell somebody! Tell your friends. Tell your family. Tell a co-worker. Tell the person next to you in line at the grocery store.

If you really liked it, please consider reviewing it on BookBub, Goodreads, your favorite online vendor, or any other social media site you frequent.

Made in the USA
Middletown, DE
20 February 2020